"What a fun read! This story is a clever romantic comedy, in every sense of the words . . . *7 Days and 7 Nights* is a fast-paced story that will have readers wanting more. It's the perfect summer book!"—*Hawthorne Press Tribune/Lawndale Tribune*

"Entertaining, lively, and engaging, this is an excellent summer read."—*Booklist*

"*7 Days and 7 Nights* sparkles with wit and humor. . . . A mix of strength and vulnerability make Olivia a heroine with which one can easily identify. Wax is an author to watch."

—*Romantic Times*

"[*7 Days and 7 Nights*] is a thoroughly satisfying read— funny, poignant, sexy, and real. This fresh, well-woven tale might teach you a thing or two about your own relationship! Put Wendy Wax on the top of your to-be-read pile."

—Stephanie Bond, author of *I Think I Love You*

"Just what we've been looking for, a wonderful guilty pleasure, sweet, smooth, and delicious, with just the right note of tartness. And not at all fattening! *7 Days and 7 Nights* is a lovely new entry in that lovely genre, the romantic comedy. This is one box of truffles you won't be able to put down until you're done."

—Mira Kirshenbaum, bestselling author of
The Emotional Energy Factor and
Too Good to Leave, Too Bad to Stay

"Wendy Wax has a hilarious take on men and women and relationships. She has a gift for creating characters and situations that are real. Readers will enjoy getting to know the different characters, and are sure to identify with many of them. I found myself laughing out loud more than once as I read Ms. Wax's first romantic comedy, and I'm looking forward to reading future books by her."—*Old Book Barn Gazette*

"*7 Days and 7 Nights* is the delightfully funny, yet very emotional, debut contemporary romance by Wendy Wax. The bickering and bantering dialogue between Olivia and Matt is delicious, as are their 'on air' personalities. This is a fast-paced and intriguing story, guaranteed to keep you turning pages long into the night."—America Online's Romance Fiction Forum

"A romantic comedy that is sure to please . . . Wendy Wax proves that she has a knack for showing us what makes her characters tick, and keeping it light yet fascinating. It's been quite a while since I've enjoyed a contemporary romance this much. It was a shock to see that this is Wendy Wax's first romantic comedy, and I look forward to more from the lady in the future. Pick up a copy of *7 Days and 7 Nights* today and settle in for a read that I guarantee you'll enjoy!"

—*Romance Reviews Today*

"Debut author Wendy Wax throws her hat into the proverbial romance writing ring with a surefire hit. *7 Days and 7 Nights*, with its quirky but lovable characters and its positively refreshing plot, is a definite winner in this reader's opinion. Kudos to Ms. Wax for her ingenuity."

—*The Word on Romance*

"A *hilarious* and romantic romp that is unforgettable! I laughed all the way through it. Highly recommended!"

—*Huntress Reviews*

by Wendy Wax

Single in Suburbia
Hostile Makeover
Leave It to Cleavage
7 Days and 7 Nights

HOSTILE MAKEOVER

Wendy Wax

Bantam Books

HOSTILE MAKEOVER
A Bantam Book / November 2005

Published by Bantam Dell
A Division of Random House, Inc.
New York, New York

This is a work of fiction. Names, characters, places, and incidents
either are the product of the author's imagination or are used
fictitiously. Any resemblance to actual persons, living or dead, events,
or locales is entirely coincidental.

Bantam Books and the rooster colophon are
registered trademarks of Random House, Inc.

ISBN 978-0-553-58795-1

Printed in the United States of America
Published simultaneously in Canada

www.bantamdell.com

10 9 8 7

Acknowledgments

Special thanks go to Kitty Gillespy for walking me through the world of advertising and for reading this work in progress. She also shared her first-hand knowledge of L.A. hotels and restaurants. I'm still trying to figure out why her life sounds so much more glamorous than mine.

I remain ever grateful to my fearless critique partners Karen White, Jennifer St. Giles, Sandra Chastain, and Karen Kendall, who are brutally honest and refuse to let me get away with the "stuff in the box."

I'd also like to thank my editor, Wendy McCurdy, and her assistant, Erica Orden, for making this feel less and less like brain surgery with every book.

Thanks also go to my agent, Pam Strickler, for her support and enthusiasm.

HOSTILE
MAKEOVER

For the first time in her thirty-three-year-old life, Shelley Schwartz faked an orgasm. On principle she was opposed to this idea and had, in debates with her friends, been very smug about always hanging in there even if the payoff was more like a blip on the Richter scale than a full-scale movement of the earth.

A woman should never be cruel or unsympathetic in bed, she'd argued, but pretending that something she didn't like might actually lead to an orgasm had potentially dangerous ramifications; how could a woman go into paroxysms of ecstasy over something one day and then fail to get off on it the next? It was Pavlovian training at its most dysfunctional—and most men didn't need any help or encouragement in failing to satisfy.

But today she'd gotten stuck between a rock and a hard place. Well, actually it had been a mattress and Trey Davenport's superbly sculpted chest.

Faking it had turned out to be her only viable option.

Because although her body had been pinned beneath Trey's very studly one, her mind had been trained on her two-thirty meeting—the one at which she intended to show her father and everyone else at the advertising agency that she was not the cream puff they believed her to be. The meeting she'd spent months preparing for, and which she was now racing to at the speed of sound.

Shelley coasted through a four-way stop then mashed down the accelerator, still trying to figure out how an innocent lunch had turned into such a sexual Waterloo.

She'd invited Trey to the Ritz for his birthday, certain they'd have plenty of time for a celebratory lunch before her meeting. Things had been going swimmingly until he dangled the room key in front of her.

She'd felt the smile freeze on her lips, but Trey was a truly sweet and very hunky guy and it was his birthday; she simply couldn't tell him she'd rather go back to the office and pitch a feminine hygiene account. "This is my chance to be taken seriously at work" wasn't going to cut it with a man who'd just turned thirty-five, consumed most of a bottle of Cristal, and was looking at her like she was the icing on his cake.

Unsure what to do, she'd acted pleased and figured if they got right to it, she'd be showered and dressed in plenty of time.

This might have worked except that Trey, ever the gentleman, kept waiting for her to go first. Only Shelley wasn't going anywhere anytime soon and Trey, who ran marathons and climbed mountains, could go for hours if properly motivated. This had never seemed like a bad thing. Until today.

But even as she'd stared at the ceiling and admitted defeat she'd realized it wasn't fair to penalize Trey just because she was throwing in the sexual towel. Surely all God's children deserved an orgasm on their birthday.

So she'd kicked up their rhythm, whispered things in his ear that actually made her blush, and urged him on, giving an Oscar-worthy performance of turned-on womanhood.

And then when she could tell he was hanging on by the very slimmest of threads she'd done it, the thing she'd argued so vehemently against. She'd impersonated herself at her free-falling, head-banging best and forced Trey Davenport to follow suit.

Despite the compromising of her sexual principles, the meeting was already under way by the time Shelley arrived. The Easy To Be Me people sat with their backs to the conference room door; the Schwartz and Associates team aligned across from them. Her father sat at the head of the table with the indispensable Ross Morgan at his left.

Both men turned as she skidded to a halt in the doorway. Her father sighed. Ross Morgan looked at her as if she were a car wreck he couldn't bear to watch. The conversation sputtered to a stop and everyone else turned to see what they were looking at.

"This is my daughter Shelley," her father announced to the now-silent room.

She swallowed and nodded then forced a smile to her lips. It was only as she moved toward the empty seat at the foot of the table that she noticed the huge run in her stocking. Her heart stopped as she realized that the jacket of her lilac Donna Karan suit, the one she'd bought specifically for this presentation, was misbuttoned, and that the contrasting aqua shell was inside out, the label clearly visible.

She might as well be wearing a sign that read "Delayed due to sex, doesn't know how to dress herself."

Shit, shit, shit. She'd showered in under two minutes, thrown on her clothes, then touched up her makeup in the rearview mirror as she raced to the office. Obviously she should have taken that extra ten seconds in the hotel room for a full-length glimpse.

"I'm sorry I'm late," she said, not even bothering to try to explain. What was there to say? "It's inside-out day at Schwartz and Associates, didn't you get the memo?"

Pulling her notes out of her Louis Vuitton carryall, she decided she'd be a very old woman before she allowed herself to go anywhere near the Ritz at lunchtime again. In fact, she'd give up the Ritz, and possibly sex, for life if Trey's birthday orgasm didn't cost her the opportunity she'd been waiting for.

Ross Morgan speared her with his blue eyes and a familiar tic appeared in his cheek, but it was her father's gaze, filled with disappointment and resignation, that sent the chill up her spine.

Shelley wanted to point out that she'd only been ten minutes late. It wasn't as if she'd blown off the whole thing, or not bothered to do her homework; she knew this client's products like she knew the clearance rack at Neiman's.

Her father gave her a "Don't say a word or you're grounded" look, and Shelley bit her lip and lowered her gaze while Ross Morgan directed everyone's attention back to the storyboards in front of them.

As the meeting progressed, her research was quoted

freely, and her ideas were presented and approved, but she wasn't invited to speak. She felt like a child who'd accidentally used a bad word in front of the adults and been banished from polite society.

If Ross Morgan had been ten minutes late, he could have waltzed right in and still taken command of the group. But of course he would have been ten minutes *early*, not late. And he wouldn't have jeopardized his career in order to give someone an orgasm. Not that he didn't know how to give a woman the "Big O," as she unfortunately knew after ending up in that supply closet with him during last year's holiday party. But he never would have risked business for one. He was always in control of his considerable faculties; always focused, always so sure. How dare he turn out to be the son her father never had!

Shelley kept her gaze fixed on the exposed brick wall of the conference room and worried at her bottom lip until she tasted blood. Forty minutes later there were handshakes all around and Ross—not her—was promising to get things under way, to be in touch, expressing enthusiasm over the opportunity to work together. He promised that they'd be glad they'd put their advertising dollars with Schwartz and Associates.

As usual, she was the Schwartz in disgrace; he was the man in charge.

The Easy To Be Me people filed out of the conference room and the rest of the staff followed.

"Shelley," her father said, "you and Ross come with me." They followed in silence and sank into chairs across from his desk in the big corner office. Still silent, Harvey Schwartz studied them both.

"Daddy, I'm sorry, I . . ."

Her father ran a hand through his graying hair and sighed again. "Never mind, sweetheart. Perhaps we expected too much of you this time."

"No." When had her father ever expected anything of her? "I can handle this. I did the research, a lot of the ideas were mine."

"Yes, Ross told me that."

Well at least he hadn't tried to snatch the credit. "This account is perfect for me."

"Yes." He smiled sadly. "But are you perfect for the account?" He let the question hang in the air. "Your prep work was first-rate, but you weren't here when the time came to close the deal. You can't pick and choose which parts of the job you're going to do."

Ross stared out the window, his expression making it clear he wasn't going to weigh in on the subject. *So why was he there?* she wondered miserably. *Why was he always there being so damned competent? And why did she keep screwing up?*

"It won't happen again, Daddy. Just let me have this account. Let me show you what I can do."

Her father sighed again. He was forever chucking her under the chin like a child, or sighing over her. "I'm sorry, Shelley, but I just can't take the chance. We're talking billings of more than a million dollars. You can work on the account, but you'll work under Ross's guidance. He'll decide what your role will be and how much responsibility to give you."

His intercom buzzed, and his secretary's voice squawked in the too-quiet room. "I've got to take this call. Why don't you two sit down over a cup of coffee and hash it out? There's plenty of work for everyone."

But not plenty of room to earn credit for the success of this campaign.

Shelley followed her nemesis out of the office and down the long hallway. It would be easier to hate him if he'd just go ahead and be a jerk, rub it in, lord it over her. But he was always polite and completely professional. Well, except for that time in the supply closet.

Why couldn't he be short and balding with a squeaky nerd voice, instead of tall and blond with that deep rumbly baritone? Life was so unfair.

Ross paused at the door to his own corner office. "So do you want to discuss this now, or would you like to go finish dressing?"

She was tempted to pull off the blouse and redress in front of him just to see the expression on his face. She hated that he was everything her father wanted and that she apparently was not. What was the point of trying to be professional? When no one expected anything of you, how long could you keep trying to prove them wrong?

"I'm as dressed as I plan to be," Shelley replied quietly. "But my nails *are* a bit ragged." She looked down at them as if they mattered then raised her chin a notch. "I don't think we need to have this same old motivational chat, do you? You don't really want me mucking around in this account, and we both know my father doesn't really care whether I help or not."

She cocked her head to the side and looked at him from beneath her lashes. "I think I'll just run out and get my nails done, maybe do a little shopping."

He didn't try to stop her, didn't argue, didn't do anything but look at her out of those serious blue eyes. As if she were some alien species that he'd never run across before.

Her pride was about all she had propping her up, so she kept her tone light and her chin up as she turned to leave. "I'm pretty sure that's what daddy's girls are supposed to do."

chapter 2

Shelley shopped until the stores closed. Like an alcoholic hanging in until the last call, she prowled the aisles of her favorite stores until the doors locked behind her at ten P.M. The hurt had begun to numb in the lingerie department of Saks. By the time she picked up a new Kate Spade bag at Bloomingdale's, she was close to philosophic. No one really expected her to work a full-time job, and her salary was clearly not dependent on her performance.

So she'd made a mistake. So she'd shown up late and embarrassingly disheveled for the most important business meeting of her life. Beating herself up about it was getting her exactly nowhere.

Letting herself into her Buckhead condo, Shelley dropped her shopping bags in the foyer, moved into the black-and-white kitchen, and dialed her voice mailbox number. Cradling the phone against her shoulder, she flipped the kitchen shutters closed on the view of midtown

Atlanta and sank onto a kitchen chair to listen to her messages.

"Shelley, it's Nina. I'm taking a personal day tomorrow. I'm thinking the nine A.M. Pilates and lunch at Panera's. Then I was thinking facial. A best friend is supposed to tell a girl when her pores look like moon craters."

The next voice belonged to her mother. As usual, Miriam Schwartz wasted no time on a greeting. *"Daddy told me you left early today."* There was a pause. *"I hope you're not too upset; there'll be other accounts. Don't forget dinner tomorrow night. We're going to do the whole Friday night thing. Marilyn Friedlander's grandson is in town and I invited him to join us."*

Shelley rolled her eyes.

"Don't roll your eyes at me." Even through the receiver and cyberspace, or wherever this message had been stored, her mother's irritation was clear. *"He's a very nice boy. An accountant. A girl could do worse."*

Yes, a girl could, Shelley reflected as she listened to the remaining messages, and often had. Her mother's steady stream of Jewish men had covered every legitimate profession and a few that told her just how desperate her mother had grown. She'd known she was in deep shit when Malcolm the Maccabee, a rising star on the professional wrestling circuit, had shown up for a family meal.

Of course, she hadn't done that well on her own, either. Her choices were almost always blond-haired, blue-eyed, and athletic like Trey. It was no fun to be out with someone you thought you could hurt or outwrestle—but their one common attribute had been their non-Jewishness and their inability to commit—at least to her.

Trey's message reminded her that some good had come out of what she now thought of as the Ritz fiasco.

"Thanks for the, uh, birthday send-off." The smile in his voice was clear.

She smiled in response as she remembered his shout of pleasure and the warmth with which he'd shown his gratitude.

"I'm leaving for that white-water trip in the morning, but I'll call you when we get back to civilization."

Good old Trey, so Waspy, so rugged. As long as he didn't expect her to rough it with him, they'd get along just fine.

Her older sister's voice came next—rushed and out of breath as usual. Most of Judy Schwartz Blumfeld's calls were placed via cell phone from car pool lines or Little League fields. And they were almost always instructional in nature. *"Shel, will you bring those fabric swatches I left at your house to Mom and Dad's tomorrow night? The bar mitzvah coordinator wants to see them. I'm thinking about using them for the central color theme."*

Her nephew Sammy's bar mitzvah, whose theme was apparently "Bigger Than Ben-Hur," was a mere five months away.

"I understand Mom found you an accountant this time," her sister concluded. *"Maybe you should bring your tax forms so it isn't a total loss."*

Ha, ha. Shelley moved to the refrigerator and pulled out a Diet Coke. Easy for Judy to joke. She'd married a lawyer and produced two sons, thereby fulfilling their parents' fondest hopes. She had done everything Shelley was now supposed to do, but didn't want to. And tomorrow night Judy would have her whole perfect family with her. If you added the accountant to the equation, you had the perfect end to the perfect week.

"So what does she have for you this time?" Dr. Howard Mellnick was in his mid-forties, and attractive in a gray-templed serious sort of way.

"An accountant." Shelley made a face as she imagined the receding hairline and glasses, the beginning-stage paunch. All that sitting and squinting at numbers rarely buffed up a body.

"And you've already written this guy off because?"

"His primary selling point is that he's related to Marilyn Friedlander—which believe me is nothing to brag about—and my mother is going to spend the entire evening shoving us at each other. He fits all her criteria: He's Jewish, he's breathing, and he's not on death row. She's probably already calling the caterer."

"So you still think all Jewish men are either unexciting or training to be ax murderers."

They considered each other across the therapist-patient divide.

"Well, I'm willing to exclude present company," Shelley said. "But to borrow your trick of answering a question with a question, why do you think my mother insists on paying for these sessions?"

He shrugged comfortably. "Because you're hopelessly stuck in rebellion and you need to grow up?"

"Possibly, but the fact that you're Jewish and divorced doesn't hurt. She's hoping you'll fall madly in love with me so that we can add a shrink to the family." Shelley smiled. "Can I tell her there'll be a family discount?"

Howard Mellnick smiled back. "Therapist-patient relationships are unethical."

"Yes, but I don't think dating scruples are part of the Jewish Mother code of ethics. You're male and Jewish and a doctor; that makes you fair game."

He coughed to try to hide his laugh. "Does it occur to you that your parents genuinely love you and want what's best for you?"

"Occasionally. But the fact that my mother pays you to talk to me makes everything you say suspect."

Dr. Mellnick went ahead and laughed, which was one of the reasons she kept showing up.

"Okay," he said, "we've spent the requisite ten minutes on your mother. Why don't we move on to what happened with the presentation yesterday? The one we've been talking about for two months, the one you prepared for like Noah prepared for the flood."

Shelley groaned. "It was Trey's birthday. We ended up in a room at the Ritz."

Mellnick just waited—a task at which he excelled—so Shelley went ahead and divulged her birthday orgasm theory.

The best thing about Howard Mellnick—after his sense of humor—was that he never looked shocked or overtly disapproving.

"So let me see if I have this straight: As of yesterday morning, you were poised and ready to turn your career situation and your relationship with your father around. Yesterday during lunch you decided Trey Davenport's sexual satisfaction was more important." His eyes behind the frameless glasses were kind and at the same time merciless. "Any idea why?"

"Isn't that what you're being paid to find out?"

He smiled, but it didn't quite reach his eyes this time. "I can keep pointing out the ways in which you shoot yourself in the foot, Shelley, but I can't keep you from loading the gun. The ultimate goal is to recognize the self-sabotage *before* you blow your toes off."

They stared at each other for a time.

"There's nothing wrong with being a Jewish American Princess if that's what you want to be. There's nothing wrong with refusing to be one, either. But you've got to declare yourself. You're stuck in that netherworld. You continue to rebel against what your parents expect, but you won't go after what *you* really want."

"I want to be taken seriously." She said it quietly, but she knew he heard and understood.

"And yet you choose to give a boyfriend an orgasm rather than show up and pitch an account."

"Well, it wasn't like I had a scale there and was weighing the pros and cons. The man was naked and it was his birthday. Frankly, I thought I could do both."

Shelley looked down at her watch and back up at Howard Mellnick. Their fifty minutes was up. "I don't suppose you'd like to go handle my mother and the accountant while I straighten out your six o'clock appointment's life?"

"No, thanks, but I'll look forward to hearing the details next week. Oh, and do me a favor. Be gentle with the accountant. Chances are he isn't any happier about this fix-up than you are."

chapter 3

Howard Mellnick was wrong. Richard Friedlander was ecstatic to be there. Ecstatic to make her acquaintance. His eyes widened at first sight of her, which told her he'd been anticipating the worst.

Since her father continued to refuse to discuss the Easy To Be Me account and had told her not once, but three times, not to "worry her little head about it," exceeding *anyone's* expectations felt incredibly nice. Of course, she reflected as she looked into his round, earnest face, this might not be the compliment she was assuming; there was no telling what kinds of women had been thrown at Richard Friedlander since he'd arrived in Atlanta.

His hand was clammy when he shook hers in greeting. He beamed at her out of relieved brown eyes, probably still thanking his lucky stars she hadn't been wheeled in on a forklift. But then, Richard Friedlander wasn't exactly God's gift to women. Or even a party favor, for that matter.

Trying to be generous, she factored out the sweaty palms and told herself that even someone who looked like a marshmallow might have something to offer.

"Just call me Dick," he said as he pumped her hand for far too long. Shelley forced herself to smile as if this might actually happen. Then she shoved a glass of wine at him, led him to her father and brother-in-law, who were jockeying for position around a plate of her mother's chopped liver, and fled to the kitchen.

The memory-charged aromas of matzo ball soup and brisket hit her as she entered. Plates of gefilte fish, each arranged on its bed of lettuce with a dollop of horseradish by its side, sat on the kitchen island waiting to be served after the soup. Miriam Schwartz didn't do Shabbas dinner on a weekly basis, but when she did she approached the meal exactly the way her mother, Nana Rose, always had—as if she were auditioning for a part in *Fiddler on the Roof*.

Tonight, every dish was intended to accomplish two things: remind her family that they were loved, and demonstrate to Richard Friedlander what kind of meals he might expect as a part of said family. Miriam Schwartz still believed that the most direct way to a man's heart was through his stomach; Shelley had reason to believe the road began somewhat lower.

Nana Rose's younger sister, Sonya, perched on a bar stool at the counter and watched Judy ladle matzo ball soup into bowls that said "Jewish penicillin." Great-aunt Sonya lived in the Summitt Towers, where she made papier-mâché animal heads and insisted the maids were sneaking in at night and rearranging her apartment.

Shelley gave her great-aunt a hug and slid onto the stool

next to her. "Can we take some things out of the oven so I can fit my head in?"

"That bad?" Judy kept ladling. Despite the heat of the kitchen and her proximity to the stove, neither her hair nor her clothes drooped. She was six years older and four and a half inches shorter than Shelley. Like their mother, Judy was petite and curvy.

Trying to follow in her older sister's too-tiny footsteps had left Shelley feeling like an ugly stepsister trying to squeeze into Cinderella's glass slipper. She'd been twelve or thirteen when she finally stopped trying.

"He *wants* to be called Dick. He's shorter than the mortician, has less hair than the chiropractor, and is pudgier than the rodeo clown." Shelley cheered briefly. "Do you remember how incensed Mom was when she found out 'clown' was his occupation and not a comment on his sense of humor?"

As if summoned, Miriam backed through the swinging kitchen door with the empty chopped liver dish in her hands. "I don't want you hiding in here, Shelley," her mother said as she grabbed a waiting replacement tray of hors d'oeuvres. "Richard's a very nice young man. Marilyn tells me he's thinking about opening his own firm."

Before Shelley could respond—not that she intended to—her mother was already hurrying back to her current and potential sons-in-law, the plate of food extended in front of her like a sacrificial offering.

Judy finished ladling. Putting the lid on the pot of soup, she poured herself a glass of wine and moved to join Shelley at the island. She looked distracted, her expression at odds with the crispness of her hair and clothes, as if she'd gone through all the usual motions but didn't really mean it.

"I liked the wrestler," Sonya commented as the door swung closed. "He looked great in tights."

"He was a total ten from the neck down," Shelley agreed, remembering how pleasantly surprised she'd been when she first spotted the blond-haired Adonis. "Unfortunately, I think that was also his IQ."

Shelley placed an arm around Aunt Sonya's bony shoulders, surprised, as always, by her increasing fragility. Her great-aunt seemed to be shedding flesh as she aged, getting rid of all the unnecessary bits and pieces.

"Why won't she give up?" Shelley asked. "Does she really think that one day I'll walk in, see a plump proctologist eating her chopped liver, and say, 'Be still, my heart'?"

"No." Judy put down her wine and picked up two bowls, motioning Shelley to do the same. "She just figures if she throws enough shit against the wall, something's going to stick."

"I definitely could have lived without that image," Shelley said as she followed her sister out to the dining room. "And, of course, if she keeps flinging shit, sooner or later one of us is going to step in it."

For the next thirty minutes Shelley annoyed her mother by being helpful. Though she normally went to great lengths to avoid housework and preferred the family dinners where her mother's longtime maid, Delilah, served and cleaned up, tonight Shelley used the cleaning woman's absence to her advantage. The first to jump up when something needed to be done, she fetched more soup from the kitchen, got up to pour refills of water and wine, and cleared the table by herself, which allowed her to avoid Richard Friedlander without being rude.

Her mother shot her pointed looks and protested every time Shelley volunteered to do something, but even a master kvetch couldn't come out and complain that a daughter was helping *too* much. Shelley had already chipped a nail and gotten a brisket stain on her white silk blouse, but the defeated expression on her mother's face more than made up for it.

As a coup de grâce, she insisted on loading the dishwasher while her mother took coffee out to the table. At a nearby counter a strangely subdued Judy unpacked Tupperware containers of baked goods and began to arrange them on silver trays.

With sure fingers she arranged perfectly formed rugelach, brownies, cookies, and strudel slices into artful patterns.

Shelley's heart sank. Someone else might look at the rows of sweets tucked into their colored paper baking cups and see dessert. Shelley saw a cry for help. Others might turn to drugs or alcohol when distressed; Judy Blumfeld baked. If her sister were to dial a suicide help line, the conversation would begin with "Help! I can't stop sifting!"

"That's a lot of goodies you've got there," Shelley said.

Judy shrugged and finished filling the first tray. Without missing a beat, she started to fill another.

Was there such a thing as a baking intervention? Should she try to start a chapter of Overbakers Anonymous?

"So how's Sammy's bar mitzvah coming along?" Shelley asked, edging closer to the rows of treats.

"Fine."

This was not good, either. If there was anything Judy normally liked to expound on, it was the progress of THE bar mitzvah.

"Did you decide on a theme?"

"I'm not sure we really need a theme this time."

There was a moment of shocked silence while Shelley tried to absorb this heresy.

"What does Mandy say about that?" Mandy Mifkin was the bar mitzvah coordinator who had implemented the Gladiator theme for Jason's bar mitzvah two years ago. The theme had allegedly been designed to dovetail with her oldest nephew's interest in wrestling and to take advantage of the popularity of Russell Crowe's movie, but Shelley had thought it an odd choice for descendants of a people who had been so heavily oppressed by the Romans. Forcing the band members and waiters to wear togas had been just one of Mandy's signature touches.

"I don't know. I guess I'm just having some second thoughts."

The theme music for *The Outer Limits* began to play softly in Shelley's head. "OK, who are you? And what have you done with my sister?"

Judy snorted and popped a brownie in her mouth, which was another thing Judy never did. For all her sister's baking, Shelley hadn't seen her consume chocolate in public since she was pregnant with Sammy, which was approximately thirteen years ago. The Schwartz women consumed their high-calorie items behind closed doors.

Back at the dinner table Shelley stirred her coffee and idly pushed a piece of strudel around on her plate. She snuck surreptitious glances at her sister while congratulating herself on minimizing her contact with Richard—who appeared slightly bewildered that she had not, in fact, flung herself at his feet.

With her last sip of coffee she decided that as soon as the meal ended she was going to get her father alone to try for one last shot at the account that had fallen so unceremoniously into Ross Morgan's lap.

She intended to be coolly professional, and had actually prepared a sort of mini sales presentation in her head while she loaded the dishwasher. She prayed her father would be receptive, but if all else failed she'd stick out her lower lip and let it quiver pathetically. If she had to, she'd cry. She was prepared to go to the mat on this one.

Shelley glanced up at Harvey Schwartz. In his early sixties, with salt-and-pepper hair and an interestingly craggy face, he was still an impressive man. She had his height and his build. Up until her sixteenth birthday, she'd had his nose.

He gave her a private wink and she smiled in return. She had always had his love; it had been the bedrock on which much of her life had been built. But recently she'd begun to crave his approval and respect with an intensity that she didn't understand. She dreamed of earning a heartfelt "well done," or the kind of look he normally bestowed on Ross Morgan.

She opened her mouth to ask him something, but before she could get the words out a strange expression washed over his face. His eyes closed briefly and he clamped a hand around his upper arm.

"What is it, Daddy?"

He started to speak, and she leaned forward to hear what

he was saying, but although his lips moved, no words emerged.

"Daddy!"

The table fell silent, no doubt at the urgency in her tone. Or maybe they'd seen the same things she had.

"Harvey?" Her mother's voice was sharp. "Do you need Rolaids? Quick, somebody get a Zantac. I told you not to eat so much!"

But no one moved. They sat there straining to hear him, waiting an eternity for him to get the words out, unsure what to do or say.

"I . . . I feel like an elephant's sitting on my chest and I can't feel the left side of my body," he finally said in a strangled voice she barely recognized.

"Oh, God," Shelley shouted as he fell face-first into his dessert, "forget about the Rolaids. Somebody call nine-one-one."

chapter 4

Shelley spent the rest of Friday night and most of Saturday morning bargaining with God. At any other time she might have questioned the likelihood that there was a supreme being hanging around up there, waiting to answer prayers or to enter into negotiations with someone who only showed up for temple on the High Holidays. But when you were sitting in a hospital waiting for your father to make it through an emergency bypass, you clung to any available straw. Right now Shelley was clinging to both God and Dr. Manny Shapiro, whose job it was to open up her father, reroute his blood around those clogged arteries, and then appear in this waiting room to utter the medical equivalent of "piece of cake."

Only they hadn't seen Dr. Shapiro for hours, and her mother—who hadn't speculated on Dr. Shapiro's marital status or uttered a single word since her father had been wheeled back to the operating room—continued to stare into space with a lost look on her face that Shelley had never seen before.

Across from Shelley, Judy slept with her head on her husband Craig's shoulder, her chin mashed to her chest. Periodically Judy's eyes fluttered open, but she didn't lift her head from Craig's shoulder. Shelley didn't blame her. If she'd had a shoulder to burrow into, she wouldn't have come up for air, either.

Trey's shoulders were even broader than her brother-in-law's, but Trey's shoulders weren't here. They were out floating down a river somewhere in Colorado. But even if Trey had been in town, would she have called and invited him into such a personal and painful place?

It was almost as hard to picture as a favor-granting God. She spent a few minutes imagining what Howard Mellnick would say about that little admission. Then she went back to negotiating with the Almighty.

She'd already promised to give up sex in return for the Easy To Be Me account while she was racing back to the office from the Ritz, but He hadn't taken her up on her offer. Which led Shelley to wonder how much God really cared who she had sex with and how often. And whether she could now rescind the offer of abstinence since the prayer accompanying it had not been answered. It was enough to make her wish she were Catholic so she could have some saints to appeal to.

Shelley repositioned herself in the molded plastic chair and contemplated her sister (still sleeping) and her mother (still staring). Maybe God was looking for something a little more G-rated. Maybe God would come through if she promised to get along better with her family.

What if she stopped arguing with them? What if, no matter how annoying they got, or what they said or did, she simply smiled agreeably and kept the peace?

She sat up straighter, certain she was on to something here. If God would spare her father, she'd turn over a whole new leaf. Kind of like Yom Kippur without the fasting and praying. If her father came through this surgery, she'd stop envying and baiting her sister. She'd go out with any Jewish man her mother . . . Shelley shot a look toward the ceiling and squashed that thought.

If God didn't care about her sex life, why would he concern Himself with the religious affiliations of the men she dated? Surely He didn't sit around up in Heaven shaking a finger at Jewish girls and telling them it was just as easy to fall in love with a Jewish man as a non-Jewish one.

Shelley unfolded her body out of the chair and stretched. Her hair stuck out in undreamed-of directions, and her mouth felt as if someone had snuck in during the night and stuck a dirty sock in it.

"Mom, do you want some coffee?"

"No." Her mother's makeup had eroded during the night, leaving her haggard expression bared for all to see. "What if he doesn't make it?" she whispered. "If that man dies on me, I'll kill him."

Shelley shook her head. "There's not going to be any dying. I'm bringing you a coffee and something to eat so you can keep up your strength." Was this really her encouraging her mother to be stronger? Wasn't that like trying to shore up Fort Knox? "You don't want Daddy to think you've given up on him."

Her mother blew her nose into a crumpled tissue. "You're right."

Shelley went stock-still. "What did you say?"

Her mother sniffed. "I said, you're right."

Shelley stole a quick glance out a nearby window to make sure hell had not, in fact, frozen over. If they'd been somewhere other than this hospital under these circumstances, she might have pumped a fist in the air or called the *Guinness World Records*. But her mother's admission only underscored how dire she thought the straits were.

In the bathroom, Shelley finger-brushed her teeth, gargled with the tiny mouthwash she kept tucked in her purse, and freshened her makeup.

In the hospital cafeteria she bought four coffees and an assortment of fruit and Danish, which she passed out when she got back to the waiting room. Numb, they sipped on their coffees and waited for the caffeine to do its job. Part of her couldn't bear the waiting another minute, while the other part preferred the fear to the knowing; once bad news was given there'd be no taking it back.

An eternity later, she looked up and spotted Dr. Shapiro heading toward them. Her heart began to pound as she took in his tired eyes and the expression on his face. Sliding into the vacant seat between her sister and mother, Shelley grabbed their hands and held on. It was clear "piece of cake" were not going to be his first words.

Judy squeezed back so hard it hurt. Her sister's eyes were caked with sleep and had black smudges beneath them. Her lips were chapped and her lipstick had been eaten off a long time ago. It was hard to decide which was more frightening:

her sister's state of dishevelment or her mother's disturbing silence.

Panic rolled off them in waves: Shelley recognized it because it matched her own. She wondered briefly what sort of bargains they'd been making and whether the sum of all the things the Schwartz women were willing to change or give up would be enough for God.

Together they raised their gazes to meet the doctor's. There was a collective intake of breath.

"The blockage was much worse than we were expecting."

Her mother gasped and squeezed Shelley's hand so hard she had to hold back a gasp of her own. At the words "much worse" Shelley's brain began to race. Was he making excuses? Preparing them for the fact that they hadn't been able to save him? If everything was all right, wouldn't he have said that first?

"The next twenty-four hours will be crucial."

Her brain stopped racing and she let out a ragged breath as one clear thought emerged. If her father hadn't made it, the next twenty-four hours wouldn't be crucial.

Oh, thank you, God, thank you. She squeezed the hands clasped in her own and drew a steadying breath.

"He's in recovery right now. Once we have him stabilized, he'll be moved to ICU."

"When can we see him?" Judy's voice was full of the relief Shelley was feeling. Their mother still hadn't spoken.

"Once they've got him situated in ICU, immediate family can see him one at a time. But he should sleep for quite a while."

"So, he's all right?" Her mother's voice was high and tight.

Dr. Shapiro adjusted his glasses. "Well, as I said, the next twenty-four hours are critical. Right now we take it one day at a time. But ultimately, if things go well he'll be looking at some serious lifestyle changes." The doctor ran a hand through his short brown hair, and Shelley realized that he'd used that hand to help save her father's life.

"But assuming he takes this as seriously as he should... well, the rest of him appears to be in pretty good shape."

They were too numb to ask any more questions, too relieved to think about details. As they watched Dr. Shapiro's retreating back, the fear began to dissipate. Shelley wanted to jump for joy, whoop it up, skip inappropriately through the halls singing at the top of her lungs.

As they began to gather their things, her mother pulled her compact from her purse and applied powder and lipstick with a shaky hand. She popped a piece of spearmint gum into her mouth and offered the pack to the rest of them. Shelley could see her pulling the tattered remnants of real life back around her. When she spoke, it almost felt strange to hear her voice again.

"Well," she said with a glint in her eye that smacked of unshed tears, "you better believe I'm going to give your father a piece of my mind for scaring us this way." She smoothed her hair back into place. "Why, I can practically feel the gray hairs sprouting."

"Mother," Shelley said carefully, "I don't think Dr. Shapiro would approve nagging and scolding as an incentive to recovery."

"Hmmph!" Miriam Schwartz snapped her purse shut and slung the strap over her shoulder. "For your information, I never nag. I only *prod* your father along when it's absolutely necessary. Subtle is my middle name."

There was a lot of eye-widening, but no one came out and countered her claim to subtlety. Miriam Schwartz had just spent the night confronting what must have been every one of her worst fears. However she chose to express her relief, it was not their place to criticize. And of course, asking her mother to stop nagging was like asking her not to breathe.

"Besides," her mother said in a deceptively reasonable tone, "your *father*'s the one who's been ordered to change his lifestyle. Dr. Shapiro, who by the way was NOT wearing a wedding ring, didn't say a word about *me*."

The dough was moist and smooth in Judy's floured hands, the weight of it comforting. Intent, she used her fingers and palms as well as the heels of her hands, pressing forward, pulling back, applying both muscle and finesse to work the dough into two perfect rolls.

It was Wednesday, four P.M., four and a quarter days since her father had come out of surgery, and she hadn't left the house once all day. The boys would be home soon and she knew she should be planning dinner, but she was making mandelbrot instead. The dog-eared recipe card, written in Nana Rose's spidery handwriting, was propped up against the flour canister. Judy knew the recipe by heart, but the card, like the smell and taste of this German/Jewish version of biscotti, brought her grandmother closer. When the mandelbrot was finished, she'd store it in one of Nana's old tins.

Nana Rose had lived to ninety-one. She'd been independent and feisty right up until the day she dropped dead in the middle of her kitchen while making matzo balls. Both her mother's and father's families were known for their longevity. Sprung from good European peasant stock, the Schwartzes and Kleins got shriveled and wizened and shrank like Great-aunt Sonya was doing now; they didn't drop dead from heart attacks at the age of sixty-three like her father had almost done.

Judy arranged the rolls of dough on the baking sheet and slipped it into the preheated oven.

She'd assumed her parents would live to ripe old ages; had assumed she and Craig would do the same. But what if she didn't have another fifty years? What if she was going to drop one day soon in the sportswear department at Bloomies? Or while letting Lars, her sadistic personal trainer, push her through yet another workout? What if it happened in a car pool line while she was waiting for one of the boys?

Her thoughts swirling, she cleared the counters and scrubbed the mixing bowls, breathing in the almond-scented warmth that began to fill her kitchen. She gathered the dirty clothes strewn across the boys' bedroom floors and deposited them in the laundry room, then hurried back to the kitchen to take the warm mounds from the oven. She had just sliced the dough and put the crescent-shaped pieces back in the oven when Sammy, her youngest, breezed through the kitchen door.

"Hi, sweetie."

At twelve Sammy had already more than matched her five feet four inches. Although he was rapidly catching up with his older brother physically, in many ways he was still her little boy and not averse to the occasional display of affection.

Judy gave him a quick hug and a peck on the cheek. "How was the social studies test?"

"Killer."

"And?"

"I knew it. I did fine."

"Good." The timer went off and she pulled the browned cookies out. "What kind of homework do you have?"

"Just language arts and science."

"All right. Pick one and get started. After dinner we'll—"

"I've got baseball practice at six-thirty. Can't I do my homework when I get home?"

"Practice? But—"

"Just a little TV and then I'll get dressed and start on my science."

She was too busy regrouping around the unexpected practice to negotiate. Had she really forgotten? Or missed an e-mailed schedule change? She'd been so busy cleaning and baking today, she hadn't even gone on-line.

Moving to the pantry she perused its contents, looking for something she could make for Jason and Craig that would be portable enough for Sam to eat in the car.

The kitchen door opened and slammed shut. Jason sauntered in and dropped his backpack in the middle of the floor.

"Do *not* leave that there," Judy said as she did every day. He grunted and kicked it approximately two inches to the left and she came around the counter to stand in front of him, knowing better than to try to hug or kiss him. At four-teen and a half, he towered over her. His shoulders were almost as broad as his father's. The child they had once dubbed "the mouth" now communicated via shrugs, grimaces, and monosyllables. She no longer had any idea what he thought or felt.

"How was school?"

"OK." He opened the refrigerator, grabbed a carton of milk, and lifted it toward his lips.

"Don't *even* think about it."

With a shrug, he pulled a glass out of the cupboard, filled it to the brim, and drained it in one long gulp. Abandoning it without a backward glance, he grabbed a handful of Oreos from the cookie jar and headed back toward the door. "Going to Joey's," he mumbled around a mouthful of chocolate.

"But what about homework?"

"Already finished it."

She checked the clock. If she made some kind of casserole, she could pop it in the oven before she left to drop Sam at practice and get back in time to put it on the table. She reached for a can of tuna. "Be back by seven for dinner."

"I have wrestling practice at six forty-five."

"*You* have practice tonight, too?"

"Uh-huh."

He was gone before she could question him further. Turning back to the pantry she reconsidered her options. She'd do a drive-through for the boys and let Craig fend for himself. Her own appetite had disappeared months ago.

"Where's my belt?" Sammy shrieked from the top of the stairs. "And my other red sock?"

Judy sighed. When you were a lone woman in a house

full of males you were pretty much the only person who actually knew where things were. Or cared.

"Try the laundry room," she shouted over the ringing of the phone. He clomped off as she brought the receiver to her ear.

"Judy?" Craig's voice was hurried and distracted. This was nothing new.

She looked up at the clock on the wall. "Where are you?"

"On my way to the Witherspoon dinner."

"But both the boys have practices tonight. I wanted to go to the hospital to see my father after dinner."

"Judy," he spoke as if to a child. "This has been on the calendar for weeks."

"No way," she protested as she walked over to the family calendar. She was the most obsessively organized person she knew. She scheduled their lives like a commander scheduled his troops; her calendar was her battle map.

She glanced at today's square just to prove her point. And clamped her mouth shut.

"You know, writing things on the calendar is only helpful if you remember to look at it on the appropriate day," Craig pointed out.

Very funny. She looked at that damned calendar constantly. She didn't make a move without consulting that calendar.

She changed the phone to her other ear. Except lately she'd become reluctant to look at all those packed squares and what they represented. She'd been reluctant to consider a lot of things lately.

Craig had his little chuckle at her expense and then said

good-bye. Judy put away the mandelbrot and told herself she should be happy she didn't have to cook dinner.

She'd just throw the boys in the car, toss something down their throats—like the seal trainers did at SeaWorld—and deposit them at their respective practices. At which point she'd have about forty-five minutes to regroup before she turned around and started picking them back up.

"Sammy, hurry up!" she shouted up the stairs. Jason ambled through the door and she waved him in, trying to light a fire under him. "You need to hurry, too," she said. "You're going to have to come with me to drop Sam. Throw your gym bag in the back of the car and let's go."

Sammy pounded down the stairs and Judy fell in behind him, shooing both boys toward the door, trying to figure out when she'd lost her grasp on the details of their lives.

At the step down to the garage she stopped to flip off the kitchen light and retrieve her purse and keys from the kitchen desk. But neither of her children was hotfooting it to the car. In fact, they'd turned and planted themselves in her path and were now considering her out of identical brown eyes.

"What?" she asked, annoyed by all that she'd forgotten and all that she still had left to do.

"Well..." Sammy looked embarrassed. Jason's expression indicated he thought she was dumber than dirt. "Well," her oldest said now. "We know we're in a hurry and all." He gave her an odd once-over and she dropped her own gaze to see what he was looking at.

"But don't you think you should go back in and change out of your pajamas?"

chapter 5

On Monday morning Shelley met Nina for breakfast at the Lox, Stocks and Bagel, a trendy new deli located above a brokerage house in Buckhead. Nina was dressed for work at the small engineering firm she'd recently joined. Shelley hadn't been able to force herself to go into the office since her father's heart attack. The idea of the office without him was more than she could take.

Pushing her mushroom omelet around on her plate and sipping halfheartedly at her coffee, Shelley watched Nina consume two eggs, an order of corned beef hash, home fries, and whole-wheat toast with the precision of a surgeon. In her methodical way, Nina packed away more food than any truck driver, yet still looked like a supermodel. Shelley had been trying to hate her for it since they'd met in Mrs. Gerber's first grade class, but her friend's unfailing good humor and practical nature generally compensated for her enviable metabolism and ability to make every other woman in a room disappear.

Nina Olson was naturally blond and blue-eyed, with Scandinavian cheekbones and an aquiline nose that hadn't required remodeling. If you looked up "shiksa" in a Yiddish dictionary it would say "non-Jewish female" and be accompanied by Nina's picture.

"How's Miriam taking all of this?" Nina reached for a piece of Shelley's untouched rye toast and slathered it with jelly.

"About like you'd expect. One minute she's fussing over him and telling him to take it easy, the next she's complaining that he's not trying hard enough to get better. He just got home from the hospital yesterday, and he's already got that hunted look on his face. I'm heading over there after breakfast."

"Well, give him a hug from me and tell him I'll stop by after work."

Nina's own father had died when she was in elementary school, and her mother had married a variety of men who'd come and gone too quickly to get attached to. Harvey Schwartz was the closest thing to a father figure Nina had.

"Then you have to tell him all your ideas for moving the agency more deeply into media. This is a perfect time to start taking on more responsibility."

Shelley shot her a look. "You're starting to sound like Howard Mellnick."

"It's just common sense, Shelley. You've been waiting for your opportunity, and your dad's supposed to take it easier. Who better than his own flesh and blood to help supervise things while he's out?"

"Gee, I don't know, let me think." Shelley struck a thoughtful pose, went so far as to rub her chin. "Ross Morgan?"

"Ross Morgan is not his flesh and blood." Nina eyed what was left of Shelley's toast and when Shelley didn't protest she helped herself. "*You* are. And there's nothing wrong with a little good old-fashioned nepotism."

The idea of asking and being turned down again belonged in the category of "too painful to contemplate." It was way too soon after her Easy To Be Me debacle to confront her father's perception of her.

Nina popped the last of Shelley's toast into her mouth. "As your father once told us both," she said after chewing and swallowing, " 'If you don't ask, you can't get.' If you don't throw your hat in the ring, Shel, you can't complain when you're not elected."

"If you don't stop quoting my father and channeling Howard Mellnick I'm going to have you exorcised. And frankly, if I had to choose between Ross Morgan and me right now, I'm not sure *I'd* choose me."

Nina narrowed her eyes at that. "Don't be ridiculous. You are totally competent when you're not sabotaging yourself." She made her voice sound large and omnipotently Oz-like. "The Mellnick and I have spoken." She signaled for the check. "You might be able to blow one of us off, but not even you are pigheaded enough to ignore us both."

The waitress came to the table and laid the check on it. "So you're the ones," she said, eyeing their plates. "The dishwashers have been trying to figure out who the cleanplaters are for weeks. I'm assuming I can take these?"

Once, long ago, Shelley might have protested her innocence and pointed the gluttonous finger at Nina. Nowadays she no longer bothered.

"Can we change the subject now?" Shelley asked when their plates had been cleared. Knowing Nina was right about approaching her father didn't make the idea any less daunting.

"Sure." Nina looked at Shelley expectantly.

"So... tell me about Tad. Are you going to take him to the firm dinner?"

"Tad and I are history," Nina said. "I mean, what kind of name is Tad anyway?"

"You dumped him because of his name?" Shelley snorted. "And you call *me* picky?"

"But he *is* his name. The guy is a skydiving instructor. He goes up in the air and jumps down. Repeatedly. What if he lands a *tad* too hard? Or opens his chute a *tad* too late?

"I'm ready for a nice solid man who goes to work every day and comes home for dinner. I don't know if you've noticed or not," Nina continued, "but we're not as young as we used to be."

"Thank you so much for that."

"Seriously, Shel. Aren't you getting tired of dating? I'm thirty-two and I started dating when I was fifteen. That's seventeen years. I've had enough."

Shelley studied her oldest friend. "But you're so good at it. Nina Olson giving up dating? Why, it would be like Betty Crocker giving up baking. Or Madonna writing children's books."

They looked at each other.

"Well, you know what I mean."

"I'm ready to settle down, Shelley. And I want a nice, solid, dependable guy to do it with. I've had exciting; exciting's not all it's cracked up to be. I want somebody like your dad..." She looked up out of blue eyes that were not joking one little bit. "And they say Jewish men make the best husbands. You can tell by the way they treat their mothers."

"Jewish men are good to their mothers because they know they'll be guilted to death if they're not. Believe me, you don't want to go there."

"But I do. And I've drawn up a list of goals and objectives along with a cursory plan of attack." Her friend pulled a sheet of computer paper out of her purse and pushed it toward Shelley. The list was organized and to the point, just like Nina. It read: 1) Place personal ad in *Jewish Singles Magazine* and on Web sites. 2) Ask Shelley for referrals. 3) Accept any and all blind dates with appropriate men. 4) Go to bookstore and study Jewish section. 5) Talk to rabbi?

"Finding a Jewish husband is now my number-one priority," Nina concluded. "The only thing I'm not sure about is whether I need to convert or not."

Shelley arrived at her parents' filled with resolve. If her father seemed up to it, she planned to broach her role at the agency one last time. If she had to, she'd pitch him like she would a new account.

That resolve weakened at the sight of Ross Morgan's shiny black Porsche parked at the top of the driveway.

Slamming her own car door, she gave the Boxster a wide berth and tromped up the drive to the front steps. His presence and his car, which was far too flashy for such an intentionally unflashy guy, irritated her. She immediately faulted

Morgan for bothering her father with business when he was barely out of the hospital, until she remembered she'd been about to do the same.

"Hello?"

There was no response as she let herself into the house, so she followed the sound of male voices back to her parents' bedroom. Her father was propped up in bed with an array of pill bottles and a stack of reading material beside him. Ross leaned against the side of an armoire, his arms folded casually across his chest. They both fell silent when she entered the room.

"Hey, Dad." Shelley went to the bed and leaned over to give her father a smooch on the cheek. "You're not looking too bad for someone who almost bought the farm."

But he didn't look all that great, either. He'd dropped weight he couldn't afford to lose and his eyes, which had new lines etched around them, were tired. This was not the man who jumped up every morning eager to see what the day would bring.

"Hello, sweetheart." He squeezed her hand, but without the usual heartiness. "We were just talking about you."

Ross Morgan nodded politely. He was always polite, which, given how big an obstacle he was, only served to irritate her.

"Ross tells me things are moving along well with the Easy To Be Me people," her father said. "They're going to shoot the TV spot and cast the radio commercials later this week."

Shelley sank down in the club chair opposite the bed. Just what she wanted to hear about—the success of an account she was no longer working on.

"That's good," she said. "Did you get Mike Moorehouse?" She referred to the commercial director she'd recommended for the shoot.

"Yes." Morgan's voice was pleasant, even-toned. "And I think we're going to go with Kylie West for spokesperson. They really liked her demo."

"Great."

Shelley and Ross considered each other. His blond hair looked recently cut and his face freshly shaven. He was dressed in rolled-up shirtsleeves and a pair of dress pants. His shirt was the same bright blue as his eyes, and his forearms were lightly muscled and covered with a dusting of blond hair.

Great. Ross Morgan was preventing her from stating her case to her father, and she was noticing the hair on his forearms. No wonder she wasn't getting ahead.

"Can I get you anything, Daddy?"

"No, honey. Your mother just ran out to the grocery store. She should be back any minute."

"OK." She looked pointedly at Ross Morgan, more than ready for him to go so that she could speak to her father alone. When he didn't budge, she motioned with her head toward the door.

"So, I guess I'll be going," he said.

"No." Her father stopped him. "I think we'd better talk about this now." A look passed between the two men that made Shelley distinctly uncomfortable. Her father cleared his throat, then looked her straight in the eye. "Ross and I have been talking about the agency and his role in it," he said.

Shelley straightened in the chair and had a brief wild

rush of hope that Ross Morgan and his lovely forearms were moving on to greener pastures.

"My heart attack forced me to face the fact that my time might be limited."

"But the doctor said you're not going anywhere as long as you take care of yourself." Shelley definitely didn't want to hear everyone's worst fears put into words.

"Yes," her father said, "and that's what I plan to do."

Shelley opened her mouth, but he cut her off.

"I'm going to retire."

"But—"

"I'm going to take it easy, play golf, learn to basket-weave or some such thing. Take your mother back to Europe."

Like that would be less stressful.

"But you'll be bored. You'll go crazy." *You'll be with Mom all the time.* "You two will drive each other mad within a month."

"It's done, Shelley."

"But—"

"I'm going to hand over the agency to Ross. He'll put a certain amount of cash up front, and pay me out over time, but he'll take charge immediately."

She swallowed around the horrible lump in her throat and blinked back tears, determined not to sound too pathetic. "But what about me?"

Ross's gaze was on her now, and she had a terrible feeling there was pity in it. How dare he come in here and steal her family's business away and then pretend he felt bad about it?

She came slowly to her feet. "I wanted to talk to you about taking a larger role. I'm ready, Dad, really I am. I can help relieve your burden. Your heart attack got through to me, too. I know I've messed up before, but I'm ready now."

"I appreciate that, sweetheart." Her father pulled himself up straighter against the pillows and smiled, completely oblivious to how cleanly he was cutting her heart out. "And that's the great thing about this. You can have as big a role as you can handle. Ross has agreed that as long as he runs the business you'll have your job. And we've worked out cost-of-living increases, medical benefits, and so on. It'll all be in writing." He smiled full-out, clearly proud of all he'd negotiated on her behalf. "So you're set, sweetheart. And if you show Ross what I know you're capable of, you'll be a very important part of his team."

His team, *his* agency. Shelley's chest ached and tears blurred her vision. No matter what she said, her father would always see her as a little girl to be taken care of. And how could she blame him when she'd never given him reason to see her any other way?

She wanted to throw herself on the floor and kick and scream out her hurt and frustration. Or better yet, beat her fists against Ross Morgan's broad chest. But she would not upset her father with some silly temper tantrum or give Ross Morgan the satisfaction of seeing how badly she hurt.

Her mother's voice wafted down the hall from the kitchen, growing louder as she neared the master bedroom. Entering, she rushed to the bed and began to cluck over her husband, seemingly oblivious to the undercurrents charging through the room.

"I hope you're not wearing yourself out talking business, Harvey. You know what Dr. Shapiro told you."

She turned to Shelley and Ross. "I've got a big bowl of

chicken soup for the patient and cold cuts for anyone who wants to stay for lunch." She cocked her head, clearly happy to have people to fuss over and orchestrate. "How many places shall I set?"

Shelley didn't wait to see whether Ross Morgan was staying. All she wanted was to get out of this house before she broke down into tears or said something that would hurt or upset her father. "I, uh, have an appointment I have to get to." She stepped forward and pecked her mother on the cheek, then leaned over the bed to do the same to her father. "I have to be going. You have a big rest this afternoon, Daddy. I'll check in later to see how you're doing."

And before anyone could stop her, not that anyone seemed inclined to, Shelley was out of the room, out of the house, and on her way to her condo, where she burst into tears as soon as the door closed safely behind her.

chapter 6

Shelley spent the next three days in her pajamas, wallowing. It wasn't a conscious decision. She just couldn't seem to make herself get out of bed. Or answer her phone. Or go to her job. Or keep her appointments. Voice mails poured in from her colorist, her manicurist, her electrolysist, her masseuse, and her personal trainer. Her misery was affecting profits at salons all over Buckhead.

In the kitchen the dishes were piled in the sink and the remnants of all the food she'd eaten lay wherever she'd consumed it. The empty quart of Cherry Garcia with the spoon sticking out of it stared her down every time she walked past the coffee table, but she couldn't summon the energy to remove it. The one time she answered the phone without checking her caller ID her mother caught her. Possibly sensing Shelley's vulnerability, she charged right through the pleasantries and then zeroed in for the kill.

"Shelley?"

"Mmm-hmm?" Lazily, Shelley examined her fingernails and was surprised to note that her polish was chipped and one of her acrylic tips had disappeared.

"Are you all right?"

"Mmm-hmm."

"You don't sound all right."

Normally Shelley would have argued or changed the subject, but her mind was moving much too slowly to successfully feint and parry with her mother.

"I'm fine," she managed. Then she yawned.

"If I'm keeping you awake, I'd better get right to the point."

It was a sign of how tired she was that this seemed like a good idea. Plopping onto the living room sofa, she put her bare feet up on the cocktail table and edged the empty ice cream carton aside with her toes, which she now realized were also unusually...ragged. When had the hair on her legs reached the Brillo stage?

"I had a call from Thelma Horowitz."

Shelley's antennae must have been as numb as the rest of her, because they failed to spring up and warn her of the danger ahead.

"Her son just moved back to Atlanta and he needs a date for..."

Shelley knew there was something she should be saying or doing now, but she couldn't seem to remember what it was.

"...a client dinner." Her mother paused for the briefest of moments as if waiting for objections to brush aside, but Shelley couldn't seem to come up with any.

"So I told her of course you'd be glad to go. And I gave her your phone number to give to him."

Shelley closed her eyes and lowered her head to her knees. She knew something bad had just happened but she couldn't summon the energy to protest.

"OK. So . . . that's all I wanted to say."

There was a stunned silence as they both recognized that Miriam had accomplished in thirty seconds what normally took a good week of nagging. Then her mother hung up before Shelley could "come to."

Shelley laid down the phone and went back to bed.

She was still sleeping that afternoon when someone started banging on her front door. Groaning, Shelley pulled a pillow over her head and burrowed deeper under the covers, but the pounding didn't stop.

Finally, she shrugged into a robe and shuffled to the front door. It was two P.M.

"You look like shit," Nina said as she swept into the foyer. "And so does your place."

"Do you *ever* not say exactly what you think?" Shelley asked.

"To you? No. Now tell me what's going on. I've been trying to reach you all week."

So Shelley told her. In detail.

"And you didn't explain how important this was to you?"

"Well, I tried, but—"

"Or how completely ready you are to buckle down and prove yourself?"

"Well, I tried, but—"

"You *are* ready to buckle down and prove yourself."

Shelley nodded, still numb. "But it's too late. He's already given the business to Morgan. And I'm an addendum to their contract!"

Talking about things was supposed to make you feel better, but that was definitely not the case. Tears pricked the backs of her eyelids. Again.

Nina picked up the empty carton of ice cream, holding it at arm's length. "Go get dressed." She sniffed in Shelley's general direction. "After you shower, we're going to Nordstrom's designer shoe sale; it just started this morning."

Shelley waited for her usual thrill at the sound of "shoe" and "sale" in such close proximity, but she didn't feel so much as a quiver of excitement.

Nina must have read the panic in her eyes, because she came over, took Shelley by the arm, and led her toward the master bedroom closet. "Don't worry, Shel. I know you, girl. When you get your first sight of those Weitzmans at thirty percent off, you're going to snap right out of this. I guarantee it."

Nina pulled a pair of black capris and a crop top off of their hangers and pushed them into Shelley's arms. "In fact, if you can make it through that sale without experiencing a complete recovery, the first pair's on me."

Twenty minutes later they were inside Nordstrom's and approaching the shoe department. Shelley's first whiff of leather was promising and so was her first sight of the racks of markdowns, but her sense of relief was fleeting.

"Blahnik...Spade...Choo." Nina repeated the designer names like a mantra while waving the gorgeous spring concoctions under Shelley's nose.

"It's not working!" Shelley tried to keep the desperation out of her voice, but she was completely surrounded by the best shoes in the universe and she didn't have the slightest urge to whip out her charge card.

"Don't give up. Here—" Nina ran to the next department and returned with a Furla handbag designed in the same bright pink and lime green as the sandals she'd just dangled in front of Shelley. "Look at this!"

Shelley tried to summon the appropriate level of enthusiasm, but it was no use.

"You've got to work with me here, Shel." Nina dashed to the accessory counter and brought back a chunky necklace and earrings that complemented the shoes and bag perfectly. "What about these? Come on, admit it." She held them up over the bag. "They're perfect."

Nina was right, but for some reason Shelley just couldn't get excited about owning them. "I'm sorry, I guess I'm just not in the mood."

Nina gasped. "I'm going to pretend you didn't say that." Her friend studied the Nordstrom sales floor. "What about a spring makeover? The Trish McEvoy counter is right over there. Or we could go upstairs for a bite and then come back down to finish shopping. You are not leaving this store without a purchase; we have reputations to uphold."

Shelley eyed her oldest friend, the one who'd preferred making mud pies until she'd been enticed into her first Little Miss Scarlett Boutique. If she didn't buy something they'd be here all night. "OK." She forced a cheerful tone. "I'll take the shoes and the bag. And that pair of Ferragamos. But I think I'll hold off on the jewelry."

Nina's eyebrow went up.

"Fine, I'll take the jewelry, too."

"That's my girl." Nina walked with Shelley to the register. "And you know what else? I think you should check your messages. I wouldn't be a bit surprised if there was one from Ross Morgan begging you to come back to work. Why, you're an important part of Schwartz and Associates. In fact, you're the main Schwartz now."

Shelley felt a mild glimmer of interest. Despite her initial misgivings, the shopping and Nina's company had cheered her up a little. If she kept hiding in her condo eating ice cream, she'd be too big to squeeze out the front door. She needed to go in and set things straight, but a little discreet begging from Ross Morgan would allow her to go back to work with her head up. After all, she had to do *something* every day.

Handing her purchases to the salesclerk, Shelley located her cell phone.

There were messages from her mother and, unfortunately, a painfully shy Tommy Horowitz, but the message she'd been hoping for proved to be...not exactly what she'd been hoping for.

"*I understood you taking off while your father was in the hospital,*" Ross Morgan's voice boomed. "*But where are you now? Shopping? Accessorizing?*"

OK, so it had been a lucky guess.

"*I can hardly wait to hear.*"

Shelley signed her name to the credit card slip, but her attention was riveted by Ross Morgan's matter-of-fact tone.

"*We both know I can't fire you. But part of your salary's coming out of my pocket now, and I think it's time you started earning it.*"

There was a pause and in the brief silence Shelley could hear her anger build. It was loud and crackling and it burned away the icy apathy that had gripped her all week.

Seeing her face, Nina reached for Shelley's shopping bags. "I'll, uh, just step over there and look at the, uh, ties. Let me know when you're done."

Shelley barely heard her. Every one of her faculties was completely focused on the voice coming to her through the receiver. And the asinine things it was saying.

"I'm assigning you your own client list, and I need you to come in and get started. Tomorrow. In the morning. Like a normal employee." There was another pause and then, *"I'll expect you in my office at nine A.M."*

Shelley waited for her head to explode. It felt as if it might just shoot right off her shoulders, kind of like those cartoon eruptions that were accompanied by the sound of train whistles.

Ross Morgan was an interfering, business-stealing pain in the butt, and she could hardly wait to tell him so.

She'd get on it first thing in the morning. Right after she finished shopping. If she was going on the offensive, she was going to do it in a knockout outfit.

chapter 7

Too keyed up to sleep, Shelley spent the night lying in bed with her jaw clenched and her fists gripping the sheet while Ross Morgan's words replayed themselves in her head.

In the predawn light she showered and dressed, using concealer to camouflage the dark circles under her eyes and gel to tame her normally curly hair into a chignon. Standing in her walk-in closet, she pulled out the Chanel suit she'd bought, and paired it with her fabulous new Ferragamo pumps. Nana Rose's antique pearls went around her neck.

She suspected Ross Morgan thought that she wouldn't show up, or that if she did, she'd come in weeping and wailing like a hysterical female. But Shelley intended to be icily genteel. Elegantly intimidating. Untouchable. Calm. In fact, she was going to do Grace Kelly with a touch of Katharine Hepburn; a persona that would allow for plenty of looking down her nose at him, even if she had to get a ladder to do it.

***

At 8:59 she swept past Ross's secretary, Mia, and into his office, grateful he hadn't yet moved into her father's office. Closing the door behind her, she posed just inside, her shoulders angled, her chin elevated. When she had his complete attention she walked to the seat across from his desk, carefully channeling both Kelly and Hepburn, then lowered herself into the chair. Crossing her ankles, she swiveled her legs to the side, folded her hands in her lap, and gave him a regal nod. She opened her mouth to begin. Only he beat her to it.

"Queen Elizabeth," he said.

"What?"

"You're doing Queen Elizabeth, right?"

She blinked in surprise.

"And it was good, too. The only thing missing was that little cupped-palm wave thing."

Shelley clenched her teeth; she may have growled.

"No? Let's see ..."

"Ross—"

"Audrey Hepburn in *My Fair Lady*?"

He had to be kidding.

"*After* the transformation, but before he starts to appreciate her."

This was not happening.

"Am I close? I don't know why, but I just can't seem to pin it down."

Good grief. They were playing charades.

"I know!" He pointed a finger at her. "It's Barbara Parkins, isn't it? In *Valley of the Dolls*."

Abandoning her pose, Shelley folded her arms across her

chest. "Are you finished with 'name that movie'? I'd like to get started."

His eyes twinkled. They were bright blue and filled with amusement, damn him.

She waited for him to wipe the smile off his face.

"You asked me to be here and I'm here," she said, her tone imperious, but not Elizabethan.

"Yes, and on time, too. I'm stunned."

She ignored the jibe. "I'm here because it's obvious that we need to clear the air."

He nodded, but didn't comment.

"We both know you don't want me around. Well, I don't want *you* around, either. In fact, I absolutely loathe the way you've horned in on my family's business."

So much for her problem with being direct. Too bad Howard Mellnick wasn't around to witness her breakthrough.

Ross folded his arms across his chest. He was so calm she wondered if he'd missed the part where she told him she wished he'd get lost.

"Funny that you call it horning in," he finally said. "I call it doing my job. Earning my paycheck. Showing up and putting forth effort. If you'd done a little more of that, there might not have been an opening to horn into."

Shelley bit back a retort and tried to imitate his maddening calm. "You don't know anything about my family's dynamics. Or me. It's not as clear-cut as you seem to think."

"No," he agreed. "I don't know your history." He paused. "Or why your father's let you get away with this spoiled princess business for so long. How old are you now? Thirty-five? Thirty-six?"

She gasped.

"Well, however old you are, you're old enough to pull your weight."

She had a horrible feeling he was going to guess her weight next. Instead, he stood and walked around to stand between her and his desk. "Fortunately, we're not family. And we don't have any dynamics to speak of."

Except, of course, that dynamic episode in the supply closet. "Thank God for small favors."

"So we're talking business here." He gave her a look. "And personal pride."

Her head snapped up. "Which you seem to think I'm lacking."

"I can understand your anger and hostility, even though I think a lot of this situation is of your own making." His reasonable tone was sending her right up the wall. "If you don't feel like we can work together, I'll understand."

There was a wonderful moment in which she thought he was going to bow out. He reached across his desk and picked up a typewritten piece of paper. "In fact, I took the liberty of drafting a resignation letter."

Her heart leapt at this piece of good news. He *was* going to step aside. Maybe he wasn't as big a schmuck as she'd thought; maybe she'd misjudged him.

Ross passed her the letter and she skimmed it, curious to see what kind of excuse he'd come up with. Then she reached the signature line. "You want *me* to resign?"

He handed her a pen. "It would make things a lot easier for both of us."

She considered doing a little palm-cupped wave right now. With her middle finger clearly extended. "Let's see," she said, still mimicking his dead-calm tone. "You've insulted my dress, my manner, my age, *possibly* my weight, my family, and my work ethic. And now I'm supposed to sign this paper so you can have the place all to yourself?" Sitting back in her chair, she folded her arms across her chest and shook her head. "I don't think so."

He studied her right back and then reached across his desk to retrieve another piece of paper. "All right, then," he said, still calm. "Here's a list of clients. I want you to contact all of them, introduce yourself, and start setting up appointments." He handed her the sheet of paper. "These are underserviced accounts that could produce a much greater revenue stream."

"But I'm an account *supervisor*. I don't service clients directly."

"Actually, you haven't serviced any indirectly or otherwise—at least not with any regularity. I think it's time you take a step back and reacquaint yourself with how this agency operates."

"But this would be a demotion." And a humiliation.

Shelley skimmed the list. It included a string of funeral homes with the unfortunate name of Forever Remembered, a low-end contemporary furniture chain whose owner insisted on serving as talent in his own television commercials, her uncle Abe's electronics business, a fledgling falafel maker who was in the process of franchising his operation, and something called Tire World. Those were the best ones on the list.

"You're joking."

"No, I'm not."

Their gazes locked as she confronted the obvious. "You're trying to make me quit."

He stared right at her out of those blue eyes. "I prefer to think of it as giving you a chance to prove yourself the good old-fashioned way."

She wanted to throw the list in his face and stomp out of the room. Wanted to rip it into tiny pieces and shove them down his throat one at a time. Which would be playing right into his hands.

He waited quietly, clearly expecting her to utter those two magic words that would free him of her and her salary. But he didn't know whom he was dealing with. Shelley Schwartz had spent a lifetime refusing to do what was expected of her. She'd been resisting her parents' plans for her since she was ten; why would she change for the man who'd stolen her business out from under her?

Wrapping her anger around her like a shield, Shelley stood. Ross Morgan did the same. Then folding the list into a tiny square, she shoved it in her purse. He didn't think she could do anything with this list. He didn't think she'd even try. What Ross Morgan didn't know about her could fill an ocean.

Extending her hand, she looked him straight in the eye, the blue ones that had turned a dark velvety color; the ones that were giving absolutely nothing away.

"Thank you so much for this incredible...opportunity," she said in her best Hepburn voice. "I can hardly wait to get started."

And then she turned on her heel and strode out of the room without a backward glance.

***

"He gave me the absolute dregs of the advertising world. The littlest, piddliest, most ridiculous waste-of-time accounts in the history of the world." She took a deep breath and told herself she would not cry. "He demoted me!"

Howard Mellnick made a note on the pad in front of him. "And you think he's just trying to make you quit."

"No, I *know* he's trying to make me quit."

"And so you dug in your heels." He studied her for a long moment. "Why?"

"Because..." Despite years in this very chair, self-examination did not come easily. "Because nobody, and especially not Ross Morgan, is going to shove me out of my family business."

Howard Mellnick looked up and out the window for a moment then back at her. "So you're staying because he wants you to leave."

"Yes! No!" She groaned. "I don't know." She stared at him, miserable. "Does it really matter why?"

Howard Mellnick sat back, crossed his legs, and propped his yellow pad up on his knee. Apparently this was one of those questions she was supposed to answer for herself.

"All I know is, I'm not quitting. And as crappy as that list is, I'm going to have to *do* something with it."

He made another note on his pad. "You know, getting rid of the family dynamic and the attached emotion could prove to be a positive. If you're not carrying any of the old baggage, you should be able to travel...lighter. It's fortunate your relationship with Ross Morgan has always been strictly business."

Shelley suspected this would be the time to tell Dr. Mellnick about her and Ross and the supply closet. Except she was still trying to blot out that memory, and there were some things that were too embarrassing to share with your shrink; even one as nonjudgmental as Howard Mellnick.

"You know, Shelley," he said, "this could turn out to be a good time to prove yourself. To yourself."

Easy for him to say; he didn't have Ross Morgan looking over his shoulder, waiting for him to fail. Still, she kind of liked the sound of it. "When I referred to my new accounts as the dregs, that was actually a compliment. I have no idea how I'm going to suddenly turn them into producers."

"I think you're up to the task." Howard Mellnick smiled. "And I can't wait to hear all the gory details." He flipped his yellow pad closed, signaling the end of their session. "Just remember that torturing Ross Morgan is only a perk—not your main goal."

"Right," Shelley said as she stood and prepared to leave. "I'll try to keep that in mind."

On Sunday afternoon Judy stood at the entrance to the Temple Kol Chaim social hall and surveyed the hum of activity inside. Today's Bar Mitzvah Expo, which was to bar and bat mitzvah planning what a Bridal Fair was to weddings, was in full swing.

Scanning the crowd for her coordinator, Judy waited for the expected rush of adrenaline, but nothing happened. Which was very strange indeed.

She could still remember the excitement of her first expo four years ago, when she'd spent an entire afternoon visiting each vendor, nibbling catering samples, watching videos, and listening to demonstration CDs.

At home afterward she'd spent a euphoric afternoon

poring over the brochures and promotional items. With wonder, she'd contemplated the caterers and event facilities, the photographers and videographers, the goody basket creators and personal shoppers, even the security companies specializing in hormonal thirteen-year-olds.

Entertainment options had ranged from a lone guitarist to the Atlanta Symphony Orchestra and included the ever-popular DJs, who came with emcees, light shows, and crates full of party favors, as well as the all-important crowd motivators.

It had all seemed so incredibly exciting.

You could have a video of your child's life. Or photos of the guests applied to buttons they could wear home. Concession stands, celebrity look-alikes, jugglers, magicians—name it, and it could be ordered à la carte or as part of a package. The sky and the depth of your pockets were the only limits.

On that fateful day she'd understood that her son's bar mitzvah was more than a ceremonial trip to adulthood. It was something she could throw herself into; something that required more than chauffeuring and cheerleading. It was her opportunity to make her mark.

Judy had read every word of every brochure, and then she'd hired the ridiculously expensive Mandy Mifkin. Together they'd come up with the Roman gladiator theme and turned Jason's bar mitzvah into the gold standard against which all other such functions were measured—at least in the highly competitive suburb of Atlanta where she lived.

But today, Judy's competitive juices refused to flow.

She was contemplating slipping out the way she'd come, when Mandy rushed up and enveloped her in a hug.

"It's so crowded I didn't see you standing here," Mandy said. "Come." She turned to lead the way back into the exhibit hall. "I want to show you the invitation I told you about."

The crowd parted before them like the Red Sea. Mandy nodded regally as they passed through the throng of women, and Judy heard the awe in their voices; "togas," they mouthed to each other. "A lion in a cage right next to the gift table." Another nodded importantly. "I heard the rabbi wore a toga under his robes."

The room was thick with their admiration and envy, but Judy felt no answering sense of pleasure or accomplishment. In fact she felt as if she were having an out-of-body experience—the kind those briefly dead people described in which they levitated up into the air and watched the hospital staff trying to revive them. Everything around her was muffled, once removed, but there was no beckoning ray of white light, only a ton of other women snapping up samples and exclaiming over chair covers. And all of them seemed to be moving and talking at warp speed, while she was stuck in slow motion.

Mandy led her to a brightly decorated table whose sign read Pinchas Paper Products. After the requisite air-kissing, Stacy Pinchas pulled out an oversized piece of card stock festooned in gold and silver foil and presented it to Judy.

"Don't you just love the type style?" Mandy gushed. "And look how the silver stands out against the black and gold. It's masculine, yet communicates the sports theme with real elegance." She lowered her voice. "The sports theme's been done to death, so doing something new with it is critical."

"Hmmm?" Judy tried to focus, but she couldn't seem to work up the energy.

"The sports thing," Mandy repeated. "If you don't do something different with it...well." The coordinator looked her in the eye. "Then you really don't need me."

Judy considered the other woman. During the planning of Jason's extravaganza, the slightest hint of losing Mandy would have triggered a full-blown panic attack. Today Judy felt only a bone-crushing weariness. And an increasingly urgent need to get out of this building. Now.

Judy looked at the invitation. Did she really care what color the foils were? Did she believe the invitation's design would appreciably affect Sammy's bar mitzvah experience?

"It looks fine," Judy said. "I guess I'm just not in the mood for all this"—she motioned around the room— "right now."

Mandy stiffened but quickly recovered. It appeared Judy was not going to be fired.

"We've already booked the important things. Why don't I stay and pick up any samples I want you to see?" She gave Judy a parting hug and made a show of shooing her off. "You just call me when you're ready to see them, and I'll run them over."

Outside, Judy drew in great gulps of fresh air. The day was bright and a slight spring breeze stirred the air, but she felt lost, unsure what to do next. Sliding into her BMW SUV, she started the car, then rooted around in her purse until she located her cell phone.

Craig picked up on the third ring. She could hear a base-ball game on in the background; heard one of her sons shout in response to something that must have happened on-screen.

"Oh, hi," he said. "Where are you?"

She used to feel a little bubble of pleasure when she heard her husband's voice; now the little bubble was filled with annoyance.

"I told you I was going to the expo."

"Oh, right."

She could tell his attention was elsewhere, most likely on the game.

"When will you be home?" he asked.

"Soon."

"Good."

Silence.

Once they might have chatted easily for fifteen or twenty minutes; now they couldn't fill five.

"I, uh, didn't really have the energy for the expo. Mandy's going to bring the samples later."

"That's good."

She heard papers shuffle in the background. A mechanical voice told him he had mail.

"I think I'm going to drive over and see Daddy before I come home. I might pick up Chinese for dinner."

"OK," Craig said automatically. "Give him my best."

Before she could respond she was listening to a dial tone and feeling annoyed all over again. Craig had been a rock during her father's emergency surgery and the frightening days immediately afterward. But once her father was out of imminent danger, Craig had made it clear he expected her to move on. Only she couldn't seem to get back to normal—not that normal had been feeling all that attractive lately.

On the way to her parents' she tried a glass-is-half-full exercise. After all, her father was going to be fine; she had a marriage that her friends envied, two healthy sons, and an upcoming event that she could afford to celebrate in a way befitting their place in life. She had no reason to be dissatisfied, and even less to keep teetering on the edge of tears.

At her parents' she fussed over her father then joined her mother, who was writing thank-you notes at the kitchen table.

"Betty Halpren finally switched florists, thank God. Did you see the flowers she had sent from Raphael?"

"Uh, no." Judy's visits to the hospital had been too fraught with anxiety to contemplate the relative merits of the floral arrangements filling her father's room.

"The roses never even opened. And it had mums in it! I hate to think what Betty spent on that puny arrangement."

Judy just nodded. "Do you feel OK about Daddy's progress?"

"As OK as I can." Her mother laid down her pen. "The doctor says as long as he rests and takes care of himself the prognosis is very good."

She straightened the pile of note cards and her eyes got...dreamy?

"We're going to stop putting things off for the future. In fact, your father and I are going back to Europe this year."

Her mother's voice sounded almost girlish. This was getting very weird indeed.

"We went to Paris on our honeymoon, you know." Judy's mother smiled. "And I've always wanted to go back. Harvey can be very romantic when he puts his mind to it."

In thirty-nine years, Judy couldn't remember more than

a handful of compliments coming out of her mother's mouth. It was always a complaint or a suggestion as to how things could be better. And here her mother was blushing over a trip to Europe with the man she'd been married to for forty years.

"Daddy? Romantic?" Part of her wanted to file this news in the "way more than she wanted to know" category. The other part was totally fascinated and dying to ask questions. Because right now, forty years sounded like a life sentence. Given how little she and Craig spoke to each other now, in twenty-five years they'd probably be communicating via sign language.

Her father was romantic and her mother, HER MOTHER, was blushing.

Which meant they probably still had sex. And *enjoyed* it.

Judy listened to the rest of her mother's chatter with only half an ear, because she was completely stuck on the fact that her parents' marriage sounded markedly better than hers.

Which made her own life even more pitiful than she had realized.

chapter 8

On Monday morning Shelley bounded out of bed and into the shower. Eager to get to the office to show Ross Morgan whom he was fooling with, she smoothed her hair into a French twist, selected a nubby turquoise suit, and stepped into matching mid-heeled pumps. After downing a low-carb breakfast bar, she drove the twenty-five minutes to the midtown warehouse, which had been so skillfully converted into the offices of Schwartz and Associates, in ten.

The receptionist's mouth dropped open when Shelley stepped into the high-ceilinged lobby. She turned to look at the clock on the wall, looked down quickly at her watch, then back up at Shelley.

"Good morning, Sandra. Did you have a good weekend?"

"Yes," the other woman managed. "It was, um, fine." She held her wrist up, shook it, and tapped the watch face. "Aren't you in a little early?"

Shelley glanced up at the clock. It read 8:55. "Doesn't the day still start at nine o'clock?"

"Um, yes. Yes, it does."

"Then I guess I'm right on time." Shelley moved past reception and walked briskly down the hallway toward her office, her heels tapping on the scored and glazed concrete floors. As she passed the glass-fronted offices along the way, her coworkers looked up in surprise. Some hung up their phones, others shut their drawers or dropped their pens. As if unable to stop themselves, they left their offices and came out into the hall to silently watch her progress.

By the time Shelley reached her own door, a sizable crowd had formed. When she turned and looked back over her shoulder, a line of fascinated faces stared back.

"Good morning?" she said tentatively.

There was throat-clearing, looks of embarrassment, and finally, a collective sort of nod. One or two people lifted a hand in greeting.

"Yes," Shelley said before stepping into her office. "It's great to see you all, too."

Despite an almost overwhelming need for caffeine, Shelley gave them a full fifteen minutes to disperse. Then she headed for the break room where, once again, conversation sputtered to a stop and eyes moved to the clock on the wall then back to her.

"It's me," she said. "And, yes, it's nine-seventeen." She watched the second hand on the clock go around. "Make that nine-eighteen. Does anyone want to make something of it?"

As the room emptied, Shelley tried to shrug off her embarrassment, but their amazement stung. She poured a cup of coffee and had just finished stirring in a packet of sweetener when Ross Morgan came through the door.

His shirtsleeves were already rolled up and his tie was loosened, and she felt that immediate burst of attraction and irritation that she always felt when she saw him. His head was bent over some sort of report, and he got all the way to the coffeemaker before he looked up and spotted her. He, too, did the automatic clock-check thing, but instead of avoiding her gaze, he scrutinized her carefully. In fact, he did a very thorough scan from the top of her head down to the tips of her shoes.

"Don't tell me," he said. "Doris Day?"

That amused glint was back in his eyes.

"Debbie Reynolds."

"Just little ol' on-time me," she replied. "Which seems to be throwing the entire workforce into a major tailspin."

He put his papers down on the counter and reached past her for a mug, giving her a faint whiff of aftershave and man. "It's just the shock of the unknown, that first stab of unreality," he said. "This is the second day in a row. They'll get over it." He lifted the pot and poured coffee. "Assuming you keep it up."

"Oh, I'm going to keep it up, all right. Now that I have that spectacular client list to deal with."

She waited while he stirred sugar into his coffee—all three spoonfuls. "Have we heard from anyone on that list over the last six months?"

He dropped the plastic spoon in the garbage. "No," he said. "If we don't call them, they don't call us. Which means nothing to bill for. Which would, of course, be why I gave them to you."

"Right."

He studied her closely. "Do you have a complaint?"

"Me? Complain? About that list?"

He sipped his coffee and studied her, and she had the disturbing sense that he could see past the flip tone right down to the raw place inside her.

"What would you say if I told you it wasn't just a punishment? That I actually thought you could do something with that list?"

She stared Ross Morgan right in the eye, not at all liking the little flutter of hope that blossomed in her chest. "I'd say you were probably lying, but on the off chance that you're not, it's really going to piss me off to have to prove you right."

Shelley spent the rest of the morning at her desk. For the first few hours she alternately played solitaire on her computer and stared into space, trying not to notice the curiosity-seekers who wandered by or in, on the flimsiest of pretexts. She realized it had been a while since she'd been in before noon, but she was getting awfully tired of being looked at as if she were some new specimen at the zoo.

At eleven her stomach began to rumble. It wasn't actually food she wanted as much as lunch, preferably in a slick upscale restaurant like Medici's, packed with men in power suits on expense accounts.

Picking up the phone she began to punch in Nina's number, then switched in mid-punch to Trey's, then put the phone back in its cradle with a sigh.

She had made no calls, contacted none of her clients. She was not going to lunch or anywhere else until she'd reached at least one. Shelley read over the list one more time, hoping that it had somehow improved since the last time she checked, but they were still the losing propositions they'd been five minutes before.

Cradling her head in her hands, she groaned in frustration. What was she doing here? What was she trying to prove? And what in the world was she supposed to do with these worthless accounts?

She thought back to Ross Morgan's irritating attempts to identify her "look" and asked herself: If this were a fifties flick and she were playing the Debbie Reynolds or Doris Day role, what would happen now?

Drumming her fingers on the desktop she seriously considered the question.

For one thing, Doris would do more than just show up. Doris would find a way to rub Rock Hudson's nose in his attitude. She'd take the lemons he gave her and make them into lemonade, and then she'd find a way to beat him at his own game. *And* make him fall in love with her.

Shelley pulled out a pad and pencil. What if she went ahead and pretended these were *real* accounts that deserved *real* attention? What if she actually thought about what she might do for them? Came up with ideas. After all, anything she produced from these underperformers would be a victory. All she had to do was start.

Closing her eyes, she concentrated on opening her mind. It had been a long time since she'd done this, so she was a little rusty, but she told herself not to panic. Giving her imagination permission to wander, she sat and thought. Slowly ideas began to form. Pictures and words began to line up into concepts.

She looked back down at the list and focused all of her energies on it. And somehow she knew where to begin.

"Mr. Simms," she said when she got the owner of Furniture Forum on the line, "this is Shelley Schwartz at Schwartz and Associates, and I just called to tell you that I love the TV spots you've been doing."

She listened to his surprised murmur of gratitude. Previous AE's had spent their time trying to talk him out of appearing in his own commercials. Previous AE's had failed.

"And I think we can add a lot of production value to what you're already doing."

She popped a Tylenol. "Your nephew Charlie is your videographer?" She wrote "nephew" next to the client's name and really listened as Brian Simms praised his nephew's production skills and explained that he'd been mentoring the boy since his sister's death. There was a lot more at stake here, as far as Brian Simms was concerned, than just production.

As she listened the solution came to her. She knew exactly how to get this client to buy her idea. "You know, Mr. Simms," Shelley said, "we use an incredible director out in L.A. He and his production company could take your spots to a whole new level. And I bet we could get them to take your nephew under their wing, maybe even work out an apprenticeship of some kind. Especially if you're going to be a long-term client."

Brian Simms couldn't agree fast enough. Delighted, Shelley penciled in a meeting with him and his nephew for the following week. A smile spread across her face as she hung up the phone.

Flush with success, she dialed Forever Remembered and

got David Geller on the line. "Mr. Geller," she said once she'd introduced herself, "have you watched the HBO series *Six Feet Under*?"

As it turned out, the Forever Remembered CEO was a big fan. Convincing him that Alan Ball, the Atlanta creator of the hit series, would be the perfect company spokesperson took a whopping two minutes. Still smiling, she placed a call to the producer's agent in L.A. and added David Geller to her schedule.

When her stomach rumbled she remembered that it was lunchtime. Suddenly she was thinking falafels—those lovely balls of chickpea and breading sold in stands across the Middle East.

"Yes, Mr. Awadallah," she said into the phone after she'd introduced herself, "I want four to five of everything on your lunch menu. Yes, yes. The time has come for us to really understand what we're selling."

Obviously thrilled, her client shouted to someone in a deep, fluent Arabic as Shelley doodled smiley faces in the margins of the menu. "And be sure to add a Fab Falafel Plate for our new president, Ross Morgan. Oh, yes, he's a great big chickpea fan."

After hanging up, she warned Sandra about the upcoming delivery. Then she called the falafel account planner. "Hi, Todd. This is Shelley." There was a moment of silence. "Shelley Schwartz. I need everything you can give me on falafels. History of, national origins, sales figures, the works."

"Falafels," he said.

"Yes."

"But I'm just heading out for lunch."

"Actually, I took the liberty of ordering you lunch. We've got enough falafels coming to feed your whole department. I'll let you know when everything's set up in the conference room."

She hung up the phone and spun joyfully in her desk chair. This AE business was a lot more fun than she'd realized.

At twelve-thirty lunch arrived, hand-delivered by Fadah Awadallah and two of his sons. Soon the smells of falafel, pita, tabouli, and other things Mediterranean filled the office.

"Lunch is now being served in the conference room," Shelley announced over the office intercom. "I'd like everyone to try at least two dishes from the Falafel Shack. Then we're going to brainstorm ideas."

She pressed Sandra and Mia into helping her serve as the staff took plates and found places to perch. The smell of a Middle Eastern street corner permeated the office; the only thing missing was the camels. Everybody ate, nibbled, and shared.

"Here, try this." Shelley handed Mia a plate of hummus (also made from the much-loved chickpea) and pita triangles. She cornered another coworker. "Put some of this tahini on that falafel ball."

"Um, thanks."

Shelley watched him bite into the sandwich and waited for his reaction as if she'd made the falafel herself.

"Mmm." He chewed enthusiastically. "S'good 'n chewy."

Shelley looked around her, pleased. Everyone was talking excitedly, their mouths crammed with food. Somebody found a Middle Eastern CD and put it on the speaker system. All they needed were some belly dancers.

She spun around at the tap on her shoulder, her mouth still full of falafel.

"What is going on here?" Ross Morgan whispered.

She held a finger out toward him, signaling that she needed to finish chewing. When she'd swallowed the last bit, she searched around in the delivery box and located his Fab Plate.

"Research." She smiled at him. "Here, you need to eat this, and then we're going to do a brainstorming session."

He flipped the Styrofoam container open, and she read the uncertainty in his eyes.

"It's the Fab Falafel Plate. From the Falafel Shack."

He squinted down at the four round balls sitting in sauce, onion, and cucumber.

"We're tasting the menu to come up with a new proposal. Fadah Awadallah was thrilled."

He looked around and she followed his gaze. There was food everywhere. People were looking very stuffed and sleepy. Shelley remembered that they slept away the afternoons in the Middle East. Possibly because of all those falafel balls sitting in the pits of their stomachs.

"I bet." His tone was dry, dry as the desert in the land of the falafel. "Who's paying for all of this?"

Fadah Awadallah's oldest son stepped forward and presented Ross with a handwritten bill. "Thanking you so much for your interest in us and for the order." He smiled at Shelley and pumped her hand. "One day Fadah's falafels and the Falafel Shack will be household names. Shelley say so." The Awadallah family left grinning broadly.

Ross handed her his Styrofoam container and looked down at the bill. "You spent five hundred and fifty dollars for lunch from a falafel stand?"

"Well, you told me to contact my list. How can I propose a plan of attack without sampling the product?"

"But food for the whole office?" He looked aghast, evidently trying to remember what other businesses were on that list. "You didn't order a funeral today, did you?"

"Don't be silly. It's just one lunch. And we need to know what we're selling." She thought about the funeral homes and bit back a smile. "Within reason."

"Yes, let's begin applying some reason, shall we?" He handed her the tab. "And let's make sure *this*"—he motioned around the room and sniffed at the accompanying smells—"comes out of your budget. I'll expect you to fill in the appropriate paperwork."

This was when Luke Skyler, the creative director, said, "Falafels—they're not just for the Middle East anymore."

"How about 'Chickpeas...who knew!'"

"We should be targeting the vegetarian market."

The comments and ideas began coming fast and furious. Shelley plucked the receipt out of Ross's fingers and handed him his falafel plate in exchange. "Not a problem," she said with a saccharine sweet smile. "Now, if you'll excuse me, I have a brainstorming session to conduct."

By the end of the day, Shelley's stomach was full of falafels, she'd reached seventy-five percent of her client list, and her head was spinning with ideas. Her little run-in with Ross notwithstanding, she felt energized enough to run a marathon, or swim the English Channel.

Unfortunately, she was scheduled to meet Tommy Horowitz for drinks, presumably as a precursor to attending a dinner for an important client. Not even her enhanced energy level and unaccustomed sense of well-being could whip up any enthusiasm for that.

Two days ago she might have dwelled on this negative, but today her brain was quick to identify a specific course of action. Picking up the phone, she dialed Nina's cell phone and caught her on her way home from work.

It only took a minute to lay out her plan.

Nina was already seated at a prime table in the front window of Epiphany when Shelley arrived. Her blond hair shimmered in the sunlight that filtered through the plate glass. Nina *was* Grace Kelly and Katharine Hepburn and Debbie and Doris, without even trying. Her white-Anglo-Saxon-Protestant nose was buried in a shiny new copy of *The Jewish Book of Why*.

"Did you know that some Jewish men avoid marrying a woman whose first name is identical to that of their mother?" Nina's tone was full of wonder.

"No, I didn't." But then, that wasn't surprising. Since being confirmed at the age of sixteen, Shelley only set foot in temple for the High Holidays and family bar mitzvahs and weddings. For the Schwartzes, Friday night dinners were as much about getting together with family as they were an observation of the Sabbath.

"I hate to spoil this for you, Nina, but there's really no reason to convert. You're already everything every Jewish man secretly covets: the exact opposite of his mother." Shelley took a sip of her martini. "And lots of Jewish men already marry non-Jewish women. Just ask my mother; I'm pretty sure she's keeping statistics on the ones who got away."

Nina looked up from the book, which she was holding almost reverently. "I don't know, Shel. It looks so interesting, and so . . . welcoming. I'm really getting excited about the idea."

"Nina, you've watched too many episodes of *Sex and the City.* Most of the Jewish men I know are not like the one Charlotte married."

"And I think you're the one who's not seeing things the way they really are. I've envied how close-knit your family is, and how everyone looks out for each other, since we were children."

Shelley finished her martini and ordered another. "That's not close-knit, that's a stranglehold."

Nina shrugged and smiled prettily, and then turned her attention to the man approaching their table. He had a thatch of carrot-red hair, matching freckles that paraded across his nose, and a shy smile on his lips. "I'm Tom Horowitz," he said to the table in general, even though his eyes were already fixed on Nina.

"It's so good to meet you, Tom," Shelley said as she signaled the waiter to cancel her second martini. When she looked at Tommy Horowitz she saw "nice Jewish boy" and nothing else, but Nina was looking at him as if he were a rare and wonderful gift.

He said something inane about feeling like cream cheese between two beautiful bagels, and Nina giggled as if he'd just said something . . . funny. Shelley was more than happy to help Nina achieve her goals, but she didn't think she had the stomach to sit around and watch.

"So," she said as she stood and prepared to leave, "I hate to have to rush off, Tom, but I know you'll understand. This is my friend Nina Olson. Maybe you can give her some advice; she's thinking about becoming Jewish."

chapter 9

Shelley was sitting at her desk eyeing her rapidly cooling coffee the next morning when her cell phone rang. She didn't have to look at the caller ID to guess who was calling at 9:05 on Tuesday morning.

"So?" Miriam Schwartz's voice was tentatively optimistic. "What was he like?"

"Mother?" Shelley asked, stalling for time.

"Of course, me. What was he like?"

There was no point pretending she didn't know who her mother was referring to. Her mother had most likely lain awake last night planning the engagement party.

"Um, he was fine."

"Fine, fine? Or fine, fine!"

"Um, just fine. You know, OK."

"No, I don't know. Why don't we go out for breakfast so you can explain it to me."

"I can't, Mom. I'm at work."

"And?"

"And, I'm actually working." Being gainfully employed had some benefits she hadn't anticipated.

"Well, you have to eat. Let's do lunch and then run into Bloomies after. You'll need something new for that client dinner."

"Well, actually—"

"How about Maggiano's at eleven-thirty, so we can beat the crowd?" She didn't wait for a response. "For now just tell me the important things. Does he like his firm? Have plans to advance? What does he look like? I keep picturing him with Thelma's coloring but without all those freckles."

Her mother was bubbling over with happiness at the thought that Thelma Horowitz might have delivered "the one" right into their arms.

For the first time, Shelley felt a small twinge of guilt at raining on her mother's parade.

Apparently noting her silence, her mother paused. "He was short, wasn't he? Thelma's practically a dwarf. But you know, sometimes good things come in small packages." Her mother paused again, this time for emphasis. "Like diamond rings, for instance."

"Yes, well, the thing is," Shelley said, "he, um, asked someone else to the dinner."

Her mother gasped in horror. "Someone else? But how could that have happened? Last night was just supposed to be a formality. What is this, *The Bachelor* TV program? Who did he ask?"

Shelley considered lying, but it would only delay the inevitable. Her mother was not going to drop the subject until she knew who had supplanted her daughter.

"He asked Nina."

There was a loud whap as her mother evidently banged the receiver on the table. Shelley's ear was still ringing when her mother spoke again. "Something must be wrong with my phone." She tapped it a few more times. "I could have sworn you said—"

"He asked Nina."

"Nina, Nina? Tall, beautiful, blond shiksa Nina? Nina-who-doesn't-need-a-Jewish-husband-like-you-do Nina?"

Shelley winced. It had seemed like such a good plan at the time, a win-win for everyone concerned. Except, of course, her mother.

"They just really hit it off, Mom. And he wasn't my type at all. I gave them my blessings."

"Shelley Rachel Schwartz. What have you done?"

"It's no big deal, Mother. Let's not turn it into one."

"No big deal?" Her mother drew a sharp breath and Shelley could practically feel her indignation leap across the phone line. "This is not cute or funny anymore. You're thirty-three years old." She might have been saying sixty, for all the horror in her voice. "You have never been married. And you're giving an eligible man away?"

"Mother, really. It's not as if he's the only—"

"I hope they invite you over for an occasional Friday night dinner. Maybe they'll let you baby-sit their children every now and then."

"Aw, Mom. You have to stop getting your hopes up every time someone tries to fix me up."

"And you need to stop treating the finding of a husband like a joke. You need one. AND you need children, too, or you're going to end up like your great-aunt Sonya. Old and alone without daughters to take care of you."

"I'm not going to start worrying about my golden years now. Besides, I can always move in with Judy and let her sons take care of me."

"Sons. Ha! With daughter-in-laws, Judy'll be lucky if she gets invited for latkes on the first night of Chanukah. And that's assuming they don't end up with Ninas. Choosing someone to spend your life with is no joking matter."

"And neither is being forced out on a blind date every time some unattached male with a drop of Jewish blood in his veins and a graduate degree on his wall passes through town."

There was a silence, but Shelley knew her mother well enough to know that it wasn't because she was actually considering what her daughter had said.

When she finally spoke, her mother's voice reeked of injured dignity and unspoken hurt. Shelley felt the stab of guilt, just as she was intended to. "Speaking of Aunt Sonya," Miriam Schwartz said, "don't forget you and Judy are going to take her to dinner tonight. She really likes that Italian restaurant over on Abernathy. And I think they're having bingo afterward at the Towers."

"I've got it! I've got it!"

"So yell 'Bingo' already and put us all out of our misery," Great-aunt Sonya said to her friend Elaine with a roll of her eyes.

"BINGO!"

"Mazel tov." Aunt Sonya turned from an ecstatic Elaine

and whispered to Shelley, "I hope she really has it. It's so embarrassing when she tries to cheat."

Shelley and Judy sat with Great-aunt Sonya and her friend in the auditorium of Summitt Towers with the rest of the white- and blue-haired women. Walkers were parked around the room and many of the occupants sat in wheelchairs, but there was nothing tame about this predominantly female crowd.

"Elaine, are you sure about that card?" The emcee, a tall egretlike man—one of the few males in the room—asked. "I don't want to make you walk all the way up here for nothing."

Shelley hid a grin. The last winner had taken almost twenty minutes to reach the stage area to claim her prize. Elaine could probably make it in less than fifteen, but evidently nobody wanted to commit that much time for a false claim. When you were in what Aunt Sonya referred to as God's Waiting Room, every minute counted.

Elaine stood, grabbed up her cane in one hand, then picked up the bingo card in her other and began hobbling very carefully toward the stage, although Shelley suspected it was her fear of dislodging the markers rather than her fear of falling that caused the extra caution.

"You'd think there was something at stake besides a free cone in the ice cream shop," Sonya muttered as they all watched Elaine make her way to the front of the room. "Last time I won, all I got was a plastic comb and brush set. It wasn't worth the trip."

Shelley and Judy exchanged glances. As Elaine triumphantly accepted her prize and worked her way back to their table, Shelley's thoughts tumbled forward forty years.

Would she and Judy still be playing their designated roles when their parents were no longer there to play them for? Judy had come first and gotten to choose her part; Shelley had been second and forced to take what was left. Growing up she would have traded too-tall-rebel-princess for petite-daughter-who-does-no-wrong in a heartbeat. Even now, playing bingo, she had to fight back the urge to do the opposite of whatever her sister did.

Their six-year age difference had left room for comparison but not much opportunity for closeness. She'd been eleven when her sister left for college; an annoying child in the eyes of the older sister who already considered herself an adult. Their sisterhood had been in name mostly, and Shelley would have felt like an only child through middle and high school, except for her parents' constant reminders of how well Judy had done at whatever Shelley happened to be mucking up at the time.

And now? She studied Judy as they helped Aunt Sonya and Elaine to the ice cream shop, where Elaine gleefully ordered her free cone. Rationally, Shelley knew it wasn't her sister's fault that she felt like the Jolly Green Giant—physically and emotionally—next to her, but it didn't exactly make her want to hang around waiting for everyone else to notice, either.

Judy was staring forty in the face, yet she was in perfect shape, flawlessly dressed and made-up, and if she'd ever had a gray hair, Shelley had never seen it.

She, on the other hand, was crumpled and wrinkled after a long day at work, could actually feel the shine on her nose and a blemish forming on her chin, and she'd eaten so much manicotti at dinner she'd had to loosen her belt a notch.

"What do you want, Aunt Sonya?" Shelley asked when the waitress appeared.

"I've had a craving for hot fudge since first thing this morning. I'll have a sundae," she told the waitress. "And make sure there's plenty of whipped cream and a cherry on the top. Last time they forgot the cherry."

Elaine ordered her free cone and proudly presented the coupon she'd won.

The waitress turned to Judy.

"No, thanks." Of course Judy would be watching her figure. As much as her sister liked baking, she wasn't much in the eating department.

"I'm going to throw all caution to the wind and have a... Diet Coke," Shelley said when it was her turn. She'd be damned if she'd chow down in front of everyone when Judy was going to be sipping on a glass of ice water. Shelley leaned toward her sister. "What do you do with all those desserts you make?"

"Hmm?"

"Well, what's the point of baking if you never eat any of it?"

"It's relaxing. And if I ate half of what I've been making lately I'd be..."

"Big as a house. Yes, that was what Mom always told me. And then she'd get that funny look on her face whenever somebody heavy walked by eating something, and say—"

"No wonder she looks like that," Judy finished.

"Where is that girl's pride?" Shelley added.

You didn't have to be a Howard Mellnick to know what those kinds of comments did to a young girl.

"That's absolutely ridiculous," Great-aunt Sonya said.

"Both of you girls are way too thin; a stiff breeze would blow you over. A man likes some padding to sink into, if you know what I mean." She waved the waitress back to their table. "These two will have sundaes like mine. And no skimping on those cherries."

"Aunt Sonya, I don't think that's—" Judy began.

"Oh, hush. I won't tell your mother," their great-aunt said as the waitress left to place their orders. "Both of you are old enough to think for yourselves, but in my opinion a life without ice-cream sundaes is barely worth living."

Elaine bit her lip, but whether it was to stifle her laughter or in anticipation of her ice cream was unclear.

Judy turned to Shelley, her look speculative. "Do you ever eat high-calorie items in front of other people?"

Shelley shook her head. "No. I go to expensive restaurants on dates or with people I don't know that well and barely eat. I can leave Maggiano's and still be hungry."

Judy laughed, but there was no humor in it. "I only eat fattening things when no one's around. And I eat them standing up so I can hide the evidence if someone comes in."

"We are too pathetic for words," Shelley said. Still, it was somewhat cheering to know that Mrs. Perfect wasn't.

When their ice cream arrived it was buried beneath hot fudge, whipped cream, and extra cherries. Aunt Sonya dug right into hers while Elaine licked a complete circle around the tall ball of vanilla ice cream perched atop her cone.

Shelley and Judy considered their sundaes guiltily.

"I'm not sure I can do this," Shelley said.

Judy picked up her spoon and poked at the whipped cream. "I think that's real whipped cream. I've spent my whole adult life scraping it off or giving it away."

"Yeah. And look at all that fudge."

They looked each other in the eye. And there was a silence.

"I will if you will," Judy finally whispered.

Shelley licked her lips and studied her older sister. "Age before beauty," she teased, even though she was already dipping her spoon into the gooey concoction, making sure to get whipped cream, fudge, *and* ice cream on it. She held her spoonful up, admiring it. "One small spoonful for the Schwartz sisters, a giant leap for womankind," she said before shoveling it into her mouth.

Aunt Sonya and Elaine applauded quietly.

"Oh, my God," Shelley groaned as the cool richness flooded the inside of her mouth. "Oh ... my ... God!"

Judy popped a cherry into her mouth and bit down with a satisfied smile.

"I could die now and be completely happy." Shelley picked up one of her cherries by its stem and offered it to her sister, who popped it into her mouth and smiled her thanks. She offered the second to Aunt Sonya.

Then Shelley and Judy began to eat in earnest while Elaine and Aunt Sonya looked on with approval. They ate fully, completely, and without reservation. Together. No competition. No comparisons. Just ice cream and hot fudge and whipped cream.

The way it was meant to be.

chapter 10

By the end of the week, Shelley understood why the phrase "Thank God It's Friday" had been coined.

She'd spent the entire week working her list and had managed to schedule three appointments for next week, and a tentative four for the week after that. They were just meetings, of course; she still had to find a way to convert them into signed business, but she'd worked long and hard to fill her calendar. Though she was tired from the concentrated days of effort, she was also savoring her success, and already anticipating the challenges ahead. Right now, though, she was headed for her standing appointment with Howard Mellnick and then going to meet Trey for drinks at the Ritz, where she fully intended to put Schwartz and Associates completely out of her mind.

At the light knock on her door, Shelley looked up from the briefcase she was packing and waved in Ross Morgan's secretary.

"I, uh, e-mailed you earlier on Mr. Morgan's behalf about your appointment schedule for next week," Mia Holmes said, "but I didn't get a reply."

"That's because I couldn't come up with one that didn't have four-letter words in it."

"Oh."

Shelley snapped the briefcase shut. "You can tell your boss that while I appreciate his offer, I don't need him to come on my appointments with me. I'm completely capable of handling things on my own."

"But I don't think that's an option. He distinctly said that—"

"Mia?" Shelley said.

"Yes?"

"I don't really care *what* Mr. Morgan said. He gave me a client list and I'm working it. Period. I don't need an escort."

"But maybe your clients do."

Both their gazes swung to the doorway at the sound of Ross Morgan's voice.

This time he was wearing a suit, a black pinstripe with a crisp pink shirt and a tie she recognized as Armani. The bold color brought out the blue of his eyes, and the cut of the jacket emphasized his broad shoulders. He was a manly man, all right; just looking at him made her think of supply closets and strong sure fingers, which was completely inappropriate and not likely to help her win this current power play.

Ross nodded to his secretary. "Thanks, Mia, I'll take it from here."

"Take what?" Shelley asked as the secretary beat a hasty

retreat—undoubtedly headed for today's equivalent of the water cooler. "I don't need or want you on my appointments." *Maybe naked in a supply closet, but not calling on clients.* She slung her purse over her shoulder and picked up her briefcase. "End of conversation."

"As the director of Account Services it's totally within my authority to meet with clients before turning them over to the account executive and/or supervisor. It makes the client feel good to know that the upper echelon of the agency is involved."

She let the fact that she was now even lower echelon than she used to be slide. She did not want to call on clients with this, or any other, man staring over her shoulder.

"Well, I'm a little confused," she said. "I thought you were the president now, and as the daughter of the former president, I happen to know that dogging, er, accompanying the staff on sales calls is not a good use of a president's time."

She walked straight up to him, only stopping when they were toe to toe and nose to . . . chest, damn it. She raised her head slowly to reestablish eye contact. "And of course these aren't exactly new accounts. Are you afraid I'll lose one of these big producers?"

He looked down at her and she realized, with some surprise, just how tightly leashed he was. As if he was holding back all kinds of things that might spring forth at any moment. "Until I find a new director of Account Services," he said quietly, "I'm wearing both hats. And whomever I go as, I'm going. I want to see how you handle yourself and how you represent the agency. I don't need permission for that."

She refused to react to this heavy-handed pronouncement; she simply couldn't give him the satisfaction. And she definitely wasn't going to blow up and quit, no matter how tempting the idea.

Casually, she took a step backward to put some physical distance between them, because even when she was steaming with indignation or wanting to slap his annoyingly handsome face, she was aware of him physically. This was not a good thing.

"Fine," she said with a shrug. "Be ready to leave here Monday morning at nine o'clock. We're meeting with Wiley Haynes from Tire World at their Gwinnett location and then going on to the corporate offices of Mendelsohn TV. The owner, Abe Mendelsohn, is an old friend of the family."

She looked him up and down, trying not to notice what a fine specimen he was. "Wiley Haynes is a good ol' boy from Alabama. Abe hasn't worn anything but golf clothes to the office for fifty years. If I were you, I'd lose the Armani."

After Ross Morgan, Trey Davenport seemed somehow... smaller. Or at least more... restful.

It wasn't his size so much, Shelley realized as she joined Trey in a quiet booth at the back of the Ritz-Carlton lounge, since both men were similarly built. It was more the force of Ross's personality. Or maybe it was the fact that she was always so angry with him, she couldn't push him all the way out of her mind.

Trey was just... sweet and... fun. With him there was no clashing of goals, no need for confrontation, none of that appalling... sizzle.

Winding her way through the bar, she searched Trey's face for any sign that he might have a room key on his person, but he smiled back easily. When she reached the table, he stood to pull out her chair and leaned over to brush his lips across her cheek. He was as blond and beautiful as ever, better looking than Ross Morgan, really, if you went feature by feature, though she wasn't all that wild about the way she kept comparing them.

"It's been way too long," Trey said in greeting. "You look great."

"Thanks."

He signaled the waitress over and they placed drink orders. Settling back into the chair, she took a handful of mixed nuts and popped one into her mouth. They made small talk until their drinks arrived.

"I was sorry to hear about your dad," Trey said as she took a first sip of martini. "How's he doing?"

"Much better now, thanks." She didn't have the energy to go into the handover of the business to Ross Morgan and how that had shaken up her world. Better to turn the subject, keep things light. She took another sip of her drink then set it down. "Tell me about the rafting trip. I can't remember who went."

Obligingly, Trey launched into a monologue about the mishaps that had befallen them, turning the whole episode into a *City Slickers*–style adventure. "I'm telling you, I was hearing the theme song to *Deliverance* at one point, but everything worked out OK."

Shelley sipped her drink and allowed herself to be entertained. The story was greatly exaggerated—Trey was too strong a naturalist and athlete to have been seriously daunted by any river—but as he spun his yarn, Shelley reflected how much easier this was than interacting with Ross

Morgan. The sound of Trey's voice washed over her, warm and fluid, and some of the tension seeped out of her body. Yes, this was much nicer and a whole lot easier than dealing with Ross. Who needed the butting of heads and the gnashing of teeth when one could sit back and enjoy the company of an undemanding, yet undeniably attractive, man?

When the waitress checked back, Shelley ordered a second martini and nibbled a few more nuts. The green olive was perfectly tart after the smoothness of the gin and vermouth. A welcome languor spread through her bloodstream and into her limbs.

"Shel?"

"Hmmm?"

"You look like you're going to fall asleep."

"Me?"

Trey smiled and took the drink out of her hands. "We need to get you something to eat." He set her drink down on the table and smiled again. "Then we can head on over to my place so I can show you how much I've missed you."

"Hmmmm..." She considered the idea slowly. It was so peaceful here with Trey in the darkened corner of the bar. It had been a long grueling week, and next week was bound to be even tougher. She deserved some attention and a firsthand reminder that some men didn't question her competency. She knew from the look in his eyes that Trey Davenport found her sexy and alluring just the way she was.

"Why don't we kill both of those birds with one stone?" Shelley asked as he called for their check. "I don't think either of us should be driving right now." She smiled up at him as the waitress approached. "And I'm a big fan of room service."

Trey signed the tab, then reached over to squeeze her hand. "Wait here." He smiled happily as he pushed back his chair and stood. Trey Davenport was as sunny and uncomplicated as the request she'd just made. "I'll go over to the front desk," he said, "and see what's available."

Judy lay in bed and pretended to be asleep. It was six A.M. on Saturday morning and not a creature was stirring—not even her spouse.

Careful not to wake him, she listened to Craig's breathing. In the early morning it was soft and regular—a far cry from the Richter-scale levels he reached during the night; snores that obliterated the soundtrack of the late-night TV shows and forced her to buy earplugs and pop the occasional sleeping pill. Unlike some of her friends, she refused to sleep elsewhere when Craig was the one making all the noise. And since moving him when he was in full snore mode was pretty much impossible, she'd passed far too many nights sleep deprived and resentful, not to mention spoiling for a fight.

Keeping her eyes slitted so that she could feign sleep if necessary, she studied her husband's face. His features were even, his mouth wide and mobile, his hairline receding. Craig Blumfeld had once made her heart race and her pulse skitter. But the reality of eighteen years of living together was a high hurdle to jump.

How did you forget the snores and snorts, the burps and farts? The toilet seats left up—or even worse, down—and the dirty underwear piled on the floor? These days when he reached for her those were the things she saw; the everyday familiarities that did, in fact, breed contempt.

Turning her back, she curled into a ball and willed herself to sleep, but her mind refused to leave the path she'd set it on. Was it possible to keep things fresh and exciting when you'd been sleeping with the same person for twenty years? Could this be done without Saran Wrap? Or greeting one's spouse at the door wearing nothing but a bow?

"Jude?" Craig's arm slid across her waist and his hand searched out her breasts, which admittedly hung a little lower than they used to. "Wanna fool around?" He asked the question as he always did, as if it were some sort of erotic invitation she couldn't possibly resist.

A wave of annoyance washed over her and she opened her mouth to refuse, but at the last moment she couldn't do it.

She couldn't even remember the last time they'd made love; absolutely could not recall the last time his request had prompted anything resembling a positive response.

Her eyes squeezed shut. How many headaches could a woman claim? How many times could she say no before her husband took that as permission to ask elsewhere?

Craig's hand skimmed over her breasts then moved lower. Judy lay perfectly still, careful not to encourage or discourage, while she tried to tap into the excitement she'd once felt for him. Unfortunately, the vein seemed to have run dry. It was dry as toast, just like her.

Of course, if she was honest, a lot of that original excitement had had more to do with his suitability as a spouse than his prowess in bed. Craig Blumfeld had been so absolutely what she'd been looking for that just having him want her had been a complete aphrodisiac. She'd been downright orgasmic—multiply so—right up until the time her honeymoon tan had peeled off.

She opened one eye and stared at the wall. She was awake; she didn't have to be up with the kids or rushing out the door. She already knew she wasn't going to say no. She was just having a hard time saying yes with any enthusiasm.

Craig nibbled on her ear and pressed his growing erection up against her bottom and Judy tried, again, to dredge up some real enthusiasm for what was about to happen.

Ten minutes later she was staring at Craig's back and listening to his contented snores, and feeling none of the lazy comfort she'd felt earlier. Getting up, she showered quickly, drew on her robe, and padded quietly downstairs wishing, not for the first time, that she'd been born second so that she could run around and have a good time and sleep with hunky men like Trey Davenport whenever she felt like it.

Their mother could harass Shelley about getting married all she wanted; Judy knew which one of them was leading the more interesting life.

chapter 11

Wiley Haynes was ferret-faced and towheaded, with two oversized front teeth that would have done Bugs Bunny proud. He met Shelley and Ross in the Tire World parking lot, barely nodding at Shelley before reaching out to pump Ross Morgan's hand. "That's one fine car you got there," he said, nodding to Ross's Porsche Boxster. "But that right rear tire's lookin' a little iffy. You want me to have my boys put it up on the rack and give it a goin' over?"

Morgan swallowed and blanched slightly, which was the most emotion Shelley had seen him display that day.

"No, thank you, Wiley," he said. "It's due for regular service soon. But I'll, uh, be sure to have them check it out."

"Suit yourself." Wiley stuck his hands into the pockets of his jeans and led them through the garage, where the blare of the radio and the clanging of tools made conversation impossible. "We'll use my manager's office," he said as they followed him through the tire showroom and entered an office, which was shaped like a shoe box and roughly the same size. It was unclear how all three of them would fit without benefit of a shoehorn.

Ross waved her into the single guest chair—which along with a battered metal desk, chair, and ancient file cabinet were the only furnishings in the room—then wedged himself between Shelley and the file cabinet, a chivalrous act that left his hip and thigh practically embedded in her shoulder.

Despite the fact that she was the one seated directly across from him, Haynes spoke to Ross. "This here was my first location, and I'm opening my sixth at the end of April. As I told your assistant here on the phone," he nodded toward Shelley, "I don't have a whole hell of a lot left over for advertisin'."

Assistant? The flush of anger worked its way up her spine. "But I'm not—" she began.

"I'm sure you don't know too much about tahrs," he said to her. "Fortunately, your boss appears to know his way around a vehicle."

"What I was trying to say," Shelley bit out, "is that I'm actually your account executive. Mr. Morgan is just—"

"Really pleased to be here," Ross interrupted. "We've been wanting to talk to you about your business for some time. We think there's a lot more we could do for you besides just placing occasional newspaper ads."

Wrestling with her annoyance, Shelley snapped open her briefcase and pulled out the proposal she'd put together. "I went ahead and worked up a—"

"Phew," Wiley interrupted. "I have got to get that AC unit fixed. It's hotter than a witch's—" He shot Shelley an apologetic look. "Sorry, ma'am." He reached into his pocket and withdrew a stack of quarters, which he set on the desk and pushed toward Shelley. "How'd you like to run on over to the Coke machine out in the garage and get us all somethin' cold to drink?" he asked. "My treat."

Shelley's mouth may have fallen open. There was a not-so-subtle pressure on her shoulder, and she knew exactly what Ross was trying to tell her. But then, it was easy for him to expect her to be diplomatic; he wasn't the one who'd just been sent out for drinks.

She closed her mouth and swallowed back her outrage. "Sure." She scooped the quarters off the scarred desk and left the office, barely resisting the urge to walk out the front door, hop in the impressive-mobile, and peel out of there.

When she entered the garage, conversation ceased, and she could actually feel every eye in the place glom on to her rear end. She moved slowly to the Coke machine and then carefully—so as not to drop any change she'd have to bend over and pick up—fed the coins into the machine. Clutching the cold cans to her chest, she made her way out of the garage and back through the showroom.

In the office she delivered the refreshments without comment and took her seat in the metal folding chair—smack up against Ross Morgan's rock hard body and the tons of heat it was throwing off.

"Thank you, little lady."

She knew Wiley Haynes hadn't really called her that, because this was, after all, the twenty-first century. The pressure on her shoulder told her that he had.

"Mr. Haynes," she said as calmly as she could. "I assure you I am—"

"Ross here tells me you prepared this report." He held up the proposal she hadn't had the chance to hand out.

"Yes." Surprised, she fumbled in her briefcase for her copy.

"So maybe you know a little more about tahrs than I gave you credit for."

"Well..."

The pressure on her shoulder was more subtle this time, but she didn't need any warning pressure to remind her of Ross Morgan's presence or their purpose here.

"I'd never pretend to be an expert on tahrs, um, tires, Mr. Haynes," she said. "But I have been doing my homework. There are a zillion tire locations to choose from here in the Atlanta area and all of them—including Tire World—are ignoring a potentially important market segment."

"Which is?"

"Well, actually..." She swallowed, already imagining how a man who still called people "little lady" and assumed all females were assistants was going to feel about this. "It's women."

Ross stiffened beside her and Wiley Haynes started in surprise.

"I assure you there are women out there who buy tires. And we want to make sure they buy them from one of your six locations."

Wiley Haynes appeared to be speechless, which Shelley decided was not necessarily a bad thing.

"That's a very interesting premise," Ross began. "Maybe we should give Wiley some time to, um, digest this idea and then..."

Shelley refused to let him backpedal on her behalf. She

was right about this; the research said so and she knew it in her gut. If they backed off now, Wiley Haynes would never agree to consider the idea. Hell, after this kind of heresy he'd probably never let them back in the door. "I'd like to see you do a huge grand opening celebration with entertainment and giveaways targeted toward women." She felt Ross's hand on her shoulder, warning, cautioning, but she ignored it. "I also think we should offer tire clinics for women. You know how Home Depot teaches people how to do home repairs and remodeling? Tire World could give free workshops to teach women about tire selection and safety. And when they've completed the workshop they get a discount coupon as a graduation gift."

Wiley winced, then snuck a peek up at Ross.

The weight beside her shifted and she braced herself.

"I haven't had a chance to read the report," Ross said smoothly, "but assuming the research backs this up, it's a very...novel approach...which is," he cleared his throat, "of course what you're looking for from an agency."

Shelley began to unclench. It wasn't exactly a rousing vote of approval, but it wasn't a slap-down, either.

"I have every confidence in Ms. Schwartz's ability to steer your account in a more profitable direction."

He did?

"You do?" the tire man asked.

"I do. And, of course, no one at Schwartz and Associates operates in a vacuum. We have a team of creative and marketing people working on each client's behalf. We're, uh, just at the idea stage. The main thing right now is that we agree to proceed."

"Well, now." Haynes leaned back in his chair and took a

long sip of the Coke she had fetched for him. "I suppose I'd be open to hearin' more about this. I already figured we'd do some sort of grand openin'." He shook his head, still at a loss. "But women?" He snorted. "I never would have thought of it."

"No, me, either." Ross squeezed out from behind her—a move she felt through the open back of the folding chair and in too many parts of her body—then placed a hand under her elbow to help her rise so that they were standing side by side in front of the desk. "But one thing Ms. Schwartz knows for sure is parties. She'll give you a call when she has a plan and a budget ready."

"Yes." Shelley stuck out her hand to shake Wiley Haynes's callused one and silently prayed that he was NOT going to call her "little lady" again. "Give me a couple weeks to put something together for you. Then maybe you could come in for lunch to discuss it when it's ready?"

As they left the office, Shelley tried to decide whether she was relieved to be leaving with a positive outcome or pissed off that Ross Morgan had taken over so completely. In the end she decided there was no reason she couldn't be both.

Morgan handed her into the passenger seat, and she pulled the door shut, laid her briefcase at her feet, and folded her arms across her chest. "You were just supposed to be an observer on this," she pointed out as he slid into the driver's seat. "But as usual you had to be the head sardine."

"If you'd gone by yourself you'd still be running out for snacks."

"Ha!"

"Do you realize what you proposed to that man?"

"I proposed a killer idea that's going to set Tire World apart from every other tire store chain in Atlanta."

"To Wiley Haynes, head of the unenlightened. You might as well have proposed that he hire all female technicians."

"Hmmmm..." She looked at him to see if he'd been joking. "Maybe he could put a few women on that we could feature in the print ads..."

He snorted and slammed the car into gear. Shelley stared out the window, refusing to be soothed by the leather seats enveloping her or the purr of the engine. She tried to picture the meeting with Haynes minus Ross Morgan, and had to admit the image wasn't a pretty one. Still, she was not going to thank him for interfering or put up with any more of it.

On the interstate, the Porsche cut smoothly through traffic. Ross drove with a light touch on the wheel, handling the car like he handled everything else: with a calm competence she didn't want to admire.

A silence stretched out between them.

"I've been trying to figure out who you are today," he said, finally, without taking his eyes off the lane of merging traffic ahead of them.

"Who I am?"

"Yes. Whenever I'm with you I feel like I've been plopped down in a fifties movie. It's not just the cut of your suits, though, or what you've been doing to your hair. It's the whole shoulders-back, chin-up, you-can't-keep-a-good-woman-down thing."

The man was much too observant. And obviously an old movie buff.

"It's Hepburn again today, right?" His thigh muscle

bunched—she just happened to notice this out of the corner of her eye—and the car accelerated as he changed lanes. "With a hint of, oh, I don't know... Sophia Loren?"

Shelley studied him out of the same corner of her eye that had noted his thigh-bunching. She'd die before admitting to her dependence on film stars for inspiration and internal fortitude, or the time spent in front of her mirror each morning trying to imitate their easy confidence. Nor did Ross Morgan need to know that today she'd been unable to settle on an individual role model and was now, instead, channeling the combined presence of every strong movie heroine she could come up with. On the bright side, if he thought she was confining herself to fifties films, he was sorely underestimating the depths of her desperation.

"Don't be silly," she said. "It's just me. Mortally offended, tired of being a second-class citizen, thinking about calling the National Organization for Women and reporting Wiley Haynes to them."

"You can deny the movie influence all you want. Just promise you'll let me know when I get it right."

Not bloody likely. "Look, let's not get off the subject."

"Which is?"

"Your interference."

He didn't respond, but a small tic appeared in his jaw.

"I want you to keep your mouth shut at the next appointment."

"You want me to remain silent?" His tone was incredulous.

"Yes, you can smile and nod but you can't talk."

"You're kidding."

"Nope." She folded her arms across her chest and continued to stare straight ahead. "I've known Abe Mendelsohn since I was born and there's no way he's going to say no to me." She turned to face Ross. "I don't need or want you on this appointment. Either agree to keep quiet or let's just skip the whole thing."

"This is ridiculous. If I go in there and don't talk, we'll both look like imbeciles."

"I mean it," she said. "Promise me now, or I make my excuses to Abe and we go back to the office."

He shook his head, irritated. "You know, you were starting to actually make sense back there at Tire World. I mean, you were preaching to the wrong choir, but at least I could follow your line of thinking. This is just plain stupid."

"I don't care what you call it." They were less than a block from the store. A few moments later he turned into the parking lot. "If you won't agree we'll just cancel the appointment."

"But what if you get in trouble? What if—"

"No matter what," she insisted.

"Fine!" He put the car in park and turned it off. "Have it your way. But don't think you can change your mind midway through. If things start heading south, you're on your own."

She rolled her eyes. "I'll take my chances."

He pulled the key out of the ignition and reached for the door handle. Both car doors slammed as they exited and crossed the parking lot toward the building.

"Just remember," he warned as they neared the entrance, "you're the one who laid out this little scenario. These will be the last words you'll hear from me until we're finished. I'll save the I-told-you-so's for later."

***

Abe Mendelsohn met them on the sales floor of the North-pointe Mendelsohn TV and Appliance store. A bear of a man with a shiny dome of a head and appraising brown eyes, he wrapped her in a great big hug, then shook hands with Ross.

Shelley had known the Mendelsohns since childhood, and had spent part of her formative years in the sandbox with their son, Paul. When she and Paul had hit their teens, their mothers had tried to matchmake, but even the most determined yenta couldn't overcome the lack of chemistry between two people who had stuffed tadpoles in each other's diapers.

Paul was married now and about to become a father—a fact her mother brought up often.

"You look great, pumpkin," Abe said.

Ross's eyebrow shot up at the reference to her childhood roundness.

"I haven't seen your father since he got home from the hospital. How is he?"

"Good," she answered. "He's taking it easy."

"Yeah, I heard he and Miriam were planning a trip." Abe smiled down at her. "Your mother called yesterday to ask if Paul had any unmarried friends."

Shelley sighed.

"Parents want to see their children settled down and pro-ducing grandchildren." Abe pulled a crumpled piece of pa-per out of his pocket. "Have you seen the sonogram?" Abe's chest puffed out with pride. "This is my future grandson."

Shelley studied the grainy black-and-white radar-looking

picture, trying to make out the body parts. "Oh, my God, is that his—"

"It's his arm." Abe chortled. "Everybody thinks that first thing."

Something resembling a laugh escaped from Ross Morgan, but when she turned to check, he'd clamped his mouth shut again. Remembering the purpose of their visit, she handed the sonogram back to Abe and began the introductions. "This is Ross Morgan, Uncle Abe. He was our director of Account Services, but is now president. He's buying Daddy out."

Ross nodded and smiled. He stuck out his hand and the two men shook, but Ross didn't say anything, which under the circumstances felt pretty strange. Nothing she'd said to him in the car should have precluded a simple greeting.

Shelley shot him a look then stepped into the silence. "Is there somewhere we can sit down and talk?"

"Of course." Abe led them up the stairs to his second-floor office and motioned them toward the far end, where a small conference table with chairs overlooked the sales floor.

"I've been given the opportunity to review your account, Uncle Abe," she said when they were seated. "And I, um," she cleared her throat, "noticed that it's been somewhat ... inactive ... for the last few years."

She turned to Ross for confirmation, but he just nodded politely. When Abe looked the other way he made a zipper motion over his lips.

Shelley's mouth went dry. She could have asked Wiley Haynes for the moon, but asking for money from someone who'd once removed a frog from your diaper suddenly seemed infinitely more difficult. "And, I, uh, think we need to do something about that," she concluded lamely.

Abe pointed down to the sales floor, which overflowed with appliances and electronic equipment. "Do you see what's going on down there?" he asked.

Shelley and Ross looked. Two salesmen leaned against a flat panel TV and talked. A lone maintenance worker swabbed at an already shiny floor.

"Nothing's going on down there," Abe said. "The big chains are squeezing us out. Best Buy, Circuit City, HiFi Buys." Abe shook his head. "I don't have enough locations to place big enough orders to match their prices. This used to be my busiest store."

This would have been the perfect time for the president of the agency to step in and discuss the basic tenets of advertising. Except, of course, that she'd commanded him not to speak. Mr. Mum shot her a look that said he knew just how difficult this was for her and expected her to deal with it anyway. Or fall on her face.

"I'm, uh, sure Dad explained to you that advertising is even more important in, uh, slow times than it is during good ones."

Abe looked back at the empty sales floor and sighed. "Yeah, but what's the point? How big a difference can a few more ads make? I'm dying here."

And so was she. She'd bragged that Abe would never say no to her, but if she didn't actually present or ask for something, there'd be nothing for him to say yes to.

Shelley straightened and folded her hands in front of her on the table. "Uncle Abe," she said firmly, "I understand your concern and your reluctance. But you can't just let them push you under without a fight. You've got to advertise, and it's got to be done the right way. You've got to make potential buyers understand why they should shop with you instead of the big chains."

"Honey, that's very nice, but people today shop for price. They'll come in here and put my salespeople through hoops, touching, trying, feeling, and then they'll go order it from the Internet or some mail-order catalogue. They'll spend two hours in research to save five bucks. I'm tired to death of all of that. There's no customer loyalty anymore."

"But research indicates people want service and a personal touch. I've started working on a campaign for you that will highlight what a family-owned enterprise can do that a chain can't."

He studied her closely, then looked back down at the empty sales floor.

"Dad once said he believed you could sell ice to Eskimos. I want to put you on the air and give you a chance to do that." She let that sink in for a moment. "You're no quitter," she added quietly. "Give me a chance to show you what we can do for you."

Abe looked briefly at the still-silent Ross Morgan then back to Shelley, who was holding her breath.

"What would it cost to do what you're suggesting?"

"I need to crunch some more numbers," she said carefully. "And I want to sit down with the Creative Department to put a formal presentation together."

He ran a hand over the bald dome of his head. He was tempted, she could tell. He wanted to believe, but he needed a final inducement; that thing that would push him off the fence and squarely onto her side.

"I can have a presentation ready for you next week," she said, "and I'll tell you something else I can do."

Abe and Ross both sat up straighter. She could feel Abe teetering toward yes. Ross looked like he was bracing himself somehow, which was kind of weird because she didn't even know exactly what was going to come out of her mouth before she said it.

"I'll make a presentation just like I would for any new account," she said, "with storyboards and projections and a complete budget."

"Okay," Abe said cautiously. "And if we go along with this plan and it doesn't pick up my business..."

Ross Morgan's eyes got really really big. Kind of like saucers or maybe more like...tahrs. But Abe looked cautiously intrigued.

"If we don't create noticeable results for you," Shelley said, "then..." She paused and considered what Abe Mendelsohn would be unable to resist. "Then I'll refund every penny above our out-of-pocket expenses, which would make our work for you pro bono. As in absolutely free."

Abe perked up at that. And Shelley felt pretty good herself. It was the right offer to the right person at the right time. She knew before Abe said yes that she had set the hook and could go ahead and reel him in.

Ross made the first sound of any kind he'd made since they'd arrived. Unfortunately it was a choking sound. Or maybe it was more of a growl.

He scraped his chair back from the table. Shelley and Abe turned to watch him stand.

"Excuse me," he said, taking Shelley by the elbow and

pulling her up next to him. "But we're late for our next appointment. Shelley will have to get back to you with details."

"But..."

He didn't give her or Abe a chance to protest. There were no handshakes, no drawn-out good-byes, just Ross Morgan's hand clamped around her upper arm speed-walking her down the stairs, through the showroom, and out of the building at a pace that had her struggling to keep her shoes on her feet.

chapter 12

The drive back to the office was many things, but silent wasn't one of them.

They were barely out of the parking lot before Ross let loose all the words he'd been holding back. "Never, in all my years of advertising, have I ever heard anyone make such a ridiculous promise."

He accelerated too quickly and raced toward the interstate with a shifting of gears and gnashing of teeth. At the on-ramp he cut off a semi. The blare of the trucker's horn followed them onto the expressway, loud and indignant.

"This was supposed to be a SALES call, Shelley. The term 'SALES' connotes an exchange of services for MONEY. 'Money' being the operative word."

He didn't raise his voice but she could tell, just from his tone, which words belonged in capitals. His driving became both more controlled and more aggressive until the

Porsche felt like a guided missile hurtling toward some unseen target.

"NOW," he continued, "would be a really good time to explain what in the HELL you were thinking. If, in fact, you were THINKING at all."

Ross downshifted as they approached the toll on 400 South then tossed coins in the basket of the tollbooth, barely waiting for the barrier to go up before roaring forward. If they'd been on the Cartoon Network, steam would be pouring out of his ears and a plume of smoke would be coming out of the car's exhaust pipe.

Shelley was feeling pretty steamy herself. "You don't believe I was thinking? Well, maybe I wasn't. Not everyone's a cold, calculating automaton." She left off the "like you," but it rang between them in the car, loud and clear.

His hands clenched the wheel more tightly and the tic in his cheek...ticked, but she didn't give him a chance to respond.

"Sometimes—especially in this business—you have to trust your gut. And my gut told me that Abe Mendelsohn was not going to put up a penny without some sort of guarantee."

"Your GUT?" Ross cut across two lanes of traffic and zoomed into the exit lane. A little old lady in a Volkswagen Beetle gave them the finger.

"Yes. I may not be the most...structured...employee, but I learned this business from one of the best. And advertising is not just numbers. It's guts and intuition and creativity, too. And my GUT told me how to handle that meeting."

He snorted in dismissal and whipped into the office

parking lot, where he screeched to a halt in the president's parking space.

"If my GUT told me to work for FREE, I'd have it ripped out," he said.

Shelley turned in her seat so that she could look him in the eye. "We only work for free if he gets no results, and I don't intend to let that happen. Don't you have any faith in this agency? Don't you believe we can deliver enough for Abe Mendelsohn to want to pay us? Or is it just ME you don't believe in?"

They got out of the car, slammed their respective doors, and stalked—side by side—through the parking lot. In the lobby they made a beeline for the elevator, barely waiting for the doors to close before lighting into each other.

"I just laid a bet on Schwartz and Associates," Shelley ground out. "And I'm going to do everything in my power to make sure we win it."

At the fourth floor, they stormed off the elevator and whipped around to face each other. Afternoon sun poured through the huge industrial window and spilled over them like a stage spotlight.

The receptionist's greeting died on her lips. People froze in the hallway while Shelley and Ross squared off.

"You'd BETTER win it," Ross said in that infuriatingly dead-calm tone. "Or those fees he doesn't pay will come out of your salary. Not your BUDGET. Your salary."

"FINE!" she said, putting all of her anger into the capitalization process, determined to appear as icily calm as he did. "I have no problem with that." She turned and took in the audience surrounding them. "I believe in these people." She turned back to face him and held him with her eyes.

"Letting people know you expect them to succeed can be a great motivator. You should try it sometime."

And then she turned on her heel and stalked away from him, down the hallway to her office, where she slammed the door as hard as she could.

It wasn't quite as satisfying as shouting, but it came damned close.

Shelley vibrated with unreleased anger for hours. Unable to get back to work and too upset to eat a late lunch, she went to the health club and worked out until some of her anger began to dissipate. Then she sat in the sauna, trying to sweat the rest of it out of her skin while she pictured Ross Morgan evaporating into a puff of steam and disappearing into the air.

By three o'clock, when she'd showered and dressed and applied a fresh coat of makeup, she knew she couldn't go back to the office. Without conscious thought, she headed toward her parents', only remembering when she saw the cars parked in the drive that Monday meant mah-jongg in her mother's world, and that it must be her turn to host the game.

Just what she needed—a whole living room of Jewish mothers.

"Come, let me have a look at you."

"I think she's lost weight, don't you think she's lost weight, Sarah?"

"What, aren't you eating, little one?"

Her mother's mah-jongg group sat around a card table set up in the living room, their tile-holders in front of them, the pool of discarded mah-jongg tiles spread across the center of the table. Bowls of snacks sat within a hand's reach, provided—in addition to the lunch they'd consumed before starting—in case anyone should grow faint from hunger.

Their voices and the clack of tiles transported Shelley back to girlhood, when she'd come home from school on her mother's Monday and find the women in the midst of their game, happily dissecting each other's lives, and the lives of their all-important children.

"One bam, three crack."

Her mother had been playing mahj with these same women, with occasional substitutions due to arguments or travel, for the last forty years. Her father played a regular Saturday morning golf game with their husbands. Like the Mendelsohns, they'd always been "Aunt" and "Uncle" to Shelley and Judy. And every one of them was as concerned about Shelley's unmarried state and eating habits as they were about their own offsprings'. But she'd been a child then. Now she was an adult on a mission.

Shelley came up behind Sally Casselbaum and plucked a chocolate-covered peanut from the glass bowl on the snack tray beside her, and hugged Myra Kurtz, whose last bout with cancer had left her with bony shoulders and a platinum wig. "Hi, kiddo," Myra said. "I gave my nephew Jared your number. A friend of his is moving to town." She smiled and threw out a tile. "Two crack," she said. "He's relocating with Goldman Sachs." Her smile broadened. "An investment banker."

The other women nodded approvingly. Shelley sighed. Myra was fighting off cancer and still had the time and energy to arrange a fix-up.

"That is, unless you're seeing someone?" Myra said.

Shelley would have mentioned Trey, whom she'd been seeing now for almost six months, except Trey wouldn't count for these women. "Seeing someone" required at least one Jewish parent and acceptability—in their minds—as a marriage partner. A buff body was not required.

"There's tuna salad in the kitchen if you're hungry," her mother said from over her tiles. "Judy's our fifth today; she's back in the den with your father."

Good, that was just what she needed. Shelley took a bunch of grapes and carried them with her into the den. Judy sat on the couch with a heavy photo album in her lap. Her sister leafed through the album, occasionally pausing to study something, a thoughtful expression on her face. Their father was ensconced in his favorite chair and had *The New York Times* open in front of him.

Shelley gave her father a hug. "You're looking good," she said truthfully.

"People wait on me hand and foot and I get to play golf whenever I want to," he said. "Who wouldn't look good?"

Shelley turned to Judy. "What are you looking at?"

"My wedding album." Judy's brow furrowed and her tone grew wistful. "It *was* a beautiful wedding, wasn't it?"

"Gorgeous," Shelley replied. "You were the one in the really beautiful white dress, right?" She came over and sat next to Judy, unable to miss the fact that even seated she towered over her. "I was the one in the taffeta torture device."

With her finger, Judy traced a picture of her and Craig standing under the wedding canopy, then turned the gilt-edged page. They both stared down at a close-up of the bride and groom's beaming faces that the photographer had superimposed over a wider shot of the wedding party. Judy's shoulders slumped.

"What's going on?" Shelley asked quietly.

"Judy?" Their mother's voice reached them from the other room. "You're in!"

Judy closed the album gently and set it aside. "Time to get massacred."

"Yeah," Shelley agreed, "you're toast. I filled in once. I still have nightmares about it. They won every penny I had with me, then refused to give me a chance to win it back."

Judy stood and straightened her shoulders. "Maybe they'll take pity on me."

They looked at each other and shared a smile. "Nahhhh," they said in unison.

Shelley watched her sister leave the room—the perfect daughter dutifully fulfilling their mother's request. It was only recently that Shelley had begun to notice that Judy's participation might be less than wholehearted. Still, she reflected as her father folded his newspaper and laid it on the ottoman, Judy Schwartz Blumfeld was a tough act to follow.

"So." Harvey Schwartz settled back in the club chair and focused his complete attention on her. "What's on your mind?"

"Oh, just the usual."

"And that would be?"

"Ross Morgan."

Her father's eyebrow went up, but he waited for her to explain.

"We're not seeing eye to eye on the list he gave me or the way I'm handling it."

"You two don't see eye to eye on the weather," her father pointed out mildly. "So I suppose that's not too surprising."

"Why did you do it, Dad?" she asked, though she'd vowed not to ask again. "Why'd you choose him?"

Her father removed his glasses and rubbed the bridge of his nose; she'd seen him do the same thing in meetings right before he pointed out something no one wanted to hear. "Because he's solid and responsible and he's got that hunger in his belly that's necessary to keep a company growing."

"And I don't."

"You're smart as a whip, Shelley," her father said, "but no, you're not hungry, sweetheart, not in the way Ross is. You've never had to go without or really fight for anything. It's not your fault, of course, but there it is."

Shelley hated the certainty in her father's voice. But he was wrong if he thought she wasn't hungry. She was absolutely starving—for Ross Morgan's head on a platter.

"Believe me when I tell you the last thing Ross Morgan wants me to do is succeed. He's watching over my shoulder, setting me up to fail. You should have seen how he reacted this morning when I told Uncle Abe that if we didn't produce results for him we'd work for free."

"You told Abe that?" Her father laughed. "I've been trying to get him to do more for years, but he's such a penny-pincher." He laughed again. "Why didn't I think of that?"

Shelley laughed with him, her heart lightening. "Morgan absolutely hated it, accused me of not THINKING. Me!" She laughed again. "Good lord, you should have seen his face."

"Who else did he give you?"

Shelley recited her list, and her father whistled. "Definitely bottom of the barrel. So what are you going to do?"

"I don't know." She shook her head, unsure. "I've talked my way into the chance to pitch, and I've got some really good ideas."

"But?"

"But trying to get him to trust me is like...I don't even know what it's like. I just know he makes me crazy."

"If it's too hard, Shelley, you can just forget it. I'd hoped you'd make a place for yourself at the agency, but if it's too difficult..." He shrugged. "Well, you know we're never going to let you starve."

She looked into her father's eyes and knew that his offer was made out of love; everything he'd done for her could be chalked up to that. But he was wrong about the lack of fire in her belly. She was not going to be defeated by Ross Morgan. Or herself.

"I'm not giving up, Daddy. I am absolutely not going to quit."

"Well, if you're serious, it's time to sit down with Luke and fill him in on what you need. We have one of the best creative departments in the southeast. I know because I recruited it."

"I can hardly wait to see Morgan's reaction to me committing serious time and money to these accounts. He almost had apoplexy over a five-hundred-dollar falafel tasting."

"The man's interested in the bottom line, Shelley, and the only way to increase that is to bring in more business. That's what *you're* being paid to do."

"Yes," she agreed, "and that sounds great in theory, but

I'm not sure how he'll react to the idea of me actually succeeding."

Not that she was exactly primed for handling the concept of success herself.

"Ross Morgan's a big boy and he wants what's best for the agency," her father replied. "Sounds to me like it's time you stop pussyfooting around and show him that's what you want, too."

chapter 13

Tuesday at noon Shelley swept into Creative Director Luke Skyler's office bearing a bottle of Pellegrino and designer sandwiches from Eatzi's.

To get there, she traveled from the end of the building that housed the hushed Account Services department, through the buffer zone of the Media Department, to the creative side, where music blared and bright color dominated. Though neither side would exist without the other and both were necessary to the success of any advertising agency, the two factions operated in a state of armed truce, each jockeying for control, all too often squabbling like children who simply could not see the other's point of view. It took a strong president to make them play nicely together.

In the beginning, before she'd grown tired of trying to prove she was more than the boss's spoiled daughter, she'd been drawn to the creative side. She was willing to take intuitive leaps that were frowned upon by her colleagues in Account Services, and totally respected the creative genius of Luke Skyler, whom his admirers had christened Skywalker. She still did, but until this morning she'd given up taking chances.

Luke was in his early forties with a head of wavy salt-and-pepper hair, an olive complexion, and sharp green eyes. When he wasn't required to deal with clients, he wore jeans—crisp designer ones—that he liked to pair with white cotton button-down shirts and Cole Haan shoes, minus socks. He was totally hip, more than a little sexy, and married—incredibly enough—to his high school sweetheart.

"Ah," he said as Shelley entered. "She comes bearing lunch. Whatever could she want?"

Shelley laid her offerings before him. Whipping a glass out of her jacket pocket, she set it next to the bottle of Pellegrino.

"I need you," she said as she placed a gold, beribboned sample box of Godiva chocolates and an artfully folded cloth napkin before him.

"And badly, by the look of it."

"Well, actually, I need your wonderful twisted brain and all that good stuff that's floating around inside it."

"Aha." He unwrapped the sandwich, lifting the edge of the crusty Italian bread to check it out. "Very good. Grilled veggies are excellent brain food."

He unscrewed the cap of the sparkling water, poured himself a glass, and gestured to the picnic she'd spread before him. "Would you like something?"

"No, thanks, I'm good."

"All right, then," Luke said. "You talk, I'll eat and think." He checked his watch. "I've got a meeting at one, but I'm completely and totally yours for the next forty-five minutes."

Her phone was ringing when she got back to her office. "Shelley speaking," she answered happily, only losing her smile when she recognized her mother's voice.

"I just wanted to remind you that you're going to be getting a call from a friend of Jared's."

"Jared?" Shelley's mind was still on the meeting she'd just had with Luke Skyler. "Jared who?"

"Jared Kurtz."

"Mother!"

"Myra asked you to speak to him and, well, this could be Myra's last request."

"Mother, Myra Kurtz is in remission and it's incredibly tacky of you to use her cancer to try to get your way."

There was a shocked silence on both ends, which was immediately filled by an attempt to inflict guilt.

"I don't know how you can speak to me that way." Her mother's tone was both wounded and indignant. "Myra Kurtz is one of my oldest and dearest friends. She's known you since you were born. She's been through a horrible ordeal—which she may have licked, though we really can't be sure—and all she's asking is that you take a call from a friend of her nephew."

A friend of a nephew. She didn't even rate actual relatives anymore. Shelley groaned. "Fine, Mother. I'll speak to him. But not today; I'm really busy today."

"Actually, I just got off the phone with him—he called to

double-check the number. Be nice, Shelley. You never know. This could be THE ONE."

Right, and she might be winning the lottery tomorrow. Or discovering the cure for the common cold.

Hanging up the phone, Shelley flipped open her legal pad and began to look over the To Do list she'd compiled during her meeting with Luke. The phone rang again.

"Shelley speaking."

"Uh, Shelley? This is Josh Stein. I understand you know my friend Jared Kurtz's Aunt Myra?"

This really sucked. Maybe she should just find someone to marry to stop all the attempted fix-ups. Like in those marriages of convenience that were so popular in romance novels.

"Yes, Josh, I was told you might call, but—"

"I don't really know anyone in Atlanta, and I've just been transferred here. I'm in town going around with a Realtor, but I wondered if you might have time to show me around the city."

That was her: Shelley Schwartz, pathetic unmarried daughter and Atlanta tour guide.

"I'm kind of busy today"—or at least she would be if she could ever get off the phone—"and this week is not good." She wished she could just go ahead and say no, but she was too well trained for that. And then there was Myra. "But if you want to meet for drinks tomorrow, I can introduce you to a friend who might be able to help."

If Nina was contemplating becoming a member of the tribe, she might as well get a taste of the fix-up business.

Shelley hung up the phone and picked up her pen, but the phone was no sooner in its cradle than it rang again.

Productivity in America had probably been much higher before the invention of the telephone.

"Shel? It's Nina. Do you want to meet for a drink later?"

"Can't." What Shelley really wanted was to get to work. She didn't even have time to think about what a novel thing that was. "But I have a new prospect for you. I can turn him over to you tomorrow at six at the Ritz."

"Where does he live? What does he look like?"

"These are the unanswered questions that make blind dating so...intriguing. He's a friend of Myra Kurtz's nephew and his name is Josh Stein. That would make him totally and completely Jewish. And he's an investment banker."

"Oh."

"I'll see you there at six tomorrow."

"Oh, OK."

"And don't say I never gave you anything," Shelley said as she hung up. She'd barely put the receiver down when the phone rang again.

"This is Shelley."

"Yes, this is the Darnell Day Spa. We wanted to let you know that you missed your scheduled manicure and pedicure this morning. And your massage and facial yesterday."

Oops. She looked down at her fingernails, which were, in fact, in serious need of shaping and polishing.

"We will, of course, be billing your account." There was a brief pause during which the woman must have noticed how much money Shelley regularly dropped there. "Would you like to reschedule?"

Yes, she would, but when she scrolled through her Palm Pilot she couldn't find an open slot big enough to fix a single body part. This work thing was wreaking havoc on her beauty regimen.

Shelley hung up, repositioned her pad, and tried to remember what she'd been doing. The phone rang. Again.

"Shelley Schwartz," she said with a groan.

"Shelley? Are you all right?" It was Trey, lovely Trey, whom she did NOT have time for.

"I would be if my phone would stop ringing."

"Oh."

"I didn't mean you," she said, apologizing. "It's just that I have all this work piled up and the phone is driving me crazy."

"Why don't I come take you away from all that? Do you want to do lunch at Hidalgo's?"

She was tempted, really tempted. But she wanted to get her To Do list down, and reach the party planner for Tire World's grand opening, and...well, that was the point, wasn't it? She had too much to do to break for lunch.

"I wish I could, Trey, but I am not budging from this desk until each item on this list in front of me has been marked off."

"I'm thinking I may have called the wrong Shelley Schwartz. Is this..." He recited her number but she couldn't tell from his tone if he was really amused or not.

"I'm sorry, Trey," she said, meaning it. "I'm just swamped today. How about later in the week?"

"OK."

Trey hung up and Shelley asked Sandra to hold her calls. Then she started at the top of her To Do list and began to work her way methodically through it. When she got to the

Tire World grand opening, she called Sandra for the number of the party planner the agency normally used.

"Oh, hi, Ms. Schwartz," the woman's assistant answered. "No, I'm sorry, Lacy's on a huge project for the next couple of months. She's not taking anything else on."

"Can you suggest someone else?"

The woman kept her on the line while she flipped through her Rolodex. "Sorry, but I have notes next to everyone's name; they're all booked. It's a really busy season."

Well, shit. Shelley hung up and thought about the grand opening. She was absolutely determined that it would be unique, and effective. She wanted to knock Wiley Haynes's socks off.

Unfortunately, despite Ross Morgan's assumption, parties were not her forte. Attending them, maybe. Planning them? No, that was definitely not her thing.

Shelley leaned way back in her chair and stared up at the ceiling, searching for answers in the shiny black plaster.

Judy, now, that was another story. Judy could outplan the best of them. There was no detail too small to interest her. And she wasn't afraid to do something different—as she'd proved with Jason's Roman Gladiator bar mitzvah. And what did Judy have to do with her time besides run her sons around and . . . bake?

Shelley didn't give herself time to think it out any further. Despite Ross Morgan's opinion, sometimes those gut reactions were the truest. She picked up the phone and dialed it, waiting impatiently for her sister to pick up.

Judy was baking again. She didn't want to be baking, but Craig was at work, the boys were in school, and her tennis match had been canceled. She didn't even have a volunteer shift on the calendar. It would be four and a half hours until Sammy got off the bus.

Her hands and kitchen counters were covered in flour, and warm wonderful smells emanated from her oven. The only problem was what she'd do with the chocolate banana cakes when they were finished. Both the freezer in the house and the one in the garage were jammed full, her friends and family had forbidden her to bring them any more baked goods, and the neighbors had begun to run when they saw her with anything in her hands. Even the staff at Summitt Towers blanched when they saw her coming.

The phone rang, startling her out of her thoughts, and she ran her hands under the faucet, hurriedly dried them, and scooped it up. "Hello?"

"Judy?" Her sister's voice cut through the silent room. "What are you doing?"

Judy's gaze swung around the kitchen, taking in the floured granite countertops, the cabinets left open, the mixing bowls and blender waiting to be washed. She knew better than to admit to Shelley that she'd been baking. Her sister viewed her... hobby... as if it were some dangerous addiction.

"Not too much." Once she'd cleaned up she'd go work out, pick up the dry cleaning, get a few things at the grocery store. She was doing a whole lot of nothing, just like she did every day.

"I've got a problem. A sort of emergency."

"And?"

"And I need you to do something for me. And, um, for the agency."

Judy stopped thinking about her errands and her kitchen. Surely she'd heard wrong. "Me?"

"Yep. I don't have time to explain all the details, but I have to plan a grand opening and the party planner we normally use isn't available."

"So…"

"So I'm wondering if you'd take over the grand opening."

"Me?"

"Yes, you."

"But I don't have any idea how to do something like that."

"Don't be silly. You give great parties and you can get anybody to do anything. People are still talking about the lion in the cage and the rabbi wearing that toga."

"But I don't plan parties. I *hire* people to plan parties."

"But the ideas are all yours. You'll just be cutting out the middleman. You're a natural-born organizer, and, well, I really need this event to be a success."

The timer on the oven went off but Judy ignored it. "No, Shelley, this is crazy, I—"

"Are you telling me you're too busy?"

Judy looked around her kitchen once more. She thought about the empty day stretching ahead of her. "Well, no, not exactly."

"Or that you're not interested in helping your poor overwhelmed sister or the agency your father founded??"

Judy snorted. "I think you'd better leave the guilt to Mom."

"Too much, huh?"

"No, not enough! Mom would have found a way to work in Myra's cancer."

"I'm saving my creativity for the job. But I need you, Judy. Come into the office tomorrow morning and I'll fill you in."

"Well…"

"Don't make me beg. My voice gets all whiny and it's too embarrassing."

"I don't know, Shel. I'm just not sure."

"I'm going to take that as a yes. I'll see you here at ten A.M. tomorrow, dressed for work. If I'm going to put you on the payroll, you're going to have to act like a professional."

"The payroll? Shelley, I don't—"

"Thanks, Judy. You're a lifesaver. I'll see you in the morning."

With the dial tone humming in her ear, Judy hung up the phone. Her kitchen was trashed, smoke was pouring out of her oven, and the clothes dryer was buzzing insistently, but she felt oddly excited. She knew now what she'd be doing for the rest of the afternoon and where she'd be headed in the morning.

Moving quickly, she pulled the ruined cakes from the oven and shoved them down the garbage disposal, then opened windows to get rid of the burnt smell. She caught herself humming as she rushed around putting the kitchen to rights.

Thirty minutes later she was showered and dressed and pointing her car toward the nearest mall. If she was going to look like a career woman tomorrow, she was going to have to go shopping.

chapter 14

"Wow, great outfit." Shelley came out from behind her desk to greet Judy, who stood in the office doorway wearing low-slung black slacks and a pale pink Donna Karan shell and cardigan set that Shelley had barely resisted at Bloomingdale's earlier that month. Judy's short dark hair was perfectly tousled, and she wore oversized silver dream-catcher earrings and a chunky bracelet shot through with black and pink. "Those earrings are fabulous."

"Thanks." Judy smiled and her lips, which were painted a matching pink, parted to reveal even white teeth. She looked bright, competent, and professional, and she hadn't had to dress like a strong-willed movie heroine to do it. Shelley looked down at the white linen pantsuit that had felt so "Bogie and Bacall" when she'd put it on and now felt so . . . wrinkled. If she'd thought her sister might look like a fish out of water in an office environment, she'd been mistaken.

After a quick hug, Shelley led Judy to the chair across from her desk. Her older sister's brown eyes sparkled with something Shelley hadn't seen there in a long time, and although she'd squared her shoulders and folded her hands in her lap, Judy's body practically vibrated with excitement.

"Thanks so much for coming in," Shelley said.

"No problem." Judy's nod sent the earrings bobbing. She fingered the bracelet at her wrist. "You mentioned a grand opening, but you didn't say for whom."

"It's Tahr"—Shelley rolled her eyes—"I mean *Tire* World. They're opening a new location and we're going to turn it into a major event."

"*Tire* as in the round rubber things that go on a car?"

Shelley nodded.

"You mean those round black things that I don't know anything about?"

Shelley nodded again.

"But I've never even kicked one, let alone picked one out or bought one." Judy sat forward. A worried frown pursed her lips. "We trade in our cars every two years. I'm pretty sure they come with tires already attached."

"Fortunately, you don't need an intimate understanding of the product to pull off a party," Shelley reasoned. "I mean, how much of Jason's Torah portion did you understand when you planned his bar mitzvah?"

"Good point." Judy nodded in relief.

"And something else we're going to promote is 'How To' workshops for women. We're not the only ones who've never kicked a tire."

"Are you sure about this?" Judy dropped her gaze. "I mean, are you sure you want me here?"

"Absolutely." Shelley stood and waited for Judy to do the same. "Come on." She slid an arm around her older sister's waist, surprised to be the one offering reassurance. "Let's go get you settled in. There's an empty office around the corner I thought you could use."

"An office?" Judy stopped moving.

"Unless you'd rather work from home." As far as Shelley was concerned, Judy could work from the bathtub as long as she got the job done.

"No, no, an office is fine," Judy said. "It's just that—" She laughed self-consciously. "I've never *had* an office before."

Whereas Shelley had always had one but only recently begun to use it. "It's actually more like a cubicle," she explained. "You know, just a desk and a phone—"

"Oh, I don't care what's in it. I mean, I'm not planning to pick out wall coverings for it or anything." Judy laughed, then paused. "Am I?"

"No," Shelley promised, "no wall coverings. No decorating. Just a convenient spot to get things going from."

There was a brisk rap on the door and the sisters turned to see Ross Morgan in the doorway.

Suddenly reminded of the discrepancy in their sizes, Shelley took an automatic step away from Judy. Ross crossed the room toward them, and she cringed inwardly at what he must be seeing—the Jolly Green Giant towering over Career Barbie.

"You remember Ross Morgan, don't you, Jude?" Shelley said as he neared them.

"Hi." Ross and Judy reached forward at the same time and Shelley watched her sister's hand disappear inside Morgan's.

He turned to Shelley. "I just wanted to check and see where we were with the Simms and Mendelsohn proposals."

"I've already met with Creative," Shelley said. "I should be ready to report back by the end of the week."

"Mendelsohn as in Uncle Abe?" Judy asked.

"The very one," Shelley replied.

"If it's not a bargain, he's not interested," Judy said.

"Tell me about it." Ross's tone was dry.

"Hey," Shelley said, turning to her sister, "say that again."

"What?"

Shelley tuned out Ross Morgan and her fear of looking foolish in front of him. "The 'If it's not a bargain' thing."

Judy complied.

"What do you think of 'If it's not a bargain, I'm not interested. And neither are you.'"

Judy and Ross were both watching her closely.

"When I met with Luke, we agreed that the biggest difference between Mendelsohn TV and the chains is Abe. As much as we've been trying to get Brian Simms *off* the air, I really feel we need to put Abe on television. And in newspaper ads. And on the radio. Because he's a great old Jewish-grandfather type who's only going to buy at a discount and pass that savings on to his customers."

Ross stared at her as if he'd never seen her before. Judy nodded enthusiastically. "He's a total character, but he inspires trust at the same time."

"Yeah. Luke thinks we should do everything in black-and-white, go completely antislick and old-fashioned so that we're countering the chains in every way."

Judy shot Shelley an admiring glance. "I don't know much about advertising, but that sounds really good to me."

"It has...possibilities." Ross studied her more closely and she had the sense that she'd somehow popped out of the box he'd put her in. The big question was how hard he'd try to stuff her back inside. "But since there's every chance we won't be making a nickel off those commercials, let's not get too carried away, hmm?"

Shelley bristled as he considered the two of them then checked his watch. "Isn't it a little early to be going out to lunch?"

"Lunch?" Shelley realized with a start of surprise that she'd never mentioned her intention to hire Judy. *Uh-oh.* "No, uh, actually, Judy's here to help plan the Tire World grand opening party. I was just going to find her a place to work."

One lone, blond eyebrow sketched upward and she felt herself go on the defensive.

"Our, uh, regular party planners weren't available." She saw Judy's face fall and felt an unfamiliar surge of protectiveness. "Judy's absolutely first-rate at putting on parties. Why, she's famous all over the northeastern suburbs for her Roman Gladiator–themed bar mitzvah."

"But this isn't a bar mitzvah."

"Same basic concept," Shelley said, wanting to end this conversation before any damage was done. "Without the chopped liver and Middle Eastern folk dancing."

"I know Wiley Haynes would be thrilled to hear that," Ross said.

"Jude." Shelley turned her sister around and gave her a gentle push toward the door. "Why don't you wait for me outside? I need to explain a few things to Ross."

Judy went, and Shelley rounded on the man in front of

her. "You know," she bit out, "I've gotten kind of used to you attacking my competency. I don't particularly like it, but I've come to expect it. But you don't have to bring my sister into it."

"*I'm* not the one who brought your sister into it. You can't just put family members on the payroll without checking first, Shelley, especially family members without experience." He skewered her with a look. "Despite the precedent that's already been set."

She took that one in the gut, but kept silent. She was afraid that if she opened her mouth, she'd quit. Which was exactly what Ross was angling for.

"In the future, all budget expenditures, including hiring staff—related or otherwise—are to be approved by me. In advance."

She kept her chin up and held her position until he turned to leave. Gritting her teeth, she fell in behind him and joined her sister in the hallway. Together they watched him walk away. He was arrogant and irritating and had the ability to yank her chain without even trying.

He also had broad shoulders, a tapered torso, and an incredibly firm rear end. When he'd rounded the corner they turned back to each other.

"That is one of the finest tushes I've ever seen." Judy let out an exaggerated sigh.

"I guess." Shelley slung an arm around Judy's shoulder, glad Ross Morgan's tirade hadn't robbed her sister of her sense of humor. "I won't tell your husband you were ogling another man's buns if you don't tell Uncle Abe I called him an old Jewish grandfather."

"All right," Judy agreed as they left to go find her cubicle.

"But I wasn't the only one ogling that rear end." She shook her head. "And to think I used to scoff when my trainer talked about buns of steel."

It was close to three o'clock when Judy checked her watch. After Shelley had introduced her around, she'd spent the hours reading up on Wiley Haynes and his Tire World, looking at the print ads the agency had been running, and trying to get a handle on how one might throw a party at a tire store that anyone would actually want to attend.

The biggest problem, she knew, was that she kept trying to picture her friends and family gathering around—well, she didn't even know what one would gather around at a tire store. Her imagination sputtered to a complete stop when she tried to picture what Mandy Mifkin, Bar Mitzvah Coordinator Extraordinaire, might do with this assignment; she just didn't know where to start.

Finally, she began making lists of the things that she knew were germane to all parties, tire-themed or otherwise. The biggies, of course, were food and entertainment. And you'd probably have to give something away to get people to come there.

In her own circle, a spa certificate or a lunch at a favored restaurant would qualify for giveaway status, but what did people who bought tires want? Tickets to a wrestling match? Raw hamburger meat? She really had no idea.

Still, it was fun to turn her mind to a challenging task, to apply herself to something other than errands and volunteer work and the mundane tasks of running a household. At first she watched every person who walked by her cubicle, listened in on snippets of conversation, and tried to decode the novel language of this business that had always hovered at the edge of her existence but never really touched it.

By lunchtime, which she spent nibbling on a sushi sampler plate that Shelley had sent in, her initial panic at the idea of occupying an office and being expected to produce something had faded, and she began to enjoy the ringing phones and the buzz of activity—not to mention being surrounded by so many adults. Here, nobody wanted her to cook for them or pick up after them or run their shirts to the cleaners. Here she was a part of the subdued urgency and the collective sense of purpose. The wonder of it slid down her spine and dug its way deep inside.

Did Craig feel this way when he went to work? Was it a relief to go somewhere and be appreciated for something more than providing a salary and showing up for school performances and sporting events? Did he walk into his office and think, "Thank God, I'm here"?

Judy set the pen down on the pad and stared out the glass front of her cubicle. She didn't have the first idea how Craig felt about his law practice anymore. Oh, she still asked about his day when he came home, still made clucking noises of comfort and nodded at what felt like the appropriate pauses in conversation. But somewhere along the way she'd stopped paying attention to his answers. She just let the words flow over her, absorbing very little; and though she didn't like to admit it, she'd seen the glazed-eye look that told her Craig did the same to her.

At three-thirty she gathered her things and walked over to Shelley's office. Knocking softly on the open door, she popped her head inside. "I have to go," she said. "Sammy gets off the bus at four-thirty, and I promised I'd be there."

"OK." Shelley looked up from the open folders spread across her desk. She'd shed the linen jacket and had totally dislodged the "up do" she'd been wearing. Judy had never seen her so unaware of her appearance.

"Do I get to, um, do you want me to come back tomorrow?"

Shelley lifted her arms above her head and stretched her fingers toward the ceiling, then rubbed at the base of her neck, obviously trying to work out the kinks. "You won't be punching a time clock or anything. Just come in as much as you need to to get things done. I'd like to sit down in a couple of days and hear where you are."

"Right now, I don't even have a theme. So far all I've got is round."

Shelley smiled. "Round, huh? That could be pizza, doughnuts, bagels, pies, meatballs, falafels..."

"Yeah." Judy smiled back. "Like I said, my next mission is to start narrowing the focus."

Judy hummed her way out of the office and into the parking lot, knowing she needed to get on the road before rush hour began in earnest. Maybe tonight she'd run out and pick up a briefcase of some kind. Or a Coach pad holder she could use in meetings. She shivered in anticipation.

Opening the car door, she tossed her purse on the passenger seat and drew in one last great breath of air, tasting the freedom of being out in the world on a beautiful spring afternoon, rather than in a kitchen or an overheated laundry room. Then she slid into the BMW and turned on the radio while her mind skittered here and there, weighing potential meal options and fiddling with the concept of round, as in tire, from which she needed to extract a theme. Then she moved mentally to tomorrow's clothing options, and how lucky she was to have somewhere to go and something interesting to do.

After a cursory glance in the rearview mirror, she began to back out of the parking space, her mind still focused on the wonder of being a part of the working world. The one thing it wasn't focused on was what other cars might be backing up at precisely the same moment, in that exact parking lot.

Which was why it was so unprepared for the sensation of slamming backward into what felt like a brick wall. And the sickening crunch of metal that accompanied it.

chapter 15

Behind her, a car door slammed and there was a quick, muttered curse. Footsteps approached. A peek over her shoulder revealed a tall male body striding toward her.

She muttered a curse of her own, not at all in the mood to deal with an accident report and insurance companies and some irate somebody who would undoubtedly give her all kinds of grief.

Dreading what lay ahead, Judy laid her forehead on the steering wheel and closed her eyes.

"Are you OK?" The voice was mercifully calm and she thanked her lucky stars she hadn't hit a raving lunatic brandishing a gun. It was also deep and masculine. And vaguely familiar.

Still hugging her steering wheel, Judy looked up and into warm hazel eyes set in the middle of an arresting face. She hadn't seen that face, except in the occasional bawdy dream, for almost twenty-two years, but she would have known it anywhere.

"Judy?" Brett O'Connor flashed the killer smile he'd slain her with in high school. "Gee, it's really great to..." he paused and his smile grew broader as he realized what he was about to say, "run into you."

She flushed and tried to smile back. "Yeah. I just wish it hadn't happened so literally."

"Good point." Still flashing that killer smile, he reached down to open her door and help her out. Together they turned and she got her first full look at his car, which was a bright red Lexus convertible. With a great big dent in it.

"I'm so sorry," she said.

He shrugged a pair of broad shoulders. "It could have been worse," he said. "It could have been mine."

Her mind was too busy sorting through the tidbits she'd heard about him over the years to focus on his words. Ancient gossip had him married and living in Chicago, but she had no idea if this was still true. A surreptitious glance confirmed he wasn't wearing a wedding ring, but too many men went without them for this to be conclusive. She pulled her gaze back up to his and told herself to pay attention.

"It's a rental," he explained as they moved to the rear of her car to examine the damage. "I have no personal attachment to it whatsoever."

"Well, that's a relief," she managed. "I hate to make a grown man cry." OK, that was nice and casual, slightly flip. She wasn't a teenage girl with a mad crush anymore.

He smiled again. He did that a lot. And, she couldn't help noticing, he did it really well.

"Well, your bumper came out ahead in that one." They looked at the point of impact. "It barely has a scratch. And you," he said, shaking his head, "you look so exactly the same. I can hardly believe it."

Judy blushed and thanked whoever was in charge of these things that she was dressed and made-up. "What are you doing in town? Have you moved back?"

"No. The investment group I'm with is buying property in midtown for development. I'm here for a closing. In fact," he looked down at her as if she were completely and utterly fascinating, "I'll be in and out of Atlanta for the next six months." He flashed the lethal smile at her. "Tell me about you."

"Me?" She smiled stupidly. "I, uh, do consulting work. I'm planning a grand opening for a chain of tire stores." She left out the fact that this was her first and possibly last project. And the existence of her husband and two children.

Leaning into the Lexus, he pulled a packet out of the glove compartment. "I just need to call the rental company and see what they want me to do." He pulled out a cell phone and began to punch in a number. "Do you need to report this?"

Normally she would have called Craig to let him know what had happened, but it wasn't like she needed towing or anything, and it looked like she was in good hands. She blushed as she remembered their high school fumblings, how their heavy breathing had fogged the windows of the vintage black Mustang he'd driven.

She dug out her own insurance card and began to punch the numbers into the phone. While she held for the next available agent, she watched Brett O'Connor start up the

Lexus and move it into the empty space next to her BMW. He walked back around the car and leaned over to take something out of the trunk, and for the second time that day she checked out an unfamiliar hard male body; it was absolutely amazing how many steel buns seemed to be wandering around Atlanta, available for ogling.

The low rumble of Brett O'Connor's voice sent a ripple of awareness through her into places that had been unaware for a very long time. Embarrassed at her reaction, she turned her back to him and called home to leave a message for Sammy.

Then she pulled out her lipstick case and applied a fresh coat of Persian Pink.

Shelley didn't have time to worry about lipstick shades or motivational clothing. She spent the week with her nose pressed firmly to the grindstone, arriving early each morning and staying late, spending as much time as possible with Luke and his creative team in order to work up presentations for the clients she'd already called on.

For the last three hours she'd been in Luke's office with his people discussing L.A. soundstages, location sites, and a realistic production schedule for Brian Simms's futuristic furniture commercials. As the meeting drew to an end, Luke shooed the rest of the staff out of his office and closed the door behind them.

Shelley was still high from the excitement she felt at being a part of the creative give-and-take, the "what ifs" that led to better ideas and cleaner concepts. She could hardly wait to present the storyboards the art department had created and to let Simms's nephew know that he'd been invited to do a full internship with Jake Helmsley, one of the best-known commercial directors in Hollywood. Her sense of accomplishment was only eclipsed by her desire to accomplish more. And to rub Ross Morgan's nose in her success.

She looked up when Luke came over and took a seat next to her at the conference table where they'd been working. Drawings and meeting notes were still strewn across the tabletop, but he was looking at her, not the work.

"What is it?" she asked.

"What would you say if I told you the most incredible opportunity is hanging out there waiting to be plucked?"

"I'd say, what kind of fruit?"

Luke smiled. "I heard from an old friend this morning in Chicago."

"And?"

"He's with BBD&O," he said, naming one of the largest ad agencies in the country, "and he spends a lot of time out on the coast, supervising production."

"And?"

"The Selena Moore Boutiques account is going to be put out for bid."

Shelley's spine tingled. Selena Moore was a high-end retail chain with billings over ten million. Coupled with Easy To Be Me, it would catapult Schwartz and Associates into the upper echelon of women's retail.

"Why would he tell you this?"

"Because BBD&O can't bid on it. They're already representing a direct competitor, so they're out of the running."

"I remember when the chain started in Atlanta. About a year ago they turned over a corner of each store to Custom

Cleavage, Ballantyne Bras' custom lingerie line, and took the whole thing national."

"Yes," Luke said, "that's when they moved their advertising to Chicago."

Shelley's spine tingled again. She shopped Selena Moore regularly and owned three of Ballantyne's custom-made creations, which had cost a small fortune and were worth every penny. "Do you think we could get a shot at it?"

"Not normally. But they're making noises about looking for a smaller ad shop and the owner wants to move their headquarters back to the southeast."

"Better and better."

"You haven't heard the best part yet." He leaned closer. "They're going to be in L.A. shooting with their old agency at the same time we're doing Simms's stuff."

Shelley could already see it; she'd find out where they were booked in L.A. and then she'd create her opportunity. She'd met Selena Moore and Miranda Smith of Custom Cleavage at a local fund-raiser. If they were staying at the same hotel it would be easy enough to renew the acquaintance.

"Have I mentioned lately how much I love you?" She threw her arms around the creative director's neck and gave him a goofy buss on the cheek. "I'm going to get right on this."

She looked down to check her watch, surprised at how quickly the morning had flown. "Just as soon as Judy and I finish our 'tahr' research."

Hurrying to the door, she stopped at the last minute and turned to face the creative director. "Let's not mention this to Ross Morgan just yet. When it comes to landing a new account, what he doesn't know won't hurt me."

An hour later, she and Judy were in a Tire World restroom looking around in dismay.

"They really need to do something about their ladies' rooms." Judy eyed the two metal stalls.

"You are so right," Shelley said as she studied the stark nondescript walls and cracked concrete floor. "If we actually get more women into these places, they'll be afraid to go to the bathroom." She remembered her unease buying cold drinks during the meeting with Wiley Haynes. "And the drink and snack machines need to come out of the garage area and into the showroom or waiting area."

Judy did a 360-degree turn, her brow furrowed in thought. "What if we got the bathrooms redone?"

"What?"

"Not overly elegant, but funky stylish—maybe with faux finishing and a few nice touches?"

Shelley could just imagine Ross Morgan and Wiley Haynes's reaction to that line item on the budget.

"You know, it might be enough of an oddity to get a feature of some kind in the Style section."

Shelley looked at her older sister. "That's a good idea." Her mind raced ahead. "Didn't you go to school with the Home and Garden editor at *The Atlanta Journal-Constitution*?"

"Mm-hmm. And speaking of getting press, what if we asked different decorators to do them, like they do for the symphony show houses?" Judy squinted one eye at the big yellow stain in the white porcelain sink. "Can't you just picture bringing Claude Gilbert or Jacques Dumas in to do a Tire World bathroom?"

As they washed their hands, Shelley looked at her sister, the one with the glow in her cheeks and the fabulous ideas spilling out of her mouth.

"Yes," Shelley said, her own enthusiasm growing, "I can. But first we need to extract the words 'little lady' from Wiley Haynes's vocabulary and find a female mechanic to present the workshops."

"You know," Judy said, digging up into the paper towel receptacle in search of a towel, "maybe the presenter doesn't have to be female. Maybe it just needs to be someone attractive to females."

"Yeah," Shelley deadpanned, trying her own hand at the paper towel dispenser when Judy came up empty, "I'm definitely going to call Brad Pitt and Antonio Banderas's agents to see if they want to come to Atlanta and teach tire classes."

They shared a laugh over that one.

"Well," Judy asked, "what about local celebrities or sports figures? Or, I know, why don't we worry less about the presenter and have female radio personalities participate in the classes. Let them give away a free class to female listeners?"

"Wow." Shelley grasped a piece of paper toweling and tried to yank it down. "I don't know where all this great stuff is coming from, but I am so glad you're a part of this team."

"You are?"

"I am."

Judy shook her hands dry while Shelley tried to use the sliver of paper towel she'd torn from the dispenser. "I'm glad someone thinks my working makes sense. Craig and the boys are giving me such grief about the hours I'm putting in." She checked her watch. "In fact, I've got to get going. I promised them an actual meal; something that doesn't come wrapped in plastic."

Shelley studied her sister's reflection in the mirror, but her expression was hard to decipher. "Why didn't you say something? You can work less if you need to."

"No, I don't want to do that. I'm having a ball. They're just not used to having to pick up after themselves, or, as it turns out, actually do *anything* for themselves. You'd think I was the only one capable of operating a washing machine; it's as if they think women are born with some sort of genetic predisposition to separate whites from colors."

Shelley laughed, wondering why it had taken her so long to notice what good company her sister was. How could she have missed that?

"I just wish someone had told me how great this working thing was sooner," Judy said, leaving the mirror and moving to Shelley's side. "I would have tried it a long time ago."

"Yeah." Shelley smiled at her sister as they used their forearms to push open the bathroom door. "That makes two of us."

It was Friday afternoon and time for Shelley to leave for her appointment with Howard Mellnick when the shit hit the fan.

She'd already packed up her things and was sprinting for the door when the intercom on her desk buzzed. Standing just shy of the open doorway—and freedom—she debated whether to make a break for it. It was the hesitation that did her in.

"Shelley?" Mia's voice squawked in the silent room.

Shelley looked longingly toward the door. She was tired and irritable and she wanted to be out of there.

"If you're there, please respond."

With a groan she went back to her desk and mashed her finger on the speak button. "Yes?"

"Mr. Morgan would like to see you."

Shelley checked her watch. It was four P.M.; her appointment was for four-thirty. She needed to talk to Howard Mellnick; she did NOT need to talk to Ross Morgan. "I'm just on my way out the door for an appointment, Mia. Can I see him on Monday?"

"Uh, hold on." There was a squawk and a brief silence. "Sorry," Mia came back. "He says it won't take long."

Damn right it won't. She stomped down the hallway and took the elevator up to the big windowed office of the president. She'd avoided coming in here since Ross had moved into it because she hadn't wanted to see anyone else—especially not Ross Morgan—sitting behind her father's hand-carved cherry desk, but there was no help for it now.

In the outer office, Shelley swept by Mia, strode through the double doors, and came to a stop in front of Morgan. "You buzzed?"

Papers were piled in front of him. She recognized her presentation notes and the accompanying storyboards as well as the budgets and requisition forms she'd prepared. He looked up at her and ran a hand through his already tousled hair. "Did you do all of this on your own?"

She couldn't tell whether he was impressed at the

amount of work she'd accomplished or appalled by what she'd done. Which made it especially difficult to tailor an appropriate response.

"Well...I've been working with Luke and the creative team. Judy assisted with some of the research." She raised her chin. "But the majority of it is pretty much me."

He nodded as if he'd expected as much. "That would explain the bathroom redecorating expenses at Tire World locations across Atlanta. And the proposed *Tire Talk* radio show. The tire as art charity auction is an interesting touch."

She started to relax a little. OK, there was some sarcasm in his tone, but even he couldn't ignore the fact that she'd generated activity in so many of the dormant accounts he'd dumped on her.

"Of course, the cost of those things is chump change in comparison to the weeklong shoot you've booked in L.A. for Furniture Forum. The one that includes," he paged through the reports until he found what he was looking for, "first-class travel and accommodations at the Four Seasons Hotel for all of Simms's people as well as our own."

She'd known he'd react to the expense, but she wasn't going to give up the opportunity to make contact with Selena Moore, nor was she going to tell him about the account until after she'd won the right to pitch it. If she told him too soon, he'd assign someone else or, God forbid, take it himself. She reined in her temper and ordered herself to stay calm.

"Do you have any idea what that's going to cost?"

"Why, yes," she said carefully, "I believe I detailed that in my budget report." She looked him in the eye and offered the only explanation she'd been able to come up with. "It's imperative that Simms know we think that highly of him. The contrast between what he's done for himself and what *we* can do for him has to be significant."

"We DON'T think that highly of him," Ross ground out. "I don't think that highly of anyone."

Shelley blanched at the capitalization, recognizing it as the yelling that it was.

"You cannot possibly justify that kind of money for production. This man's NEPHEW has been shooting his commercials with the equivalent of a family video camera. He'll never spend this kind of money on a commercial shoot."

"But don't you see?" She was determined to stay calm and professional—at least on the outside. "It *has* to cost a lot more. If we're just going to do what he's been doing and charge him more money, he'll never agree. I promised him a giant leap and this is it. Plus I got his nephew the coolest production gig in the world."

Ross shook his head. "You know, I keep telling myself that your enthusiasm is a good sign, that it makes up for your lack of experience and spotty work history. You've put in long hours and Luke seems impressed with some of your ideas." The last was offered reluctantly. "But you have NO CONCEPTION OF MONEY. You can't go throwing it around this way." He held up the budget reports and actually shook them at her. "I'm not your father and I'm not going to approve a shopping spree."

Being treated like a child who'd asked for an unwarranted increase in her allowance made her blood begin to boil. Really. She could feel the heat coursing through her veins. She had to clamp her lips together to keep them from opening. Her brain formed arguments, all of them beginning with "Listen, you big jerk," and escalating from there.

She bit back the words, swallowed them whole. Nothing she wanted to say right now would help her achieve her goal.

"Has Brian Simms seen this proposal?" he asked.

"I'm not sure if he's seen it yet, but it was sent to him at the same time it came to you."

"I told you I wanted to see everything first."

She shrugged and tried to look regretful. She'd thought out how to handle this, too, and in the end had decided to take her chances with Brian Simms. Ross might be pissed off for a while—well, OK, there was no *might* about it—but what was he going to do, fire her?

"Sorry," she said. "It was an accident."

"You'll have to call him first thing Monday morning and tell him this was a mistake. That it was just a preliminary and that you did NOT have approval to send it out and that you are going to rework the budget."

"I can't do that. He'll lose all faith in me. It's vitally important that we do this the way I've laid it out."

"No. You'll call Brian Monday and explain the situation." He picked up the Simms budget, the one he'd shaken at her, and dropped it in the trash can.

She stared at him, mute, while the blood rushed to her brain and made her light-headed. She closed her eyes and began to count to ten, but abandoned the idea when she got to twelve and couldn't remember what number came next. She was too far gone to count herself back to normal.

"Talk to him, Shelley. Do it first thing Monday morning. Or I will."

Ross's phone rang and with a curt nod of dismissal, he reached for the receiver.

She wanted to scream at him. Or punch a hole in the wall with her bare fist. Or find a quiet place to cry. She was tempted, so tempted, to shove her anger in his face and quit right there on the spot.

But that was what he wanted, wasn't it?

His eyes slid over her as he brought the receiver to his ear and without so much as a return nod, she left. Her heart was pounding and her legs were shaking. The picture of him sitting behind her father's desk was now embedded in her brain forever. She hoped like hell Howard Mellnick could help her dislodge it.

chapter 16

From the hallway, Shelley called Howard Mellnick's office to say that she was running late, then called Nina from the car to let her know she couldn't pick her up as planned. They agreed to meet in the psychiatrist's waiting room instead.

Nina sounded a little strange on the phone, but Shelley was too upset herself and in too big a hurry to get into it. Plus it was really hard to hear over the grinding of her teeth.

She was supposed to be at dinner at her parents' at seven, but she should be able to fit in a drink with Nina beforehand. After the day she'd had, she needed a psychiatrist AND alcohol before she had to deal with her mother.

Ten minutes late, Shelley raced into the empty waiting room. Finding the reception area empty as well, she knocked on Dr. Mellnick's office door and was ushered inside.

Where she immediately burst into tears—great honking sobs that came from somewhere deep down inside.

Helping her to her usual seat, he plucked a tissue from the box on his desk and pressed it into her hands. Then he waited quietly while she cried, handing her a new tissue when the one she had grew soggy, making it clear through his silence that there was no rush.

Shelley sobbed loudly and thoroughly, slightly surprised at the racket she was making. She avoided his gaze as the tears streamed down her face and the sounds of her jagged breathing filled the room. Finally the pressure in her chest and behind her eyelids began to ease, and she licked the salt from the corner of her lips.

Dabbing ineffectually at her wet cheeks, she drew in a shaky breath and let an even bigger one out. Her heartbeat began to slow. Drained, she dashed away the remaining tears and looked beyond the psychiatrist to the clock on the wall. Unbidden, her brain registered the time elapsed and began to convert it into dollars. If her math was correct, she'd just blown thirty-five dollars crying. She could do that on her own time for free.

For a long moment, she and Howard Mellnick contemplated each other in the now-silent room.

"Let me guess," he finally said in a teasing tone, "they didn't have your size at the Saks trunk show?"

Shelley shook her head.

"Somebody else required a birthday orgasm at an inappropriate time."

Another no, but she felt a smile tugging at her lips.

"Things aren't going so well at work."

Shelley nodded and she sniffed one last time. Thank God for Howard Mellnick. "Work," she said, "is a total disaster."

"Now, is this because it's so new, or—"

"Actually, it's not the work that's a disaster. As it turns out, the *work* is pretty great. It's my new boss who sucks the big one."

"And that would be," he looked down and flipped back through his notes, "Ross Morgan?"

She nodded emphatically. "He's so concerned with the bottom line, he can't see what's in front of him. And he doesn't trust me at all."

Mellnick listened and nodded, his solid presence offering its own form of encouragement.

"It's clear that he's trying to make me quit, even though I'm working my butt off and Judy and I have come up with a really novel approach to the Tire World campaign."

"Is this your sister, Judy, you're referring to? The baker?"

"Yeah, only she doesn't have time to bake anymore. I've got her scoping out Tire World bathrooms and planning a grand opening party."

Mellnick made a note on his legal pad.

"And she's not the Goody Two-shoes I thought she was, either." Shelley hiccuped and brought the tissue up to the corner of her eye.

He smiled and scribbled something on the pad. As always, Shelley wondered how he knew which things merited a notation when everything seemed to pour out of her mouth in one long, equally important, stream.

"And the worst thing is that even when I'm so mad at him I want to scream, I'm totally aware of him," she sniffed, "you know, as a male. And he's got these really incredible buns." She did a sort of half snort, half sniff, and her voice trailed off. "Of steel."

She started to cry again although she was fairly certain it

wasn't because of Ross Morgan's rear end. Through the sheen of tears, she ventured a peek at the therapist and was relieved to see he wasn't writing that part down.

"So." Howard Mellnick sat back in his chair and crossed one leg over the other, studying her from behind his frameless glasses, his intelligent brown eyes both appraising and comforting. "What happens now?"

Shelley mirrored his body position and tried like crazy to imitate his calm. The crying had left her slightly numb, and she had to sort through all the soggy nerve endings in her brain to get to the possible options. As it turned out there weren't a whole lot of them. "I guess I just have to keep slogging along, trying to do my best."

She heard the words and considered them. They didn't sound like nearly enough.

But Howard Mellnick froze for an instant. Then he broke out in a smile and did his own imitation of a, well, she thought it might be a bugle or a trumpet. "Da-da-da-dah!" he announced, "Shelley Schwartz has just had what we in the mental health field like to refer to as a breakthrough!"

"Me?" She looked around as if there might be another Shelley Schwartz somewhere in the room.

"Yes, you." He looked, well, happy. Or at least incredibly pleased. Which might have made her feel better if she'd had any idea why.

"Do you realize what you just said?" he asked.

"That I have to keep trying?"

"Yes, that." He smiled again. "Don't you dare shrug that off as if it's nothing. A month ago if you'd had a run-in like this with Ross Morgan you would have quit, or sabotaged yourself. Or ditched our appointment to go shopping."

She wanted to deny it, but he was absolutely correct.

"But today you did none of those things. And you're not quitting. You're gritting your teeth, and soldiering on. That's huge, Shelley. Absolutely huge."

She wished she could feel as good about this as he apparently did. Howard Mellnick was practically glowing. She, frankly, still felt like shit.

And she really wished she hadn't brought up Ross Morgan's buns.

There was a noise out in the waiting area and they both turned toward the door.

"I don't have any appointments scheduled after yours and I know Irene's gone for the day," Dr. Mellnick said. He rose.

The sound became more distinct. Someone was crying. There was a loud sob and what sounded like boo-hooing. Shelley was very glad no one had been outside while she was sobbing her guts out. At their next session, she was going to suggest soundproofing.

"Nina," Shelley realized. "I asked her to meet me here." Looking down at her watch, she realized the session was pretty much over. The crying grew louder. "Can we make sure she's OK?"

Together they opened the door and walked into the waiting room. Nina sat hunched forward in a chair, her blond hair forming a curtain around her face. She looked up as they entered the waiting area and her hair fell perfectly back into place. Her blue eyes were moist and dewy and her lips, though quivering, still looked plump and pink. The nose against which she'd pressed a wad of tissue paper didn't look even the tiniest bit red or runny. Shelley didn't have to look in a mirror to know that her crying jag hadn't left her looking anywhere near as tragically beautiful.

"Oh, Shelley," Nina wailed as she stood and wobbled over to throw her arms around Shelley's neck.

"What is it, Nina? What happened?"

Her friend drew in a ragged breath. "I saw Rabbi Jordan today." She looked up and her face crumpled ever so delicately as Howard Mellnick looked on. "He won't let me join his conversion class. He said I don't have a good enough reason for wanting to be Jewish."

Too drained for serious drinking, they left Nina's car in the parking lot and Shelley drove the two of them to her parents' for Friday night dinner.

"Don't you worry," Shelley soothed on the way. "You heard what Dr. Mellnick said. You just have to do a little research on your own so that you can express your reasons for wanting to convert more...convincingly. You probably shouldn't have been quite so honest with Rabbi Jordan."

"But I couldn't lie to a rabbi!" Nina looked horrified. "I might burn in hell for that!"

Shelley smiled, her first real smile in hours. "There's no hellfire and brimstone in Reform Judaism, Nina. That's one of the best parts. But I didn't mean you should *lie*, exactly. You just need to come up with a few more reasons than snagging a husband."

Nina nodded slowly.

"You do have other reasons, don't you?"

"Um, sure."

Shelley didn't press the point. Chances were, once Nina grasped the realities of conversion, she wouldn't be quite so eager to become one of the "chosen people." "Mom's setting an extra place right now. I bet we can get her to help with your Jewish education. And maybe we could get Dad to speak to the rabbi on your behalf."

Nina sniffed one last time and smiled. Despite all her crying she looked like a movie star ready for her close-up. It was a good thing she was such an old friend.

Shelley spent the rest of the drive complaining loudly about Ross Morgan, but her session with Howard Mellnick and the flood of tears she'd released seemed to have extracted some of the poison. If the good doctor thought she'd made some kind of breakthrough, who was she to argue?

When they arrived at her parents' they found the usual cast of characters preparing for dinner. Craig and her father sat in the living room debating the economy while Shelley's nephews argued about which one of them was going to fill the water glasses.

In the kitchen Delilah, their longtime maid, ladled out matzo ball soup and passed the bowls to Judy and Great-aunt Sonya. Her mother flitted in and out supervising the final touches to the table, refilling drinks, and hunting down a pack of matches to light the Sabbath candles.

Shelley and Nina plunked their purses on the kitchen table. "We're here!"

Delilah turned from her place at the stove. The affection reflected on her mahogany features was in direct contrast to her flippant tone. "Well, look who the cat done dragged in." She motioned to both cheeks and Shelley and Nina, used to this ritual, came over to the stove to peck the spots she pointed to. She studied their faces for a long moment, and

Shelley was glad they'd repaired their tear-streaked faces in the car. "You two been up to mischief again?"

Shelley filched a black olive from a bowl of crudités on the counter. "Who, us?"

"Don't you pull that innocent face on me. I've known you girls since you was wearing pigtails." She turned to the others. "What you think, Aunt Sonya? You think they're up to something?"

"That's a pretty safe bet," Sonya replied.

Shelley accepted her great-aunt's hug and did a quick scan for any sign of excessive baked goods. "So, what's for dessert?" she asked the room at large.

Judy smiled over the bowls of soup she was juggling. She was still dressed from her day at the office, and it was a trifle disconcerting to see Career Barbie in their mother's kitchen. "I don't know. I think Delilah made an apple pie or something. Between the kids and my slave-driver boss I don't have time to bake."

As if summoned by their mother's words, Sammy and Jason stormed into the kitchen and accosted Judy at the counter. She looked like a pygmy in the center of them; a tired, harassed pygmy.

"Mom, why do I have to do the water? Jason was supposed to do the ice cubes and he hasn't done anything."

"Why do we have to do it at all?" Jason countered. "I want to play Game Cube. It was my turn."

Judy set the bowls on the counter. "Stop this right now," she said. "You have to do it because I asked you to. It'll take you two minutes."

"Hey, Jude? Can we get some more of that snack mix out here?" Craig's voice carried into the kitchen, his tone as petulant as his children's. Judy sighed and went to the pantry to look for the snack mix.

"Are his legs broken?" Shelley joined her sister in front of the pantry. "Why does he need you to wait on him? You worked all day, too."

Judy's smile was not a happy one. "I think that's the point. All three of them seem totally pissed off that I have anything on my mind or in my life besides them." She located the box, poured out the snacks at the counter, and turned to take them out to the living room.

"Don't you dare," Shelley said, snatching the bowl out of her sister's hands. "*I'll* take them."

She carried the snacks out to the living room. Craig looked up as she bent to put them on the table. His smile fell when he realized it was her. "Oh."

"Your wife's busy in the kitchen. And tired." She didn't wait for a response but set the snacks as far away from him as possible, then moved to give her father a passing hug. Her next stop was the dining room, where her nephews were now arguing about the ice-to-water ratio.

"Hey, chill out," she admonished as she surreptitiously checked the number of place settings against the number of people already present, sighing with relief when the two jibed. The last thing she wanted to deal with tonight was one of her mother's marital candidates. "And cut your mother some slack. She worked hard today."

When Jason and Sam left, grumbling, for the kitchen, Shelley poured a glass from the bottle of Mogen David Concord grape wine that would be used for the blessings, and downed it in one gulp. Its sticky sweetness slid down her throat and warmed her belly, its very lack of sophistication comforting in a way that defied explanation.

At the table the traditional blessings over the candles, bread, and wine were quickly dispensed with. They moved more slowly through the soup course, conversing easily while Delilah cleared their empty bowls. Shelley continued to help herself to the Mogen David. It was Miriam who raised the issue of Nina's husband hunt.

"You know," she said as she reached for a slice of challah, then passed the basket of twisted egg bread around the table, "if you really want to convert, we'll do what we can to help. But whatever you end up being, you're going to have to find your own men; no more going out with the ones I dig up, er, find for Shelley."

"But I don't want those men, Mother," Shelley pointed out as her Mogen David glow began to kick in. "So there's no reason for Nina not to date them. They'll just be going to waste."

For some reason this struck her as excruciatingly funny. "You're always telling me not to be wasteful." She giggled. "Waste not, want not." She poured another glass of the sacramental wine.

"I certainly hope you're not getting tipsy like this when you're out on dates." Her mother's tone was disapproving.

"It's a real turn-off," Craig observed.

Shelley looked more closely at her brother-in-law. He'd always been a little too acceptable for her personal taste, but she didn't remember him seeming so . . . stodgy. "I try to keep the Mogen David guzzling to a minimum when I'm out." She dissolved into a fit of giggles as she pictured Trey Davenport ordering a bottle of Mad Dog at a favored

Buckhead eatery. "Here, Nina." She refilled her friend's wineglass. "If you want to be Jewish you're going to have to learn how to drink this stuff; it takes the edge off the religious holidays. And certain family gatherings."

"Shelley, that's enough," her father said. "Let's find another topic of conversation."

"Sorry," she mumbled, noticing for the first time how avidly her nephews were watching her. But there was something driving her that she didn't quite understand. "And what about you?" she asked her nephews. "What kind of husbands will you be if you make things so hard on your mother?"

"Shelley." Judy's voice held a warning tone that Shelley totally disregarded.

Craig sat up and leaned in closer.

"You could make things easier on her, you know," Shelley said, somewhat amazed that she was trying to use guilt in the same way that her mother did. And that she felt so protective of her sister. "Let her enjoy the project she's working on. She's always been there for you guys."

"It's not like she *needs* to work," Craig pointed out reasonably, which for some reason put Shelley's teeth completely on edge. "Why are you dragging her into the office all of a sudden? It's not like you've ever taken your job all that seriously." It was a long speech for Craig Blumfeld. And not at all the genial sort of conversation he normally put forth.

Shelley looked at her brother-in-law, then at Judy's stricken face. "People change," she said quietly. "I have it on good authority that breakthroughs are possible at almost any stage. If somebody wants to change and you try to hold them back, you can get left behind."

The phone rang, releasing some of the tension that filled the air. Her mother scraped her chair back and went to answer it. Slowly things returned to normal at the table. Shelley got up to help Delilah serve the next course. Judy picked up the water pitcher and offered refills around the table.

Miriam came back from the kitchen with a smile plastered on her face and a determination to change the atmosphere at her dinner table clear in her eye. "That was Abe Mendelsohn," she said to the table at large. "The bris for their new grandson is going to be at Abe and Sarah's next Wednesday."

Shelley smiled and went along with the buzz about the news, but she watched Judy and Craig as she did so. A bris, the ceremonial snipping off of the foreskin of a newborn's penis, was the first covenant a Jewish male child entered into with God.

In her current mood there were a few men she'd like to help snip down to size. And she wouldn't be doing it with anesthesia or the traditional sacramental wine. Tonight, Craig Blumfeld was an attractive candidate. She grinned wickedly as her imagination took off. Ross Morgan was second in line.

chapter 17

Trey Davenport had inches to spare. He also had charm, a washboard stomach, and a set of buns that might, in fact, have been made of steel. He possessed all the equipment needed to get a woman off.

The only thing he didn't have was Shelley's complete attention.

"Earth to Shelley." He lifted his head from between her legs.

"Hmmm?"

Sighing, he lowered his body on top of hers, braced his weight on his forearms, then nuzzled his face into the crook of her neck. "Where are you, Shelley Schwartz?" His teeth nipped gently at her ear. "I'm ready for liftoff, and I don't feel any of your engines revving."

In answer—and apology—she looped her arms around his neck and pressed her breasts tightly up against his chest. With a little gasp, she took him inside her and felt herself stretch to accommodate him. They began to move together, their hips automatically moving in sync, but he was right; even though her body was now fairly happily engaged, her mind was elsewhere.

Trying to bring it back to the matter at hand, she wrapped her legs around his buttocks, and matched his increased pace. The sensations were entirely pleasurable. Trey was a strong, enthusiastic lover and she was feeling friction in all the right places. If she just turned off her brain and focused, she'd come.

"Yeah, that's it." Trey didn't seem to be having any trouble keeping *his* body and mind together. He was completely and utterly focused. On her—or at least on that spot where their bodies were fused together. He moved faster, driving deeper, and she felt the first stirrings of possibility. Soon, wonderful little tendrils of pressure built inside her. There was an orgasm out there with her name on it. All she had to do was reach for it.

Her body writhed beneath his. It bucked and pressed in its search for greater contact and friction. Their pace quickened and their skin grew slick with sweat.

Yes, she thought, *that's good*. And then she thought about the Simms budget, and the Tire World grand opening, and Nina's husband hunt. She absolutely refused to think about Ross Morgan while Trey Davenport was buried inside her and panting in her ear.

"Oh, God, Shelley. That's it. Oh, God." He pumped harder. "Oh, God!"

Oh no. Shelley tried to whip her brain back to what was happening, tried to center it on her ... center ... so that she didn't get left behind, but she was too late.

Trey groaned and his body went rigid above her. The buns of steel clenched under her hands. A heartbeat later he gasped his release in her ear and collapsed on top of her.

Trey had crossed the finish line and she hadn't even entered the race.

Ho-kay.

Trey pressed a kiss to the nape of her neck and pulled himself off her, flopping on his back beside her—all liquid and happy and sated. "Sorry." His arm went around her shoulder as he drew her closer. "I was too far gone to wait." His hand dropped idly to her breast, but his breathing was already evening out. His tone was drowsy. "What can I do for you?"

What *did* she want from Trey Davenport? An orgasm would be nice, but then, that was what he always gave her. One missed trip to the moon was not really a disaster; the fact that she couldn't seem to pay attention long enough to get there with him was.

He drew a finger over her nipple then circled it. He would do whatever she asked, do his best to satisfy her sexually. That had always been enough to keep her totally tuned in. Until now.

His breathing slowed further and when she looked over to study him, his eyes were closed. Her gaze traveled down his body and she noted the broad shoulders, the perfect pecs, the awesome abs. What lay below that was equally impressive. Like most men, Jewish and not, Trey had been circumcised. She studied his flaccid penis for a few moments, wondering why it was no longer . . . enough.

Her contemplation of Trey's penis led to contemplation of the Mendelsohn bris. Which shouldn't be too surprising since she'd thought about everything else in the world over the last twenty minutes.

She tried to picture Trey there with her, surrounded by her family and their oldest friends. Trey was fun and personable; he'd make conversation, be polite. Women would sigh after him and envy her. But he would be the one, as they said on *Sesame Street,* who was not like any other, the one that did not belong. It wasn't just that he wasn't Jewish; other women married non-Jewish men and it worked out fine. They exposed their children to both religions and backgrounds and found a way to meld both cultures into their lives.

It was his complete and utter WASPness, that white-bread lack of ethnicity that she seemed to be drawn to over and over again, but which she could never quite picture herself eating for the rest of her life. This was her MO, to continually reject the rye bread with its hard crust and slivery caraway seeds in favor of the bland and flavorless white bread, only to complain that her choice didn't "taste right." That he didn't fit into her world.

Maybe she was wrong about that. Maybe Trey could fit, maybe he'd want to. She didn't even know what he'd be willing to be a part of because she never even asked.

In his sleep he pulled her closer. Slipping her arm across his chest, she breathed in his scent and settled her head in the crook of his neck. "Trey?" she said.

"Hmmmm?" His voice was half asleep and his eyes stayed shut.

"I was wondering," she began snuggling closer to his side, "have you ever been to a bris?"

***

Shelley didn't call Brian Simms on Monday. She justified this by keeping busy enough to claim a lack of opportunity, and tried to stay out of Ross Morgan's way. On Tuesday she tiptoed around the office until she heard that Ross was out. Convinced that Simms would go for her proposal, she waited as patiently as she could to hear from him while moving ahead with the booking and coordination for the shoot and putting the finishing touches on the presentations she would make later in the week.

On Wednesday morning, she got to the office early so that she could afford the time off for the Mendelsohn bris. Trey was going to meet her downstairs and then they were going to pick up Nina, who'd known the Mendelsohns through Shelley most of her life and who absolutely could not resist the chance to witness this aspect of Judaism in action. Shelley was starting to see it as a kind of Judaic field trip.

At ten o'clock she went to the ladies' room to freshen her makeup. When she got back to her office, Ross Morgan was waiting for her. He was wearing a black pinstriped suit with a crisp white shirt and the Armani tie, and sat in the chair across from her desk.

She'd barely had time to acknowledge his presence or line up her excuses when a knock sounded on the door. They both turned to look as Mia stuck her head into the office.

"Excuse me, Mr. Morgan, but I've got Brian Simms on line one."

Shit. Shelley walked around her desk and sank down into her chair. Still clutching her purse, she sat ramrod straight and braced herself.

Ross gave Shelley a look that pretty much shouted "Gotcha" and leaned across her desk to punch on the speakerphone. A moment later Brian Simms's voice reverberated through the room.

"Morgan?"

"Yes, I'm here," Ross replied smoothly. "Shelley's here, too."

"Oh." There was a brief pause. "Good, good."

There was another pause and then, "I got the proposal."

Shelley drew in a breath and held it. She couldn't tell from Simms's tone whether he was preparing to yank the account or simply ask a question. The look on Ross Morgan's face told her he was expecting the former.

The sound of paper shuffling reached them in the completely silent office.

"If you're calling about the production budget..." Ross began.

"I am. I spent the weekend going over it. And the last two days in meetings about it."

OK, this was not necessarily a bad thing. Shelley swallowed, not an easy task while holding one's breath.

"It's completely fixable," Ross said. "If we just scale down the—"

"Fix it?" Brian Simms's incredulous voice boomed into the room. "You want to *fix* this?"

Shelley winced. Ross closed his eyes briefly then opened them. They stared at each other, both now expecting the worst.

"Why, I wouldn't change a thing. You should see my nephew, Charlie. I can hardly pry him off the ceiling, he's so happy. An apprenticeship with Jake Helmsley at Hightower

Films? He's practicing his Academy Award acceptance speech."

"So you're OK with the budget?" Ross asked.

"Never been to Rodeo Drive or rubbed shoulders with any celebrities. And I see here we're booked at the Four Seasons Hotel!" He snorted happily. "Shelley promised us a big step up, and it sure as hell looks like she's delivering."

She was, wasn't she? Shelley dropped her purse and scooted forward in her chair as relief flooded through her.

"Hi, Brian." She let her pleasure ring in her voice. If it hadn't been for the set of Ross Morgan's shoulders and the tic in his cheek, she would have pumped a fist in the air. Or done a little happy dance around her desk. "Thanks for the vote of confidence." She shot Ross a triumphant look. "I'm really excited about your shoot."

There, she thought, as irritation flashed across Ross Morgan's face. *Take that.* She had a completely childish urge to stick out her tongue at him and add nyah-nyah-nah-nah-nah, but she managed to resist.

She schmoozed for a couple of minutes and ended the call with promises to courier over the travel itinerary when it was ready. Then she and Ross contemplated each other across the wide divide of her desk. He was shocked, that much was clear, and she braced herself once again. But Ross Morgan didn't lash out, unload, or try to slap her down to size. In fact, he was disappointingly calm.

"I guess you read that one better than I did."

"That's it? That's all you have to say?" Her victory would have tasted much sweeter if he'd shouted just a little bit. Or used a few capitals. Or broken down and cried.

He shrugged and stood. "You made a client happy. We're

spending way too much money to do it and you disregarded every directive I gave you. You gambled and won." He cocked his head. "But the agency wins, too."

He turned to leave the room but stopped in the doorway. It really bothered her that he was being so gracious in defeat.

"Just make sure I'm booked on that trip. There's no way in hell I'm letting you loose with the company funds in Beverly Hills."

"Right."

He started to leave, but turned back once more. "I need directions to the Mendelsohn bris."

She blanched and told herself she must have heard wrong. "You're coming to the Mendelsohns'?"

"Abe Mendelsohn is a client." He shrugged again. "And he can, in fact, sell ice to Eskimos. How long will it take to get out there?"

Shit. She was already responsible for Trey and Nina. Adding Ross Morgan to the mix was decidedly stress-inducing.

"About twenty-five minutes," she said, already picturing him there cramping her style. The only way she'd be glad to see him there was if he were the one whose penis was on the block. So to speak.

chapter 18

In the Jewish religion a bris is a joyous occasion right up there next to a wedding or graduation from law school. When Shelley and Trey and Nina arrived, Abe and Sarah Mendelsohn's home was stuffed with people. Its spacious rooms rang with laughter and good wishes and a bartender mixed mimosas and poured champagne.

People milled everywhere, dressed for the event, circulating with their drinks in their hands and hugging and kissing as if they hadn't just seen each other the night before for dinner at the club. Or tennis or golf. Or bridge, or mah-jongg.

Baskets of bagels and assorted cream cheeses shared table space with lox and whitefish. Herring and chopped liver sat alongside egg salad. By the time all the food was put out, there would be enough of it to feed a small army. At all such events the hostesses' biggest fear was the possibility of running out of food, or that a guest might leave hungry, not that Shelley had ever seen this happen. The eating would commence after the ceremony.

The guests got to eat; the baby got to give up a part of his penis.

Nina had spent the entire drive regaling them with the rationale behind circumcision and other Jewish rites of passage. Trey, who had evidently thought a bris was more like a confirmation or honorary event, rather than the minor surgical procedure that it was, was looking a little green around the gills by the time they arrived.

"Are we really going to watch an eight-day-old baby—who's never done anything to anyone—have part of his penis cut off?" he asked for the third time.

"Yep," Shelley said. "Although I don't intend to actually watch. I generally pick a spot in the back of the room and make a point of not watching."

"Is there going to be a doctor here?"

"No," Nina interjected, eager to share her knowledge. "They're going to use a *mohel*—that's a specialist who just does circumcisions."

"He goes from place to place cutting off the tips of penises?" If possible, Trey's face went a shade greener.

"Well, it's not a random thing," Shelley promised as she led him over to introduce him to the proud grandmother. "I think your manhood is safe."

Shelley leaned over to hug and kiss Sarah Mendelsohn. "Trey," she said, "this is my aunt Sarah." Trey stuck out his hand, but Sarah enveloped him in a motherly hug. "So you're the one Shelley's seeing." She looked him up and down. "Very nice, Shelley." She winked. "I'd make sure he's standing at the back of the room."

"Where's Uncle Abe?"

Sarah pointed toward the bar area. Abe stood with his back to her, her father on one side. Ross Morgan was on the other. Shelley decided those greetings could wait.

"Have you seen Paul yet?"

"No," Shelley said.

There was a loud baby's wail.

"I don't blame him one bit," Trey said under his breath as they turned toward the sound. "Maybe he's heard what's going to happen."

"Oh, here's Ilana." Sarah motioned her daughter-in-law over.

Shelley hugged Paul's wife and gazed down at the baby. "Very cute."

The new father joined them and slid an arm around his wife's shoulders.

Shelley kissed her old friend on the cheek. "You did good. And fortunately for everyone he doesn't seem to resemble you at all."

"Ha!" Paul gave Nina a hug and shook hands with Trey. "And I'm not letting any bossy girls put frogs in his diaper, either."

Shelley smiled. "Ha, yourself!"

Her mother descended on them, a plate of desserts intended for the sweets table in her hands. "There you are," she said to Shelley with an air kiss. "Nina."

Shelley braced for the "See what Paul and Ilana have produced, when are you going to settle down and start producing grandchildren" conversation, but her mother just stepped back and contemplated Trey for a moment. "And this is?"

"Mom, this is Trey Davenport. Trey, my mother, Miriam Schwartz."

Trey extended his hand and bowed his head formally. "It's a pleasure to meet you, ma'am." His manners were automatic and were probably honed at cotillions and debutante balls. Trey was very cute and formidable in his own way, but she didn't think he'd ever gone mano a mano with a Jewish mother before.

Sarah looked on with interest. Miriam stepped closer, an Inquisitional gleam in her eye.

"Stockbroker," Shelley replied before her mother could get started. "Morgan Stanley. Ole Miss." She flashed them both a warning look. "*No.*" The last was intended to keep the question of religion unasked.

"Well, then." Her mother's smile was brittle. "It's a pleasure to meet you, too. You won't want to miss the blintzes and sour cream. I make them from an old family recipe."

Shelley found herself hoping Trey wouldn't ask what a blintz was. Maybe she should have given him a study sheet or sent him to the rabbi with Nina.

"Yes, ma'am." Trey loosened his tie a bit and flashed his beautiful smile. He towered over Miriam physically, but he was sunny and unencumbered with any noticeable sort of agenda. There was no question in Shelley's mind which of them possessed the greater force of will. Her mother could have him for breakfast. "I'll be sure and do that."

Her mother's lips pursed. "Sarah, come take a look at the dessert table and tell me what you think."

The two women smiled, nodded, and scurried off, though Shelley doubted it was a food emergency that propelled them. More likely a dating dilemma they were going to try to solve—hers.

She spotted Judy carrying a coffee urn toward a table and sent her a quick wave. Craig stood with a group of other businessmen, but though Judy passed by her husband on numerous occasions as she helped set up the food tables, neither ever moved into the other's orbit. The sight of them so separate niggled at Shelley; there'd been a time when neither of them could have passed by the other without a smile or a touch. She knew, because she could still remember the stab of jealousy she'd felt at their obvious attraction—as if some sort of compass or magnet drew them into each other's sphere whether they meant to or not.

When she could avoid it no longer, Shelley led Nina and Trey toward her father's circle.

"Hi, Daddy. Uncle Abe. Ross." She gave and received hugs and kisses from the two older men. Nina did the same. Trey nodded genially and shook hands all around.

She watched Ross Morgan assess Nina and relaxed slightly when he didn't light up like most men automatically did in her presence. Then she watched him consider and dismiss Trey, which rankled. His gaze ended up on her.

"Ross tells me you've sold Brian Simms on an L.A. shoot. And got him to agree to use professional talent. Never thought I'd see that day." Her father turned to Abe. "You, I understand, are going to be a star."

"Our Shelley is very impressive when she puts her mind to it." Abe Mendelsohn beamed at her. "I didn't even know

Ross here had vocal cords the first time I met him." He slapped Ross on the back and grinned.

Ross raised an eyebrow at her. "I'd been threatened with a fate worse than death. She wouldn't let me get a word in edgewise."

Shelley snorted at the understatement, but she didn't call him on it. As the six of them conversed, she felt him dominating the group, and that rankled, too.

It wasn't that he monopolized the conversation or sought attention, but somehow everyone seemed to address their comments to him. In response he made these dead-on observations and flashed his incredibly droll wit. He and Trey were both tall and blond and blue-eyed, but while Ross exuded an air of command and a total ease with his surroundings, Trey looked like a sweet, towheaded schoolboy who had somehow wandered out of his milieu.

The swirl of conversation in the room changed slightly and people began to move.

"Oh, boy." Nina gestured toward the other end of the room. "It looks like they're getting ready to start."

"Excuse me." Abe left to go find Sarah. Her father went to join a group of his cronies at the other end of the living room, where the rabbi and mohel were preparing for the ceremony.

"Come on," Nina said. "I want to be up front."

Trey put down his drink and swallowed. His face turned a bit greener and his blue eyes telegraphed his panic. Ross's eyes glinted with amusement.

"It's OK," Shelley said, taking Trey's arm. "We're going to stay back here." She shot Morgan a look. "I don't like to get too close."

Trey licked his lips nervously and fell back a step. "How can you look so calm, Morgan?"

Ross shrugged. "You just put your mind somewhere else, and before you know it," he snapped his fingers merrily, "it's over." He looked from Trey to Shelley and his smile turned wicked. "It's the adult male converts I worry about. Imagine getting ready to go through this, knowing what's going to happen. There's not enough sacramental wine in the world to make that palatable."

Shelley gritted her teeth. "Very funny." She waved him off. "Go away. We're staying back here. There's no rule that says you have to watch."

"Ross can come with me," Nina said. "I don't want to miss anything. Maybe I can score a few brownie points with Rabbi Jordan by showing him how comfortable I am in this setting."

The two of them made their way to the front of the room, and took a spot right behind the baby's godfather, who was now taking the baby from its mother and stepping forward toward the mohel. Silence fell as the baby's gown was lifted and his diaper undone. The ancient Hebrew words, repeated in this very situation for thousands of years, rang out.

"Oh, God," Trey groaned. "Is it hot in here?" He clawed at his necktie.

The chanted Hebrew was a distant murmur in the back of her mind as she turned her thoughts elsewhere. Trey's discomfort, the Simms shoot, the pride in Paul Mendelsohn's face as he looked down at his son. Ross Morgan.

Realizing her gaze had strayed along with her thoughts,

she pulled it back from the broad shoulders and blond head at the front of the room next to Nina. Spotting Great-aunt Sonya perched on a couch to her right, Shelley took Trey's now clammy hand in hers and signaled him to follow her. Leading him quietly through the press of bodies, they sank down next to her great-aunt.

"I prefer this view myself." Aunt Sonya nodded toward the sea of backs in front of them.

"Yeah, me, too."

"Your young man doesn't look so good."

Shelley looked over at Trey. Aunt Sonya was right. "I think he's got some sort of stomach bug."

Aunt Sonya cackled. "You could have picked an easier family occasion to expose him to." She gave her a considering look. "Unless you're trying to drive him off?"

Was she? She considered the questioning gleam in Aunt Sonya's eyes. A baby naming, a Friday night dinner, even a temple service might have felt alien to Trey, but not quite so inherently threatening. Had she *wanted* him to be uncomfortable?

"Does he play tennis?"

"Hmmm?" Shelley refocused on her aunt. She knew her mind had wandered, but the leap from circumcision to tennis was pretty astronomical.

"I organized a mixed doubles game for Saturday morning, and the other team canceled. Would you two come play?"

Her eighty-two-year-old great-aunt Sonya on a tennis court? Shelley blinked and tried to picture it. "Trey's into extreme sports, Aunt Sonya," Shelley whispered as a loud wail split the room. "I don't think he plays tennis."

A loud female wail followed the baby's, and there was a collective gasp at the front of the room. Then came the thud of something solid hitting the floor.

"Oh, God, what was that?" Trey moaned.

Before she could reassure him the sound was way too loud for a falling foreskin, his eyes rolled back in his head. There was another moan as he crumpled and slid boneless to the floor.

Shelley fell to her knees to try to revive him while her great-aunt Sonya sprang up and craned her neck for a better view. A shocked silence gave way to a buzz of excited conversation.

"Trey, get up," she whispered in his ear. "It's all over."

Beside her, Great-aunt Sonya went up on tiptoe in an attempt to see over the people in front of them. The murmuring grew. Soon it was accompanied by muffled laughter.

Shelley was still trying to revive Trey when the crowd parted. She dropped Trey's hand and looked up as Ross Morgan stepped in front of them. He had a body slung over his shoulder and a pair of long legs hanging down his chest. He held them in place with a hand across the backs of the thighs just below the buttocks.

The buttocks were Nina's.

"Where do you want her?" Ross didn't laugh, even though it was clear he wanted to.

Shelley motioned to the sofa she and Aunt Sonya had just vacated and he deposited Nina in a corner of it. Without asking, he bent down and hefted Trey off the floor and propped him against the opposite arm. They looked like a pair of blond bookends.

"What happened?" Shelley asked, though it was obvious.

"The same thing that apparently happened here. I guess the reality was a little too . . . real."

"Oh, my God," Nina moaned. "I am *so* humiliated. Did the rabbi see me go down?"

Shelley looked at her friend, then over at Trey, who was also starting to come to. "Can somebody get a glass of water?" she shouted.

Ross looked from Nina to Trey. Shelley wanted to wipe the smile off his face, except she was having a hard time beating back her own.

"It looks like you're zero for two today," he observed. "Not exactly a staunch showing for the Schwartz contingent."

"Very funny."

Aunt Sonya stepped forward and swept her gaze down Ross Morgan's body. Shelley blushed on his behalf.

"What about this one?" her aunt asked. "Does *he* play tennis?"

"Aunt Sonya, I have no idea, and I don't think—"

Ross got that wicked gleam in his eye again and she knew she wasn't going to like what came next.

"I've been known to swing a racquet now and then," he said smoothly.

"Good." Her aunt gave him a nod, then turned back to Shelley. "Bring him with you Saturday morning at ten, and we'll see what he's made of."

"Aunt Sonya," Shelley said, "this is a really bad idea. Ross and I have never even played together." Why did everything seem to spiral out of control when he was around? She shot him a "Get lost" look, which he ignored, so she was forced to turn her back to him and practically whisper to her aunt. "We don't even really like each other."

"Save your excuses for the court, girl," her great-aunt Sonya said with a smile for Ross. "I'll see you both there Saturday morning. Horace and I haven't lost a match this season. And I don't intend for us to start now."

chapter 19

Because it was a weekday, the crowd at the Mendelsohns' thinned quickly. Shelley and her contingent were among the first to leave, but Judy stayed to help clean up. She took a break from her duties to walk Craig out. On the Mendelsohns' wraparound porch he placed an underwhelming peck on her cheek and patted down his pockets in search of his car keys.

"I was thinking about chicken on the grill tonight," she said to his chest. "What time do you think you'll be home?"

He stopped patting and looked at her with barely disguised impatience. "I have a dinner tonight with the new client I told you about—the investment group out of Minneapolis. It's been on the calendar for weeks."

"Right." When had their schedule become too much for her to keep up with? What had happened to her organizational zeal?

His cell phone rang. As he pulled it out of his pocket he

focused on some point just to the side of her. "Can you pick up my gray suit from the cleaners?" He was already bringing the phone to his ear as he added, "And don't forget the red tie. I hope to hell they got the gravy stain out of it."

She stood on the porch and watched him drive off, torn as she always was lately, by a vague sense of disappointment and a not-so-vague flash of anger at how easily he dismissed her.

After a few steadying breaths, she forced herself back into the kitchen, where her mother and Sarah were dissecting the morning's happenings. Picking up an empty Tupperware container, Judy began to spoon chopped liver into it.

"I still can't believe they both fainted," her mother said.

"Amazing, wasn't it?" Sarah said. "I thought that Trey business was made of sterner stuff. He looked too...buff... to pass out."

Judy looked up from the chopped liver. Had Sarah Mendelsohn really used the word "buff"?

"Pfft." Her mother dismissed him. "All of Shelley's dates are tall and blond and...buff." The word sounded just as strange on her mother's lips. Her tone made it clear the word was not intended as a compliment. "What good is buff when the going gets tough?"

"She's young yet. She'll figure it out." Sarah dipped a knife into the container Judy was filling and smeared a thin layer of chopped liver onto a piece of bagel.

"She's not so young." Miriam shook her head. "And if I left it to her she'd never go out with anyone remotely appropriate. Look at your Paul, all settled down and giving you grandbabies." She smiled at Judy, then reached over to bracket her cheeks in one hand. "Thank God I raised one sensible daughter."

Sensible. Normally Judy would have taken pride in the word, would have accepted her mother's approval as confirmation of the rightness of her life. Today the word rang hollow.

"I've got to get going." Judy covered the container of chopped liver and shoved it into the refrigerator, then pulled off the apron she'd drawn on over her new suit. "Mazel tov, Aunt Sarah." She bent and pressed a kiss to both women's cheeks. "Mom." She collected her purse and moved to the kitchen door. "I'll call you later."

And then she was sprinting out the door, trying to escape the horrible stifling fact that her whole life could be summed up in that one suddenly unappealing word. "*Sensible.*"

That was her, the eminently sensible and completely dismissible Judy Schwartz Blumfeld.

Shelley arrived at Howard Mellnick's office for her Friday afternoon appointment rushed and out of breath. Taking her seat, she contemplated the therapist with affection. Actually, she seemed to be contemplating the whole world through some strange rosy glow. She tried to stifle her smile as he contemplated her back, but the corners of her lips kept tugging upward.

"You look...happy," he finally said in wonder. "Are you feeling all right?"

"I feel fabulous."

He didn't comment, just let one of his eyebrows go up, but she could see an answering smile playing on his lips.

"I hope that's not going to be a problem," she said.

"I'll try to get over it." He went ahead and smiled. "To what do we owe this startling situation?"

"Well..." She thought about it for a moment, but even trying to analyze it didn't dim the internal glow. "For one thing, I blew everybody away this morning with my presentations. Uncle Abe signed on to everything I suggested. And he kept shaking his head and rubbing his chin and saying how he couldn't wait to call my father and tell him what a great job I was doing. That was my nine o'clock meeting."

Mellnick's smile grew.

"At ten-thirty, Fadah Awadallah told me he loved the proposal for his Falafel Shacks. We're going to concentrate on building his Atlanta presence and then look at introducing him around the southeast. Then Wiley Haynes came in for lunch. He was a little harder to sell, but he's agreed to my plan to market Tire World to women. Judy's doing an incredible job on his grand opening, and I know the coverage is going to be huge."

Howard Mellnick made a few notes, but mostly he was smiling.

Shelley continued happily. "I've got a little over a week to prepare for the L.A. trip. Brian Simms and his nephew are ecstatic, and I'm doing research right now for my approach to Selena Moore, who owns a nationwide string of upperend boutiques. I'm not leaving L.A. until I get her to agree to let us pitch the account."

"Very impressive." Howard Mellnick's smile was almost as big as hers. He made a final note and looked up, letting her see his delight. "So you've managed to work things out with Ross Morgan. I'm glad to hear it."

Her smile dimmed at the mention of Ross's name. "Well, we haven't exactly worked things out."

"But you're functioning together," he pointed out reasonably. "You're not using him as an excuse, and unless I'm missing something, I don't see you getting ready to blow off any toes." He made a show of examining her Ferragamo sandals.

This would definitely be the time to tell him about the fantasies she kept having, the ones in which she either slapped the arrogant smile off Morgan's face or licked her way down his naked body. She had no middle ground where he was concerned; the switch between anger and lust happened quickly and without warning, generally at the most inopportune times. Like while she was pitching her Uncle Abe, or holding up flow charts to illustrate the potential market share for falafels.

To say that her reactions to him were conflicted would be like saying Mick Jagger had lips. It didn't even begin to cover it. But Mellnick looked so happy she kind of hated to rain on his parade. And she didn't need him to tell her how suicidal giving in to either of those fantasies would be.

"He's hard to figure out," she said. "I think he still believes it would be easier if I just folded up my tent and went home, but he doesn't seem to be actively trying to trip me up anymore. And he seems genuinely pleased that these accounts are producing revenue.

"It's so strange, one minute he's giving me grief and making life miserable, and the next he's agreeing to tennis with Great-aunt Sonya."

"Excuse me?"

"Ross and I are playing a match against Aunt Sonya and her mixed-doubles partner tomorrow morning."

"But isn't your aunt in her eighties?"

"Yes, she is." Shelley snorted at the ridiculousness of it. "It's got disaster written all over it. And since Ross and I have trouble agreeing on what time it is, I don't know how we're going to play on the same court. But when I gave him a chance to back out, he said he wouldn't miss it for anything, that Great-aunt Sonya reminded him of someone and he didn't want to disappoint her."

The rest of the session flew by with small forays into her sister's strained marriage (they agreed Shelley should try to stay out of it), Nina's determination to win permission to convert (they both smiled over the fainting, though Shelley kept Trey's swoon to herself) and her parents' plans to relive their honeymoon in Europe (maybe the distraction would keep Miriam out of Shelley's life). They ended back on the next day's tennis match, which Shelley realized was producing both a wave of irritation and a hard-to-squelch sense of anticipation.

"All you have to do is show up and play," Dr. Mellnick advised her. "You're not responsible for Ross Morgan's motivation or his performance on the court."

"That's easy for you to say," Shelley said as they concluded the session. "I can't figure out whether we should try to win or lose tomorrow. I mean, smearing a pair of octogenarians all over the court doesn't sound particularly sporting. But losing to them would be pretty humiliating."

She went to bed that night trying not to think about Ross Morgan in tennis shorts or how Great-aunt Sonya might react to losing the match. After tossing and turning until almost two A.M., she started praying for rain.

Which pretty much accounted for the unrelenting sunshine that greeted her when she woke up the next morning.

"Great," she groaned as she pried her head off the pillow to the sound of birds chirping outside her window. "Noah got forty days and forty nights and I don't even get one measly Saturday morning rain shower?"

Clubbing her hair back into a ponytail, she washed her face and brushed her teeth. It took three cups of coffee to get her sufficiently revved up to paw through her tennis clothes for the plain white halter top and tennis skirt that gave her the best range of motion. Back in the bathroom she brushed through her hair and put it back in its ponytail, then applied the minimum of makeup before hunting down her racquet. She'd decided that they had to go ahead and win, since Aunt Sonya would call them on it if she felt they weren't trying, but not by too much. She sincerely hoped Morgan wasn't going to be the chest-thumping sort who had to annihilate all competitors regardless of their age or ability to walk unaided.

When she arrived at the Summitt Towers tennis courts, Aunt Sonya and her partner, whom Shelley recognized as the egretlike bingo caller, were already on the court warming up. Her great-aunt was wearing white shorts that showed off her still long, if slightly bowed, legs, and a V-necked white sleeveless T-shirt over a still full, if sagging, bust. Her visor read "Take No Prisoners" in bright red letters, and her eyes were hidden behind a pair of Gucci sunglasses. They were smacking the ball around pretty soundly with a minimum of chatter. In the bleachers, a small white-haired crowd—comprised mostly of women—watched Shelley walk onto the court. A last look at the sky confirmed that it was bright blue and dotted with cotton-ball clouds. There was not a thunderbolt in sight.

Aunt Sonya linked elbows with her partner and the two walked up to the net. "Horace Zinn, this is my great-niece Shelley." Horace stepped forward to shake her hand. His was big and leathery, not the hand of an aging egret at all. "And that's her partner," she nodded at a point over Shelley's shoulder, "Ross Morgan."

The women in the stands began to whisper, and Shelley could see why as she turned to watch Ross Morgan approach. His blond hair glistened in the sun, and his white teeth flashed a smile of greeting. His shorts were a bright blue, and his white T-shirt, which had a matching blue abstract pattern, hung from a pair of impressive shoulders and skimmed down an equally broad chest. She couldn't see his eyes behind his sunglasses, but he didn't appear the least bit worried about the weather, their audience, or the prospect of playing an opposing team who might require oxygen during the match.

There were handshakes all round and a kiss for Aunt Sonya. *A kiss for Aunt Sonya?*

Shelley and Ross walked back toward the baseline. "Listen," she said, trying to figure out his real motive for being there, "let's not embarrass them in front of their fans. All we have to do is win by a respectable margin."

He shot her a smile. "Agreed. What side do you want?"

She took the forehand court and left the backhand to Ross. He tossed her a ball and they began to warm up. He had beautiful strokes and moved with assurance—not out to prove anything, just returning the ball easily to Horace, keeping it in play. He looked like a poster boy for the physical benefits of the sport; all solid planes and angles, with a burnished glow to his skin.

They moved from the baseline to take some shots at the net then took a few overheads, both of them being careful not to hit too hard at their opponents. Aunt Sonya and Horace took a few serves—they were little dinky things that barely made it over the net—then it was time to begin.

Aunt Sonya positioned herself at the service line and Shelley, who was set to receive, moved up in the box, not wanting to be caught unprepared for one of those dinky serves.

"OK, these are good," Aunt Sonya yelled, bouncing the yellow ball a few times in front of her.

Shelley was still taking in the sight of an unexpectedly bulging tricep beneath her aunt's age-spotted skin, when Aunt Sonya tossed the ball, looped her racquet behind her head, and slammed the ball into the inside back corner of the service box.

Shelley blinked, shook her head. She hadn't even gotten her racquet back before the ball kicked up over her shoulder and bounced off the court.

Horace and Sonya did a high-five in the middle of their court.

She and Ross eyed each other. "Did you see that?" Shelley yelped. "She aced me."

"Yeah." Ross's bark of laughter was tinged with awe as he moved back to receive the next serve. "How old did you say they were?"

Before Shelley could answer, Aunt Sonya angled herself toward Ross and began her toss.

THWACK!

This time the ball sliced into the backhand corner of the service box and spiraled off the court.

"Shit!" Ross's stunned whisper reverberated with disbelief.

"That's thirty-love," Aunt Sonya called with delight.

"I think we've been had," Ross said as the next serve slammed down next to Shelley's feet and died.

"Big-time," Shelley agreed.

Sonya and Horace did what looked like a Native American war dance in the center of the court. The spectators started whooping it up in the stands. Two women in the front row began to do the tomahawk chop.

"If they start the wave, I'm going home," Shelley said.

"Forty-love!" Horace Zinn's voice rang with satisfaction.

"That's it, Schwartz," Ross said. "I don't know about you, but I'm not prepared to get slaughtered by someone on Geritol."

"Right." Shelley moved into position near the net. "But we can't exactly cram it down their throats." She got in the ready position. "What do you suggest?"

"I'll return it, then if it comes back you just get a racquet on it. I'll put it away. Then we're going to check their Social Security cards."

"Right."

This time Ross returned the serve, and when the ball came back Shelley managed to get to it, but her racquet came up underneath it and sent the ball shooting up into the air. She watched in horror as the elderly duo changed sides with the grace of longtime ballet partners so that Horace could drop back and smash the overhead right at Ross's . . .

Morgan danced to the side, and the ball smacked harmlessly at his feet.

"Jesus!"

"That's game!" Aunt Sonya and Horace leapt into the air, their fists pumping. The crowd in the bleachers went wild. "Whoo-whooo-whooo-whooo!"

"*This* is humiliating," Shelley said as they walked around the net to the other side. She couldn't bring herself to watch as Aunt Sonya and Horace helped each other jump the net.

"Tell me about it," Ross replied. "I was the captain of the Dartmouth tennis team. If this ever gets out, I'll never live it down."

Shelley took a long swig of water. Aunt Sonya and Horace were already in position, ready to grind them into dust. "Well, it's clear we need a strategy of some kind," she said. "Do you want me to distract them? Maybe we should shout 'Fire.' Or fake a Wayne Newton sighting."

Horace did a little running in place. His knees practically touched his chest.

"I hope I look that good at his age," Ross said.

"I'd like to look that good now," Shelley said. "Did you see that topspin lob?"

"Maybe if we look really pathetic, they'll give us a few points."

They looked at each other and laughed at the sheer ridiculousness of it. "I wouldn't count on it," Shelley said.

"Come on, you two. Let's play," Aunt Sonya yelled.

"OK." Ross gritted his teeth. "They got the first one

through the element of surprise. I say we give them maybe one more and that's it." He looked at her, his blue eyes lit with humor. "Are we together on this?"

"Aye, aye, Captain. But how do you suggest we accomplish that?"

He turned and studied their opponents. "You take the net, and I'll hang back. If you can get to the ball, go for it. Don't worry about poaching. It's going to take both of us to tame these unruly heathens."

Shelley laughed. The sun caressed her bare shoulders and there was a light breeze. Ross Morgan was a good sport and, it turned out, he had a sense of humor. Who would have guessed it?

"All right, let's go for it," she said. "We have some old folks to trample."

"Don't feel badly, darling. You made a valiant effort." Great-aunt Sonya's tone was soothing, but there was a disturbing glimmer of satisfaction in her eyes.

"Right." Shelley had an arm around Ross's shoulder and was leaning against him so as not to put any weight on the ankle she'd twisted. Ross limped beside her. He had a gash on his knee from the racquet she'd accidentally whacked him with and a black eye from the ball she'd miss-hit in her rush to the net.

"I'll get you two whippersnappers some ice for your wounds," Aunt Sonya offered.

"Tennis is not supposed to be a contact sport," Ross pointed out as they hobbled off the court together. His shirt was covered with clay from the spill they'd taken when their feet got tangled up with each other's. Blood still dripped down his shin. "It felt like World War Three out there."

Horace came up to join them, and the audience fell in behind them.

"Most entertaining match I've seen in years," one of them said.

"Reminded me a little bit of Laurel and Hardy," said another.

"You got two games off them," someone else said. "Their last opponents didn't even get one."

"Well, at least we put on a good show." Ross stopped, which brought her to a halt as well.

"They'll be talking about us for weeks." She looked up into his face. It was covered with scrapes and bits of clay from the court. She wanted to laugh, but she was too tired. And way too battered.

"I think it goes without saying we won't be mentioning this at work," Ross said.

"Agreed."

"And I don't think we should be allowed on a court together again for any reason," he added.

"Absolutely not."

He smiled and reached over to wipe something off her cheek. "I have this weird sense that we're lucky to be alive."

"Yeah, I'm sure I'll feel more thankful later."

They hobbled toward the parking lot. "Right now I just want to get home and soak my bruised and battered body." Something slightly wicked flashed across his face. "You want to join me? My Jacuzzi's big enough for two."

She studied his face, trying to read the expression on it

and failing completely. Although she questioned his motive, the idea was strangely appealing. They'd been horrible
on the court together, completely out of sync and unable to
make anything happen. But she'd actually enjoyed being
enmeshed in the disaster with him. Despite the punishment
they'd taken physically, despite the humiliation of being
beaten by a couple who didn't even have their own teeth,
he'd kept his sense of humor right up to the final point.

"Sorry," she said. "I have plans." She and Trey were going
to a barbecue at the home of one of his friends; a function
at which, he'd been quick to point out, no one would be losing part of his manhood. And the only passing out would
be the result of too much alcohol.

They said good-bye to Aunt Sonya and Horace, took
some final ribbing from their fans, and then hobbled slowly
toward the parking lot.

"I'll see you at the office on Monday, then," Ross said as
he opened her car door for her and watched her slide carefully into the driver's seat.

Shelley nodded as he closed her door and moved equally
gingerly toward the black Boxster. She watched him stow
his tennis bag in the trunk and slide into the Porsche, and
was not at all happy to realize she wished she were going
home to soak in a Jacuzzi with Ross instead of out with
Trey.

chapter 20

Shelley drove to work with trepidation on Monday morning. Almost as confusing as being stomped into the dirt by the Aged Duo was Morgan's suspicious metamorphosis from company-stealing irritant to upbeat tennis partner.

Ross Morgan's good sportsmanship and humor had thrown her; she had been a lot more comfortable when the only emotions he was triggering in her were anger and resentment. What in the world was the man up to?

In the lobby she waved hello to Sandra and couldn't help noticing that the receptionist's gaze did not stray to the wall clock. A look of amazement did not wash over her face.

Her coworkers' greetings were equally ordinary—just a wave or a nod or a smile here and there; Shelley couldn't get over how good their casual acceptance felt.

At her desk, she wasted a few minutes weighing her need for additional caffeine against her desire to avoid Ross

Morgan, and finally opted for the smushed Snickers bar she found in the bottom of her purse, reasoning that the chocolate would provide at least as much caffeine as the cup of coffee she was coveting, not to mention a nice little sugar rush to get her day rolling.

Pleased with her decision and the candy bar, she worked her way through her e-mail, then started on a lengthy To Do list.

As she worked, images of Trey Davenport and Ross Morgan flitted through her brain. The pictures of Trey were less than flattering; mostly she saw his eyes roll up in his head and the unexpected crumple to the floor at the Mendelsohn bris. A snapshot of Ross Morgan picking Trey up and tossing him, limp, into the corner of the sofa followed.

The mental images of Ross Morgan were mostly rearend shots and consisted of that fine posterior moving under tight-fitting tennis shorts. Occasionally her mental camera cut away to the twinkle in his blue eyes as they'd attempted to strategize during their ill-fated tennis match. The images of Ross Morgan brought a reluctant smile to her lips; the images of Trey Davenport did not.

Shelley frowned as she confronted the truth: Seeing Trey faint at the bris, and facing how out of place he'd been there, had underscored all the reservations she'd been burying. Good-looking and attentive no longer felt like... enough.

And good-looking and annoying did?

Applying herself to her work, Shelley managed to avoid both Ross and Trey until Wednesday afternoon, when she accidentally picked up the phone without first checking her caller ID.

"You have become scarcer than...well, I'm not sure what you're scarcer than, but I'm starting to think you're a figment of my imagination." Trey's voice was both sexy and chiding.

It took her a few moments to regroup. She used those moments to try to assess the feelings Trey's voice pulled up in her, but the only feeling she could identify was regret. Trey was so perfect on paper and so unfailingly sweet in person. Why was she having so much trouble whipping up enthusiasm for being with him? "Oh, I'm real, all right," she said. "Just busy getting ready for the Furniture Forum shoot in L.A."

As she listened to him talk about his day, she did feel a faint stirring. Encouraged, she focused on the feeling until it developed into an actual gurgle. Shelley smiled in relief, glad that her feelings for Trey were not, in fact, dead but just...resting somehow in the pit of her stomach.

"Would you like to go out to lunch?" Trey's question produced another gurgle, louder this time, and Shelley's smile faded as she recognized the gurgle for what it was: a hunger pang.

A glance at the clock on her computer screen confirmed that it was lunchtime. She was hungry, all right; she just wished she was hungry for Trey rather than a tuna melt.

"I wish I could," she lied. "I've just got too much to do."

"You know what they say about all work and no play, Shelley. Wouldn't want to let life get too dull."

"No, we wouldn't want that." She looked down at her watch.

"How about dinner tonight, then?" His tone made it clear he was offering more than a meal.

"I'd, uh, love to, Trey, but I can't. I've got a late meeting to go over the storyboards and then we've got a conference call with the production people out on the coast. The three-hour time difference really pushes things back."

There was a silence and Shelley felt a stab of guilt—which she figured was pretty much hard-wired into her DNA. If she was losing interest, she should speak up right now and say so. Wouldn't she want him to do that if he had lost interest in her?

No, she realized, she would not.

"I'll give you the week to get organized," Trey said, "but Friday night's mine. OK?"

She hesitated longer than she meant to. "Sure. Friday night would be great." Swallowing, she forced some of the missing enthusiasm into her voice. "I'll be looking forward to it."

Hanging up, she dropped her head to her desk and groaned in disgust.

She was such a wuss.

Her head was still cradled in her arms when the knock sounded on her office door. Her entire body snapped to attention as Ross Morgan's voice reached her from the now open doorway. Formerly dormant juices began to stir.

"Sleeping on the job?"

Lowering her brow, she told herself the stirring had been caused by the fight-or-flight instinct that Ross Morgan's presence produced—a sort of Pavlovian reaction to him over which she had no control. Or maybe it was that hunger pain.

Deep down, though, she was afraid it was something equally elemental, like plain old animal magnetism or... lust.

"No, of course not. I was just thinking. With my eyes closed." She sat very still. "Do you need something?"

"Just an explanation." He walked to her desk and shook a sheaf of paper at her. "I'd like to know why everyone's flying first class."

"Hmmm?"

"Is there ANYONE on this bloody shoot who's NOT flying first class to L.A.?"

Oh, good, he'd moved right into capitalization. Shelley breathed a sigh of relief as she braced for a fight. What would she do if he ever stopped being annoying? "Only you, if you want to change your reservation."

The tic appeared in his cheek.

"But I think there's quite a large fee. For changing a reservation."

"And of course everyone has their own suite," he growled.

"That's right."

"Because?"

"Because we're adults and this is not summer camp?" She looked up at him. "I can check with the counselor, though. Who were you hoping to bunk with?"

He gritted his teeth. "It's not the sleeping arrangements I'm concerned with. It's the money we're wasting."

His eyes were a turbulent blue, and there was that tic in his cheek, the set of his jaw. She scurried into the safety of the anger that crackled between them. And stoked it just a bit.

"Just so you know," she said sweetly, "I'm not going to be counting pennies while we're out there. In this case, we're spending money to make money. I'm thinking of it as a kind of investment strategy."

"Spoken like someone who's always had too much of everything and never had to work for it."

The jab didn't hurt any less just because it was true.

"Well, then, this is the perfect account for me, isn't it? The more I spend, the happier Brian Simms seems."

"Only you could think that made sense. This is a business, not a shopping spree."

"Obviously you know nothing about retail therapy," she snapped back. "Believe it or not, there's comfort to be found in shopping." She glanced meaningfully at the doorway, willing him away before he saw beneath her anger and irritation to the raw attraction she couldn't seem to get rid of. "Some of us just need more comfort than others."

By Friday afternoon there was nothing else to do. Every *t* had been crossed, every *i* dotted—except for her inability to reach Selena Moore to set up an appointment in L.A. The woman was proving surprisingly difficult to get ahold of.

Shelley had just picked up the phone to see if she could get a last-minute manicure and pedicure, when Judy strode into her office and dropped into the chair across from Shelley's desk. Her body was knotted as tightly as a pretzel.

Shelley lowered the phone and considered her smoldering sister. "Do we have a tahr emergency?"

"Tire World is not a problem." Judy folded her arms

across her chest and became even more pretzel-like. "My husband is a problem."

This was new territory; territory Shelley had no idea how to traverse. "Craig?"

"That would be him."

"Was it something he said?"

"Oh, yeah."

"Something bad?"

"Most definitely."

Shelley tried to picture Craig Blumfeld hurling obscenities and failed miserably. "What did he say?"

"He said he couldn't pick up Sammy from practice or Jason from his friend's because he was tied up. Even though he promised he would. He also told me that that was my job." Her eyes snapped with hurt and indignation. "And I still have work to do."

"I'm sure you can finish it later or at home if you want to."

"But I don't *want* to." Judy looked ready to cry or strike out; it wasn't clear which. "I want to finish my work *here*, like I'd planned. And I want him to take what I'm doing seriously." Her eyes glistened. "But he just talks to me as if I'm some child playing at having a job or gets mad that I'm not there to wait on him."

She jumped up and began to pace in front of Shelley's desk. "I'm tired of waiting on everyone and doing everything for everybody else. I'm a person, too!"

Shelley watched the emotions wash across her sister's face. Perfectly buttoned-down Judy Schwartz Blumfeld had popped a few of those buttons. "Have you tried telling him what you're telling me?"

Judy looked her in the eye. "He doesn't want to hear it.

We barely talk to each other anymore anyway." She flailed at the air dismissively. "He just wants things the way he wants them—which is exactly the way they've always been. He won't even consider what I want. And this project? Pfft!" Judy made the sound their mother made when she was upset, which Shelley was very careful not to point out. "You'd think I decided to take on this grand opening just to inconvenience him."

Shelley didn't know how to respond. If this had been Nina or another friend of hers, she'd be advising her to dump the guy, let him know in no uncertain terms that she wouldn't put up with this kind of bullshit. But this was Judy, happily married Judy—a ray of hope on the marital horizon that Shelley now realized she had somehow been clinging to.

And then there was Craig, who might be a little stodgy and apparently averse to change, but whom Judy had always treated like the grand prize. Not to mention Jason and Sammy, who had always made Judy *kvell*—to use the Yiddish term—with pride.

"Dump the guy" was not going to cut it.

"OK." She eyed Judy carefully. "Maybe the two of you need to take a weekend off somewhere to reconnect. Or if you can't get all the way out of town, why not spend a night or two at the Ritz?" The Ritz was great as long as one wasn't pressed for time or late for a meeting.

"Pfft!" This time Judy noticed her word choice. A look of horror washed over her face. "Oh, my God, I'm starting to sound like Mom!"

Shelley winced.

"I do, don't I? I sound just like her!" Judy clasped her

hands together. "I am not our mother. I refuse to be. And he can't make me." She paced a few steps to the right, then turned and headed back in the other direction.

"Judy, just calm down. I have to leave now for an appointment, but we could go out for a drink afterward."

OK, so she was supposed to be getting ready for her evening with Trey after she finished at Dr. Mellnick's. But blood was thicker than...dating. "We'll have a couple of glasses of wine and consume a large quantity of hors d'oeuvres. I promise you'll feel much better."

"I can't go for a drink," Judy bit out, "because my husband is not available to pick up our children. If he won't help me get my work done, you can bet your ass he's not going to drop what he's doing so I can go out and have a drink!"

Once again, Shelley didn't know what to say. She'd never heard the word "ass," or anything remotely like it, come out of her sister's mouth.

"Jude..."

"No, don't worry about it!" Judy reached down to retrieve her purse. "I've got to go."

"Judy, just let me—"

Her sister reached the doorway, then whirled back around. "It's OK, Shelley. I'll be fine. Really. I'm not completely sure I can say the same for Craig."

Shelley arrived at her appointment with her sister's words reverberating in her head. When Dr. Mellnick motioned her to her usual chair, she sat slowly, trying to figure out how much to say. It wasn't really her place to discuss Judy's problems with her therapist. But then, it hadn't been her place to discuss Nina's, either, yet she'd given her friend part of her session.

"What's wrong?" Dr. Mellnick asked.

"With me?" Shelley stalled. She'd already decided not to bring up her unwelcome attraction to Ross Morgan or her lack of one for Trey. If she put her feelings into words, she was afraid she'd have to act on them. And she was nowhere near ready for that. "Nothing."

"So why the face?"

Howard Mellnick was nothing if not patient; she knew this from experience. If she didn't respond in some way, he'd just wait until she couldn't take the silence anymore and started spilling her guts. For a moment she considered denying she was making a face, except, of course, she'd been gnawing at her bottom lip all the way over here and it felt like she'd drawn blood.

"Well, to tell you the truth," she began, still stalling, still trying to decide whether to confess to her own conflicted feelings or offer up her sister's as a distraction. "I, um…" She paused, unsure, but unable to push away the mental picture of Judy headed home for certain confrontation with Craig.

She'd come to know Judy better in the weeks they'd been working together than she had in a lifetime. If Howard Mellnick could give her some insights that might help Judy, then surely that would be a good thing. Besides, the Mellnick was sworn to secrecy as surely as a priest in a confessional; whatever she said to him would never leave this room.

She met Howard Mellnick's gaze and gnawed once more

on her already raw lip. This was not an attempt to avoid dealing with her own problems; for once her sister's problems loomed much larger than her own.

"The thing is," she said quietly, "I'm a little bit worried about my sister, Judy."

chapter 21

Judy picked Sammy up at practice and Jason from his friend Joey's, and drove them home spoiling for a fight. The boys were smart enough to disappear into the basement the minute they reached the house. Craig wasn't home yet, so Judy stomped around the kitchen preparing dinner and venting her fury on the cans she slammed onto the can opener, and on the roast she yanked out of the freezer, defrosted in the microwave, and slapped into the oven.

Unfortunately, none of these things helped her chill out to any noticeable degree.

By the time Craig got home an hour and a half later, she was too mad to make small talk or pretend that she was anything short of furious. She'd been nursing her hurt and anger since their phone conversation that afternoon and there was no way she could have acted as if things were normal. Even if she'd wanted to.

She finished the dinner preparations in silence, too angry even to try to harangue one of the boys into setting the table.

"What's for dinner?" Craig asked.

Judy looked at her husband, the one who had graduated with honors from Emory University Law School, but didn't seem to realize how close to the precipice he was standing. "Food."

She picked up the glass of Merlot she'd just poured and rammed it toward him, taking real satisfaction from the sight of it sloshing down his coat sleeve and onto the cuff of his crisply starched white shirt. "Maybe you'd like some wine while you're waiting."

Leaving him in the kitchen, Judy stalked to their bedroom suite and slammed the door behind her. There, she paced the perimeter of the room and tried to redirect her thoughts, but there was no room in her brain for anything other than anger and unhappiness. In the bathroom she splashed cold water on her flushed face and told herself to calm down. Unfortunately, her self didn't seem to be listening.

"Judy, the bell's going off on the oven," Craig shouted through the locked bedroom door. She was beginning to think the man had a death wish.

Steaming, she threw the door open, brushed past Craig, and marched into the kitchen to pull the roast out of the oven. Craig followed a few steps behind her and stopped on the other side of the kitchen island, his silence indicating that he had finally noticed that something was amiss.

She set the sizzling pan with its unintentionally blackened hunk of meat on a trivet and pulled the instant mashed potatoes out of the microwave. The peas were boiling madly on the stove. She shoved the cutting board and a meat fork and knife toward him then rummaged in the cupboard for a platter. "Please cut the meat" was all she could manage.

The four of them sat at the table staring at what was supposed to be dinner. The roast looked like leather. The peas were shriveled beyond recognition, and the mashed potatoes had coalesced into one large lump.

"I had a snack at Joey's, and I'm not hungry." Jason scraped his chair back. "May I be excused?"

"I don't feel so good." Sammy stood, too. "I think I might have that stomach thing that's going around."

The boys hotfooted it back down to the basement.

Judy filled Craig's plate with slabs of shoe-leather meat, a mound of ceramic-strength peas, and several golf balls of potato. With a direct challenge in her eyes, she sat back in her chair and waited for Craig to make an excuse and flee, but he surprised her by picking up his fork and beginning to eat.

"So," he said tentatively. "How was your day?"

He swallowed a piece of meat—a feat that took several minutes and half a glass of water—and eyed the mashed potatoes and peas, evidently trying to determine which to attempt first.

She waited, eyes narrowed, while he opted for the peas. It crossed her mind that if he kept eating the garbage she'd placed before him, she might have to perform the Heimlich maneuver or call 911, but, frankly, she wanted him to suffer.

He raised a golf ball of potato to his mouth, hesitated briefly, and then slipped it between his lips.

"Are we talking *before* you called and reneged on your promise to pick up the boys, or after?"

He choked on the mashed potatoes and reached for his glass of water. Convulsive swallowing followed.

"I told you I was sorry, but I had to take care of something for a client."

"Well, I have news for you," Judy replied. "I have a client now, too. And an apology doesn't just make your ... breach of promise go away."

"Breach of promise?" He stopped pretending to eat and pushed his plate away. "What about your breach of promise? You promised to love and honor. You promised to stay home and raise our sons and run our house. I don't see any of those things happening anymore." He wiped his mouth with his napkin and crumpled it onto his plate.

"I signed on to a partnership, not a lifetime employment contract. My terms have changed. It's time to renegotiate."

"You can't just change the terms of an agreement, even an unwritten one, without discussion. You've turned all of our lives totally upside down without even asking how we feel about it. I don't *want* to negotiate."

He scraped his chair back and stood so that he towered over her. His even features were sharpened by anger, while his clear brown eyes were clouded with—she didn't know what.

Judy stood to face him. She had to tilt her head back a bit and look up at him, but she met him glare for glare. She'd never seen Craig this angry or unsettled, and she was a bit surprised that she'd been able to rock his world so completely. She'd been raised to give in, concede the point, smooth things over, but deep down where she rarely delved, she knew that she couldn't back down now. She was just starting to get a sense of what she was capable of. Who knew what she might accomplish now that she'd set out on this new path? If she gave it up now she'd never forgive herself. Or him.

"You are not going to keep me locked in this box," she said.

Craig looked around the state-of-the-art kitchen then gestured toward the rest of the house. "You're calling a three-quarter-of-a-million-dollar home in a gated community a box?" His features hardened until she barely recognized him. "I've lost count of how many times you've redecorated this . . . box. Have I ever once said no to you, or stood in your way?"

She was too mad and too hurt to come up with a response. He was turning this all around, making her out to be the guilty one, when all she wanted was a chance to find out what she was made of. Leave it to a lawyer to go on the offensive and argue it until the other person threw up her hands and quit. But she was not going to surrender to Craig Blumfeld; she was not going to give up the work that gave her so much pleasure just because he missed having the little woman at his beck and call.

"I think I need to go somewhere and cool off for a while."

A look of relief flickered across his face; it was brief, but she saw it.

Judy left the table and, once again, brushed past him. In the bedroom she retrieved a suitcase from the closet and laid it on her side of the king-size bed. Then she went and got her makeup case and set it on the bathroom vanity. Her mind began racing through her wardrobe, considering what she would take, but her brain was all muddled with the need to escape.

Unable to make specific choices, she pulled her lingerie drawer out of the chest of drawers and dumped it into the suitcase.

"What are you doing?" Craig leaned against the bedroom doorjamb. His tone was casual, but his body language was too taut to pull it off.

"Putting a few things together to take with me."

"To take with you?"

"Yes." Returning to the closet, she retrieved a drawer of exercise clothes, which she also dumped into her suitcase. "I told you I needed some time to cool off and think things out."

"Cooling off is a walk around the block, maybe a long drive. This is," he watched her walk back into the closet and return clutching her favorite dress and casual shoes, which she zipped into a second suitcase, "leaving."

"A walk's not going to cut it. I'm too upset to think that quickly. I need some time away to . . . evaluate . . . our relationship."

"Evaluate? What is there to evaluate?"

Two drawers later, Judy zipped the bulging suitcase and then rummaged in the closet for the matching garment bag. It took several trips back into the closet to fill it.

"For one thing," she said as she moved into the bathroom to start packing up her cosmetics, "you don't want me to work, and I don't think I can give it up." She reached past him to get her hair dryer and curling iron. "I need some time to figure things out."

"But what about the boys?"

Judy refused to be sidetracked. Surely her sons were old enough to survive without her for a few days. "I'll let them know that I have to be away for a little bit. They're so busy they'll probably hardly notice I'm gone."

"But who'll take them to their activities? Who'll keep up the house? Who'll—"

"My mother will help, and I'm sure Eva will be glad to come in and clean a few more days a week. You'll be fine."

"But you can't just…leave us here. Where will you go? What will you do? How will I reach you?"

"I don't know," she said as she zipped the makeup case and grasped the handle. "The boys can reach me anytime on my cell phone. I'd rather not hear from you unless it's an emergency."

"Judy, this is the most ridiculous thing I've ever—"

She turned and raised a hand, cutting him off in midsentence. His look of shock was almost comical.

With a small start of satisfaction, she realized that she now had his complete and undivided attention. "Could you put those suitcases in the car for me, Craig?" she asked in as friendly a tone as she could muster. "They're a little bit heavier than I'd anticipated."

Shelley spent most of Friday evening alternately trying not to sleep with Trey and trying to want to.

They began with drinks in "their" spot—a table in a dark corner of the bar at the Ritz, where Shelley consumed two

Cosmopolitans and a handful of peanuts while trying to see Trey Davenport in the same light she'd seen him in before he'd hit the floor at the Mendelsohns'.

By the time they reached the end of a wine-infused dinner at Veni Vidi Vici she was starting to realize what an uphill battle she was waging.

She slipped the last spoonful of tiramisu into her mouth and took a final sip of brandy. Trey's gaze caressed her bare shoulders and lingered on her décolleté before moving up to meet hers.

Shelley tried to lose herself in the blue of his eyes. She stared into his face, with its finely chiseled features, and imagined it positioned over hers. Then she imagined the feel of his lips and the warmth of his breath on her cheek. When that failed to produce the desired...desire, she scoured her memory for a picture of the washboard abs and rock-solid thighs, closed her eyes to better remember the weight of his perfectly toned body settling on top of hers.

She could have that body for the night or for the weekend; she could enjoy it for as long as she chose with no major strings attached. All she had to do was get in the mood and let Trey make love to her. Sex now, reassessment later. It had worked for Scarlett O'Hara, it could work for her. She did not have to figure everything out tonight.

And she definitely did not need to keep comparing Trey Davenport to Ross Morgan as if she were playing some sexual version of eenie, meenie, minee, mo in which she could point out which man she preferred without having to face Trey's disappointment or Ross's potential amusement. Not for the first time, she wished she were a man and didn't have to muddy up the sexual waters with the complications of feelings and expectations.

She didn't need happily ever after, the perfect mate, or some warped version of Hepburn and Tracy, or Doris and Rock. She just needed to get her head around the concept of having sex tonight with Trey Davenport.

"Your place or mine?" Trey's voice was husky and his eyes were warm. His lips were turned up in humor as he delivered the pickup cliché.

Shelley winced. Even as a joke, the line was pretty uninspiring. *Come on, Trey*, she thought, *help me out here.*

Trying to put herself in the mood, she smiled in the sexiest way she knew how and licked her lips suggestively. She could see in Trey's eyes that her act was working for him. It wasn't doing a damned thing for her. "Let's go to my place," she said in her breathiest voice. At least that way if the evening ended badly, she'd already be home.

Trey covered her hand with his and called for the check. Five minutes later they were in his car racing toward her condo and she was trying to get pumped for what was about to happen.

Were there cheers for this sort of thing? Focusing exercises? Maybe she needed to find her inner child and threaten to spank it.

In the elevator of her building, Trey pressed her up against the back wall. She could feel his erection through the thin barrier of her dress. His hands snaked behind her, inched her dress up, and cupped her buttocks, which had been left bare by the black satin thong.

All she felt was a faint glimmer of interest. And the certain knowledge that if she had been in this elevator with

Ross Morgan, she would be reaching for the emergency stop button right now.

"No!" She tried to push the thought from her mind, but pushed Trey away at the same time.

"What?" Trey looked up, startled. "What's wrong?"

The elevator door slid open.

"We're here." Shelley smoothed her dress down and followed Trey off the elevator. The idea of sleeping with someone, even Trey, when she was so not in the mood made her slightly nauseous. Or maybe she'd just had too much wine?

Faking an orgasm had been bad enough. Having sex with someone she wasn't sure she wanted to sleep with felt decidedly . . . yucky.

Shelley fumbled the door key out of her purse and fit it in the lock.

Inside, Trey wrapped his arms around her and walked her backward into the foyer, kicking the door closed behind him. He kissed her for what felt like a long time. With their lips still locked, Trey loosened his tie and began to unbutton his shirt. "I thought we'd never get here," he breathed as he dropped his shirt and tie to the floor and slipped his hands inside the front of her dress.

Shelley shivered, but not from excitement. If she didn't stop this right now, they were going to end up in bed. And although she didn't understand her reasons, she simply didn't want to sleep with Trey tonight. Or possibly ever again.

"Trey, I—"

He didn't give her a chance to finish, but swept her up into his arms and braced her against his bare chest. He was whirling to head for her bedroom when the doorbell rang. The sound of it resonated through the marbled foyer. There was a thud against the front door and then the sound of something landing on the carpeted floor of the hallway.

Trey stopped where he was and disengaged their mouths. "Let's pretend we didn't hear that."

He took a step toward the bedroom.

"Trey, it's midnight. We can't just ignore it."

The bell rang again. Whoever was ringing held their finger down and the echo in the foyer made it feel like they were trapped in the bell tower at the cathedral of Notre Dame.

When the sound subsided a muffled voice reached them through the door. "Shelley? Shelley, it's me."

Trey's smile faded. His shoulders drooped. "I guess we can rule out Jehovah's Witnesses or Girl Scouts?"

He set her on her feet with obvious reluctance then moved beside her as Shelley straightened her dress and pulled open the front door.

Judy stood in the center of a perfectly matched set of luggage. It was midnight and tears streamed down her face.

"Oh." Judy took in Trey's bare chest and Shelley's disheveled state. She sniffed and swiped at the tears on her cheeks. "I'm sorry. I should have realized. I—"

"Shhh," Shelley said, stepping forward to draw her sister inside. "It's OK. Don't even think about it."

Without being asked, Trey walked into the hall and started carrying in Judy's luggage.

"I'm so sorry," Judy said again as Shelley led her to the couch and helped her to sit down. "I'm really sorry to interrupt."

Trey brought in the last of the suitcases and closed the front door.

Judy's sobs filled the living room. "I wouldn't have come here. But I've been driving around for hours and I couldn't think of anywhere else to go."

chapter 22

The sisters watched Trey shrug into his shirt and loop the tie over his shoulders. Shelley hoped her feelings didn't show on her face; concern for her sister warred with her relief at having been saved by the bell. If she was no longer attracted to Trey she should simply say so, but she couldn't exactly end their relationship in front of Judy. Nor could she do so without any warning; how could she be about to sleep with him one moment and ready to end things the next?

She looked up into Trey's disappointed face and sighed. Was she afraid of hurting his feelings or afraid that if she didn't have Trey as an excuse she'd end up in another supply closet with Ross Morgan?

"Have a good trip to L.A.," Trey said.

"Thanks." She stood and went up on tiptoe to give him a peck on the cheek.

"Bye." Judy waved dispiritedly from the living room

couch as Shelley walked him into the foyer and locked the door behind him.

Back in the living room, Shelley sank into a club chair. Judy's luggage was everywhere. "Are you headed out of town?"

Judy shook her head.

"It's after midnight and you seem to have your entire wardrobe with you," Shelley observed. "You must be going somewhere."

A lone tear slid down Judy's cheek. She shook her head again. "I left Craig. And I didn't have anywhere to go." She began to cry quietly. "How pathetic is that?"

No more pathetic than not being able to tell a guy you didn't want to go out with him anymore. Certainly no more pathetic than almost sleeping with that guy in order not to have to tell him yet.

"You left Craig?"

"Well, I'm not sure I *left* him, left him. I just had to get away for a while." She sniffed again. "Everything's such a mess."

Shelley watched her sister struggle for control. "Do you want to talk about it?"

Judy shook her head and swiped at her cheek.

"All right, but I don't ever want to hear you say you don't have anywhere to go. I'm your sister. You always have a place to go."

Judy sniffed. "Really?"

"Umm-hmm." Shelley wasn't sure which thing alarmed her more—the fact that her sister had left her husband and brought what looked like all her worldly possessions with her, or the way she seemed to be clinging so tightly to every word Shelley uttered. "It's late and you look dead on your feet. We can talk in the morning."

Judy yawned and blinked. "I definitely need to go to bed." She looked at the suitcases surrounding her.

"Come on." Shelley stood and helped Judy do the same. "Just bring your overnight case. We'll deal with the rest of it tomorrow."

Slipping an arm around Judy's shoulder, Shelley led her to the guest room, then pulled down the covers and plumped the pillows while her sister went into the adjoining bathroom to brush her teeth and change into a nightgown.

Struck by the odd rightness of it, she tucked her sister into bed and drew the covers up over her. "Good night, Jude. Sleep tight."

Turning off the bedside lamp, she tiptoed toward the bedroom door. By the time she reached it and turned to pull it closed behind her, the sound of Judy's even breathing already filled the room.

Shelley awoke at nine A.M. to the smell of freshly brewed coffee. Pulling on her bathrobe, she followed the scent through the living room, which was already devoid of luggage, and into the kitchen, which was full of wonderful smells. "Oh, my God, is that what I think it is?"

"Yep." The skin under Judy's eyes was dark and shadowed, but she appeared showered and dressed and completely made-up. She wore black hip-hugger capris and a clingy black-and-white-striped T-shirt. Except for the dark circles, she didn't look like an almost-forty-year-old woman who'd left her husband. "All I could find was bread, milk, and eggs, so I made French toast."

"Great."

The kitchen counters had been wiped clean and two places were set at the kitchen table. Shelley didn't know where Judy had found the bottle of syrup that was already sitting in the center of the table, and she didn't care. They were having French toast and coffee and she didn't have to get dressed to get it.

"Sit down, I'll bring you a cup of coffee." Without waiting for a reply, Judy poured coffee into a mug, added half a Splenda, and gave it a quick stir.

Before Shelley could protest, the coffee was sitting in front of her, that wonderful aroma wafting up to tickle her nostrils. "Thank you."

Judy flipped the French toast onto their plates and carried them back to the table. "Can I get you anything else?"

"I think that's supposed to be my line." Shelley lifted the coffee to her lips and sipped gratefully. "But I really appreciate you doing this." Commanding herself not to salivate, she took her first bite, which was heavenly. The second bite was even better.

"It's nothing. If you'd had cheese or veggies I could have made you an omelet. Craig loves feta, tomato, and onion in his—he calls it My Big Fat Greek Wedding Omelet." Her voice faltered and she jumped up to flip something on the stove.

"Well, you didn't have to do this for me."

Judy returned to the table, her eyes suspiciously moist.

"But I'm very glad that you did," Shelley hastened to add.

"I hope your family realizes how lucky they are to have you taking care of them."

Judy stabbed at her French toast, but Shelley noticed she didn't actually eat any of it. She shook her head sadly.

"Sometimes I feel like the hired help, except, of course, I'm grossly underpaid. I drop things off and pick them up, I cook, I carpool. And what do I get when I want to do a little something for myself?"

Shelley waited.

"I get kicked in the teeth."

Shelley took a long pull on her coffee and waited some more—a technique that always seemed to work for Howard Mellnick.

"I work out, I stay in shape, I read up on parenting techniques. I try to give my children quality parenting time, even though they hardly want to be with me anymore. But does anyone notice me? No. All they notice is when I'm not there, or not prepared, or God forbid, want to do something of my own."

Shelley got up and retrieved the pan from the stove. She offered the last piece of French toast to Judy, but her sister declined. "It sounds to me like this whole wife-and-mother thing is not all that it's cracked up to be." Shelley watched the syrup slide down the sides of the French toast and form little pools on the plate.

"You've got that one right."

"So what's your plan?"

There was a sharp intake of breath on the other side of the table. "Plan?"

"Well, the Schwartz women have never traveled light,

but you brought a full set of luggage. You must have had a plan of some kind."

"My plan was to leave the house before I fed my husband rat poison. And I almost didn't make it."

Shelley laughed. "I wonder if Craig knows how narrowly he escaped death. How long are you planning to be away?"

"I don't know. I don't even know what I'm hoping to accomplish. I was just so mad that I had to make some sort of statement."

"How long do you think it'll take Craig to figure out where you are and beg you to come back?"

Judy snorted. "Craig isn't exactly a 'sweep you off your feet' kind of guy. He doesn't make grand gestures." She moved the pieces of French toast around on her plate. "I didn't think I did, either."

"Well, there's no way he can ignore the fact that you're gone."

"I don't know, Shel. He's been doing a pretty good job of ignoring the fact that I'm there."

"Aw, Jude..." The hurt and disappointment in Judy's voice were painful to hear.

Judy jumped up and started clearing away their dishes. "It's OK," she said. "I just need some time off. If I go back right now I'll make everyone, including myself, completely miserable. I can check into a hotel or something after breakfast. And I suppose I have to call Mother and tell her what's going on. Craig'll need help with the boys."

This, Shelley knew, was not going to sit well with Miriam Schwartz. Shelley was very glad she was going to be out of town when Judy and Craig's shit hit the Schwartz Family

Fan. "You don't have to go to a hotel. I've got the extra bedroom, and I'm leaving tomorrow morning for L.A. For the
next week at least, you can have the apartment to yourself."

Judy watched Shelley leave the apartment for a pretravel
shopping trip with Nina. She'd been invited to join them,
and though she also suffered from the Schwartz women's
compulsion to shop on the eve of a departure, regardless of
the destination or the actual need for anything, the outing
sounded much too lighthearted for her current state of
mind.

With Shelley gone, the apartment rang with silence. Judy
breathed it in and absorbed it. As the mother of boys, with
their penchant for shouted communication and even
louder music and television, she barely recognized it and
rarely experienced it.

Moving into the living room, which had been done in
blacks and whites with vibrant splashes of color—so unlike
her own eclectic mix of antique and contemporary pieces—
she fought back the urge to dust and straighten. This was
not her home; she was not responsible. Now, there was a
novel thought.

Why, she could plop right down on this sofa like Jason
and Sam did, flip on the television, and do her own imitation of a couch potato. She could close her eyes and take a
nap. She could go read the best-seller she'd been unable to
find time for. Today was hers, and what she chose to do with
it was up to her as well.

Like the ones before it, this thought was both strangely
frightening and incredibly wonderful.

Judy moved to the telephone and lifted the receiver, but

there was no one she wanted to call. She wasn't ready to talk to her mother. Her children, if they weren't still sleeping, would either feign indifference or assume she'd left because of them. And she damned well wasn't calling Craig.

She could call a friend, except then she'd have to confess she'd moved out, because however she wanted to sugarcoat it, that was, in fact, what she'd done. Still, doing it was one thing; admitting it was another. She was much too raw and uncertain to discuss it with anyone else. And what if after a few days she decided to go back home? Once the news was out in the world, she wouldn't be able to change her mind and pretend this hadn't happened. She knew women who'd only been testing the waters and found themselves heaved out of the boat. She needed to proceed with care.

Wandering into what was now her bedroom, she took in the pile of suitcases. She could hunt down an iron and press anything that had gotten wrinkled, hang her dresses in the closet, and put her cosmetics away in the bathroom, but she didn't want to do that, either.

So many things she didn't want to do; perhaps the time had come to find out what she did want.

Moving to the bookshelf near the window she perused its contents, waiting for something to grab her attention. Ultimately she sank onto the window seat and stared down at the traffic below, unsettled and empty, yet somehow... hopeful.

What did she want? Was it as simple as being noticed and appreciated by her family? Or something darker, more demanding? Was she wrong to want something of her own? Wrong to enjoy working and going out into the world?

Wrong to want to be more than somebody's wife or mother?

She simply didn't know. But she'd taken this first step; it had been a wobbly, not particularly well thought-out step, but still she'd taken it. It only made sense to take another and, if necessary, another one after that. Somehow she'd have to hang tough until she saw where those steps were taking her.

chapter 23

Late Sunday morning, Shelley strode through the crush of people at LAX and headed for the rental car desk. Luke Skyler had flown in on Friday for the final casting call, and Ross and the Simmses were due in midday tomorrow. The shoot would begin on Tuesday, which left her a little over twenty-four hours to make contact with Selena Moore.

Countless palm trees later, she drove past a not-yet-awake Rodeo Drive, located Doheny, and pulled into the circular entrance of the Four Seasons Hotel in Beverly Hills.

Entering the lobby, she breathed in the luxury that immediately surrounded her. Here you might run into Brad out by the pool or Matt Damon in the lobby lounge. There'd be any number of well-known faces whom you would not accost or approach under any circumstances. The cost of rubbing shoulders was overlooking their celebrity and treating them like regular folk.

At the front desk she double-checked the reservations

for the rest of the party. Brian and Charlie Simms would have a suite on the fourth floor. Ross Morgan, who she'd briefly toyed with putting at a Motel 6, would have the smallest room in the worst possible location, which hadn't been easy since the Four Seasons prided itself on its accommodations. Skywalker was on the sixth floor, just below her. She'd learned the hard way that spreading people out was the best idea during a shoot; after a twelve-hour production day, you didn't necessarily want to find yourself next door to an irritated client or a temperamental creative director.

In her room, she waited impatiently for the bellman to place her luggage and point out the amenities. As soon as he'd left, Shelley called the hotel operator and asked to be put through to Selena Moore. Once again she was forced to leave a voice mail, and once again, she was brief and upbeat and stressed how much she hoped they'd have a chance to talk while they were both here in L.A.

Determined to find the elusive Ms. Moore, Shelley left no plush stone unturned. She loitered in the lobby, took beauty treatments at the spa, worked out in the exercise room, sunned at the pool, and managed to consume food or beverage in every one of the hotel's restaurants and bars. She even jogged the route around the hotel she'd learned Selena Moore favored.

But at the end of her twenty-four hours, all she had to show for her efforts were a first-name relationship with the hotel staff and a bill guaranteed to give Ross Morgan apoplexy.

At two o'clock Monday, not knowing where else to turn, she expanded her search zone to include the shops on

Rodeo Drive. When the going got tough, the tough went shopping.

After a mad dash upstairs to stow her purchases, Shelley still managed to arrive at the hotel's Windows Lounge ten minutes before the preproduction meeting was scheduled to start. Ross Morgan was already there.

He stood as she approached, and remained standing as she moved to a club chair as far away from him as she could get. He was wearing form-fitting khakis and a black Ralph Lauren polo shirt. A black leather belt circled his trim waist. As they sat, she noted that the black set off his blue eyes and blond hair. In fact, now that she thought about it, bright color always intensified the blue of his eyes. He must be a winter.

Shelley grimaced. Ross Morgan was a big pain in the rear end and she was deciding what season he was.

"How's your room?" she asked sweetly.

"Great. Except that I seem to be near the Dumpster and the elevator. The bellman seemed surprised. He said they almost never put guests there."

"Gee, that's too bad." She bit back a smile and dropped her gaze to her briefcase. Pulling out the client file and her notes, she placed them on the cocktail table in front of her. "I trust the Simmses fared better."

"Right down to the fresh-cut flowers and artfully arranged fruit basket." He speared her with a look. "The limo was a nice touch, too. Except, of course, neither of them had ever *been* in a limo before." His look became pained. "So we had to stop a passerby and ask him to take pictures of us in it."

"Oh, God." She gave up trying to hold back her laughter. "I'm so sorry I missed that."

"Yeah. I can see that."

Still smiling, she turned and saw the production company people heading toward them. Tracy Evans, the producer, was close to six feet and the production assistants with her had to scurry to keep up with her. Luke Skyler, looking like a film star in his own right, strolled in behind them.

Shelley made the introductions and there were handshakes all around. They were still at it when Brian Simms and his nephew, Charlie, arrived.

"Oh, my God, this hotel is UN-believable." Charlie was out of breath with excitement. "I saw John Travolta in the lobby—just sitting there talking to someone. And Meryl Streep was coming out of the elevator!"

"It's cool, isn't it?" Shelley shook Charlie's hand. He was tall and gangly and though he was in his mid-twenties, he carried himself like a teenager who hadn't yet grown into his body. "Hello, Brian." She kissed Brian Simms on both cheeks, then directed everyone to their seats. She could feel Ross Morgan's gaze on her, assessing, considering. She placed Charlie next to Tracy. He looked so happy, she was afraid he was going to hyperventilate.

"Tracy's the go-to person on the shoot," Shelley explained as Charlie took his seat. "She'll be assigning you to work with different people during the week. If you have a question or a problem, Tracy will definitely have an answer or a solution.

"And this," she held up one of the production books Tracy was now passing out, "is known as the bible. Tracy's going to take us through it now, but everything you need to know about the shoot is in this document."

Charlie opened his book with reverence and she felt a warm little glow. As Tracy began to walk them through the details of the shoot, Shelley's gaze met Ross's across the table and they shared an unexpected smile.

Appalled at the warm little glow that ensued, Shelley yanked her gaze away and let it skim around the room. She'd be better off trying to find Selena Moore and Miranda Smith than trading glances with Ross Morgan; the last thing she wanted to feel in his presence was warm.

When the meeting broke up, Shelley lagged behind so she could scan the room once more without calling attention to herself. Near the entrance she spotted a table occupied by a blonde and a brunette of the right height and age.

Heart racing, she reached forward and tapped Luke on the shoulder. "I think I've got a sighting," she whispered. "Can you take the Simmses and Morgan on to the restaurant? I'll catch up later."

Casually, she turned and headed back in the direction from which they'd come. A second glance out of the corner of her eye confirmed the identity of the two women.

Reminding herself to breathe, Shelley continued to the ladies' room, where she reapplied her lipstick with a shaky hand and ordered herself to calm down. Pushing everything but the success of her mission out of her mind, she raised her chin and strode out of the restroom. As she neared the entrance, Shelley stopped and took notice of the table as if for the first time. With what she hoped looked like a surprised, yet casual, smile, she headed directly toward it—and her finally cornered quarry.

"Selena?"

"Yes?" Selena Moore tilted her head sideways. Her makeup was flawlessly applied and she had the classically perfect features that only Mother Nature or a gifted plastic surgeon could provide. Miranda Smith, who had also gotten more than her fair share from the good looks fairy, smiled tentatively.

For the span of several heartbeats Shelley felt short and frumpy. With a stab of irritation she shook off the feeling. "We met at a fund-raiser in Atlanta last fall." Shelley extended her hand. "I'm..."

There was a movement directly in front of her, and for the first time she noticed that a man was sitting across from the two women. He swiveled to stand and face her, and she noticed he was wearing a black Ralph Lauren polo shirt.

"...Shelley Schwartz," Ross Morgan finished for her.

Shelley's smile faltered.

"Yes, I remember," Miranda Smith said. "Wasn't it the—"

"Woodruff Arts Center Gala," Selena finished.

"Yes." Shelley found her voice. Ignoring Ross, she shook hands with both women.

"Did you leave me a message?" Selena Moore asked.

"Yes," Shelley said, striving to remain casual. It wouldn't do to let the woman know she'd been hunting her like wild game. "I was hoping we'd run into each other." She made a point of including both women in her smile. "I'm a huge fan of Custom Cleavage and the Selena Moore Boutiques. You're always my first stop at Phipps Plaza."

Both women smiled and Miranda Smith invited her to join them.

"Here..." Ross pulled out the vacant chair for her.

"Do you know Ross Mo—"

"Yes." Shelley tried not to let her irritation show. "Ross and I, um, work together," she said as they took their seats.

She prayed he wasn't going to point out that she actually worked *for* him now.

"Shelley and I are both with Schwartz and Associates. Her father started the agency."

"Oh, how interesting." Selena Moore was looking into Ross's eyes when she said it.

Shelley's back went up. Not, she assured herself, because he was leaning forward and staring right back into Selena Moore's eyes, but because if she wasn't careful, he was going to steal this account out from under her just like he had the Easy To Be Me account.

Selena Moore looked at him from beneath her lashes. Then she leaned back in her chair and crossed her long legs so that her short black skirt rode up even higher on her thigh. Ross Morgan's gaze dropped to take in the display.

"So how do you and Ross know each other?" Shelley asked carefully.

"Oh, Ross and I go way back." Selena's voice had gone all silky. "Don't we, sugar?"

Morgan spoke quietly. "You could say that."

Great. Now she was picturing the two of them tearing up the sheets; silk ones, no doubt. Selena Moore didn't look like the sort of woman who would let a man drag her into a supply closet.

Shelley reminded herself it didn't matter if Selena and Morgan had once been joined at the hip—or a more obvious body part; these women were hers, just like their account was going to be.

"Miranda's leaving on the red-eye in the morning," Selena said, "but I was hoping to get in some tennis before I have to be at the studio. We're finishing up a series of national spots."

"Isn't that funny," Shelley said. "We're here for production, too. We're shooting a new campaign for an account of mine. Jake Helmsley's directing."

Selena and Miranda's eyes widened at the mention of Helmsley—an acknowledged genius when it came to shooting retail commercials.

"He's a friend of my father's," Shelley offered casually. "I've known him since I was a baby."

Ross turned and looked at her. She wasn't sure what was going to happen when he figured out what she wanted from Selena Moore.

"You know, if you'd like to get in a few sets early tomorrow morning, I'd be glad to play," Shelley offered.

Selena turned back to Ross. "Actually, I was thinking mixed doubles. Ross used to play a pretty good game." The woman's words and tone were loaded with innuendo. "Why don't we pick up a fourth and play together."

Ross shook his head and smiled apologetically. "I really don't think that's a good idea." He looked pointedly at Shelley. "We need to make sure the client gets to location on time tomorrow. In fact, we're supposed to be meeting them right now for dinner." He pushed back his chair and prepared to stand.

Shelley didn't move. "Actually, we have a late start in the morning. If we meet at the courts at seven, we'll have plenty of time."

There was a brief silence as Selena Moore smiled and Ross Morgan glowered.

"Great. I'll see you both then," Selena said. After signing their check, she and Miranda left.

Shelley and Ross watched them go.

He waited until they were in the car to make his displeasure known.

"We didn't come all the way out here to PLAY TENNIS."

"Don't capitalize at me."

He muttered something under his breath, but she couldn't tell what case he was using.

"And it's not about the tennis anyway," she said.

"Then you better tell me what the hell it *is* about. Because I'm pretty sure we swore we'd never set foot on a court together again."

She turned to look at him. She'd hoped to pull this off without him knowing until it was a done deal. She wanted no question as to who was responsible for reeling Selena Moore in. But given the way the woman had looked at Ross, there was little question he was the perfect bait. Shelley wasn't going to be able to shove him out of the way even if she wanted to.

"Selena Moore is looking for a new agency. And I intend to make sure it's us."

He turned to study her then, his expression turning thoughtful as the lights on the L.A. freeway whooshed by. "You've stopped dressing up," he murmured. "I kind of miss Doris and Katharine. And you're starting to act like a real account executive. It's a little unnerving."

His words gave her a nice little buzz; one she definitely

didn't want to acknowledge. "Don't get all sappy on me now, Morgan. We still have to get through the tennis match."

"Yeah," he said with a slow smile. "Let's split up so nobody gets killed."

chapter 24

Well, that was fun." Ross drove into the roundabout at the hotel and turned off the engine. Slowly he levered his bruised body out of the car and walked gingerly around the front of it to give the keys to the attendant. "Can you keep it out, please? We'll need it again in about thirty minutes."

Shelley used her upper body to swing her legs around and scoot toward the door so that she could get out of the front seat without putting weight on her left knee. Which was throbbing painfully.

Together they hobbled toward the front entrance and into the marbled lobby.

"I thought I'd be safer on the opposite side of the net."

Shelley rolled her eyes. "If you hadn't been so busy flirting with Selena Moore, you might have gotten out of the way."

"For your information, *she* was flirting with *me*. And you're the one who insisted on playing kamikaze tennis."

Unfortunately he had a point.

"Normally, when you want to win an account, you don't slam a ball into the potential client's rear end."

"I had already started sending the ball over when she turned around. That was *not* my fault."

It took forever to reach the elevator. She was tired and in pain and she hated that he was right. Her great stab at establishing a rapport with Selena Moore had been a disaster. She was lucky she hadn't killed the woman.

Until Ross Morgan appeared in her life, she'd never been considered dangerous on a tennis court. She had a decent game; she'd played on numerous Atlanta Lawn and Tennis Association teams. But there was something about him that acted like a magnet for the simplest miss-hit ball. Selena Moore had simply gotten in the way. On more than one occasion.

When they arrived at the soundstage, Charlie Simms was waiting for them, his face wreathed in smiles. "I'm supposed to show you where to sit."

They followed him past a house exterior, designed in sleek futuristic lines to look like a twenty-second-century home, then past two room interiors filled with the ultra-contemporary furniture that would be featured in the commercials. The tag lines would read *Furniture for Your Future.*

The exterior was lit and ready. A cameraman and dolly operator were practicing a tracking shot. Actors chosen to portray the home's space-age "family" were being "touched up" by the makeup and hair people, while a handler put their equally space-age canine through its paces.

"You'll get to look at each shot through the camera before they shoot it, Uncle Brian," Charlie explained as he led them to director's chairs grouped around a television monitor. "And then you watch each take as it happens on this monitor. Is this cool or what?"

He bounded back to the set, and Tracy Evans came over to greet them.

"Hi, everyone," the producer said. "We'll be ready to roll film in a few minutes. In the meantime, breakfast's right over there." She pointed toward a cloth-covered banquet table piled high with food, then turned to Shelley. "Jake asked me to bring you to him when you got here."

"Good, excuse me." Shelley followed the producer to the edge of the lighted set where Luke and the director were locked in an argument.

"We agreed on a Benji type," the creative director said. "I approved a Benji. That's a dachshund."

Jake shrugged. He had a beak of a nose and a mane of salt-and-pepper hair that he wore clubbed back into a ponytail. His sixty-something body was rock hard—a testament to his "Your body is your temple" philosophy and his taste in women. All four of his wives had been starlets and none of them, to Shelley's knowledge, had pumped him full of matzo ball soup or artery-clogging chopped liver.

"Benji was up all night with a migraine. His trainer assures me he's not fit to work today." Jake pointed to the dachshund. "He's a friend of Benji's."

Luke, who was known to dig in his own heels on occasion, shook his head. "You wanted the dachshund all along, but I approved Benji."

Jake Helmsley was an incredibly gifted and sought-after commercial director, but he was not a schmoozer. In fact, he had a reputation for either terrorizing or ignoring his clients.

"I don't think Brian Simms really cares what breed of dog we use," Shelley said.

Jake and Luke looked at her as if she had committed a blasphemy, then went back to arguing, except, of course, all three of them knew that Luke didn't stand a chance.

"Luke, let's just live with the dachshund," she said. "It's not worth the time we're wasting."

The creative director shot her a wounded look.

"Jake?" she spoke quietly after Luke stormed off. "This shoot is excruciatingly important to me. I need you to make nice with the client. And please don't shout at"—she located Charlie Simms scurrying around with a great loopy smile plastered on his face—"that one. He's the client's nephew and one of the main reasons this shoot is happening."

"Darling," Jake said. "When have I ever shouted at a client?"

She gave him a look. "No kidding, Jake. Good behavior. Or I'll sic my mother on you."

He pretended to quake. "OK, I'm all smiles today," he said, though the expression on his face looked more like a grimace. Then he waited semi-patiently while Shelley got Brian Simms and Ross Morgan and brought them over to meet him.

"This is Jake Helmsley," she said with pride as the men shook hands. "Here, on this set, he's pretty much GOD," she teased, though it was, in fact, the truth. "And we don't question GOD directly. If you have a question or something you want to communicate, you tell me; I tell our creative director, Luke; and Luke communicates with GOD. Sort of like a priest or rabbi, depending on your persuasion. OK?"

Brian Simms nodded. Ross just checked his watch. "GOD's expensive. Can we get started?"

She smiled apologetically to Jake and shot Ross a cease-and-desist look, which he ignored. Then she led him and Brian Simms back to their director's chairs and out of the line of fire.

There, Ross pulled her aside. "What the hell are they waiting for? And where's Benji? I don't remember seeing a dachshund in the storyboards."

The tiny French restaurant was crowded with people when Judy arrived for lunch with Brett O'Connor. She stood in the marbled entrance, jostled by the throng around her, and took it all in. This was not your suburban lunch spot peppered with housewives in tennis clothes. This was your upscale, expense-account eatery filled with suited men and women and hostesses dressed in body-molding black. Here in the leather banquettes, deals were struck and alliances formed. The hum of male voices dominated the room.

Judy shifted nervously and waited behind the line at the hostess podium, asking herself for the hundredth time why she had agreed to come.

Someone brushed up behind her and Brett's voice sounded in her ear. "Sorry I'm late." He put an arm around her shoulder and gave it a light squeeze. Guiding her forward, he gave the hostess a blinding smile, then kept his hand at Judy's back as they followed the woman to a dark corner booth.

Judy slid in first and Brett followed. She expected him to

stop across from her, but he slid all the way around until they were shoulder to shoulder and thigh to thigh. She could actually feel the heat coming off his body.

"Would you like some wine?" Brett asked.

Wine seemed like a very bad idea, given the heat and all. It was already late March; you'd think they'd turn the AC up in an expensive restaurant like this.

"Maybe a Shiraz?" she heard herself say.

Brett ordered the wine, and moments later a basket of crusty bread and a crock of creamy butter arrived. The wine steward presented Brett's selection and Brett performed the ritual of tasting and approval; his casual confidence was in stark contrast to her own discomfort.

It was only lunch, she reminded herself yet again, not an act of treason. If she didn't relax soon she was going to shatter into a million pieces.

She visualized Craig here in the booth beside her. He'd like the place, but he wouldn't be staring into her eyes like Brett was now. In fact, he'd probably spend half the meal on the phone with a client and the other half quizzing the steward about the wine list, while she worked to make conversation so that no one would suspect they were one of those long-married couples with nothing left to say to each other.

The steward finished pouring and disappeared. Judy sipped her wine and eyed the bread and butter, but couldn't bring herself to eat it in front of him.

"How's your project coming?" He smiled one of those really sexy smiles that lifted the corners of his mouth and then went all the way up to darken his eyes. "Do I need security clearance to hear the details?"

Judy checked his face to make sure he was really interested. Craig occasionally asked, but rarely listened.

Judy turned in the banquette to face him more squarely, using the move to put a couple of inches between them. "So you want to hear about Tire World," she said. "I wish you could have been there yesterday when Siegfried Simone, one of Atlanta's foremost interior designers, attempted to make Wiley Haynes—he's the good ol' boy who owns Tire World—understand why he chose gold lamé wall coverings for the Tire World ladies' room he's decorating."

Brett laughed as she replayed the conversation, imitating both men, trying to do justice to each of their mannerisms and accents. As she warmed to her story, her discomfort began to fade.

"Gold lamé in a tire store bathroom?" Brett asked.

"Well, only in the ladies' room. We're leaving the men's rooms alone."

"No faux fur or imitation crocodile for us?" He grinned in delight. "So how do I get an invitation to this opening?"

"You have to be really, really nice to me," she teased.

"Funny, that's exactly what I had in mind," he replied, caressing the double entendre with his voice.

Judy felt a tiny quiver deep inside. It was emanating from a place that Craig no longer bothered to go.

"We got tahrs with art on them," she mock-drawled in an attempt to dispel the quiver. "And food that's shaped like tahrs. In fact, tahrs most definitely are us."

"I had no idea tires could be so...haute couture," he said, his eyes and smile growing even warmer. The man was a veritable space heater. But even more impressive than his heat and good looks was how enthralled he appeared to be by...her.

"Consider yourself invited." She smiled. "I'll make sure you get an invitation." She could not believe she was flirting back.

His gaze locked on hers and he leaned closer.

She felt incredibly attractive and suddenly wicked. "The invitations are..." Her voice trailed off as he caressed her with his eyes.

"Round?" he murmured.

"Yes." She wanted to look away, but couldn't. His gaze was like a tractor beam dragging her toward him.

"And made of rubber," she managed. "They've even got tread."

He was throwing off heat and light. And she, she was a flower experiencing full sunshine after a long, dark winter. Why, she could practically feel her petals opening and straining toward him, reaching for... she didn't know what.

Now, there was a load of fertilizer.

When the food arrived, she barely tasted it. Too soon, the bottle of wine was empty and the dishes were removed. He was looking at her as if she were dessert.

"So," she finally said. "Tell me about Chicago..." she swallowed nervously "...and your life there."

"Well." He flashed a white-toothed smile; one of many he'd bestowed on her throughout the meal. "I'm divorced—mostly amicable. No kids. No pets. Currently trying to remember why I left Atlanta in the first place." He looked into her eyes when he said it. "Some of my best memories were made here."

Judy blushed; she could feel the prickly heat stain her

cheeks and knew they were both picturing the backseat of his Mustang and the gymnastics having sex in it had required.

This would be the time to tell him about Craig and their sons. And why she shouldn't be here.

He laughed lightly. "Do you remember the Mustang?"

Did she remember the Mustang? Did Texans remember the Alamo? Napoleon his Waterloo? Custer his last stand? It had been the scene of her sexual awakening; her one mad grasp at completely forbidden fruit.

"It was a great car, wasn't it?" He grinned. "A little cramped, but where there's a will..."

There was no way she was following that with "My husband doesn't understand me," or "I've moved out."

This needed to remain what she had told herself it was: a casual lunch with an old friend; an unexpected opportunity to catch up on old times. Not a reliving of old intimacies or the beginning of new ones. She'd have to be an imbecile to encourage Brett O'Connor's attentions. But that didn't mean she had to spoil their lunch with brutal honesty.

She smiled, relieved by the rationalization, and then, feeling someone's gaze on her, looked up to see one of Craig's law partners staring at her from a nearby table. As their eyes met, his expression turned frosty. Embarrassed, she dropped her gaze and looked away.

"Are you all right?" Brett turned to see what she'd been looking at, but when she finally followed his gaze back toward the other table, a busboy was clearing the dishes and the back of Joe Hirsch's head and shoulders was moving toward the exit.

Her stomach lurched as she realized how the man would

probably interpret what he had just seen. He might already be on his cell phone, calling the law firm. It would take about ten seconds for the news to spread around the office that Craig Blumfeld's wife had been spotted having lunch with another man.

chapter 25

It was the day that would not end. God, in the form of Jake Helmsley, was in a bad mood; the dachshund, possibly irritated that everyone would have preferred Benji, refused to perform; and Ross Morgan continued to be a great big pain in the tush—taking exception to the expense of everything, from the elegance of the food the caterer served to the amount of film shot for each scene to the number of times Jake rehearsed the actors. Since all of these complaints were funneled through her to Luke and then on to the deity himself, she spent the day on edge and swallowing great big buckets of irritation that she couldn't let spill out on anyone.

She supposed she should be grateful that Brian Simms seemed blissfully unaware of the strife on the set, but by the time she and Ross loaded the Simmses into the car to take them to dinner at a popular seafood restaurant in Santa Monica, she did not want to relay another request to anyone or hear another word about how much anything cost.

And she definitely didn't want to deal with her appallingly conflicted reactions to Ross Morgan. Loathing and lust were not supposed to be opposite sides of the same coin.

Their table on the terrace of Lobster overlooked the Santa Monica Pier and the stretch of Pacific beyond, above which a magnificent sunset was shaping up.

"This whole trip is kind of like a dream," Charlie said in wonder.

Brian Simms ruffled his nephew's hair. "I'm real proud of you, Charlie. I can see you just soaking it all in." He turned to Shelley, his smile warm. "I sure am glad you worked all this out."

"Me, too." She could feel Ross's gaze on her, but kept her attention focused on the Simms. "The spots are going to be fabulous. We're very lucky Jake was available."

Ross Morgan snorted, and then fell blessedly silent. But even when he didn't speak she was constantly aware of him.

They ordered drinks while the sky streaked red. Snatches of music floated over from the pier, and they could hear the waves kissing up to shore. Shelley tried to relax and soak it all in, but the thought of kissing brought her right back to Ross Morgan.

He was saying something to the Simmses, and though she tuned out the particulars, she actually shivered as the timbre of his voice washed over her. Shivering over his voice? How ridiculous was that?

She studied him from beneath her lashes, trying to understand his effect on her.

OK, so he was good-looking. Lots of men were good-looking, and as she had discovered with Trey, good-looking didn't always lead to heart-pounding.

What was it about this particular man?

Why couldn't she just shrug him off and stop reacting? Shove him into the no-longer-pertinent place in her head where she had filed poor Trey?

She needed Ross out of her thoughts so that she could better focus on her current goals and objectives. With her eyes on the Pacific, she breathed in the ocean air and tuned out his voice completely, and began to examine her failed pursuit of Selena Moore. Which led her to this morning's humiliating tennis fiasco. Which brought her thoughts right back to the all-too-present Ross Morgan.

No! She looked back out over the beach and drew in another steadying breath. It was time to heed Howard Mellnick's advice; time to catalogue the positives, not dwell on the negatives. She'd made the Simmses happy and was going to walk away with a string of award-winning commercials. On top of that, she no longer needed to dress up like old or dead movie stars to get through the day. And, for the moment anyway—she stole a quick glance to confirm it—Ross Morgan was behaving himself.

As she watched, he pulled a hunk of lobster from its claw and popped it into his mouth.

He had a great mouth. And long sure fingers. She looked up as he slid one of them between his lips to catch a drip of butter. His gaze met hers and the word "SEX" popped into her consciousness. "HOT" and "STEAMY" followed.

"What time do you have to be on location tomorrow, Charlie?" she asked, though her gaze remained on Ross Morgan. Tomorrow they were shooting in a backyard in

Beverly Hills—a scene with the child actors and Benji's friend.

"They're picking me up at five-thirty, and..."

She didn't hear the rest of Charlie's answer. She was trying too hard NOT to think about how Ross looked in the moonlight with his eyes as dark and inscrutable as inkwells. *Inkwells?*

When he didn't speak, Ross Morgan was way up there on her list of all-time attractive men. His silence allowed her to fantasize all kinds of things.

On the way back to the hotel, she contemplated her silent-male theory. When a man was silent he could be mysterious. He could be strong, yet soft; virile, yet sensitive. If a man kept his mouth shut, a woman could imagine him to be anything—and everything—she'd ever wanted. It was only when he opened his mouth that a woman was forced to admit he might be none of those things.

Perhaps someone should conduct a study of male silence as an aphrodisiac. Or so she thought, as they parted in the lobby and headed for their separate floors.

Back in her room Shelley cased the minibar for a drink, finally selecting a miniature bottle of red wine. Setting it and a glass on the nightstand, she toed off her shoes, plumped two pillows behind her head, and stretched out on the bed.

The room was still and quiet, in stark contrast to the day just spent on the set. She was trying to work up the energy to remove her clothing when she noticed the blinking message light on the telephone. Worried that it might be an emergency call from Atlanta, she swiveled over to pick up the receiver, then punched in the numbers to access her voice mail.

"*Shelley?*" She'd been expecting Judy, whom she'd been unable to reach by phone, or possibly her mother. The voice was Selena Moore's.

Unable to read the tone, Shelley sucked in some air and scooted into a sitting position. What if she'd decided to sue for her tennis injuries? What if she was trying to find Ross Morgan? What if . . .

"*I'm tied up today and I'm leaving in the morning. But I wanted you to know that I found out today just how persistent you've been.*"

Shelley groaned and swung her legs over the side of the bed.

"*I picked up all six of your messages from the Chicago office. The trainer, the spa receptionist, and the bell captain here at the hotel informed me that you've been on my trail since you arrived.*"

Great. Next would come the part about the restraining order.

"*Of course, I've also got a black-and-blue mark on my rear end and one on my arm from our match this morning. And I'm not too happy that Ross barely notices me when you're around.*"

Annoyed, bruised, and unhappy were not the kind of adjectives one wanted to hear from a coveted client. Shelley broke open the bottle of wine and took a great big slug of it, not bothering with the glass. Could the part about Ross Morgan be true?

"*I expect what I should do is just put as much distance*

between us as possible. Because you're dangerous, girl, in lots of ways."

Shelley groaned and gulped more wine. She'd traveled all the way across the country to piss off the client whose advertising account she wanted. She could just imagine what Ross would have to say about this. She'd validated her father's faith in him over her; proven once and for all that she couldn't land an account on her own, let alone run the agency.

She closed her eyes and lay back on the bed, the receiver clutched to her ear.

"But I like that about you. I like that you don't give up," Selena's voice continued.

Shelley's eyes flew open.

"I can't stand quitters. I didn't open as many retail outlets as I have by giving up when things got difficult."

Shelley sat back up, held her breath.

"So if you're interested in pitching my account, I'm interested in hearing it."

There was a moment of silence. Then the smile was gone from Selena's voice and she was all business. *"I've got a lot going on over the next few weeks, with the move back to Atlanta and all. But if you call my assistant in Chicago, she'll get you on my schedule."*

Shelley whooped out loud and sprang from the bed.

"I've heard good things about your agency. And nobody's better than Jake Helmsley. I'll look forward to seeing what you come up with."

Shelley pumped a fist in the air. She did a victory dance around the room. She could not wait another moment to share the good news.

Checking the bedside clock, she realized it was too late to call home. If her mother heard the phone ring at two A.M., she'd assume someone had died. Skywalker would be excited, but he was notorious for having early nights and he had to be on set at the crack of dawn tomorrow. That left only one option.

Without allowing herself to think it through, she threw open her minibar and pulled out everything that possessed alcohol content. Then she took out everything that had chocolate in it. Scooping the celebratory goodies into her arms, she rushed out into the hallway and took the elevator down to the bottom floor. Barefoot, she traversed the back corridors until she found the room she was looking for.

She could hardly wait to rub in . . . er . . . share her good news.

Ross Morgan opened his hotel room door wearing a pair of pinstriped pajama bottoms. And nothing else.

The cocky words of victory Shelley had planned to utter stuck in her throat. Unable to stop it, her gaze traveled from his bare feet up the loose-fitting cotton that encased his muscular thighs, to the drawstring that hung just below his navel. His stomach was flat and well muscled, and his bare chest was broad, with a light dusting of curly blond hair. She stared stupidly at that chest hair for a moment then finally forced her gaze up to meet his.

He looked at the food and drink clutched to her chest. "Did I miss the party memo?"

She had a brief flash that Selena Moore had probably seen him with even less on than this. Then she had another flash: Selena Moore thought Ross didn't look at her when Shelley was around.

"What do you see when you look at me?" she asked.

He let his eyes skim up her body in the same unhurried way hers had skimmed his. "Bare feet. A fortune in minibar charges." His gaze settled on her face. "And a mouth that says such blatantly annoying things that I sometimes forget how perfect it is."

Oh. It was just like him to compliment and insult her at the same time.

He reached out and pulled her inside. Without asking or moving, he took the bottles and candies from her hands and set them on a nearby dresser.

Once again, he was taking charge, expecting her to follow, even though she was the one who'd knocked on his door. Her eyes narrowed. "Don't you want to know what I see when I look at you?" she demanded.

"No." He took a step forward so that their bodies pressed together. Her back was up against the door. "We do better when we don't talk."

Silence as an aphrodisiac. She cocked her head sideways. "Hey, that's my theory."

He lowered his head so that his mouth skimmed the hollow of her throat and continued to the V of her blouse. His hair brushed the side of her face, tickled the underside of her chin.

Oh. She opened her mouth, still planning to give him an argument for stealing her theory, but then his fingers moved to the top button of her blouse and his mouth covered hers.

His kiss pushed the silence-as-aphrodisiac theory and an

incredibly pithy comeback right out of her head, and she was forced to settle for, "What in the world do you think you're doing?"

He didn't say anything, which proved both maddening and, as her theory postulated, incredibly exciting. When his hands slipped inside her bra to cup her breasts, the irritation and annoyance she normally felt for him combusted into an unwelcome jolt of desire.

"Oh!" The door was hard and cool against her back. Ross Morgan was hard and hot. She locked her arms around him and dropped her hands down to cup his buttocks. Holding on, she spun them around until he was the one pinned to the door. And then she pressed up against him until all of them touched.

"Which part are you finding confusing?" he breathed in her ear.

Before she could even consider answering, her blouse and bra landed on the floor, and the tiny part of her brain not currently ooohing and ahhhing over what was happening to the rest of her shrieked warnings like "This is a mistake," "Don't be stupid," and "Step away from the bed." But she could barely hear them over the whooshing of blood through her veins and the hammering of her heart.

He stepped out of his pajama bottoms. A heartbeat later she was down to her thong. As he carried her to the bed, she tried to formulate an argument, but she couldn't come up with a single complaint. She liked, make that *loved*, every damn thing he was doing to her, and might have to kill him if he stopped.

By the time she was spread-eagled on the bed with his

hard body poised above hers, she was a quivering mass of nerve endings clamoring to be silenced.

Then all thinking ceased.

She lost track of time, and everything else except the things they did to each other. A kiss demanded a kiss and a groan begat a groan as they urged each other on to a series of mind-bogglingly silent crescendos.

It was only hours later, when they collapsed together in an exhausted, sweat-soaked heap, that she remembered her alleged purpose in knocking on his door.

She spooned up to his back and buried her face in his shoulder. Her last waking thought was that she had, in fact, rubbed plenty of things in Ross Morgan's face last night. Unfortunately most of them were body parts.

The shrill ring of the phone woke them. Disoriented, they rolled toward the middle of the king-size bed and collided. Their eyes opened and they took note of each other. The first words out of both of their mouths were "Oh, shit!"

Ross got a hand on the phone. With a groan he removed the receiver from the cradle and brought it to his ear. He was naked, and not worried about it. Shelley gathered the sheets in front of her and sat up.

There was nothing like a six-thirty A.M. wake-up call to bring the real world crashing back into focus.

He hung up and they looked at each other. If Ross's face was any indication, he was experiencing the same flush of horror and disbelief that was currently washing through her.

"We can't even blame it on alcohol," he said with a groan, nodding toward the dresser where he'd deposited the unopened minibottles.

"Or a sugar high," she agreed. The miniature candy bar wrappers were still intact.

He shook his head and ran a hand through the hair she'd been raking her fingers through most of last night. "When a woman knocks on your hotel room door in the middle of the night armed with alcohol and chocolates, you don't normally stop and question her motives."

"I came to tell you that Selena Moore asked me to pitch her account."

"Oh."

There was a long silence as they both thought about what had transpired between them. She had no idea where they were supposed to go from here.

"Congratulations."

"Thanks."

The silence stretched out and took on a life of its own. Only this time it was anything but sensual. She didn't know what to say. Or how to find the words that would assure him their lovemaking had meant nothing more to her than it apparently meant to him.

Except, of course, that it had been incredible. And not just physically, either, though she'd cut out her tongue before she mentioned that little tidbit.

She watched him shrug into the hotel-provided terrycloth robe and run his hand through his hair. Again. His obvious discomfort made her own unease grow.

So what had she expected? she chided herself. Admissions of undying love? Confessions of feelings long kept bottled inside and only now allowed to spring forth?

They'd had sex in a supply closet over a year ago, and then pretended it never happened. This time the sex had taken place in more comfortable surroundings—even the dregs of the Four Seasons were decidedly first-rate. But what had really changed?

"Listen," he began, "I'm really sorry. What happened here between us never should have taken place. But—"

Humiliation washed through her and her gut twisted. She absolutely did not want to hear what was coming next. Pretending relief, she interrupted, "You are so right. This was definitely a mistake. And I really need to get going."

Unable to meet his gaze, she clutched the top sheet around her and left the bed to hunt for her clothes. Getting out of here before more damage was done was feeling increasingly urgent. "Let's just forget this ever happened," she said as she bent to retrieve the clothes she'd been so quick to shed. They formed a trail straight from the door to the bed.

Her own little bread crumb trail, leading straight to the one place she shouldn't have gone.

chapter 26

The awkwardness between Shelley and Ross intensified. They tried to cover it up, but it was there, lying in wait, crackling in the air between them for the rest of the week. She could barely look at him without remembering the things they'd done to each other and his look of horror when he'd woken up beside her. A mistake? No kidding! Neither of them mentioned it again, but it was like the purple elephant in the corner; they could pretend all they wanted, but the elephant was still there.

She went out of her way to charm the client, and expended considerable energy jollying Jake and Luke along. In between, she maintained phone contact with her accounts back in Atlanta and tried, unsuccessfully, to get ahold of her sister. She found a way to do everything except interact normally with Ross Morgan. This was why fooling around in the workplace was such a big no-no. Why sleeping with a boss who already considered you frivolous made you too stupid to live.

If she could have ducked out of the Friday night wrap party at the end of the shoot, she would have. Instead, she found herself trailing behind the group into Shutters on the Beach, where she'd booked a table that would allow the Simmses one last view of the ocean.

She managed to keep the rest of the party between Ross and her as they entered the high-ceilinged dining room. Luke and Jake and Tracy fanned out between the Simmses, while she kept her eye surreptitiously on Ross in order to maintain that much-needed distance. The end, at last, was in sight: The shoot was over, and all she had to do was get through this meal and deliver the Simmses back to the hotel. Once they were back in Atlanta it would be much easier to stay out of Ross's way. She intended to make sure of it.

"Ross," Brian Simms said as they prepared to sit, "would you mind switching with Jake? Charlie wants to pump him for information about postproduction."

Shit. She shot the director a "Behave yourself" look, and stood stock-still as the others rearranged themselves. Despite her prayers to the contrary, and the odds against it, Ross ended up directly on her left. Next to her. With no buffer zone of any kind.

This was not good.

Without comment, he pulled out her chair, and she had no choice but to sit. As he eased her chair, and her, toward the table, a whiff of his cologne reached her nostrils and taunted her. A moment later he took his seat beside her.

Panicked, she turned to Brian Simms on her right and began to talk. "I understand the Dungeness crab salad is to die for," she began. "And the rock shrimp ravioli and George Banks seared scallops are equally famous." Not pausing for breath, she worked her way through the menu then started on the decor. "You know, I think they keep that fire in the fireplace going all year round. Doesn't it feel wonderfully northeastern seashore in here? Have you ever been up to the Cape?"

Shelley peppered him with questions and babbled on unchecked, and Brian Simms looked at her as if he'd never seen her before. She sounded inane even to her own ears and knew she should shut up, but she also knew that if she let the conversation end, she'd be forced to interact with Ross.

Stop me, she thought wildly, *before I speak again.*

Simms's eyes had begun to glaze over when Ross slid an arm across her shoulder. He leaned closer so that they were both facing their client. As he had so long ago in Wiley Haynes's office, he squeezed her shoulder in a silent signal. But while her reaction then had been annoyance, her reaction today was much more visceral.

She wanted to run as far away from him as possible. And she wanted him to lean closer and whisper hot sex words into her ear.

This was not good. This was definitely not good.

She remained silent while the two men spoke, and smiled occasionally when it seemed appropriate, though none of what they said actually registered. His arm remained slung casually across her shoulders; the places where their bodies touched were electric and alive.

When their food came and he took his arm back, she

missed its weight. And when he turned to his left to talk to Luke, she felt oddly alone.

The next morning, as she boarded the plane for Atlanta, she told herself she was relieved that he'd taken an earlier flight.

It was early Saturday evening by the time Shelley dropped her bags in her foyer and kicked the door shut behind her. "Judy?" she called, but got no answer. "Are you here?"

There was still no answer, but as Shelley moved through her condo, signs of Judy's occupation were everywhere. Fresh flowers spilled out of a cut glass vase on the cocktail table, and a bowl of perfect fruit sat in the center of her kitchen table. Opening the refrigerator, which normally echoed with emptiness, she encountered neat stacks of Tupperwared leftovers.

"Jude?" She ventured into the guest bedroom and found the bed crisply made and the closet full of color-grouped clothing. The bathroom counter was neatly lined with cosmetics.

In the living room, the sound system remote had been neatly arranged with the TV and DVD remotes in a new acrylic holder. When she went to the living room shelf to choose a CD, she discovered that everything she owned had been alphabetized.

Her sister had been alone here for the last seven days and the results were . . . impressive. If Judy stayed much longer, she might be able to get her to redecorate the whole condo.

Wondering where her sister was, Shelley picked up the phone, plopped down on the sofa, and began to retrieve voice mail.

The message that made her heart pound wasn't from, but for, Judy. It had been left that morning.

"*Hi, Judy, it's Brett O'Connor,*" the deep male voice said. "*I really enjoyed lunch the other day and I wanted to confirm our plans for tonight.*"

Shelley froze.

"*We have a reservation for seven-thirty at Bluepointe. Are you sure you don't want me to pick you up?*"

Brett O'Connor was taking her sister to Bluepointe? But who was Brett O'Connor? And why was his name so familiar?

"*I can't tell you how glad I am we collided that day. It feels just like old times. Only better.*"

Shelley gasped. That Brett O'Connor? The Brett O'Connor Judy had mooned over in high school? The not-Jewish and way-too-sexy Brett O'Connor their parents had put the quash on as quickly as possible?

Judy had a date with Brett O'Connor.

Hoping she'd misunderstood, Shelley replayed the message. But unless Judy had come to her senses and told him to get lost, her sister was with Mr. Too Charming right now. Aghast, Shelley tried her sister's cell phone. When she got no answer, she dialed Nina's.

"I hope this is important," Nina said as she answered the phone.

Shelley could hear the clink of glasses and the occasional burst of laughter in the background.

"I'm at the Jewish Family Services fund-raiser, and I've got a bead on Rabbi Jordan."

"Well, you've got an hour to impress the man and get over here. Judy's gone wild and I need your help."

The sound went muffled for a second and then Nina was back. "OK, but it may be more like an hour and a half. I think that's Dr. Mellnick over by the hors d'oeuvres."

Nina made it in under an hour. She arrived in a to-die-for ice blue Oscar de la Renta cocktail dress with her blond hair hanging down her bare back; Shelley felt a stab of sympathy for the other women at the fund-raiser.

"I came as fast as I could. What is it? What's happened?" She took a closer look at Shelley's face and grabbed on to Shelley's arm. "Is it your dad? Does somebody have cancer? Judy's not pregnant, is she?"

Shelley stopped in her tracks. "That was very Jewish of you, Nina," she said, startled. "You hit right on the worst-case scenarios immediately; none of that dilly-dallying around and working your way up to it."

"Really?"

"Really." They moved into the living room and sat in their usual seats.

Nina studied her for a long moment. "Are you going to tell me why you look like someone just died?"

"Judy's out on a date."

"And?"

"And it's not with her husband."

"Oh!"

"No kidding, oh! She's having dinner with her high school heartthrob. At Bluepointe. This is their second meal together this week. I figure they're into their main course about now. And I'm afraid she's going to be dessert."

"So do you want to go over there and wrestle her out of the restaurant?" Nina looked ready to do it.

Shelley shook her head. "It's tempting. But if it's innocent we'll look like something out of a *Seinfeld* episode."

"Even if it *is* innocent," Nina's voice and face indicated
her doubts about this, "I think you need to be prepared to
offer a little guidance when she gets back."

"Me? Offer Judy advice about her marriage?" Shelley
snorted. "You may not have noticed, but she's always been
the role model in the family. This isn't exactly my area of
expertise."

"Well, then," Nina said, "maybe someone should talk to
Craig."

"Yes, someone should. That someone is Judy."

"Look, Shel, you may not be perfect, but you may be all
she's got. If you had left your husband and were acting stupid, do you think I'd just let you muck around and screw
everything up?"

"God, no! You'd be whipping everybody's butt into
shape."

"And you'd do the same for me. Don't you think you owe
your sister as much?"

Shelley got up to forage for a bottle of wine. Could she
actually be the butt kicker rather than the kickee? Should
she weigh in on this? Judy was feeling unloved and unappreciated, but Shelley couldn't believe she was uninterested
in preserving her family. She set two glasses down and
poured them each a healthy glassful of Merlot. "Well…"

"There's no 'well' about it. You need to get on top of this.
Tonight."

Shelley looked at her friend, the Scandinavian Butt-
Kicking Goddess, and marveled at the core of certainty
inside the soft blond exterior. She'd give a lot to be that

certain. In the meantime, she was incredibly lucky to have Nina in her corner. "OK," Shelley said, "enough of the Schwartz family chronicles. If I think about all of this any more right now my head is going to explode. Tell me how the Jewish husband hunt is going. Any breakthroughs with the rabbi?"

Nina took a sip of her wine and settled back into her chair; Cocktail Barbie with balls of steel. "Well," she said, "my personal ad in the *Jewish Singles Magazine* netted two mama's boys, one not-actually-divorced father of three, and an Israeli transvestite named Shlomo, but I'm cautiously optimistic."

Shelley barked with laughter. "Start with Shlomo and work backward. I can't wait to hear about this."

Shelley's tension began to seep away as her friend described the six-foot-two Shlomo, who had been racked with envy for her Stuart Weitzmans.

"The rabbi," Nina sighed in conclusion, "is a less entertaining story; that man is proving a very tough nut to crack."

She and Nina drank another glass of wine and discussed the advisability of putting Miriam on the rabbi's tail. When her friend paused to take a sip of her wine and settle more deeply into her chair, Shelley said, "Well, since we're being unflinchingly honest tonight, I might as well tell you that I slept with Ross in Los Angeles."

Nina gave her "the look." "Shelley," she said, "have I taught you nothing? Repeat after me: 'An intelligent woman does not sleep with coworkers. An intelligent woman does not sleep with—'"

"Yeah, well, I can write it on the chalkboard a hundred

times if it'll make you feel better, but it's already a done deal." She wanted to groan but settled for an eye roll.

"That bad?" Nina asked sympathetically.

"No, that good. In fact, it was pretty much the best sex I've ever had, right up until the moment he woke up, found me in his bed, and shrieked in horror."

"No way."

"Way. After which he informed me that what we had just done with each other was a mistake."

"Oh, my God, what a jerk. How humiliating."

"Yeah. Tell me about it. Why would God waste all those good looks and sexual ability on someone so annoying? It's like some sort of cosmic joke."

"Poor Shelley. What are you going to do now?"

"I don't know, but I guess I'll have to make sure he understands that our 'unfortunate mistake' will never be repeated, and then retreat with what dignity I can muster."

Nina drained her glass of wine and got ready to leave. "The very best sex of your entire life?"

"Yep," Shelley admitted, her face glum. "It pains me to admit it, but the man is completely gifted."

After Nina left, Shelley settled down to wait for her sister. Though venting and discussing had helped, Shelley still didn't have an actual plan or strategy in mind when Judy finally came home at eleven forty-five. Hearing the key in the lock, Shelley put the paperback she'd been trying to read on the cocktail table and sat up on the couch. She felt like a worried parent waiting for a teenager to make it home in one piece.

The front door opened and closed. The deadbolt was

thrown and Judy Schwartz Blumfeld entered the living room. She was wearing a clingy black jersey sheath and three-inch come-and-get-me heels. She came to a screeching halt when she spotted Shelley.

"Oh!"

Oh, indeed. "Where have you been, young lady? Another fifteen minutes and you would have missed curfew." Shelley tried to make her imitation of their mother flip, but she could hear just how flat and accusing she sounded. And her mother thought she hadn't learned anything from her!

"Out."

"Married women aren't supposed to go out with their old boyfriends on a Saturday night," Shelley said. "It's very bad form."

Judy leveled a gaze at her. "Don't start with me, Shelley. I've had about as much as I can take from the *real* Miriam Schwartz."

"I'm sure you know how much it pains me to admit this," Shelley replied, "but she's got a point!"

"It was just dinner."

Shelley rolled her eyes. "You're glowing, Jude. When you're married, you're not supposed to glow for anyone but your husband."

"Well, there hasn't been much glowing going on in the Blumfeld household for a while now." Judy kicked off her shoes and sat in the club chair, putting her bare feet up on the ottoman. "I get zero attention or interest from my family. It's nice to feel like something more than a piece of furniture for a change."

"So you've decided to get your attention from Brett

O'Connor." Shelley shook her head. "What does Craig have to say about that?"

Tears formed in Judy's eyes. "He doesn't say anything. He won't even talk to me." She crossed her arms over her chest. "I went to Sammy's baseball game this morning—I've been at all their activities all week—and he pretended I wasn't there."

"Why would he do that?"

"Joe Hirsch saw me at Jacques' Bistro with Brett the other day. I'm sure he made it sound like I was giving him a lap dance or something."

Judy lap-dancing? Shelley did *not* want to go there.

"Look, Jude, I'm the last one to give marital advice, but you and Craig have been together for too long to chuck it for a Brett O'Connor."

"It's not as simple as that."

"No, of course it's not. But you're only seeing the downside, the negatives of your situation." Lord, she sounded like the Mellnick. Maybe all those years of counseling were starting to pay off. "I think you've forgotten how hard it is to find someone worth spending your life with." She had no idea if she was saying the right things; she only knew they had to be said. "And what about Jason and Sammy? You're messing with their lives, too."

Judy started to cry in earnest. Tears slid down her cheeks and landed on the black jersey, making uneven splotches. Shelley remained silent. She wanted to go over and put her arms around Judy and tell her not to worry, that everything would be OK. But who was she to tell her that? And some of her most therapeutic sessions with Howard Mellnick had been tear-driven. Those sob-filled fifty minutes when he supplied the tissues and the lack of judgment. She could give her sister that.

"Brett at least finds me interesting," Judy said. "He actually *listens* when I talk."

"Well, of course he does. He doesn't live with you!"

"Gee, thanks."

"What I mean is, it's easy to be attentive for a couple hours a week. The man wants to get in your pants, Judy. He *has* to be on his best behavior."

"You get this sort of attention all the time. You don't realize how lucky you are."

"Luck, schmuck! You want the truth? Nina and I would trade places with you in a heartbeat. Nina—who can have any man on the planet—wants someone exactly like you've got. The woman is running ads in the personal columns and stalking a rabbi to get him to convert her. Because she wants what you're getting ready to give away."

Shelley handed her the box of tissues. "If things aren't working, shouldn't you try to fix them rather than throw them out?"

Judy sniffed, but she was listening.

"I've seen you get the designers and suppliers to do exactly what you want. You've even got ol' Wiley Haynes wrapped around your little finger. Can't you sit down with Craig and explain what you need from him? Don't you at least have to try?"

Judy crumpled the soggy tissue in her fist and swiped at her cheeks. "When did my little sister get so wise?"

"Hey, twenty, thirty thousand in therapy . . . and you, too, can see what other people should do."

Judy laughed. The sound wasn't exactly mirthful, but it beat sobs any day in Shelley's book.

"You know, in all the years I've been dating," Shelley said, "and believe me, they don't call it a battle of the sexes for nothing, I've always been able to look at you and think, 'It's possible. Judy found someone; one day I will, too.'"

"But you've never acted like you wanted that." Judy wadded up her tissue and took another. "You've been running in the opposite direction so fast you've made everyone's head spin."

Shelley shrugged. "Maybe I've just been afraid to admit I wanted something I didn't think I could have. Maybe I've just been stupid." She thought about Ross Morgan and the pull she felt toward him despite all the reasons to stay away. Yes, she was definitely stupid. "We both seem to have a bad case of the grass looking greener on the other side."

Judy leaned forward to pick up her high heels. "Right now it all looks like crabgrass to me." She stood. Without the heels, Judy looked small and waiflike, much too uncertain and vulnerable for Shelley's peace of mind.

"Believe me, I wish I knew what to do," Judy said quietly.

Shelley stood, too, and started turning off lights. "You'll figure it out. I know you." She realized with some surprise that she really did. Not in the casual jealous way she'd known her older sister, but really. "You'll find a way to do the right thing.

"In the meantime, be careful, Jude," she warned. "Not everything can be repaired. I'd hate to see you do anything you're going to regret."

***

Shelley had her own regrets, and she spent most of Sunday reviewing them. That afternoon she met Trey Davenport for a drink and, as tactfully as she could, explained that their relationship was over. Then she spent the rest of the evening trying to come to grips with her biggest—and most pressing—regret: the night she'd spent with Ross.

On Monday morning, a subdued Judy left the condo early for a meeting with her bar mitzvah coordinator. Shelley, who wasn't feeling all that exuberant herself, passed the drive into the office debating her next move.

The idea of skittering out of Ross's way and flushing with embarrassment every time they ran into each other was simply unacceptable. And so was all the sexual energy that kept zinging between them; a current like that could electrocute a person. Better to get this out in the open and lay out a few ground rules. So he'd taken over her father's company. And might still want to see her out of there. So no matter how annoying she found him, she couldn't seem to ignore him.

So they'd had sex—possibly the best sex of her life—and then he'd ruined it by apologizing.

What mattered was where they went from here. And where they had to go was nowhere.

Pulling into her parking spot, she grabbed her briefcase off the passenger seat and gave herself a quick once-over in the rearview mirror. Then she strode through the parking lot and into the office, enumerating all the reasons she could think of NOT to let sex interfere with all she planned to achieve.

She, Shelley Schwartz, was about to put Tire World on the map and make Fadah Awadallah's Falafel Shack a household name. Then she was going to pitch the Selena Moore Boutiques account and win it for the agency.

Ross Morgan would simply have to understand that just because she'd gone to bed with him didn't mean she wasn't serious about her work. Or capable of standing on her own two feet.

Dropping her things on her desk, she dialed his secretary's extension. "Mia, is Ross in?"

"Well, he is, but he's—"

"Good, I'm on my way up."

"But—"

Two minutes later she was in his outer office with her eyes fixed on the big double doors.

"Shelley, wait," the secretary said, "he's—"

Afraid that stopping would weaken her resolve, Shelley continued past Mia. "It's OK," she said as she threw open the double doors, "I'll just announce myself."

Ross looked up in surprise as Shelley, gaze fixed on his face, crossed the room to stand before him.

"Listen," she said without preamble, "I'm sure I'm not the only one feeling a little…awkward…about our, er, sexual encounter in L.A."

The expression on his face changed. He looked as if he'd swallowed something that didn't agree with him. "Shelley, you don't understand, there's—"

"I know, I know," she waved him off, "it was a really bad idea and it never should have happened."

His eyes widened. She'd never really understood what people meant when they said that, but as she watched, his eyes actually did get…wider. And bigger. In fact, they looked as if they might pop right out of his head. "Right, but—"

"Not that it wasn't great, of course," she interrupted. "I mean, I thought the supply closet was pretty incredible, but California was..." she paused again to look for the right word, "um, well, actually, I think it was...stellar."

"Shelley, stop."

"No, don't be modest. You were, it was..." she shook her head in wonder, "really and truly...um, you know... mind-boggling."

"But the thing is..." She paused again to search for the words she needed, but her knees started to shake, and she knew if she stopped too long she wouldn't be able to finish. "For all I know, you're still hoping you can make me quit."

He got up and started around the desk. "What you need to quit is talking. *Now.*"

Shelley refused to be silenced. She really, really wanted to get this off her chest. Not that she was doing it all that eloquently, of course, but still, she needed to get it all out. "Please don't interrupt until I'm done."

A look of exasperation passed over his face. In two strides he was beside her, grasping her by the arms. "Shelley!"

"So, um, I just want to make sure you understand that while I did, um, enjoy myself thoroughly, I think—"

He turned her around so that she was staring at his chest. She looked up into his eyes. There was a warning there that she didn't understand.

"Shut up."

"Of course, I want you to know that I'm going to sit down with Luke immediately about the Selena Moore account. And if I get it, I expect a full partnership."

He put a finger to her lips. "Shelley," he said softly. "Be quiet."

"But—"

"I've been trying to tell you that we're not alone."

There was a complete and absolute silence as the enormity of what he'd just said and what she'd just blurted out sank in. And then someone cleared a throat in the back corner of the room.

"Oh, my God." Shelley squeezed her eyes shut and leaned hard to her left. When she thought she'd cleared the screen of Ross's body, she opened them. One at a time.

And then most definitely wished that she hadn't.

chapter 27

Shelley watched in horror as her father rose from what used to be *his* leather couch in the seating alcove and began to walk toward them.

With every step another emotion appeared on his face, and none of them were emotions she wanted to see. Shame warred with embarrassment, then gave way to dismay. Resignation followed. They blended with the shock to form a road map of a father's disappointment.

It was the resignation that frightened her the most.

He came to a halt in front of them, and if she hadn't known better, she would have thought that Ross was trying to shield her. He turned and drew slightly in front of her so that they faced her father almost side by side.

"Now, Harvey." Ross's tone was reasonable, almost placating.

"No," Harvey Schwartz said, "no explanations, no excuses."

She wanted to shout, "It's not what it sounds like," but of course it was. She'd been trying so hard to clarify everything, there could be no doubt what had taken place between her and Ross.

"I've been trying to protect her for as long as I can remember," her father said. He spoke to Ross as if she weren't even there. "She doesn't have to think before she acts, because there are never any consequences. She just leaps without a net."

"Daddy, I—"

"No." He turned and looked at her and his face was horrible to see. Her heart hurt inside her chest. She could feel each individual beat reverberating in there, like a gong struck by a mallet. How ironic it would be if she was the one who succumbed to a heart attack. Right now, it felt entirely possible.

Or maybe she could just die of humiliation and be done with it.

"I think we should all just take the day and cool down," Ross said. "Maybe tomorrow—"

Harvey Schwartz shook his head. "No."

Everything was so off. Her father was supposed to cluck his tongue over her, pat her on the head, and tell her to try harder next time, while Ross jeered and pointed a finger. But her father had turned into an implacable stranger, and Ross looked . . . regretful?

"I thought things had changed. I'd heard you were working hard, producing results," her father said.

She didn't ask him where he'd heard these things. "But I am, Daddy," she said. "I've got all the accounts I was given back on track, and I've been invited to pitch the Selena

Moore Boutiques account. We can become their agency of record."

"But you're still playing at this, Shelley," her father said, "still letting men and...whatever else comes up...get in the way of your professional judgment."

OK, she was not going to have a conversation with her father about sex. They were all already suffering from way too much information. Still, the injustice of the double standard rankled.

"So this is *my* error in judgment? Despite all the things I've accomplished, you're going to focus on my sleeping with Ross? What about him? What about his sleeping with me?" Even in her own mind she sounded like a child trying to place the blame elsewhere.

She pointed to Ross even as she took a step away, needing to put distance between them. "I didn't think Jews bought into the whole Immaculate Conception thing."

Ross actually laughed.

She shot him a look. "You! You're lucky I'm not suing for sexual harassment. And you know what else? I take back all the things I said earlier. Stellar? Ha! I spit on stellar!"

Ross stopped smiling. Harvey Schwartz cleared his throat again. And everything plunged the rest of the way down the hill.

"I came in this morning to discuss the offer from Miller Advertising," her father said, looking at her.

"Offer?" The hair on the back of her neck popped up. Between the hurt and anger and embarrassment, it was hard to imagine summoning another emotion, but fear managed to rear its ugly head.

"They want to buy us out and merge the two agencies," Ross clarified.

She was having a hard time catching her breath. Each of their comments struck her like an unexpected body blow and left her gasping for air.

"They approached Ross six weeks ago. I'd be paid off. Ross would stay on as president. Others," her father looked at her, "would be out."

Others meaning her. They'd been talking about selling for six weeks and this was the first time they'd bothered to mention it to her.

"Your father's been resisting," Ross explained. "He wasn't willing to agree to some of the terms I was. He wanted to see you taken care of."

So she'd been the holdup. Her father had tried to protect her once again.

Looking at her father made her want to cry, so she looked at Ross instead. Then the full realization hit her. She'd been jumping through hoops to try to prove herself to Ross Morgan while he'd been lobbying to sell the agency, to an agency he knew she wouldn't be a part of.

Ross could afford to pretend regret; he would get a big fat payout and be named top dog. She would be out.

Because she'd slept with him and spoken out of turn. Because she didn't know how to keep her mouth shut at the appropriate time.

"You've just helped me make my decision," her father said. "Ross, contact Chase Miller today and tell him to have the papers drawn up."

She looked at him. "That's it? Have the papers drawn up?

Shelley slept with the wrong person, so she can't possibly be serious about her work? I guess I'll go ahead and sell out?"

She looked at her father again, trying to understand. "No matter what I do, you still see me as a child, treat me as a child. You'll never see me any other way."

Her father sighed and set his shoulders. She absolutely could not bear the look of disappointment on his face. "We'll talk about this another time, when we've both calmed down." Without waiting for an answer, he turned and walked slowly out the door.

Stunned, Shelley watched him go. Then she turned to look at the man beside her; the one she'd resented and fought with and been unable to resist. The one who'd wished her gone and whose dreams had all just now come true.

"Well," she said as her anger and anguish built, "this must feel like Christmas and Easter rolled up into one." Too agitated to stay in one place, she began to pace. "It's not every day you get to watch someone destroy herself quite so completely." Her stomach was churning so violently she was afraid she was going to be sick. "I waved my sex life in my father's face. And then I handed you everything you wanted on a silver platter! Me! I gave it to you!" She absolutely could not believe it.

Incensed, she rounded on him, prepared to tell him off some more. But he beat her to it.

"I hate to break it to you, Shelley, but every move I've made has not been about you." He sighed and ran a hand through his hair. "Sometimes things don't work out the way we plan, or even the way we want them to."

He came over and bent his face to hers. His eyes were full of emotion she didn't understand.

"And don't you dare try to tell yourself that our sleeping together was some ploy to get rid of you. This thing, whatever it is between us, has been brewing since we laid eyes on each other. I'm not wild about it and I sure as hell wished it would go away, but it won't. I should never have touched you. Never."

He shook his head as if he still couldn't believe it. "But I couldn't resist. And look what's happened."

He sounded almost as unhappy about it as she felt. "You know, if you had acted like a grown-up for once, instead of a spoiled little girl, your father wouldn't have had our mistake stuffed in his face. A grown-up might have resisted storming in here unannounced. Or taken a moment to make sure we were alone before launching into such intimate detail." He shook his head again and snorted in disgust. "Just a little bit of self-restraint, and we wouldn't be standing here having this conversation."

His last words were whispered, but they rang in her ears as if they'd been shouted. He might as well have capitalized every one of them. "I have a final news flash for you: Your father treats you like a child because you insist on acting like one."

He speared her with his blue eyes so that she couldn't look away. "I was never a serious threat to you, Shelley. The only real threat you've been facing is yourself."

She stared into his eyes, completely aghast, and knew that at this moment she hated him more than she had ever hated anyone.

Most of all, she hated that he was right. She'd never forgive him for that.

Mandy Mifkin was...miffed. Someone who didn't know
her might not have noticed, but Judy could tell just how
ticked off the bar mitzvah coordinator was. She held her
small overexercised body very still; there was no fluttering
of the hands, no overt physical indication. But if this had
been a cartoon, lightning bolts would be shooting out of
her eyes.

They were seated at the Bagel Nosh, a small delicatessen
not far from Judy's neighborhood, where the waitstaff did a
fair imitation of surly New York and you could get chopped
liver with the bagels that were baked fresh daily.

"I don't understand what's going on," Mandy said. "I explained at the Bar Mitzvah Expo that if you're not planning
to go all out, you're wasting my time and your money."

Judy understood the woman's dilemma; an event planner was only as good as her last event. Mandy Mifkin's reputation and ability to attract future clients were constantly
on the line.

"If you're going to do the sports thing, you've got to DO
the sports thing. Let's divide the banquet room into National League and American League, or NFL and AFL, let
each table be a different team, make the kids' buffet look
like a concession stand. We could even dress the waiters like
concessionaires or referees. It does no good to do these
things halfway."

Mandy Mifkin could sell. She hadn't gotten where she
was by letting clients shy away from the spectacular, and the
larger the spectacle the better. Other coordinators might

turn out nice, tasteful events. A Mifkin bar mitzvah was an extravaganza. But Judy no longer felt all that extravagant.

"We can put baseballs on the yarmulkes and edit Sammy's video to make it look like an episode of *Baseball Tonight*. We've already booked the whole ESPN Zone. You've got to embrace this theme and make it your own."

Judy took a bite of her bagel. At a nearby table, a group of women from her temple glanced their way and then put their heads together. Whether they were whispering about the obvious falling-out between planner and client or the state of Judy's marriage was unclear. Taking a sip of coffee, Judy tried to focus on the woman across from her.

Mandy was right. The first decision was the theme of the event and everything else simply flowed from that. It just felt so unimportant at the moment. What did any of this have to do with Sammy becoming a man? She suspected her son would rather have two parents and the life he was used to than a big-ass bar mitzvah. She put down her bagel as her appetite disappeared.

"Look," Mandy said more quietly, "I know your life has been a little . . . *unsettled* . . . since your father's heart attack." The coordinator did a semi-tiptoe around her marital situation. "And I know sometimes things . . . change. If you can't afford to do this . . ."

Judy looked the coordinator in the eye; she was tempted to shoot a few cartoon lightning bolts herself. All this woman cared about was making her outrageous fee and enhancing her own reputation. She didn't care about Judy or Judy's family; she simply didn't want a client who couldn't or wouldn't go all out.

Or worse, a soon-to-be-divorced client whose standard of living might be about to drop.

The words "You're fired" hovered on Judy's lips, but she knew better than to make a rash decision; she'd made too many of them over the past few weeks. "It's not about the money," Judy said, her tone brittle. "Or my personal life." Which, of course, was none of Mandy Mifkin's business. "I understand what you're saying, and I'll give it some serious thought."

"But—"

"It's only April; Sammy's bar mitzvah isn't until August."

"I know, but . . ."

It was clear Mandy Mifkin craved closure. She wanted to know that they were moving ahead under her terms, or parting ways. Judy could identify completely, but she wasn't interested in Mandy Mifkin's issues; she could barely keep up with her own.

Judy put enough money to cover both their meals down on the table. "I have to go. I've got some things to take care of at—home." She stumbled over the last word. "And then I need to get into the office. I'll give you a call later this week."

Judy hurried out of the deli. Out of the corner of her eye she saw Mandy Mifkin pick up her phone and start dialing. The ladies at the corner table put their heads back together.

Two left turns and a traffic light later, Judy was in her neighborhood, sailing past the elaborate clubhouse to the cul-de-sac on which her family lived. She didn't pull into the garage and enter through the kitchen door of her home as she would have just a week ago. Instead, she parked in the driveway and came in through the front door, like the stranger she'd become.

The front rooms felt musty and unused. If Craig had had Eva in this week, he'd neglected to ask her to dust. Pausing in the foyer between the formal living and dining rooms, she tried not to think about the family dinners that had taken place there. Or the cocktail parties and fund-raisers they'd hosted. She'd put such time and effort into decorating these rooms, into creating the public face they presented to the world. Perhaps she should have spent more time on the guts of their family, shoring up the parts that they kept stuffed inside.

She went up the front stairs and into the boys' rooms, where mounds of dirty clothing covered the carpet and discarded candy wrappers and food-crusted plates littered every flat surface.

Leaving things where they'd been dropped, she padded down the back stairs. In the master bedroom, the unmade bed and clothing-strewn floor confirmed that her two apples hadn't fallen far from their father's tree.

The kitchen made her gasp. It was clear Eva had never been called and that neither Craig nor the boys had lifted a finger in her absence. It took every ounce of willpower she possessed not to clean it up. Or choke on the tears of hurt and anger that filled her.

Instead, she picked up the phone to check messages. They were all the detritus of her old life, and she couldn't find the strength to write any of them down. Then she heard the one from the temple Hebrew school that had come in last Friday. She cleared a pile of junk from a bar stool so she could sit down and listen.

"Hi, Mrs. Blumfeld," the B'nai Mitzvah administrator's voice said. "I'm calling to make sure Sammy's OK."

Judy went still at the woman's words. What could be wrong with Sammy?

"He hasn't been in Hebrew school the last two Thursdays. And his Sunday school teacher says when he is there, he's not, if you know what I mean." There was a pause. *"Can you give me a call to set up an appointment?"*

Judy jotted down the phone number, but her mind was already racing. Craig drove the boys to Sunday school, but she drove Sammy to Hebrew every Thursday afternoon. In fact, she'd driven him right up to the front entrance the last two Thursdays and watched him amble toward the front doors. It had never occurred to her that he hadn't gone inside.

Her son was playing hooky from Hebrew school, and she hadn't even known it. She'd always scoffed at those news stories in which children came to harm or did outrageous things and their parents acted so surprised. Like the mother of a serial killer she'd once heard interviewed who'd said, "I don't know what happened. I talked to him this morning and he sounded just fine."

How could a mother not know? Knowing was a mother's primary job.

Maybe the serial killer's mother had been off trying to find herself, too.

Hollow-eyed, Shelley sat across from Howard Mellnick. Drowning in hurt and anger, she'd rushed to his office when he'd offered to fit her in during his lunch hour. Now she waited for him to throw her a life preserver; something, anything she could cling to in order to keep her head above water.

"So," he said quietly after she told him what had happened. "What now?"

"What now?" she asked. She was afraid she might go under and not come up again and he was asking "What now?"

He nodded.

"I was *really* hoping you were going to tell me that."

Dr. Mellnick smiled gently. "It's your life, Shelley. That makes it your decision."

"Look," she said, madly treading through her emotional waters, "I don't have the energy for major analysis right now. I just need to get through this day. And then I need to get through tomorrow."

"Then answer the question."

"Fine." She sat back in her chair and pretended to think. All the while, in her mind, she was bicycling her legs, sculling her arms, trying to stay afloat. Trying not to think of her father's dismissal and all the horrible truths Ross Morgan had hurled at her.

"Let's see," she said, "my father, who gave his business to someone else and allowed that someone else to demote me, torture me, and make me jump through all sorts of, as it turns out, unnecessary hoops, has now decided to sell his business to people who will get rid of me. On top of that, one of the main reasons this is happening is that I slept with the person he gave the business to in the first place and then flung that fact in my father's face."

She shuddered anew over the memory and treaded harder.

"So even though I've been working my ass off for the last two months and have actually managed to do a really great job, I'm going to be out. And Ross Morgan, the double-crossing job-stealer, whom I had the bad judgment to sleep with, is going to make a ton of money from the sale and end up being president of a much larger agency."

The knowledge of her stupidity and his perfidy churned in her stomach and left a horrible sour taste in her mouth. She'd been had in every sense of the word. And pretty soon she was going to be a have-not.

Howard Mellnick simply looked at her, still calm. "That's a pretty good recap of what's already happened, Shelley. My question was, what are you going to do about it?"

"You mean other than crawling into my bed and assuming the fetal position?"

"I mean, what do you plan to do *now*?"

Shelley stopped treading water. It was way too hard anyway, and she wasn't getting anywhere. Putting her head in her hands, she groaned like a very old person and rocked back and forth once or twice for good measure.

The Mellnick just looked at her. She sensed he wanted to roll his eyes, but he just waited.

"All right, all right," she groaned. "God, you're merciless."

"So, I repeat," he said quietly, "what do you plan to do now?"

Shelley forced herself to think about it. No treading, no dodging. It wasn't easy with all the emotional garbage churning around inside: Ross's betrayal, her father's abandonment. All of it hurt so badly. And she felt so stupid.

But as she prodded her wounds, she began to notice a very strange thing. While they were tender to the touch, were, in fact, quite painful, they didn't feel...fatal.

She might want to curl up in a ball. But she was not going to die.

"What?" he asked.

"I think I'm going to be OK," she whispered, hearing the wonder in her voice.

He smiled. "Could you say that a little louder?"

"I'm...OK," she said, amazed that it was true. "Kind of bruised and bloody. But OK." She smiled back at him. "I mean, I'm not going to jump up, throw away my crutches, and shout 'I've been healed!' but I'm not going to fall apart, either."

"Good." Again, his manner was calm and straightforward, but approval and pleasure were evident in his voice. "That's very good."

Shelley sat up straighter. And somehow the load that had been weighing her down lightened. She was going to be OK. She was not going to run out and shoot herself in the foot. Or suddenly revert to the screwup she'd been. Her father might not be able to see the changes that had taken place in her, but that didn't mean they weren't there.

Dr. Mellnick looked into her eyes and gave her a last encouraging smile. "All you have to do now is move forward. Today you took two steps back, but as I believe Scarlett O'Hara once said, 'Tomorrow is another day.'"

chapter 28

Shelley spent the afternoon wrestling with her thoughts.
Most of them were unpleasant and many were humiliating;
she had to keep fast-forwarding past them so that they
didn't drag her all the way down. By early evening, she'd
drafted a letter of resignation. It was curt and to the point,
as coldly professional as she could make it. She intended to
deliver it to Ross Morgan in the morning; her only regret
was that she couldn't nail it onto his forehead or superglue
it to his ass.

She spent the rest of the evening at the kitchen table
composing a letter to her father. For hours she agonized
over each word of each draft, until she gave up at midnight
with nothing to show for her time but a pile of crumpled
paper.

Riddled with regrets, she paced her living room, unable
to halt the litany of if-onlys. If only she'd taken herself seriously from the beginning, if only she hadn't let others' as-

sumptions about her become reality, if only she'd stayed away from Ross Morgan. There were a million of them, but those three stood head and shoulders above the rest. They formed a recriminatory loop that replayed endlessly in her mind. Sinking into her club chair, she stared out her window into the darkness, and tried not to listen.

"Are you all right?" Judy sat down on the couch. She wore a pale pink peignoir and matching bedroom slippers. Her eyes were sleepy, and she, too, appeared to be focused inward.

"Not really. How about you?"

"I feel like I'm standing at this great crossroads and the next step I take will alter things forever. I'm so afraid of stepping out in the wrong direction."

"I know what you mean." Shelley's first step had been her decision to resign before they chucked her out, but choosing a new path meant taking more steps. This time she was determined to weigh her choices carefully; no more leaping before she looked.

"You know," Judy said, rising, "I ended up here with you sort of by default. But despite the reasons for my coming, and the fact that my life seems to be pretty much in the toilet, I'm glad we've had this time with each other." She stopped in front of Shelley.

"Me, too," Shelley said, reaching out her hand and letting her sister pull her up. "I can't believe it took me so long to figure out what a dynamite sister I have."

Judy's hand was smaller, the bones more delicate, but Shelley imagined she could feel Judy's inner strength. It was then that the realization hit her: The Schwartz sisters were a whole lot stronger than they'd been led to believe.

"Gee," she said, slipping her arm around Judy's shoulder, "I feel like we should break into a chorus of 'We Are Family' or something."

Judy hugged Shelley with all that hidden strength. "If I could reach the top of your head, I'd give you a couple of noogies to make you appreciate the solemnity of this moment."

"Right." Her sister's acceptance warmed her, made her stronger still. "You and what army?"

In her room Shelley slipped into bed and felt a new resolve fill her. Judy was facing her new life head-on; there was no reason why she couldn't do the same. The time had come to stop talking and dithering about what had been, and focus instead on what might be.

In the morning Shelley deposited her things on her desk and marched to Ross Morgan's office.

"Is he in?" she asked his secretary for the second day in a row.

Mia looked nervous, which was understandable in view of yesterday's fiasco. "Yes, um, let me let him know you're here," she said.

Shelley offered no argument. One office-storming and humiliation per week seemed sufficient.

This time when Mia nodded her in, Shelley walked sedately through the double doors and looked carefully about the room before she approached the desk. Which was kind of like closing the barn door after all the horses were gone.

"So," he said.

"So." She dropped the letter on his desk and waited while he opened it. "This is my resignation. I'd like to stay for the next two weeks so that I can see the Tire World grand opening through and interface with Brian Simms while his commercials are in postproduction. I'll get my other accounts ready for whoever's going to take them over."

She could see she'd managed to surprise him. Evidently he'd assumed they'd have to drag her out the door screaming and kicking.

"There's no reason to rush this." His voice was devoid of emotion. "It'll take months for the sale to go through, and another few months for everything to get sorted out."

"No, thanks. Two weeks should do it."

"You know, I didn't mean for—" Ross began.

"Don't worry about it." She gave him her best Kate Hepburn shrug. "You won, I lost. Game over."

She'd accomplished what she came for. Now was the time to spin around on her heel and leave. But her feet felt rooted to the floor.

He considered her for a moment out of serious blue eyes. She would have felt better if he were laughing, or thumbing his nose at her. A shouting match would make things even easier. But all he said was, "What will you do next?"

This, of course, was the sixty-four-thousand-dollar question, the very one she kept asking herself. But she didn't owe Ross Morgan any explanations. "That would belong in the category of 'none of your business.' "

He took the jab without flinching. If she'd hoped to stir his anger, she'd failed. But then, what was a little lip from her at this point? He'd already won all the marbles; she was going to have to pack up the few she had left and go home.

"For what it's worth," he said, "you surprised me. I think you've been doing a good job. If it were up to me I'd—"

"What?" she snapped, not at all interested in his pity. "Tell my father he made a mistake? Admit there were two of us in that bedroom? Warn me we weren't alone?"

Silently she dared him to acknowledge the intimacy of the night they'd spent together. Or allude again to the unwelcome chemistry that even now filled the air between them. He did neither.

"You can't pretend I didn't try to warn you." His laugh was totally devoid of humor. "I did everything but duct-tape your mouth shut."

She hated that he was right; hated that she'd been the instigator of her own demise; hated that she'd been so focused on him and what she'd wanted to say that she'd been oblivious to everything else. Hated that even now, when he was the victor and she was the vanquished, she was so completely and totally aware of him.

She wanted desperately to pace, to move, to work off some of her tension, but she forced herself to stay put. "I guess you can comfort yourself with the fact that I came to your hotel room. Maybe you should sue me for sexual harassment. Pick up a few extra bucks. But then, you won't need any more money, will you? The sale of my family's company should set you up for life."

He flushed, but whether it was with anger or embarrassment she didn't know. Nor did she plan to stick around and find out. She turned and left the office. Two weeks from now she'd walk out of this place forever. Then she'd never have to set sight on his face again.

***

Shelley spent the rest of the morning in her office making lists and plotting out her last two weeks of employment. The Tire World grand opening would take place the Friday night of her last day of work, and there were a slew of details she wanted to go over with Judy. Then she needed to meet with Luke about the status of Creative on her other accounts, and begin initial conversations about the presentation to Selena Moore.

Someone else would take this over when she left, but for the next two weeks the project was hers. Even the *possibility* of landing the Selena Moore Boutiques account would up the price Miller was willing to pay Harvey Schwartz for the agency. The fact that Ross Morgan would also benefit was a great big cross she'd have to bear.

Again, thoughts of her father swamped her, threatening her resolve. His low opinion of her hurt and though she continued to remind herself that it was, at last, unfounded, it continued to hurt all the same. She feared she'd relive the look of horror and disappointment on his face until her own dying day; some sick sort of karmic retribution for all the times she'd promised to change, but hadn't.

She'd cried wolf one too many times.

At eleven her phone rang. Lost in her To Do list, she reached for it automatically and brought the receiver up to her ear.

"When are you going to send your sister home where she belongs?"

"Hi, Mom. How are you? Beautiful weather we're having." She sighed. When her mother was on a mission, she wasted no time on niceties.

"Beautiful, shmutiful! I don't know what's going on with

this family. Your sister's acting like a silly schoolgirl, you're sleeping with the help, and your father is absolutely beside himself, which we all know is not good for him. And on top of that your friend Nina's out there snatching up all the available Jewish men. This has got to stop."

Shelley switched the phone to her other ear. For the first time she almost appreciated her mother's ability to cut through the details to succinctly state her complaints; a breath of fresh air after her own endless agonizing. "And what would you like me to do about all those things?" she asked.

"Fix them. Send Judy home. Make up with your father. Otherwise I'm going to have to take things into my own hands."

The ultimate threat; her mother rewriting everyone's parts in the Schwartz Family Soap Opera.

"And tell Nina to leave a few men for you."

"OK."

There was a stunned silence while her mother processed Shelley's too-rapid capitulation. "What did you say?"

"I said I'll try." Shelley smiled to herself. For the first time in memory her goals and her mother's were very much the same. "Although I'm not sure I'm the one who needs to be making up with Dad. And of course I'll need a few things in return."

There was a silence while her mother processed this. In dealing with her mother, negotiation was often required but it was rarely acknowledged. "For one thing, I need you to invite a few extra people for Passover."

This year Passover began the week after the Tire World

grand opening—the point at which she would no longer be gainfully employed.

"Passover?" her mother asked.

The Schwartz family celebration of the Jews' freedom from slavery in Egypt was legendary. Every year her mother filled tables full of friends and family as well as others with nowhere else to observe the holiday.

"I'll make sure Nina leaves a few men 'un-wowed' if you'll invite her, Rabbi Jordan, and Howard Mellnick to the seder." Shelley could practically hear Miriam Schwartz's mind working. "But only if you think you can squeeze them in," she said, trying not to smile. Three extra people at this year's Passover seder would be the equivalent of three additional grains of sand in the Sahara.

"I'll invite them," her mother said. "As to the rest, I'll give you two weeks before I step in."

There was a brief pause. "Nina doesn't really want to be Jewish, does she? I mean, don't get me wrong, we *are* the chosen people. But it doesn't always feel like such a privilege."

"I know, Mom. I don't really understand it myself," Shelley replied. "But for some wacky reason, Nina Olson wants a family just like ours."

Despite Shelley's attempts to set up a meeting by phone, her brother-in-law managed to dodge her for a full day and a half. By noon on Thursday she realized her mistake; she'd been trying to make an appointment like a civilized human being. It was time to pull a sneak attack.

Trying not to think about how badly her storming of

Ross's office had gone, she presented herself to Craig's secretary right after lunch.

"Is he tied up?" she asked.

The secretary consulted the agenda in front of her. "Um, no." She reached for the intercom. "Let me tell him you're here."

Shelley's hand reached the buzzer first. "Let's not do that." The secretary pulled her hand back and Shelley took advantage of her momentary confusion. "I've got a surprise for him from my sister. And I don't want to spoil it."

"But—"

"It'll be fine." She was already headed for Craig's office door. "I'll take full responsibility."

When she entered, Craig was leaning back in his chair, feet up on his desk, staring out the window at his impressive view of downtown Atlanta. At the sound of the door, he turned and dropped his feet to the floor. He didn't look at all happy to see her.

"Gee," she said, "I hate to interrupt when you're so busy."

He flushed.

"Is this what you were doing when you said you were too busy to see me?" She plopped down into the chair across from his desk, uninvited. "Or when Judy wanted to talk?"

"That's none of your business."

"Well, actually, it is. Because your wife is my sister. And she's living in my home, which by the way is now incredibly well organized. And she's looking real hard at her marriage. Don't you think you should be a part of that?"

He straightened and his face flushed again. "I can't believe you, of all people, are trying to tell me what to do about a relationship. When's the last time you actually *had* a relationship that lasted longer than six months? Or went out with anyone who was even remotely suitable?"

"Strange, isn't it?" she agreed. "But the fact is, Judy's left you and if you don't DO something to convince her otherwise, she might not be coming back."

That one definitely rocked him. He sat back in his chair, his brow furrowed. "I don't know what's come over her. She's not at all the woman I married."

He looked so perplexed Shelley almost felt sorry for him. Almost, but not quite. The man had been taking her sister for granted and he needed a good, swift kick in the rear end.

"No, she's not the same woman you married. She's growing and evolving; I think she's become interesting as hell. All you really have to do is open up enough to discuss what she needs from you. And you could tell her what you need, too. It doesn't have to be a one-way street."

She almost choked over the words. They were so obvious, yet when had she ever followed such advice? She'd never even been in a situation that warranted the effort.

She could see that he found the idea shocking, too. But his reluctance was tinged with something else.

"You don't think she's slept with that O'Connor guy, do you?"

It was clear he needed the answer to be no, but Shelley wasn't in the reassurance business. "I don't actually know, Craig. But if I were you I'd get in touch with Judy as soon as possible and let her know you want to try to work things out. Then I'd try a little groveling. And flowers, flowers are always good. Judy deserves to feel appreciated."

Craig's shoulders slumped. When she met his eyes, they

were troubled. "I just don't get it. I love her and I thought she loved me. How did everything get so complicated?"

"I don't know," Shelley said as she stood and drew her purse over her shoulder, "I've been asking myself that question a lot lately. I'll let you know if I come up with any answers."

Judy studied her younger son surreptitiously as she drove him to Hebrew school. On the outside, Sammy looked the same; he had the same unruly dark hair that he refused to have cut, the same dark eyes that were so much like her own. But there was a new fragility about him that hadn't been there before. He was careful of what he said, as if he was thinking out each word before he uttered it. Jason had grown surlier and more independent, seeking more and more attention in her absence; Sammy had done just the opposite; shrinking into himself and becoming quieter by the day.

"So how was school today?" she asked too brightly.

"OK."

"Did the math test go all right?"

"Yes."

Judy turned onto Mayfair, the street on which their temple was located, and slowed for a light. "What does your Hebrew tutor say about your progress?"

The light turned red, so she was able to watch his face. He blanched and swallowed. Sammy had always been the world's worst liar.

"Good. He said I'm, um, right on track." He turned his head and looked out the passenger window.

"You know, if you feel you need extra help, we can always

set that up. Steve Reinholt had lessons twice a week right up until the week before his bar mitzvah."

He turned back to face her and she thought he might say something more revealing, but then the light turned green and she was forced to pay attention to the road.

"I'm fine," he said, as she pulled up to the circular drive of the temple. "You don't need to do anything or call anyone." He gathered his book bag and grabbed the door handle. "Everything's going OK."

She leaned over and kissed him on the cheek and breathed in the scent of boy. "Good," she said, "I'm glad to hear it. Give my best to Mr. Pinkhas. And call me tonight before you go to bed."

"Sure, Mom. Thanks." Then he was out of the car and walking up the walkway, his skinny shoulders squared and set. She waited until he went inside. Then she drove out of the temple parking lot and into the crowded lot of an office building across the street, where she'd have an unobstructed view of the temple.

Turning off the car, she settled in to wait.

chapter 29

In less than ten minutes Judy saw her son exit the rear of the temple. He looked both ways before stepping outside, then walked quickly to the sidewalk and took a right toward the closest intersection.

His clothes were baggy and the oversized button-down shirt he wore open over his T-shirt flapped backward in the breeze. Feeling slightly silly and more than a little afraid of what she might discover, Judy merged into traffic and followed at a discreet distance. No one had ever told her that motherhood would require surveillance and shadowing. She drove along, afraid he'd suddenly turn and spot her before she discovered where he was going, but Sammy Blumfeld just kept trucking, his body and head bopping to whatever song he had blaring from his iPod.

With her heart in her throat, Judy followed through two intersections. He was headed toward Upper Roswell, a four-lane highway, where it would be harder to follow. She tried to guess where he might be going but all her guesses scared her to death. He was only twelve and a half, but she'd heard all the suburban horror stories.

Her heart beat faster. Some drug dealer had lured her little boy into an ugly world; worse, some unscrupulous girl had sunk her claws into him and made him her sex slave. Oh, how had she let this happen?

On the corner before the major intersection, Sammy took a right into a strip mall parking lot. Head still bobbing to the music, hands shoved in his sagging pockets, he walked without hesitation. It was obvious he'd traversed this route before.

Her son, her baby, was headed for who knew what.

Waiting in the turn lane as long as she could, Judy scanned the strip mall, which she'd passed a million times but never really paid attention to. A beep from behind forced her to make the turn into the lot. Slowly, careful not to call attention to herself, she slid her BMW into a spot between two parked cars.

Leaving the car running, she held her breath as she watched Sammy bop across the lot, oblivious to everything around him.

He went into a McDonald's.

Trembling with relief, she drove closer to the fast-food restaurant. Her child might overdose on French fries or caffeine, but it was unlikely he was going to have his virginity snatched or good name sullied under the golden arches.

After taking a few minutes to compose herself, she took a parking space on the opposite side of the McDonald's and entered.

She spotted him right away, sitting at a two-seater near

the window, wolfing down a super-size combo meal. He was still wearing his headphones. His head bopped occasionally to the beat.

Judy walked up and stopped in front of him.

The bopping stopped. A French fry froze halfway to his mouth.

Shock and horror crossed his face, and then she saw something that resembled relief. She reached over and removed the headphones from his head. The tinny, once-removed sound of a rap song blared out.

"What are you doing here?" Sammy asked.

"That's my line." Judy sank into the molded plastic seat across from him. "What happened to Hebrew school?"

"They canceled today. They—"

"Don't," she said. "Mrs. Kaplan called me. I know you've been skipping. And I don't believe it's because you had a Big Mac attack."

Sammy pushed the food away.

"Tell me what's going on, Sam."

"I hate Hebrew school and I don't want to have a bar mitzvah."

Judy looked at her son. Her first instinct was to inform him that what he wanted didn't matter. She prepared to mow down his objections, just as her mother would have mowed down hers. But how could his objections not matter? "Why not?"

"Because I don't want some big fancy party with people pinching my cheeks and gushing all over me. Because I'm not Jason, and I hate performing. If I go up there and do this, everyone's going to be comparing me to him."

He looked her directly in the eye and she saw the anguish

in his. "Because I can't pretend we're some big happy family when everything's falling apart and you don't even live with us anymore."

"But—" Judy began, but stopped herself. All the things she was getting ready to say, every glib phrase that sprang to her lips, were things her mother would have said. Some of them would be true, but none of them were valid. She had spent her entire life trying to please her mother. And then she'd expected her own children to please her.

Her normally silent child had spoken. Quite eloquently. How could she ignore what he'd said?

"I'm so sorry," Judy said quietly.

"What?" Sammy stopped slumping. He sat up and looked at her.

"I said, I'm sorry. I should have asked how you felt about this before I went off and started planning everything. And I should have talked to you about what's going on between your father and me. I've been an absolute imbecile."

Sammy smiled. It was, she realized, the first time she'd seen him do that in a very long time.

"I haven't been paying attention." She reached out to take her son's hand, and felt herself smile in return when he didn't shake her off. "Why didn't you say something sooner?"

He dropped his eyes then and looked embarrassed. "Everything's been so weird with you gone. And I didn't think it would make any difference."

Judy's heart ached for him, for her family, for the state it was in. She wanted to reassure him, but she didn't want to lie. "You have to speak up about what's important to you.

You have to tell people what you want, especially the people you love. And who love you."

A tear slid down her cheek. "I love you and Jason more than anything. And I need you to tell me when something's not right. How you feel, what you think and want. Otherwise, how can I help?"

She squeezed her son's hand hard, and held on to it as the realization hit her. She'd complained and stomped out of the house, but in the end she hadn't done any better than her twelve-year-old son. Sammy hid out at McDonald's; she was hiding at Shelley's. But both of them had given up without communicating, both of them had expected the other party to understand what they needed and somehow provide it without specific direction.

"I'm sorry, Sweetie-P." She called him by the nickname she'd used since she brought him home from the hospital. "I dropped the ball. You needed me and I wasn't there for you. That won't happen again."

He smiled again; a sweet smile that spoke of what was inside him. "It's OK, Mom. But you better come home soon. We had pizza and hamburgers every night last week and the house looks awful; I don't think any of us have any clean underwear left."

Judy speared him with a look. "Your father made it through Emory Law and you and your brother are on the honor roll. I have complete confidence that between you, you can figure out how to run the washing machine."

He wolfed down the rest of his Big Mac and drained the last of his drink. Then he gathered up the wrapper and empty cup. She waited as he dropped them in the garbage.

"I'm not exactly sure what'll happen next, Sammy. Your

daddy and I have a lot of things to work out. But we both love you; we'll figure out the whole bar mitzvah thing. In the meantime, no more skipping class or tutoring, OK?"

He nodded solemnly and she reached out to cup the smooth curve of his cheek. It was still downy-soft and sweet to the touch. "Come on, I'll drive you back to temple. The size of the 'event' is open for discussion; the studying isn't."

Now that Shelley had turned in her notice, time somehow both telescoped and flew. Her last two weeks passed in a blur of meetings and crisis management as she discovered, to her amazement, just how unhappy her clients were to see her go.

In between meetings and client hand-holding, she did her best to avoid Ross Morgan, but suddenly the place was much too small for the both of them.

Every time she turned around, he was there, being in charge, the epitome of a fearless leader. Or she was forced to hear someone talking about him.

Gossip about the upcoming sale and merger filled the halls of Schwartz and Associates, which would soon be known as Miller-Schwartz; everyone buzzed about who would stay and who would be forced to go. Since her fate was already known, Shelley occupied a position slightly above the fray, and, she discovered not at all happily, outside the loop, so that she was reduced to eavesdropping over the coffee machine like everyone else.

"I heard Ross is going to be worth a bundle before this is all through," said one wide-eyed sales assistant.

"That man is hot," agreed another.

The two giggled.

"Even without the money he's a keeper," one of Luke Skyler's trainees chimed in.

Shelley gritted her teeth and moved on, but wherever she went, the talk was the same.

"I can't believe how well Morgan is going to come out of all of this," an account executive remarked.

"A born leader, that's what I think."

"The transition went so smoothly, I hardly noticed the old man was gone."

Everyone had an opinion or some small piece of Morgan trivia to add. Everyone kept buzzing. It was enough to make a girl sick.

Shelley kept her head down and tried not to think about what would come next. She tried not to dwell on how little of her father she saw. Or the fact that when they met they were both so painfully polite.

The truth was, she'd made no progress with any of the things she'd promised her mother. Judy, who had not yet heard from Craig, continued to dither over her next move. They sat at Shelley's kitchen table hashing it out over Thai takeout.

"Every time I think about Sammy sitting in that McDonald's hiding out from Hebrew school, it makes me want to cry. And if Jason gets any surlier, I swear I'll scream."

"Maybe you should go home."

"I can't."

"Why not?" Shelley didn't even want to think about how empty her condo would feel when Judy was gone.

"Because that would be admitting defeat. Craig and I have to discuss this, figure things out. But I keep trying to get him on the phone and he refuses to talk to me." She dropped her chopsticks onto her plate. "Oh, God, what if he's decided he's happier without me?"

"Are you happier without him?" Shelley asked.

Judy looked at her hopelessly. "No. It's just all so caught up together, you know? The anger and resentment got so big it became impossible to separate it all out. I hate not being there for the kids, but I'm so confused about how to get through to Craig. Why hasn't he called?"

Why indeed? If he didn't act soon, Miriam Schwartz was going to get out her cattle prod.

"But you're not, um, seeing Brett O'Connor anymore?" Shelley broached the subject carefully; she'd cut out her tongue before she asked how far that had gone.

"No. Well, not exactly."

Shelley was afraid to ask what that meant. "But Craig and the boys will be at the Tire World grand opening, right? Maybe you can talk there." Even Shelley could hear what a stupid idea that was. A grand opening was not the place for soul-searching.

"I sent them an invitation," Judy said, "but I sent one to Brett, too."

"Great," Shelley said. "If things get slow we can have them duel it out at forty paces."

"Ha!" Judy didn't sound or look at all amused. "Craig's more likely to ask Brett what he sees in me. I don't think my husband's exactly lying awake nights trying to figure out how to get me back."

On her last day at Schwartz and Associates, Shelley walked out of the building with a cardboard box full of the "stuff" she'd accumulated: her favorite chipped coffee mug, an ancient gap-toothed photo of her nephews, a travel-size box of tampons. She left early, ostensibly to get prepared for that night's grand opening. Her sister, whose "stuff" fit in her Louis Vuitton bag, went with her.

"I can't believe how strange this feels." Shelley stopped to look back over her shoulder at the office building. "I mean, I'll probably never set foot in that place again."

"Yeah," Judy said as they let their gazes travel over the converted warehouse. "I don't understand what's going on with Daddy, but it's their loss."

"Too bad it took me so long to figure out how good I am at this." Shelley repositioned her box on one hip. "Who knows what I might have accomplished if I'd been serious from the beginning."

They began to walk across the parking lot.

"Well, it's not as if you're too old to find another job," Judy pointed out helpfully.

"That's true." Shelley put her box in the trunk of her car. "But who's going to hire me? My own father pretty much sold the business out from under me. That's not what I'd call a glowing reference."

"It'll work out," Judy said, though Shelley couldn't help noticing her voice didn't exactly ring with certainty.

"Yeah, definitely." Shelley's voice didn't sound particularly full of certainty, either. They leaned against the trunk of Shelley's car, both of them oddly reluctant to leave.

Shelley studied her sister for a long moment.

"I hope I don't look as droopy as you do," Shelley said.

Judy snorted. "You'd have to perk *up* to be droopy."

Shelley took in her sister's sagging shoulders, the chin

tucked into her chest. They were acting like whipped dogs, slinking away with their tails between their legs. If Ross Morgan was looking out his window right now, he'd know how completely he'd beaten her.

She definitely shouldn't have canceled her standing appointment with Howard Mellnick.

"I hate to admit it," Shelley said, "but I am *so* in the mood for one of those famous Jewish whines."

"Oh, no." Judy shook her head.

"Oh, yes. Are you with me?"

Judy looked over her shoulder, she looked all around to make sure they were alone. "Oh, all right. But just one."

"OK." Shelley was already starting to smile. "On the count of three." Three fingers later they began to whine in unison: "I don't waaaaaaaant to go to Miami."

The whine hung in the air around them and then began to dissipate. They were both smiling.

"Feeling any better?" Judy asked.

Shelley straightened. "Actually, yes. And you know what?" She brushed her skirt and hunted in her purse. "I'm not showing up tonight feeling sorry for myself." She pulled out her cell phone. "I'm going to have a facial. And then I'm going to get my hair and nails done." She hit speed dial for the Darnell Day Spa. "And while I'm there I'm going to get everything waxed." Shelley looked at Judy. "Are you with me?"

"Oh, yeah." Judy straightened, too, and moved toward her car. "See if Joseph's got an opening. Otherwise, I'll take Maria. Tonight's our night. We are required to look hot."

"You've got that right."

Shelley booked every afternoon appointment available.

Then they both turned to take one last look at Schwartz and Associates. "I don't know what it is," Shelley said, "but I'm feeling this really strange compulsion to shake my fist at Ross Morgan's window and say 'I'll be baaaaack.' "

Judy laughed. "You go, Shelley Schwarzenegger. That man hasn't heard the last of you."

That night, freshly buffed, gowned, and made-up, Shelley and Judy stood side by side in the middle of the sales floor of Atlanta's newest Tire World. To their right, the line for the ladies' room snaked halfway out the door as Atlanta society matrons and Jewish suburbanites waited their turn to oohh and ahhh over interior designer Jacques Dumas's Rococo Revival bathroom.

Well-dressed movers and shakers stood three deep at the buffet tables and cocktail bars, while others discussed the tire art and wrote in their bids for the silent auction.

Tonight in Atlanta, "round" was in, and success was spelled with a *T* for "TIRE."

"Pinch me," Judy said, "I can't believe this turnout."

Shelley smiled prettily for a passing photographer and continued their conversation without actually moving her lips. "Forget the pinching. Your arm is already black-and-blue." She sent a small beauty-queen-type wave to a reporter from *Southern Living*. "It's real. And when these photos hit the design magazines, you'll be THE hottest event planner in the southeast. Get ready to write your own ticket."

Judy shivered with excitement. "There's Craig and the boys." She smoothed the bodice of her dress. "Do I look OK?"

"You look mah-ve-lous." Shelley laid a hand on her sister's shoulder. "But we have a small problem. Isn't that Brett O'Connor at three o'clock?"

Judy's gaze followed Shelley's. "Oh, God, they're both headed this way. What do I do now?"

Shelley took a step forward. "You stay here and talk to Craig. I'll nab Brett."

"OK." Judy licked her lips, nervous. "And try to rescue Wiley Haynes on your way. Ellen Farnesworth has him cornered again."

They peered toward the buffet table, where Wiley Haynes was knee-deep in women. The orchestra guild chairwoman was fending the others off with the occasional sharp elbow, but it looked like things might get ugly. There was evidently something unexpectedly alluring about Haynes's buck-toothed smile and redneck ways. He was calling them "little lady" right and left and no one had taken a swing at him yet.

Giving Judy's hand a squeeze, Shelley strode forward to intercept her sister's old flame. "Hi, Brett," she said, linking her arm through his, "thanks so much for coming." She smiled up at him and fluttered her eyelashes a little for good measure, then led him toward Wiley Haynes and his harem. Out of the corner of her eye, she noticed Ross Morgan leaning against a tire display. He was talking to a dark-haired woman but his eyes were on Shelley. She stumbled slightly under his regard. Recovering, she clung tighter to Brett's arm and batted her eyelashes at him again, determined not to let Ross Morgan know how he affected her.

"Wiley," she said as she and Brett drew nearer, "I want you to meet Brett O'Connor." She shoved Ross Morgan out of her mind and focused on the two men she was introducing. "Brett knows Atlanta real estate." The two men shook hands while the harem looked on admiringly. "Didn't you tell me you were looking at several other locations?"

She got the two talking, then extracted Ellen Farnesworth. "Ellen," Shelley said as she led the woman toward the designer, "have you met Jacques yet? I overheard him saying how much he'd like to work on next year's Dream Home." She stayed with them a few minutes to help break the ice, then left them chatting amiably. When the throng of women moved in on Brett, she drew in a relieved breath. Despite her determination NOT to think about Ross Morgan, she did a quick scan for him all the same.

The garage door opened and a stream of people poured in. Shelley tensed when she spotted her parents. She and her father had barely spoken since that day in Ross's office, and she didn't know what to say to him now. She was still mulling it over when Fadah Awadallah planted himself in front of her, his face covered in smiles.

"Ees a wonderful party, Shelley. We are thanking you so much for including our falafels in your buffet."

"Including them?" Shelley motioned to a group of guests happily digging into their falafels, which someone had labeled "veggie balls." "We've replenished the falafel tray twice already. They're a total hit."

Awadallah beamed at her. "We are so happy with what you do for us." His smile faded. "But my son tells me you are leaving this agency."

"Um, yes, I am." She looked up and saw her father approach Ross. Ross bent his head to listen, but his gaze remained on her.

"You are going to other agency?" Awadallah asked hopefully.

"I, um..." She turned slightly so that she didn't have to watch Ross watching her. For all she knew, the man could read lips. "I'm not sure where I'll be."

"Well, please to let me know. I bring falafel account to you."

"Oh." She tuned in completely then. Fadah Awadallah wanted to be her client. "Thank you, I'll do that."

He bowed and turned. Careful not to look back at Ross, she moved in the opposite direction, which pointed her toward the ladies' room. The line still snaked out the door.

"Don't even think about cutting in," a familiar female voice said.

Shelley looked up to see Miranda Smith from Custom Cleavage standing in line beside a tall, good-looking man. "This is Blake Summers," Miranda said. "He's only going as far as the door."

The man smiled one of those blinding flashes of white teeth. "Another hope dashed. Here I thought I was finally going to see the inside of a ladies' room."

"Not in this lifetime." Miranda leaned closer to talk to Shelley. "Selena asked me to come and check out the grand opening. She was very impressed by you."

"I think she was just grateful I didn't kill her on the court."

Miranda grinned. "Well, that, too." She dropped her voice to a whisper. "We heard you're leaving the agency. We still want you to pitch."

"But—"

"Wherever you end up. I hope you're taking Luke Skyler with you."

The other woman's gaze slid beyond her. Shelley felt a

prickle of awareness run up her spine, and knew without being told that Ross was headed their way. Straightening, Shelley fought the urge to flee. This was her night, hers and Judy's. She didn't have to run just because he was coming. But she didn't have to stay and talk to him, either.

Telling herself she was simply feeling too good about the evening to let him spoil it, she smiled at Miranda and Blake and prepared to bail. "Thanks so much," she said, already beginning to move. "Tell her I appreciate the vote of confidence. I'll keep you posted."

Moving as quickly as she could without appearing to be in a hurry, Shelley looked for Judy. She caught a glimpse of her and Craig, their heads bent in conversation. This, she thought, was good. Or at least it would be if Brett O'Connor, who had apparently freed himself from the throng of women around Wiley Haynes, wasn't headed directly their way.

chapter 30

Judy Blumfeld looked into her husband's eyes. And he looked into hers. He was still dressed in a business suit, and his tie was slightly rumpled. It sounded corny, but it was as if someone pressed the mute button and carved out a slice of quiet around them. She felt the rest of the room recede.

His face was both achingly familiar and horribly unreadable.

"You've created quite an event," he said.

She searched his eyes, unable to tell from his tone of voice whether he'd meant it as a compliment. "Thank you. I think."

"I didn't realize the magnitude of what you were doing." He paused. "I didn't understand at all."

Once again, she was unsure of his intent. She felt him treading with care, as if she were some unknown client he didn't want to offend, but wasn't quite sure how to handle. His uncertainty gave her hope.

"I wasn't sure when I started that I could make this"—she motioned to include the space filled with people—"happen. But I did it. I created this."

He nodded. "It's very impressive."

There was another silence; one she wanted to fill with questions. But something told her to go slow.

"How've you been?" she asked.

She was expecting an automatic "fine," but he surprised her with honesty. "Hurt," he said quietly. "Angry." He paused. "Confused."

She smiled sadly. "Me, too."

They contemplated each other for a few long moments. She had what she'd been wanting: his complete and undivided attention. This was not the time or the place she would have chosen, but it might be the only one she'd get.

"We need to sit down and talk," he said.

These were the words she'd been waiting for, but suddenly they seemed ominous, unwelcome. What if what he wanted to say wasn't at all what she was beginning to realize she wanted to hear?

"Craig, I—"

"There you are!" Brett O'Connor's voice sliced into the quiet surrounding them and ripped it to shreds. Music and conversation poured in as Brett stepped up next to her. Shelley was with him.

"Hi, Craig." Shelley clung to Brett's arm, but whether she was trying to make it look as if they were together or attempting to haul him out of there, Judy didn't know.

"What's *he* doing here?" Craig asked.

"He who?" Shelley began. "You mean—"

Judy cut her off. "I invited him."

Judy looked away from her husband to study the other man. Brett was taller and broader, and everything about him was bright and shiny. He might have stepped out of the pages of *GQ*, or arrived on a white horse. He was the great unknown, and therefore exciting and mysterious.

But he hadn't contributed to her children's DNA. Or held her hand through two hard labors and a miscarriage. Nor had he sat up all night with her in a hospital waiting room while her father underwent bypass surgery. Or listened to her complaints about her mother while knowing not to chime in himself. He hadn't seen her in the morning without makeup. Or lived through twenty years of redecorating.

What in the world had she been thinking?

"Well, uninvite him." Craig's voice was firm, the one he normally reserved for the courtroom.

"Who's he?" Brett O'Connor sounded confused, as well he might. And slightly belligerent.

"He's my husband," she said. "And those two boys over there"—she pointed out Jason and Sammy, who were stationed at the dessert table—"those are my sons."

Craig gave Judy a look she'd never seen before. "Get rid of him, Judy. Get rid of him now. Before I forget myself and take a swing at him."

"Hey!" Brett shook off Shelley's arm.

"And if you want to talk about *us*—our family—our life—I'll be at home tomorrow between two and five." He gave Brett a withering glance and then turned back to Judy. "I'm going to assume you remember how to get there."

***

Craig stormed off to find Jason and Sammy. Shelley stayed with Judy while she stammered out an explanation and an apology to Brett O'Connor. Together, they watched him leave.

"Well," Judy managed. "That was fun." Her voice shook and her eyes were bright with unshed tears.

"Yeah, a total barrel of laughs."

Judy offered a lopsided smile and drew in a shaky breath. "OK, I'm going to go close out the silent bids. And then we need to end this sucker."

"I'm with you." Shelley gave Judy's shoulder a squeeze. She wanted to offer more but had no idea what. Craig had placed the ball squarely in his wife's court. "Just let me know what I can do."

"Thanks."

Shelley watched her sister move through the crowd, small yet mighty. She, too, was ready to call it a night; all of the personal drama had left her oddly keyed up.

She was still watching Judy when she felt a presence materialize beside her. When she heard Ross's voice, she realized she'd been both avoiding and waiting for this moment.

"You left early today."

Shelley turned slowly and looked up into his blue eyes. Her heart was racing, but he didn't need to know that. "Gee, if I hadn't already quit you could fire me. For breach of manners. Or, I don't know, maybe for acting like a child?"

He looked at her as if she were, in fact, some silly little girl. Which made her want to stamp her foot and carry on a bit. Even under the best of circumstances, he had that effect on her.

He shrugged and smiled. "If the Prada fits..."

"Good grief." She didn't actually stamp her foot, but it was a close thing. "Do you really still believe that's all I am?"

His eyes twinkled briefly then grew serious again. "No, I don't. I think you're a hell of a lot more than you let on."

She relaxed slightly, which was the most she could manage when he was standing this close.

"And I'll tell you something else." He spoke softly, just for her. "This thing between us? It's not over."

"Oh, yes, it is," she said. "Because I'm not interested. Not even a little bit."

He leaned closer so that she could feel his warm breath on her cheek. She was a complete sucker for warm breath, especially his.

"Liar." He said it so softly she had to lean closer to hear him, which allowed that warm breath to tickle the sensitive spot at the nape of her neck.

The pure male force of him held her there; the tickle of his breath welded her feet to the floor as surely as a fly caught in the sticky weavings of a spider's web. This was how one ended up in a supply closet or the wrong room at the Four Seasons.

The screech of a microphone, followed by the sound of Judy's amplified voice announcing the winner of the first piece of tire art, released her. The wave of applause reminded her of where she was. And with whom. Shelley took a step back. "The only thing I'm planning between us is distance," she said.

And possibly some competition. She had three potential clients right here in this room. Atlanta was a big city, full of potential clients. "Excuse me. I need to go help Judy."

She walked away from him feeling virtuous and, she

assured herself, not the least bit regretful. She was NOT thinking about what might have been.

Like the carriage reverting to a pumpkin in *Cinderella,* Tire World turned back into a tire store at midnight. The auctioned art had been taken, the sound system removed, and the buffet tables and bars broken down and carted off. Only the Schwartzes and Wiley Haynes remained.

With Harvey and Miriam looking on, Shelley and Judy said good night to their ecstatic client.

"Ya'll did an outstanding job, that's for sure," he said. "I never would have guessed you little ladies had all that in you, but it was bang-up."

Shelley gritted her teeth at the "little ladies" and saw Judy do the same. Smiling their thanks, they walked out of the tire store side by side, bracketed between their parents just as they had so often been as children. The symbolism was not lost on Shelley. But she was thirty-three, too old to be so defined by her family; too old to be craving approval she couldn't seem to earn.

In the now-silent parking lot their footsteps crunched loudly on the pavement. They stopped under a streetlight; her parents' and Shelley's cars were the only two left in the lot.

"Mr. Haynes is right," her mother said, "the evening was a great success." She looked pointedly at their father.

He cleared his throat and Shelley tensed anew. Materially, Harvey Schwartz was generous to a fault, but he could be a tightwad with his praise. Two weeks ago he'd found her so wanting he'd decided to sell his company. This was the closest to alone she'd been with him since then. She was very much afraid of what might—or might not—be said.

When her father didn't speak, her mother shot him another look. Then she turned to Judy. "Why don't I give you a ride home?" she asked. "I have a few things I'd like to talk to you about."

Panic crossed Judy's face and she turned a beseeching look toward Shelley. Then her mother said, "Shelley can drop Daddy at the house," and Shelley and Harvey Schwartz's features sprang into matching mirrors of panic.

A desperate scan of the deserted parking lot confirmed that there was no way out. It had been two weeks and Shelley had failed to produce measurable results; it seemed Miriam Schwartz was already taking over.

"All right," Shelley blustered, "but I'll have my cell phone on if you need me, Jude."

"Right," Judy said, though all four of them knew Judy would never get the chance to call for reinforcements.

In her BMW, Shelley and her father passed the first few blocks in silence. Her father stared out the window at the darkness while she attempted to brace for whatever was going to come.

As she slowed for the first red light, he cleared his throat and shifted uncomfortably in his seat. "I, um, I believe I owe you an apology."

Floored, Shelley stared straight ahead at the light, which was a very bright red and seemed to last forever.

"Your mother has pointed out to me that my expectations of you may have been too, er, low for too long."

The light turned green, but she couldn't seem to lift her foot off the brake pedal.

"And," he cleared his throat again, "then, when you were finally trying to stand on your own, I, um, judged you too quickly."

Headlights came up behind them and Shelley was forced to find the gas pedal. Her mind was fully occupied with her father's words. She drove in silence, trying to process them.

"Actually, you were right," he continued. "I did impose a double standard. I didn't give you a fair shake."

She remained silent, letting him speak. His words flowed over her—stilted, yet soothing at the same time. They began to fill in the empty spot inside her that she'd been trying to plug with all the wrong things.

"I, um, used your involvement with Ross as an excuse to sell the company." He continued to look at the passing scenery, but his words picked up speed, became more heartfelt. "You've proven yourself, Shelley. I saw the rough cut of the Furniture Forum commercials today—they're first-rate. And tonight was a huge success, huge. You have what it takes to make it in this business. You finally got it together and I forced you to quit."

He looked at her then. She could feel his gaze on her in the darkness. Pressing lightly on the brake, she slowed for the turn into her parents' neighborhood and actually held her breath.

"I'm so sorry, sweetheart."

"Oh, Daddy." Her heart squeezed painfully. "After all my screwups it's no wonder you couldn't recognize a true breakthrough when I had it."

His apology touched her and she felt love and gratitude flood through her. But it was his acknowledgment of her ability, his sincere praise, that freed her from something heavy and clanging she hadn't even realized she'd been carrying around.

"If you want to become the Schwartz in Schwartz and Associates, the firm's still mine to do with as I will."

The moisture pressed against her eyelids as she pulled into her parents' driveway. The house was dark; her mother hadn't gotten back from dropping Judy off yet. She hoped her sister's ride home had been as liberating.

"What about Ross Morgan?"

Her father studied her calmly. "Ross Morgan's a survivor. And he understands what family means."

It was a non-answer, but at the moment Shelley didn't care. She was too busy examining the new paths now stretching out before her. Her options kept expanding, but instead of feeling anxious about the choices she faced, she felt a stirring of anticipation. Whatever path she traveled, she'd be taking her hard-won knowledge and her father's approval with her.

Her father. She considered him now, the beak of his nose, the determined chin, the intelligent brown eyes. He'd been carrying her in one way or another since she'd played in this driveway as a child. Perhaps it was the lack of expectation he'd just apologized for, or maybe she'd just taken longer than most to grow up. The past no longer felt so important, because she was no longer afraid of the future.

"You go on ahead and sell, Daddy. You don't need to worry about me."

"Now, sweetheart..." He paused as the garage door went up in front of them and her mother drove past them and inside to park. Their mother had apparently whipped Judy into shape in half the time it was taking her father to deal with her. She hoped Judy had survived.

"No, I'm serious. You created that agency and you deserve every penny Chase Miller is willing to pay you. I could never live with myself if I thought I'd stood in the way."

They sat together and watched the garage door go down. Lights flickered on in the house. The last was the lamp in the front window, the one that had always been left on when one of the girls was out.

She leaned across the seat to wrap her arms around her father's neck. "I love you, Daddy. And I appreciate everything you've done for me. But it's time for me to make my own name instead of trying to live up to yours."

He pulled back and looked right into her eyes, trying to read them there in the dark. "You sure?"

"I'm sure. Now, you'd better get on inside before Mom comes out and hauls you in."

She waited while her father walked slowly up the driveway, and waved back to her mother when she opened the front door for him. Her parents hugged in the sliver of light from that lamp in the window, their heads bent in conversation. And then the door closed behind them.

Shelley drove home with her thoughts.

chapter 31

The next day at 4:59 P.M., Judy rang the doorbell of her home. Mouth dry, palms sweaty, she waited on the welcome mat, in front of her stained-glass sidelights, for someone to open the door.

Then Craig stood in the open doorway. He took note of her lack of luggage, saw that she'd left her car in the driveway rather than the garage. He didn't comment, but stepped back so she could enter.

Wiping her palms on her pants, she followed him through the entry and past the formal living and dining rooms. The scent of lemon and freshly polished wood teased her nostrils, and she sighed with relief at the first sight of her kitchen; Eva, or at least someone with ovaries, had put it back to rights.

"Where are the boys?" she asked, noting the bottle of red wine breathing on the counter. Arrangements of fresh flowers sat on the counter and in the center of the kitchen table.

"Out." His look was steady. "With friends." He locked his gaze with hers. "They could be spending the night out. That's kind of up to you."

Judy swallowed and slid onto a bar stool. The granite countertops gleamed and the copper flecks sparkled. Her husband seemed so sure, so forceful. So completely focused on her. It was what she'd wanted; she didn't want to blow it.

"About Brett," she began, wanting to get what she knew would be Craig's biggest issue out of the way. She'd spent the day practicing how to explain the flirtation, and had imagined segueing into a cozy heart-to-heart.

Craig walked behind the counter and poured them each a glass of wine, then came around to take the stool next to hers. "Did you sleep with him?"

"No." She met his gaze straight on, accepted a glass of wine. "I'm married."

He digested her answer. There was a flicker of relief in his eyes. "Good. Me, too." He leaned forward to set his wineglass down and she caught a whiff of the Boucheron cologne she'd bought him for his last birthday.

Through the kitchen window she could see their next-door neighbor getting ready to mow his lawn. She couldn't understand how everything could look so ordinary when the future of her marriage hung in the balance. She studied Craig, pondering her next move. Her mother had given her her marching orders last night, but Judy didn't want to march anywhere. She intended to communicate her needs and expectations, and then she was going to listen to his.

"OK." She checked Brett O'Connor off her mental list. "Shall we move on?"

"Absolutely." He looked deep into her eyes. "Talk to me. I'm listening."

"Say that again."

"I said, I'm listening."

She blinked. She'd been prepared for argument or evasion, but not for total cooperation. She hadn't expected the wine and flowers, either. Or the way her heart was pounding in her chest.

Please God, she prayed silently, *don't let either of us screw this up.*

"I want to hear everything you have to say."

Judy blinked again and tried to regroup. She'd allotted a good half an hour to getting Craig to utter those words; he'd done it in five minutes.

He was still looking into her eyes, still completely focused on her. "If you tell me what you want, Jude, I'll do my best to deliver."

OK. She tried to fast-forward past all the rational arguments she'd prepared and didn't seem to need. She took a sip of wine to give her brain time to get to the bottom line. "I want—no, I need to work. I'm good at it."

He took a sip of his wine and nodded, but she was too nervous to count on nonverbal communication.

"This is not negotiable."

"Not a problem," he said.

His total capitulation was throwing her completely. She searched her mind for her other points.

"And, um, we need to talk more and spend more time with each other," she said. "I can't stand how we've been taking each other for granted."

"Agreed."

"And we have to make sure the boys understand that I'm not a servant here. Everyone has to help and contribute to our family."

"Yes, that's important, too."

He was utterly sincere; she could hear it in his voice, see it in his eyes. He was looking at her as if she were the most interesting woman in the universe. Something deep and primal stirred inside her.

"You," she whispered, "you have to tell me what you want, too."

His gaze was steady. "You," he said softly. "Just you. The house felt so empty while you were gone. You're the center, Jude, the heart of us. You're all I want. The rest is just . . . details."

He leaned forward and brought his lips to hers. And then he kissed her. Completely. Thoroughly. And with such gentleness it made her want to weep.

Judy pressed as close to Craig as the bar stool would allow. She wanted him—both physically and emotionally—with a certainty that took her breath away.

His lips brushed the side of her neck and his teeth teased at her earlobe. He pulled back to look into her eyes.

She couldn't believe how turned on she was. By Craig Blumfeld. And the life she wanted with him.

At her nod, he kicked his bar stool out of the way and moved to stand between her thighs.

"OK," she whispered as she looped her arms up around his neck, "sex now, details later."

His hands slipped under her buttocks and he lifted her up against him. Judy wrapped her legs around Craig's waist and held on with her thighs as he carried her to their bed.

The next morning she snuggled up against him and breathed in the scent of husband and home. She didn't think she'd ever get enough of either.

With a contented groan, Craig flipped onto his side to face her. Idly, he traced the curve of her hip with his hand. "Do you want to go out for breakfast and then over to Shelley's to get your things?"

She shook her head and cuddled closer, molding her body to his. She was home, where she was meant to be. This morning she didn't intend to set so much as a foot outside. "Let's stay right here for as long as possible."

Later, she thought, when the boys were home and it was time to start putting their new life together, would be soon enough to admit that her bags were already sitting outside in the car.

"Are you sure Rabbi Jordan is going to be there?" Nina slid into Shelley's car and tucked the hem of her black dress under her legs. A beautifully arranged plate of chocolate-covered matzo sat on her lap.

"Nobody turns down an invitation to my mother's seder." Shelley looked at the offering in her friend's lap. "Did you make that?"

"Um-hm. Right after I got rid of all the *chametz* in my apartment." She pronounced the *ch* sound with the correct Hebrew inflection.

"*Chametz?*"

"You know, all the food products that contain wheat, barley, oats, spelt, or rye that has leavened," Nina explained.

"Yes, I know, but . . . did you say *spelt*?"

"I'm assuming that's some sort of grain."

"Nina, where did you learn all this?" She herself tried to eat matzo during the week of Passover, but had never actually gone through her condo to get rid of all traces of... *chametz*.

"Askmoses dot com. You can actually e-mail questions to rabbis and scholars. It's very informative."

Shelley turned to her friend. "Nina..." She wanted to warn her friend that rabbis, especially the old-school sort like Rabbi Jordan, might not be impressed with her command of Jewish trivia, or her burning need to...belong. Unlike other religions, the Jewish faith didn't seek converts and often made conversion difficult.

Nina's desire to marry the very men Shelley had been so arduously avoiding had seemed amusing at first, but it had become clear Nina was actually looking for something more than a man; she was soaking up the details of Judaism like a sponge, throwing herself into the knowing, striving to carve out a place for herself. Nina's quest humbled her; Shelley was simply Jewish by birth. And while she'd never been ashamed of or tried to hide her heritage, she hadn't really embraced it, either. Or made it at all central to her life.

It was just a part of who she was, like her eye color and the part of town in which she'd grown up. Something she'd taken for granted and never had to prove herself worthy of.

Like her job in her father's firm, it had been handed to her and unappreciated.

The truth smote her: Like Moses and the Children of Israel, she had wandered aimlessly in the desert. It was time for her to find her own Promised Land.

When they arrived at her parents', cars already filled the

driveway and spilled out along the curb in front. Shelley saw Judy's car alongside Delilah's vintage Cadillac. Sarah Mendelsohn's Mercedes was parked near the mailbox, and a florist's delivery was loading table arrangements through the front door.

"We're here," Shelley cried as they walked through the kitchen door.

"Hello, darlings." Her mother poked her head into the kitchen. "Has anybody seen Harvey? He was supposed to pick up those extra folding chairs and now he's disappeared." She flew back out without waiting for an answer.

Delilah bustled over and took the chocolate-covered matzo from Nina and set it with the other desserts. Hands on hips, she gave Nina a once-over. "Why, I do believe you're starting to actually *look* Jewish," she said. "Before you know it, you're going to be standing under a *chuppah*"—she pronounced the Hebrew word for a wedding canopy with the appropriate *kh* sound—"I'm going to get me a front-row seat for that."

While her mother flitted in and out of the kitchen with Sarah Mendelsohn at her heels, Delilah put Shelley and Nina to work setting up the seder plates that would be placed on each table. Judy peeled hard-boiled eggs while Great-aunt Sonya counted out bowls for saltwater and broke off tiny branches of parsley. Matzo ball soup simmered on the stove, and jars of gefilte fish sat on the counter next to plates dressed with lettuce leaves and horseradish.

Shelley moved to her sister and gave her a hug. "My condo's getting kind of messy. Anytime you'd like to come over and organize me again ..."

"Ha," she said. "My focus right now is teaching my husband and sons how to organize themselves. No more picking up after everyone and feeling like a doormat." Her eyes glowed; Shelley couldn't remember ever seeing her so happy. "I'm taking a month to whip them into shape, and then I'm putting out my event-planning shingle."

"Good for you." Glad her sister had found her way, Shelley fought back the automatic twinge of envy. Her sister's life was so together—for real this time, not just on the outside—while hers was still so uncertain. Her eyes narrowed. "What did you bring for the seder?"

Judy laughed and reached for the grocery bags beside her. One by one she lifted out the boxes of matzo that were her contribution to the meal. She crossed her heart and raised her palm solemnly. "I did not bake a single thing."

"No flourless chocolate cake? No sponge anything?"

"It never even crossed my mind."

They high-fived and went back to work.

An hour later the tables, which stretched throughout the living room and dining room like some great cloth-covered train, were set and ready, and the rest of the guests began to arrive. The men, knowing better than to set foot in the overcrowded kitchen, milled together in the family room. They munched chopped liver on matzo crackers and pretended not to watch the Braves game on Harvey's big-screen TV.

Shelley left the kitchen to hug her father hello and have a word with Rabbi Jordan. Great-aunt Sonya's egretlike boyfriend, Horace Zinn, was talking to Howard Mellnick. Shelley's brother-in-law arrived with her nephews, and she couldn't help noticing he wore the same loopy smile her sister had on. Soon a small herd of kids were romping through the house, tromping down to the basement for Ping-Pong and video games. A baby's cry pierced the room, and she found Uncle Abe cradling his newest grandson in his arms.

On her way back to the kitchen, Shelley swooped down on the head table and switched two place cards. Even God had sent an angel occasionally to set things up for him.

Just when the decibel level threatened to reach the breaking point, Miriam Schwartz came out of the kitchen with her bevy of helpers clustered around her. "Shall we begin?" she said, and then everyone went about searching out their seat assignments, settling kids at age-appropriate tables—close enough for supervision, far enough away to allow for enjoyment.

"Oh!" Nina yelped with pleasure when she saw her dining companions. Shelley was pleased to see that the rabbi's small frown of displeasure was countered by Howard Mellnick's warm smile.

Shelley took in the faces surrounding her, most of them as familiar as her own, but with a few unknowns to help leaven the meal. Thank God her mother had not felt the need to shove someone acceptable at her right now; she had all she could handle trying to figure out her life and forget about Ross Morgan. The thought of beginning anew both energized and terrified her.

Her father, as leader of the service, reclined slightly on a pillow. At the opposite end of the head table, Rabbi Jordan did the same. Soon her youngest nephew would ask the first of the four questions: "Why is this night different from all other nights?" The evening would be spent in the ceremonial answering of those questions.

It was then that she noticed the two empty seats in the middle of the long table; a heartbeat after that, the doorbell rang. Her father stood and walked to the front door.

When he opened it, Ross Morgan and a woman who looked old enough to be his mother stepped into the room.

Shelley gasped as her father clapped Ross on the shoulder, embraced the older woman as if she were a long-lost friend, and led them forward. "Everybody, this is Patricia Morganstern and her son, Ross."

Ross smiled a casual hello. "Sorry we're late. My mother's flight was delayed."

Conversation resumed around her, but Shelley barely heard it. She watched in amazement as Ross Morgan politely seated his mother and then took his own chair opposite her. Ross Morgan had a mother and her name was Morganstern. And they were here for Passover.

That meant Ross Morgan was . . .

He placed his napkin on his lap and picked up his Haggadah, the Passover prayer book, not having to think twice about the fact that it would be read from right to left.

Ross Morgan, the tall, blond, athletic man whom she wanted to hate and whom—much to her dismay—she continued to lust after and think about, was JEWISH.

How could she not have known this?

And why did she have to know this now?

She swung her gaze to her mother, who made a point of not looking back. Her father avoided her gaze, too. The only one looking right at her was the one person she couldn't believe was here. He sent her an inappropriately saucy wink and then settled back in his chair. A moment later the seder began.

Shelley heard none of it. Not the retelling of her ancestors' backbreaking life under the cruel Pharaoh of Egypt, not the ten plagues that God brought down on the Egyptians to free the Jews, not even the parting of the Red Sea after Moses, with God's help, forced the Pharaoh to let his people go.

She roused momentarily when Nina, who was called on to read responsively during the service, did so in flawless Hebrew, much to Rabbi Jordan's amazement. And again later when Howard Mellnick offered a thumbs-up to Nina, who was chosen to open the front door for the spirit of Elijah and who led the singing of the hauntingly beautiful Hebrew song that was sung to him.

But mostly her mind was stuck on one unavoidable fact: Ross Morgan was JEWISH, and her parents had known it all along.

Worse, Ross Morgan was exactly the sort of man her parents would have chosen for her had she not been rejecting the exact sort of man her parents would have chosen for her. He was exactly the sort of man her father would have— make that HAD—chosen as a son and successor.

It was absolutely and completely MACHIAVELLIAN. Which meant there was only one person in this universe who could have come up with it.

chapter 32

At the conclusion of the seder, Shelley got up from the table and walked, on rubbery legs, upstairs to her childhood bedroom. She stayed there for a long time, sitting on the pink floral-covered twin bed and staring at her reflection in the white oval mirror over the dresser.

She ignored Nina and her sister when they called to her through the door. Howard Mellnick knew better than to try to talk her out.

Downstairs, the kitchen door swung open and closed and there was the murmur of voices and the clatter of silverware as the tables got cleared and the evening drew to a close.

The spoiled, immature part of her wanted to fling herself down the stairs so that she could shriek out her anger and humiliation. She pictured her family's faces if she were to do that, then imagined Howard Mellnick's embarrassment; imagined him handing her parents back all the money they'd spent on her counseling sessions. "I tried," he'd say, "but she refuses to grow up."

"No," she said aloud. "No more steps back." She'd taken so many she should be in Florida by now.

And why, exactly, was she so upset? Because she'd been manipulated and kept in the dark? Her mother's specialty was manipulating the members of her family for their own good. It was a fact of life. What would having a scene about it accomplish?

By nine-thirty people had started to leave. She knew she should go down and at least pretend to be an adult, but she couldn't seem to make herself move.

"Shelley?" Ross Morgan's voice startled her out of her reverie. "Are you coming out?"

"No!"

"Don't be silly."

"Go away!" she shouted, feeling incredibly stupid. "And don't call me silly!"

She waited for the sound of retreating footsteps but there were none. The doorknob turned and the door opened. Ross Morgan stepped inside.

"I'm Jewish," he said, "and I have a mother. It's no big deal."

"Yeah, which must be why no one bothered to mention it to me."

He came closer and stopped in front of the bed.

She didn't ask him to sit down. She was too angry and embarrassed to make anything easy for him.

"There are a few other things that haven't been mentioned yet," he said, "and I guess this is as good a time as any to mention them."

She shrugged. Her reflection in the mirror told her she was putting on a pretty good show of indifference.

"For one thing," he said, "I didn't come into Schwartz and Associates with the goal of ousting you. I was given an opportunity that meant everything to me at the time, and I took it." He paused, obviously searching for the right words. "I wasn't attempting to take your place or steal your father's affections—not that I ever could. Believe me, if anyone understands the importance of a father/child relationship, it's me."

She stared at him, mute. It was one of the first personal things he'd ever told her. She sensed its importance, saw the promise of more in his eyes, but she was holding so tightly to the shreds of her indignation she couldn't grasp on to anything else.

"I'm sorry you got hurt," Ross said. "I wasn't trying to string you along or make you jump through hoops. It just seems to have worked out that way."

He smiled, but it wasn't the cocky grin she was used to. "You definitely proved yourself, Shelley." His smile turned rueful. "You may have done it just to spite me, but you did it. You'd be dammed good at running an agency. I'm truly sorry it won't be your father's."

She felt herself soften, but resisted it. Much safer to let him remain "the obstacle" or "the enemy." Lust was one thing, the feelings he was tugging on right now were much more vulnerable.

Shelley rose to face him. Ignoring the promise she saw in his eyes, she reminded herself that she was the injured party; she was the one who'd been duped. It was easy enough to be magnanimous when you had won so handily. "Is that it?" she asked.

"Just one more thing," he said carefully, "because I don't want you to be confused about my intentions. The supply closet," he said, looking into her eyes, "was all about sex." He paused. "Los Angeles wasn't."

So what in the world did that mean? How dare he turn everything so upside down and then expect her to react to it? Her eyes narrowed and her body went still.

"The thing is..." He paused, and she could tell he was waiting for her to chime in, but she couldn't for the life of her think of the right thing to say. "I'm really bowled over by who you've become. The old Shelley Schwartz was a little girl looking for attention; the new Shelley Schwartz is one hell of a woman. I'd like to know her a lot better."

He stood, waiting while she tried to process what he'd said.

Part of her wanted to tell him to get the hell out of here and leave her alone. The other part wanted to beg him to stay. In the end she couldn't do either.

"Well, thanks for the insights." She hated how cold she sounded, but she was holding on to her emotions by some really slim threads. Anger, humiliation, hope, affection; everything was all jumbled up and seething inside her.

Unable to sort it out, she raised her chin and took a step away. "Only I'm not a before-or-after choice. I'm sort of a package deal. And I think there's been a little too much water over our dam to try to start from scratch."

He looked at her steadily as if he could see right through her bravado to the churning mass of uncertainty inside.

And then he nodded. "Got it." His smile was brittle. "I guess I'll be going, then."

He turned and a moment later he was gone.

Shelley stared at her reflection in the mirror for a while. The murmur of Ross and her father talking drifted up the stairs. Then there was a female voice that had to be Ross's mother's. The front door opened and closed.

She sank back down on the bed, stunned. If she let herself think about what had just happened she was going to flip out. She grabbed a pillow and hugged it to her chest. She needed to put her mind elsewhere; needed to put it somewhere productive where it wouldn't keep replaying all the stupid things she'd just said. Or wondering what might have happened if she hadn't shut Ross Morgan down so thoroughly.

YOU'D BE DAMNED GOOD AT RUNNING AN AGENCY. Ross's statement flickered through her consciousness. Ross Morgan thought she was ready to head her own firm. Shelley closed her eyes and focused on his words. In her mind, they were capitalized and had a line underneath them.

Ross thought she could run an agency. She released her hold on the pillow. And so did three potential clients.

Breathing deeply, Shelley attempted to let go of her anger and embarrassment. She tried to picture it floating up into the stratosphere and out of her life. Slowly her mind opened and cleared until the only thing filling it were Ross's words: *YOU'D BE DAMNED GOOD AT RUNNING AN AGENCY*. And her father's *You have what it takes to make it in this business.*

The correct path stretched out in front of her, obvious

and unavoidable; just like Ross Morgan's Jewishness would have, if only she'd bothered to look.

Ross Morgan and her father were right.

Her brain began to race as it sorted through ideas. She could do it; she could start a small boutique agency with an emphasis on media accounts; one that would allow her to stay on the cutting edge creatively. There was no reason to try to duplicate her father's success when what she really wanted was to create her own. And she could invite her sister to join her.

Clinging to those thoughts, she left her room and started down the stairs. The sound of female voices reached her from the kitchen. Delilah's could be heard above the others, organizing and cajoling; Delilah's sister Delores was in there, too, helping wash her mother's crystal and fine china. As Shelley crossed the foyer, they began to sing an old slave song they'd taught the women of Shelley's family one year in recognition of the Hebrews' years of bondage.

The words of the song seeped inside her. Shelley felt freer than she had in years; free to move forward, free to be her own person. If she hadn't just rejected him so completely, she would have called Ross Morgan to thank him.

The dining room was empty, the tables already cleared. Shelley found her father alone in the living room. Waiting. She walked to the sofa and dropped down next to him.

"I feel like I was caught on *Candid Camera* with my pants down, and everyone was in on the joke but me."

Her father smiled. "It wasn't like that."

"No?" she asked. "What was it like?"

"Long version or short?"

Shelley glanced toward the kitchen door. "Does Nina need a ride home?"

"No, your mother asked Dr. Mellnick to drop her."

It was Shelley's turn to smile. "A very busy woman, my mother." She crossed one leg over the other and folded her arms across her chest. "Tell me."

"Well, let's see." Her father settled back into the sofa. "Benjamin Morganstern was my roommate in college. We were fraternity brothers, best men in each other's weddings. But it turned out my friend had a gambling problem that none of us knew about."

"What happened?"

"In the end it devoured him and destroyed his family. He left them one day and never came back."

"Oh, God."

"Yeah. My friend left his family drowning in debt. The only thing standing between them and homelessness was his seventeen-year-old son."

"Ross?"

Her father nodded. "Ross had already managed to put himself and one of his younger sisters through college before I learned what had happened."

Ross Morgan had become his family's sole support at the age of seventeen. Shelley's heart ached for the boy who had been forced to become a man. Just this evening she'd pretty much told him to get lost.

"I tried to help then, but the only thing he ever accepted from me was a job; and he's more than earned that."

"No wonder he's so frugal."

"His only indulgence is that car; everything else he's made has gone to take care of his mother and sisters."

Shelley shook her head, still trying to wrap her brain around it. How could she have been drawn to someone she'd understood so little. "Good God, watching me throw money around must have been pure torture." She was embarrassed at how unabashedly frivolous she'd been. Ashamed by how childishly she'd pushed him away.

And how had Ross felt, watching Harvey Schwartz stick by his daughter no matter how badly she behaved or how often she screwed up? How painful that must have been for someone whose own father had abandoned him so completely.

"Yes, I think we can safely say you drove him crazy. But that's not always such a bad thing." Her father's smile faded. "I'm sorry Ben didn't see how well his son turned out. But then, maybe he didn't deserve to."

"I guess Mother assumed I'd never appreciate a man like Ross." And of course she wouldn't have before; hadn't even an hour ago. Not in a way that counted.

"I told her not to bother; that our approval coupled with a man's suitability was the absolute kiss of death for you. And she finally listened." He smiled, remembering. "In her own very twisted way."

Shelley sighed at the ironic beauty of her mother's plan. If her mother had tried to push Ross Morgan on her, she would have run as far and as fast as possible, would probably have turned him over to Nina. So they could produce perfect blond Jewish babies and live happily every after. Nina would have found out and appreciated him for what he was. Her mother had had to trick her. And even then Shelley had managed to screw it up.

Standing, she dropped a kiss on the top of her father's

head. Then she walked across the room and grasped the kitchen door handle. Without warning, she pulled it toward her.

Her mother straightened quickly. She looked a bit sheepish, what with the empty drinking glass still raised to her ear.

"My mother, the Jewish Lucy Ricardo." Shelley leaned against the doorjamb. "Where's Ethel?"

Sarah Mendelsohn straightened beside her.

"Well, I hope you two are happy," Shelley said to her parents as she hunted down her keys and bid farewell to Delilah and Delores. It was all she could do not to cry over how badly she'd bungled everything. "The first perfectly-not-Jewish Jewish guy I've ever met and you let me go and muck it all up."

She kissed them both on the cheek and left. But it was hours later before she could fall asleep.

The thing about life, Shelley thought, as she raced to lunch with Nina two weeks after her Passover debacle, was that just when you got one part of it under control, some other part of it went all to hell.

Her plans for an agency were coming together almost effortlessly. It turned out that as the Miller-Schwartz merger progressed, the creative shake-up proved much larger than anyone anticipated. Chase Miller was driven and opinionated. Luke Skyler had had one meeting with him and his creative director and decided to jump ship.

Ross Morgan was evidently still riding the waves there; her father kept her posted in that offhand way of his as if she weren't hanging on every word or wishing she could wind the clocks back to just before she'd told Ross Morgan to take a hike. Her father was taking her mother on an extended trip to Europe as soon as the sale went through. And Judy had agreed to hang her shingle beside Shelley's.

Right now she was watching Nina eat and living vicariously through Nina's torrid love affair with Howard Mellnick.

"He says he loves to watch me eat, that most women have a hang-up about eating and that it's a pleasure to see someone enjoy her food."

"Boy, does he have the right girl."

"He's taking me home to meet his mother, Shelley." Nina reached over and helped herself to Shelley's last few French fries. "I'm scared to death."

"Of what?" Shelley pushed her plate toward her friend. "You've been handling my Jewish mother since childhood; they're all pretty much the same. Just let her know you think her son is God's gift to the universe and that you plan to offer daily prayers of thanks that you met him. Then ask for her brisket and baked chicken recipes and make sure you don't cook them as well as she does. Oh—and try not to eat off her plate."

"And have you tried any of those things on *Ross's* mother?"

Shelley drained the last of her Diet Coke before Nina could get to it. "No, and I don't intend to."

"Don't be an ass, Shelley." Nina reached for the bun Shelley hadn't yet eaten. They tussled briefly over it; Shelley got a mouthful, Nina took the rest. "So he's Jewish and nobody told you. So you fell for him anyway. You're signing a lease this afternoon on your very own office space; your competition with him pushed you to greater heights. And you told me it was the best sex of your life. What exactly is the problem?"

The bread felt rocklike in her stomach. How did you tell your best friend, who was wild about a great guy who felt the same way about her, that the person you couldn't stop thinking about wasn't likely to call? That after she'd told him she wasn't interested, he'd taken her at her word? That now that she knew what a hero he was, there was no way he'd think she was a big enough hero for him.

Shrugging, she passed the bill to Nina, who'd eaten most of both their lunches anyway, and gathered up her things.

In her car her cell phone rang and she drove to her new office with her sister's happy voice trilling in her ear. "I signed my first event, Shelley. Oh, God, this feels great. And guess what? It was a referral from Craig. I'm going to come in tomorrow and lay out my office." She was still singing her husband's praises when Shelley pulled up in front of her new building.

Stomping into the shiny new lobby, Shelley took the elevator up to the sixth floor. Removing the For Lease sign, she used her key to open the door. Inside, she breathed in the smell of brand-new carpet and paint. Closing her eyes she envisioned furniture and people; Luke and her sister working beside her. She could hardly wait.

How ironic that now when her professional life was about to take off, her personal life was so totally nonexistent. It wasn't that she wasn't happy for Nina and Judy and her parents. It was just that her old kinds of choices were no longer attractive, and her current choice—well, the choice didn't seem to be hers to make.

Her footfalls were muffled on the carpet. Down the hallway, she poked her head into the small kitchen/lunchroom. Next to it was a supply closet. She opened the door and took in the empty shelves that ran along two walls. She planned to put the copy machine she'd just leased along the far wall.

Her eyes fluttered shut and she was transported back to the supply closet at Schwartz and Associates, where Ross Morgan had made love to her up against the Canon iR400. She supposed she should be grateful they hadn't accidentally copied any body parts during their mad coupling; not that she would mind a reminder of Ross Morgan's body parts right now. Or any other part of him, for that matter.

She missed him more than she could have imagined. Missed the calm reasonableness that had always set her teeth on edge, the quick wit on which she'd sharpened her own. It pained her to admit it, but she'd rather argue with Ross than agree with anyone else.

Because she'd been thinking about him, his voice didn't sound out of place at first. It came to her as if in a dream, a very yummy dream from which she did NOT want to wake.

"You know, for the longest time after that night in the supply closet, the faintest whiff of toner would make me think of you," he said.

Her eyes flew open. Without moving, she watched him walk toward her. He had a faint smile on his lips and a definite twinkle in his eye.

"I couldn't even drive by a Kinko's without getting an erection."

She fought the answering smile that tugged at her lips.

As he approached, her flesh goose-bumped with anticipation and her pulse kicked up.

Experimentally, she reminded herself that he was eminently suitable and that her parents wanted her to want him, but her ardor didn't dampen one bit.

He was tall and broad and incredibly sexy. Without the labels she'd always attached to him, he was much too attractive to resist.

"Stop where you are," she said.

If he got any closer she was going to wrestle him to the ground and have her way with him. And what would that accomplish?

He stopped where he was, which was almost right in front of her. "Just out of interest, I feel compelled to ask 'or what?'"

This was a good question. "Or we're going to have sex and probably regret it."

He shook his head. "I'm not going to regret it. And I don't mean to brag, but I'm pretty sure I can keep you from regretting it, too."

He took a step closer and sniffed. "You're not wearing toner right now, are you?"

Her heart was racing and she was pretty sure she could feel the blood rushing through her veins. "I don't think this has worked out so well for us in the past," Shelley said. "I mean, the last time we slept together you told me it was a mistake."

"It was."

"But it's not now?"

"We were working together then," he said reasonably. "That's never a good idea."

"And now?"

"Now the closest we're going to get to that is competing for accounts."

"It's not even going to *be* a competition," she corrected as a burst of adrenaline shot through her. "I plan to leave you choking in my dust."

"Yeah, I heard you got Skyler," Ross said. "He's good. But then, so are you. I don't have a problem with a little healthy competition." He was standing so close she could feel his warm breath on her cheek.

She wanted him, wanted him badly. And she wanted more than repartee and incredible sex. "The last time we saw each other I believe I told you to get lost." She swallowed. "And you did."

"I wasn't lost." He inched closer so that they were toe to toe and chest to chest. She could feel her body straining toward his.

"No?" She wasn't sure how a person's voice could break on a one-syllable word, but hers did. He seemed so calm and confident. She seemed to be quivering.

"So where were you?" She tried to match his confident tone and failed miserably.

He put a finger under her chin and tilted her face up to his. His blue eyes were clear and warm. "I thought I'd give you a little time to get over the fact that I'm perfect for you."

"Perfect? You?" She wanted to scoff, but couldn't quite pull it off.

"Well, you did once refer to me as stellar."

"No." She shook her head, but gently so as not to dislodge his finger. "I'm pretty sure I spit on stellar. And of course, you were awfully secretive about being Jewish."

"It wasn't a secret. You just weren't paying attention." He moved his hand to cup the side of her cheek and pulled her face close to his. Then he kissed her—one of those long, deep, soulful kisses that touched her everywhere at once.

OK, so maybe she'd have to give him stellar.

"I've wanted to apologize for Passover," she said. "I was just so surprised. And angry. Nothing seemed to be what I thought it was."

He kissed her again, and then he placed his hands on her waist and pulled her closer. Their bodies melded in all the right places. "No apologies needed," he said. "I just hope this whole religion/common background thing isn't going to be a problem for you."

Her breath caught in her throat as he sank to his knees and took her with him. "Well, I wouldn't call it a problem, exactly." She kissed him back with everything she had inside, delighted by what had sprung up between them. "But I do have a small request."

His lips were warm on hers, and his body promised all kinds of things that she could tell he was ready to deliver. "I'm willing to give whatever is . . . between us . . . a shot," she teased. "But you have to promise to keep it to yourself."

Shelley kissed him again and reached for his belt buckle as he held her tight. "We are definitely not mentioning this to our parents. After everything my mother put me through, there's no way I'm ready to make her this happy."

About the Author

Wendy lives with her husband and two sons in a testosterone-laden home in the suburbs of Atlanta. When not at one ballpark or another, she spends her time either writing or attempting to invent an automatic toilet seat-dropping device.

Readers can contact her through her Web site at www. ' authorwendywax.com.

Can't wait to join

Wendy Wax

in her next hilarious and sexy novel?

———————

Read on for a preview of
her new book...

Single in Suburbia

*On sale now
from Bantam*

Single in Suburbia

In the car lot of life, Amanda Sheridan decided, she was a Volvo station wagon with about 80,000 miles on it.

People said a woman should look at how a man treated his mother when deciding whether to marry him, but Amanda now knew, from painful personal experience, that a man's car-buying habits were a much better indicator.

In her family men bought good-quality cars and drove them until they stopped running; they racked up the miles and bragged about their odometer readings. And in most cases, their marriages lasted just as long.

In Rob's family, which Amanda had been a part of for almost twenty years, the men traded up. Every year they chose a new car and passed the year-old vehicle down to their wives. Occasionally a car might last a little longer if there was a teenager in the family, but as a rule, if you were a Sheridan, when your car's ashtray got dirty it was time to trade that sucker in.

Which went a long way toward explaining why Rob was test driving a BMW Z-3 convertible named Tiffany while Amanda, whose bench seats were sagging, appeared headed for the used-car lot.

Amanda scooped Wyatt's baseball socks out of the clean-clothes basket and tossed them on his bed then stashed a fresh stack of towels in the kids' linen closet. Pithy car metaphors notwithstanding, Amanda had no idea how she was supposed to get Rob, who appeared to be in the throes of a monumental midlife crisis at the age of forty-five, to come to his senses, and even less idea of how she'd go on alone if she failed.

It was now almost two months since that January morning when her husband admitted to lubricating another woman's carburetor; two long months since he'd moved out to park his, er, car, in a strange garage.

Amanda had spent the first month in denial and the second in a semi-comatose state from which she roused only long enough to take care of Meghan and Wyatt. She'd steadfastly kept her chin up in public, had even managed to adopt a "men will be boys" attitude that belied the gaping hole she felt in her heart and the knife wound in her back.

Still, despite the evidence to the contrary, she simply could not believe that Rob had stopped loving her when she wasn't finished loving him; could not believe that he'd looked her in the eye and told her that his feelings for her had died. Died! As if they were living, breathing things that she'd somehow managed to kill.

Her chest tightened.

Rob had moved out "to look for himself," but as far as she could tell, all he'd found was a fancy town house in a singles complex and the zippy little Tiffany.

In the kitchen she brewed a pot of coffee and pulled out a thermos to take to the ball field. She'd let two whole months slide by without resolution and had been spectacularly unsuccessful at forcing Rob to discuss the situation. But she'd been wrong to let Rob call all the shots. Two months was more than long enough to live in limbo; too long to be at the mercy of Rob Sheridan's libido.

If there was one thing she knew about her husband, and given his current behavior it might be the *only* thing she knew about him, he would be at Wyatt's season opener tonight. Which meant it was time to straighten her backbone and stop being such a wimp; time to give Rob an ultimatum: her or us; alone or together.

She'd just have to find the words that would make him realize what he was giving up and she'd do her best not to include the word "asshole" while she was doing it. But by the end of the evening, one way or another, she intended to regain control over her life.

"Are you ready, Wyatt?" She took a last look in the hall mirror and tried to squelch the butterflies tumbling in her stomach. She refused to dwell on the small wrinkles that radiated out from her eyes, the deepening grooves that now stretched across her forehead and bracketed her mouth. Better to focus on the unexpected weight loss that made her jeans fit the way they were meant to and the new cashmere sweater that she'd bought for the occasion.

"Just have to get my bag and cleats." Wyatt clattered down the stairs behind her and went into the garage. At thirteen, he was tall and lanky, already matching her five-eight and on his way toward his father's six-two.

Outside, the sun was setting and the temperature had started to drop. In Atlanta, the end of February was tricky; some days felt like spring, other days bit like mid-winter. She poured the entire pot of coffee into the thermos and took an extra moment to add cream and sweetener, though the way those butterflies were cavorting, she wasn't sure she'd be able to drink a drop.

"Last chance, Meghan!" she called up the back stairs.

Her daughter's door opened and a cacophony of what was supposed to be music billowed out around her. Meghan leaned over the balustrade, her dark hair falling forward to obscure her face. At fifteen, sarcasm was her friend. "Normally I'd love to go freeze my butt off for two hours just for the thrill of watching Wy play. But I've got a project due tomorrow." She offered a flip smile and a shrug. The beat of the music pulsed behind her.

"Your dad will be there."

Meghan went still. The flip smile fled and was replaced by a look of hurt so stark that Amanda had to look away. "Do you think I should come so he can pretend like he cares about me for a minute or two?"

Amanda made herself meet her daughter's pain-filled eyes. She watched Meghan's gaze sweep over her, taking in the new sweater and carefully made-up face.

"You're wasting your time, Mom. He's written us off like yesterday's news. And I, for one, am not planning to run after him."

Shrugging into her leather jacket, Amanda picked up the thermos and blankets. "No, no running," she promised as she said good-bye to Meghan and headed for the door.

And no begging, she added silently to herself.

Rob was the one who needed to beg their forgiveness and ask to come home.

And if he didn't?

Then she'd find the backbone to tell *him* to get lost. Right after she shoved his dipstick where the sun didn't shine.

The ball field parking lot was almost full by the time Amanda and Wyatt arrived. It was seven P.M. and the smell of hot dogs and burgers cooking on the grill outside the concession stand reached them as they got out of the van. There was no sign of Rob's car, but from one of the far fields came the crack of the bat and a huge cheer. Amanda smiled, remembering the first time Wyatt had knocked one over the fence. Even all these years later, she could still remember the thrill of amazement at her son's ability, the high-fives from the other mothers perched beside her in the stands. Wyatt had been playing at this park since the age of five, and had been madly in love with the game from the first time he stepped up to the T and made contact with a ball.

Amanda gathered up the blanket she'd brought and cradled the thermos in it while Wyatt put on his cleats and lifted the equipment bag from the back of the van.

"I'll see you down there, sweetie." Amanda watched him walk down the concrete stands toward the dugout, keeping him in her sights until he disappeared from view.

She was tempted to leave and not come back until warm-ups were over and the game had begun, when attention would be on the field, but she was here and she suspected running would feel even worse. She leaned against the side of the van, trying to build her courage, but all she could think of was all the hours they'd spent together in this place. They'd always come here as a family and had been part of the crowd whose kids played not only fall and spring but well into summer. They'd spent countless hours in these stands and others just like them, munching peanuts, cheering their children on, and inevitably picking over the latest gossip.

Gossip. She'd watched other baseball families come apart, seen the children walking around wounded, shuttled back and forth.

At games, the parents, and ultimately their new significant others, would stake out opposite ends of the stands and try to act as if nothing had changed, while everyone else tiptoed around them, trying not to declare too obvious an allegiance to either side.

She'd observed all this. Selfishly, she'd hated how it complicated the pure joy of baseball, but she had never for a moment imagined it happening to them. She'd never imagined any of the things that they were living through.

Amanda snorted at her own naiveté. Straightening her shoulders, she walked directly toward the knot of women already seated in the stands.

"Hello, Susan," she said. "Helen." Amanda knew when the entire row of women stopped talking exactly who they were talking about. Helen Bradbury, whose son Blaine was Wyatt's best friend, blushed and gave her a small wave. Karen Anderson, with whom Amanda shared team mom duties, gave her a tentative smile. There were some other nods and murmurings, but mostly the other mothers watched her face, their own eyes wide, as if they could hardly wait for the entertainment to begin.

Through sheer force of will, Amanda kept a smile affixed to her lips. As normally as possible, she placed her blanket on the far end of the fourth row and went about settling in as if she weren't suddenly the most fascinating thing in these women's world.

Out of the corner of her eye she saw a flash of sympathy on the face of the statuesque blonde who was now dating the boys' coach. At any other time Amanda might have found the idea of such a sweet man dating such an apparently sophisticated woman intriguing, but today all she could think was, at least Coach Donovan had waited until he was divorced before he started dating.

Scanning the crowd for a glimpse of Rob, she caught Brooke Mackenzie, Hap Mackenzie's dewy-skinned trophy wife, assessing her with interest. Amanda's heart lurched as she realized that this was probably what that Tiffany business looked like—all pampered and polished. Amanda's eyes teared up, and she dropped her gaze, unwilling to give anyone the satisfaction of seeing her falter. As Tom Hanks said in *A League of Their Own*, and as she'd often reminded Wyatt, there was no crying in baseball.

Swiping the moisture from her cheek, Amanda checked her watch and then did what she hoped was another casual scan for Rob. She caught Wyatt's attention and sent him a thumbs-up. Wyatt smiled briefly but then his gaze moved past her toward the parking lot. He flinched and turned away.

Unable to stop herself, Amanda turned to glance over her shoulder. Rob was crossing from the parking lot and heading toward the field, his gaze locked on his son. She watched him bypass the stands altogether—he didn't even bother to check for her presence—and trip happily down the concrete steps toward the dugout.

He looked like Rob, but not. He had the same blond hair, the same even features, the same lanky build, but the hip-hugging bell-bottomed blue jeans, the spotless white T-shirt, and the red sweater knotted around his neck were new. And so was the skip in his step.

The heat rose to her face and her hands clenched at her sides. The rush of blood to her brain was so loud she barely heard her own gasp of shock or the sudden silence that now surrounded her. Because trailing along behind him was what could only be the new Z-3 in all her tight-chassised, glove leather glory.

Speechless, Amanda watched them go by. The girl—calling her a woman would have been a stretch—actually looked like she'd stepped off the cover of a magazine. In this case, probably *Teen People*.

She had a cloud of blond hair that moved with her as she walked and a body that made you look even when you didn't want to.

She had perfectly sculpted limbs, high jutting breasts, and an absurdly tiny waist. Her stomach was unfairly flat over her low-slung jeans; it had never been stretched by childbirth and then expected to snap back. Her silk blouse was white and the burgundy leather blazer was beautifully tailored, but it was her face that sucked all the breath out of Amanda's lungs as she passed. It was the most perfect face Amanda had ever seen.

"Holy shit!" The expletive left the mouths of the group of women seated around Amanda; it was torn from their lips and infused with both wonder and horror. Several made the sign of the cross. In their sweats and sneakers, wrapped in their blankets, and bedraggled from an afternoon of shuttling their children all over creation, they were a set of serviceable pearls, chipped and unpolished; Tiffany was a four-carat diamond in an antique platinum setting sparkling in the sun.

The theme song from *Jaws* began to play in Amanda's head. "Da dum...da dum..."

The appropriately named Tiffany grabbed Rob's arm as they reached the dugout. Stopping at the chain-link fence, Rob leaned forward to say something to Wyatt and the hot flame of anger ignited in Amanda's stomach.

Leaving them had been unconscionable, but showing up here with this...*child*...was beyond belief. Amanda's anger built; every move they made, Rob's laugh, Tiffany's flick of her hair, the fact that they were *breathing* when she could not, stoked that flame into a billowing inferno.

How could he do this? How *dare* he do this? No longer caring what kind of show they put on for those assembled, Amanda rose and walked down the steps and directly toward her husband. It was hard to see him, what with the red haze before her eyes and all, but she continued to move forward as if some unseen hand pushed from behind. She could not let this travesty continue.

Suddenly understanding the concept of second-degree murder, Amanda imagined the headlines if she were to give in to the bloodlust she felt right now: DISCARDED WIFE GOES BERSERK AT BALL FIELD. BASEBALL MOM BATS CHEAT-ING HUSBAND OVER LEFT-FIELD FENCE. No jury with a married woman over thirty-five on it would convict her.

Every eye in the stands was focused on Amanda's back, but she told herself it didn't mat-ter because this couldn't possibly be happening. As she reached the ground and began to move toward the dugout, the whole situation turned surreal; this was not just her facing down Rob, but Won-derWife facing down every dastardly husband who had dared to spit in the face of his family.

"What do you think you're doing?" she hissed when she reached them. "How could you bring her here?"

Tiffany flushed with surprise and Amanda wondered exactly what the girl had expected.

From the corner of her eye, she saw Wyatt swivel around on the dugout bench to watch them. His face was white, the freckles across the bridge of his nose stood out in stark relief.

"It's OK, Wy," she said, though of course it wasn't. "You just focus on your game, you hear? We're going to work this out."

The coach stepped up next to Wyatt. He placed

a hand on her son's shoulder and gave Rob a steely look. Thank God for Dan Donovan. "You all right, Amanda?"

"Yes, thanks."

Donovan led Wyatt to the other end of the dugout, out of earshot. She looked Tiffany in the eye.

"You're dating a married man and you come to a place where his wife and child will be?"

"Oh, Robbie's going to...."

She stepped closer, needing to invade their personal space in the same way they'd invaded hers. "Shame on you!" Amanda said, angered anew by the inadequacy of her words. "Shame on both of you!"

"But, Robbie, you said—" the girl began.

"It's not *Robbie*." Amanda put every ounce of disdain she was feeling into the nickname. "His name is Rob, and at the moment he's still married to me. He and I need to have a conversation. We're not going to have that conversation here in front of an audience. You can go sit down until we're done, or you can go play on the slide, I don't care which. But if I see your face again tonight, I'm going to rip every one of those blond hairs out of your head and stuff them in your mouth."

Tiffany gasped and stalked off. Without looking to see if Rob followed, Amanda marched off in the other direction. She walked until she reached a tree beyond the stands and out of the others' line of sight. When she turned around Rob was standing in front of her.